Praise for Ka

Cl

Challenged - winner of the Crowned Heart award for Excellence from InD'tale Magazine

"This first-time author has a wonderful read in *Challenged*! ... Suspense and sabotage are juicy..."
– 4.5 stars, InD'tale Magazine

"Readers who enjoy sweet, but smoking hot romance, and a little mystery besides, are going to love this one!"
– Tracy Broemmer, author of the Lorelei Bluffs series

"There was something in this book for everyone - drama, intrigue, romance and a happily ever after ending."
– Sierra Hill, author of the Physical Touch series

What readers are saying about *Challenged*

"Sophie and Jackson's story is full of twists, turns, and steamy tension."

"For a first time writer, marvelous! Good story line and interesting characters, two thumbs up!"

"A wonderful first novel...I can't wait to read more!!!!"

Books by Kate Carley

Challenged

Consumed

Chased

Chased

A Changing Krysset Novel

Book 3

By Kate Carley

Chased

Cover Art by 4Gems Designs

Edited by Alicia Street

For information contact:

kate@katecarley.com

Acknowledgements

To my awesome beta readers—thank you for boldly critiquing my work. It's hard sometimes—for you to say and for me to hear—but I know that each of your sweetly phrased suggestions has made my book better in the end.

To Tracy—thank you for the daily check-ins and the encouragement to keep writing. You know that somedays can be lonely and frustrating—writer's block, re-reading the same chapter for the 100th time, countless hours of marketing, and uncontrollable interruptions.
It's always nice to know that I'm not alone in this crazy world.
Thanks for your friendship and support!

And to my husband—I couldn't have done this without you.
You've supported and encouraged me when I might've quit.
You've listened to hours of babbling about my storylines,
and then you've read and critiqued on demand
at the oddest hours of the day and night.
You've had to tell me,
"Dude's don't say that!" on more than one occasion,
and you've been the best one-man tech-support
department I could ask for.
Thank you for all you've done! I love you!

Since this is a work of fiction, intended for entertainment purposes only, I may have stretched the truth a bit. So, any mistakes I've made or liberties I've taken during the process of writing this book are strictly my own.

Chased

PROLOGUE

Ben cast his gaze upward to the tops of the crimson and gold trees set against the pristine blue backdrop of the sky and wondered how such a horrible day dawned with such spectacular color. If heaven held a limited store of brilliant pigment for displays of this magnitude, today it had been wasted on the weeping hearts of Krysset.

And that constant drone of words—completely lost on him. Yeah, some tiny fraction of his brain probably heard it, but he wasn't really listening. But without a doubt, those words would replay themselves with crisp clarity each and every day for the rest of his life.

Haunting him in the quiet moments of night.

Goading him to linger in memories of the past.

Laughing at him when normalcy threatened to make its grand reappearance.

Yes. He'd been assured by countless thoughtful people that the painful emotional wounds would heal and life would return to normal once again.

He wanted to laugh at the stupidity of their words, but the overwhelming weight crushing his chest made it impossible to breathe, let alone draw in enough oxygen to laugh. Those sincere words of comfort, spoken in the gentlest of tones, served as insurmountable conjecture, inconceivable speculation. The simple act of his heart mending itself and his brain blurring the sharp memories of the past week into some faded watercolor snapshot seemed out of the question at this moment. Or at any time in the foreseeable future.

Ben swallowed past the lump in his throat, only to release a small sob. It shuddered through his body, and he forced it back. He felt his dad's strong grip on his left shoulder tighten while his mom stepped closer on his right, her shoulder brushing his upper arm as she clasped his hand in hers. His best friend, Jackson, stood behind with his hand planted on Ben's right shoulder. His support system hadn't left his side for the past five days, and at this moment, he was grateful.

No one would fault him and he wouldn't be alone if he broke down right now in a show of uncontained grief. Soft weeping and sniffling sounds with the occasional loud sob filled the air around him. Everyone here came because they wanted to say goodbye. Not because they wanted to see if he could keep his shit together. Which he obviously couldn't.

Ben blinked back the tears and allowed his eyes to wander over the crowd to the small contingent that stood across from him. The same visceral agony that threatened to gut him was reflected on their faces. Five strong young men and one little girl.

The tallest of the men, a Norse giant with sharply pronounced features. A stone-cold expression masked his face in an attempt to hide the pain evident in his icy-blue eyes. The harshness seemed to soften when he glanced down at the eight-year-old girl clinging to his hand.

Long blonde braids hung well past her shoulders. With each blink of her eyes, the watery blue pools released a tear that rolled down along her fair cheeks and dripped off her chin to land on her navy sweater. Her pain-filled eyes caught Ben's and held his gaze until she squeezed both eyes shut and gave an agonizing sob, leaning into the strong body that stood beside her.

Cameron knelt in the grass, uncaring of the formality of the ritual that occurred around them or the monotonous voice that rambled endlessly. He wrapped his arms around Kendall's slight frame and, overwhelmed by his own grief, allowed tears to stream down his face.

Ben forced his gaze away from the two cousins, feeling like an intruder in their private moment. Gulping mouthfuls of air, he stared at his black dress shoes. But deep breaths and redirected eyeballs weren't enough to hold back Ben's sorrow. Cameron and Kendall's effortless show of emotions, coupled with Ben's own stifled grief, released a floodgate.

Ben rubbed at the annoying tears, wishing the damn things would just stop, and he fixed his eyes on the row of four shiny caskets. All in a light oak. All covered in bouquets of flowers. His gaze riveted to the one on the end, draped in sixty red roses. His red roses. One rose for each month that she'd been a part of his life.

Tears streamed unchecked while he gazed at the bold red petals and deep green leaves. Like brushing at the never-ending tears to magically halt their flow, the insignificant floral arrangement was a feeble attempt to say goodbye to the girl he loved. He could only imagine Jenna's delight with dozens of romantic red roses.

She'd have been tickled to receive the garden-full of roses in life, but he'd foolishly waited until her death.

CHAPTER 1

Sixteen years later

Ben stumbled out of the Brawling Bear Bar and nearly face-planted on the frozen sidewalk outside. His firm hold on the swinging door was the only thing that kept him upright. Barely.

He glared at the offensive doorway before taking a gander downward in the general direction of his boots. Same brown leather work boots he'd worn into the bar tonight. That was a good sign, right? But his feet felt sloppy, loose. Or maybe that was his brain.

God, he was messed up.

Maybe Ethan Bearbower had been right, cutting him off. Ben had probably had plenty. How many shots had he downed? Nine? Ten? After several beers. His gaze wandered over the piles of snow heaped on either side of the street. Judging by his blurred vision alone, he'd most definitely had enough.

"Ben, close the damned door," someone shouted from inside the bar.

"G'night, all," Ben said and then released the door, allowing it to drift closed.

He scrubbed his hand over the scruff on his jaw. He hated when Ethan refused to serve him like this. It didn't happen often. But when it did, it made him feel about ten years old.

Ben squinted up at the streetlight ringed by a shimmering halo of light. Like an angel.

Well, that just about cinched it, didn't it? If he was seeing angels, he was completely shitfaced.

When was the last time he'd gotten this drunk? A while back. He scratched at his face again. Hard to say. The last six months or so had sucked—worse than his usual life if that was even possible. He'd done plenty of self-medicating in the form of alcohol. He'd hooked up with a fair amount of women—because really, what was better than a hot round of sex with a friendly brunette? And when neither of those options had been available, he'd exercised until he'd puked.

Nothing helped.

The door swung open, hitting him in the shoulder and nearly knocking him into a snowbank. Dani Bearbower stuck her head out the door. Even she looked like an angel tonight. And she was a brunette. Although she was off limits. Ethan's wife. But in Ben's humble opinion, Dani—fretting over everyone—was just too damned sweet to play the part of a saloon owner's better half.

"Ben, you need help getting home?" Great. Now the barkeep's wife was offering to escort him back to his front steps.

"No. S'all good." He flashed what he hoped was a thumbs up. Couldn't tell. But it made her smile.

"I could get one of the guys to walk you home. I know it can be...confusing sometimes."

Like when you're drunk. She didn't say the words, but he knew exactly what she meant. Ben had to agree with her on that one. But then there were those times when everything was confusing, and there was no alcohol involved.

Like why the hell had Kendall Aasgaard come back to town?

Okay, maybe she hadn't *actually* returned to Krysset. Ben had no idea, really. But that was the hot news on the street tonight. Some jerk had moseyed into the Brawling Bear, claiming to have seen a woman who looked just like Sylvia Aasgaard, Kendall's late mother. He'd insisted it was Kendall at the Kwik Trip on the edge of town.

She'd been gone for years, so Ben couldn't even say with one hundred percent certainty that he'd recognize Kendall if she walked past him on the street. But that simple speculation by a big-mouthed jackass had punched Ben in the gut, wrenched at his hardened heart, and knocked him headfirst into a bottle of scotch.

And he wasn't the only one who'd had an adverse reaction to the dubious news. Ben had never seen Cameron Aasgaard flip out like he had tonight. Ethan had gotten in the big guy's face and told him to calm the fuck down, which somehow managed to transform Cam into a calmer version of his generally uptight self.

"Really, Ben. You can't just stand there. It's too cold. Come back in." Dani, still worrying for his wellbeing, stood shivering in front of the door.

"Nope. Going home now." He turned right toward the parking lot. Where the hell had he parked his truck?

"Other way, Ben. You walked here. Now go straight home."

"Yes, Mom." Couldn't a guy enjoy his drunken buzz in private on the street corner? He puffed out an annoyed breath, and the white cloud of moist air gave him his own personal fog bank. Yes, he should definitely go home now.

"You got this?"

"Good night, Dani." He stepped into the road and jaywalked to the park. Dani was right. It was so cold his eyelids were freezing to his eyeballs. He could hardly enjoy the glowing halos around the streetlights in this condition.

And worse yet, the biting cold had a way of making his drunken numb feel…less.

The arctic air forced Ben's feet to hustle along the crisp snow, the crunch loud and sharp in the silence of midnight. It wasn't far now. Just down the block. He could see his house from here—doing its best impression of a radioactive Christmas tree. What the hell? Yellowish light pooled on the white snow outside each window, illuminating the house like the noontime sun. The front porch light burned, as well as the back floodlights and every window in between.

He picked up his pace, cursing himself for standing in front of the bar for so long in this subzero weather. When he obviously had a visitor. Or an intruder. He spotted an eco-friendly sedan parked in front of his house. It hadn't been there when he'd left. And once he got up close, he noted the Oregon plates.

Kendall. The only person he knew who lived in Oregon. Although he couldn't imagine her driving a car halfway across the country. Or driving at all, for that matter. And he certainly couldn't picture that little girl in the ultra-shiny shoes and lace-trimmed ankle socks resorting to breaking and entering.

He climbed the steps of the wraparound porch and headed to the backdoor. The welcome mat had been peeled from its frozen position in front of the door by his determined intruder searching for a key. Somehow the boldness of her search and uninvited entry pissed him off when he should just be thankful that she hadn't broken a window to get inside.

He keyed the locked door and entered, stumbling over a pair of high-heeled boots left just inside the door. His ire skyrocketed. Couldn't she have waited till morning to barge into his life?

Ben slipped off his own wet boots and shrugged out of his parka, hanging it on one of the pegs near the door before he stepped out of the small mudroom into the kitchen. A puffy down jacket hung on the back of one of the dining chairs with a large tote-style purse sitting next to it. Ben snatched up the purse and withdrew a thin leather wallet from the main opening. A tinge of guilt washed over him at the invasion of privacy, but he shook it off. She'd invaded his space first, and he needed confirmation that it was really her.

Kendall Aasgaard.

The minuscule picture on her driver's license revealed a stunning beauty graced with long blonde hair.

The exact type of woman he'd avoided his entire adult life.

What the hell was she doing here? That drunken buzz he'd been appreciating when he'd stepped out of the bar? Yeah. Gone.

Damn. His hands were shaking. He grabbed an open bottle of Southern Comfort off the counter, twisted the top, and took a long pull. God, he couldn't handle this. Kendall would spark all his memories. Hell, just the rumor of her return had caused him to go overboard on the shots tonight.

He looked at the bottle in his fist and took another swig. No, nothing good could come from having Kendall waltz into his life. Things had been so damned messed up recently, he had little to offer Kendall in the way of emotional support or friendship. Besides, she probably battled her own boatload of ghosts every day.

"Huh?" He grunted out a little laugh. Maybe they could be drinking buddies? Yeah, probably not. He went to take another chug but stopped short and set the bottle back on the kitchen counter.

"Kendall?" He made his way toward the front of the house and into the foyer, pausing to peek into both the formal parlor and his media room. He'd half expected to find her curled up on the sofa, watching TV or reading a book, but like every room on this level, it was empty. As a matter of fact, he hadn't heard a sound since he'd stepped into the house. Damn, he was going to be pissed if he got a lamp to the back of the head simply because she thought he was an intruder.

Just to be on the safe side, he called her name again. Upstairs he checked the two spare bedrooms—both empty, doors open and lights on. He flipped the lights off and headed to his favorite room in the house—the grand master suite. As he rounded the corner into his bedroom, Ben stopped midstride and backpedaled two paces.

Kendall. At home and quite comfortable. In his bed.

Forget that question about what Kendall was doing back in Krysset. What the hell was she doing in his bed?

Letting out an exhausted sigh, Ben leaned his shoulder against the doorjamb. He'd always hoped to meet up with Kendall again someday, but it'd never seemed like the right time to barge into her life. Instead, he'd received occasional updates from Cameron. However, it seemed as if Cam had an inability to string together more than a few words in polite conversation in Ben's presence, so the updates had been unembellished synopses. Short. To the point. Most often containing and usually consisting of no more than the word "good."

Now here she was, asleep in his bed. Of all places. Nothing like what he'd have expected from the little girl he remembered eating pink cotton candy at the Wahnata County fair sixteen years ago. Judging from the voluptuous pink lacy bra and matching scrap of fabric topping a pile of discarded clothing, not only had she maintained her affinity for that color, but she'd grown up.

And taken to sleeping naked in strangers' beds.

Ben breathed a weary sigh. Oh, Kendall.

He studied her form as she lay sleeping, captivated by the sight so different than what he'd anticipated when he'd first entered the house. Sound asleep on her back, Kendall's arms were flung wide above her head in a gesture of complete abandon as though she'd collapsed onto the mattress and hadn't moved an inch. For some odd reason—probably because of the quantity of lights she'd used in her attempt to chase away the deepest shadows—he'd expected her to sleep curled on her side in the fetal position to protect herself from the monsters that stalked the night.

The sheets covered the roundness of her breasts, although her shoulders remained bare. The thought that she was naked under those covers excited him, and he shifted a bit, making more room at the front of his jeans.

He gave himself a mental kick. What was wrong with him? He was behaving like some creepy old man instead of counting his blessings that she hadn't pushed off all the covers in her sleep. There'd be no hiding with the ceiling light and both bedside lamps on, not to mention the brightness that poured through the open door of the adjoining master bathroom—all casting enough light to perform surgery by.

On silent steps, he advanced to the far side of the room, clicked off the small lamp, and then crept around the bed to the opposite side. He reached to shut off the light that shined on her face and paused to gaze at her peaceful features. Her face was the shape of a heart, her nose was small and turned up at the tip like a ski slope, and her lips were pink and full. Odd shadows fell across her shoulders, but her skin looked soft and smooth—

touchable. With her arms thrown above her head, however, he noticed raw marks on the inside of her arms—the only inconsistency in her flawless skin. It almost looked as if she'd been playing with a mad cat. Those marks aside, she'd grown into a beautiful woman, although he could still see a resemblance to the young girl of his memories.

And to the woman that he'd once planned to marry.

He pinched his eyes closed, attempting to block the flurry of pictures that flashed through his mind. But after sixteen years, he should've known it was useless. Memories of Jenna were etched into his brain. Ingrained and permanent. No action as simple as squeezing his eyes shut would erase them.

He gave another weary sigh. Shutting off the lamp, he turned and headed for the door. Stopping, he took one last glance over his shoulder at the woman in his bed, and then he switched off the overhead light.

She stirred. "Ben?" Heavy with sleep, her voice was a different, richer tone than he'd expected. "Is that you?"

"Hi, Kendall. I'm sorry I woke you." Talk about different tones. His words came out husky like his best seduction voice.

"No. Don't be. I tried to wait up for you."

"Why are you in my bed?" Damn, that sounded like an invitation, not like the serious inquiry he'd intended it to be.

"I thought I'd surprise you." She stretched like a languid cat fresh from a nap in the sunshine.

He chuckled at the words at the same time he cringed at the sight. "Well, you did that. I'm exhausted, Dolly. I'm going to bed. I'll sleep in the guestroom since you've commandeered my room. Good night."

"No. Don't leave." The panic in her voice startled him, forcing him to stop midstride.

Ben's heart pounded in his chest while he searched her face. A hint of fear touched her eyes while her expression begged him not to leave her side. His stomach twisted while his own massive bout of panic set in, and although his body acted eager to become better acquainted with this bold and beautiful stranger, his heart and brain agreed he needed to keep his hands off of her.

Then Kendall lifted the covers on the side closest to the door, and his heart nearly stopped beating altogether.

"I don't want to kick you out of your bed. We'll share. Come cuddle with me."

Ben gritted his teeth as the bulge at the front of his jeans tightened. "Not happening, Kendall. It's late, and I'm tired." Frustratingly, his body didn't seem to care what his mouth was saying. She was naked. In his bed. It seemed like a perfect opportunity. And she *had* invited him to join her.

No. He shut down that line of thought, which was only being incited further by the quantity of alcohol he'd consumed over the past several hours.

Damn, what was wrong with him? He shoved his hands into his front pockets to adjust himself again. This young, naked woman in his bed should've brought out his protective nature, but no, here he stood hard as steel, leering at her while carnal thoughts raced through his mind. The title creepy old man no longer fit. Time to try on pervert for size.

He exhaled sharply and forced himself to turn from the sight of her body. "We'll talk in the morning. Good night."

CHAPTER 2

Even with her eyes closed, Kendall knew precisely where she was.

The opulence of Ben's bed linens was a dead giveaway. She had to admit the man had excellent taste in furnishings if her perusal through his home last night was any indication. And she'd looked. In every nook and cranny. She'd turned on lights, peeked in closets and under the beds, and surveyed just about anywhere someone could hide—except the basement. She didn't do basements. Ever.

Kendall stretched and forced her eyes open, feeling every stiff and sore muscle in her body. If she didn't know better, she'd think that she'd run halfway across the country instead of driving for twenty-five grueling hours. She was fairly certain that the long hard push had paid off. Nick would've never expected her to abruptly leave town like that, and since she'd ditched her cell phone back in Portland, he'd have no way to track her to Krysset. But he was an intelligent and resourceful man, so Kendall had no doubt that eventually he'd figure out where she'd gone. It was only a matter of time before he'd show up in town, thinking he could manipulate or manhandle her into coming back home. Not. Happening. Ever.

How could she have fallen in love with him? Hopefully, she'd bought herself some time to rest and regroup before she had to face that cruel man again. And maybe she could convince Ben to help her.

Reluctantly, she threw back the covers. Given an option, she'd stay in bed for a few more hours on these awesome sheets, but judging from the loud clanking downstairs that wasn't going to happen. The not-so-subtle wake-up call forced her to drag herself from bed to face what sounded like an angry man making breakfast.

She quickly rummaged through Ben's closet and pulled on a soft flannel button-down shirt that hung midway down her thighs. And then she dug through her tote for a change of underwear before pulling her hair back into a ponytail and securing it with an elastic hair tie.

Kendall padded down the steps and out to the kitchen. Quietly she stood, drinking in the sight of the man she hadn't seen in sixteen long years. He wasn't as tall as she remembered, although he must be close to six feet with broad shoulders that stretched that long-sleeved thermal shirt to its limits. All that upper bulk narrowed down nicely to his trim waist, showcased by the way he stood before the stovetop in snug-fitting jeans that hugged his bottom. The ends of his dark brown hair, still damp from his shower, curled over the top of his collar.

Jenna's three journals had gone to great lengths describing Ben as she'd seen him, but regardless of the number of words her sister had used, they hadn't done him justice. The sight of him here and now flat-out took Kendall's breath away. Perhaps it was the flesh-and-blood reality of the moment or maybe the years of maturity, but Benjamin Montgomery was an incredible specimen of maleness.

Kendall stepped up behind him and wrapped her arms around his stomach, pressing her cheek against his back, inhaling the fresh clean scent of man, woodsy and masculine.

"Good morning, Kendall." His words rumbled deep through his chest, and she smiled before releasing him and taking one tiny step backward, giving him room to turn and face her.

Ben was as handsome today as in her childhood memories, but far more serious. A stern expression was plastered on his freshly shaven face. That smooth clean look made her fingers tingle with the need to caress his jaw. But the way his cheek muscles twitched—as if he'd clamped his mouth shut in frustration—had her curling her overeager fingers into tight fists by her side.

He definitely seemed annoyed with her presence, although his chocolate-brown eyes held her gaze while an underlying heat flared to life within their depths. His intense scrutiny sent a surge of excitement racing through her body while he searched her face. His gaze dipped to her mouth, and he pursed his lips for the briefest second as if considering a potential kiss.

Kendall's heart thundered at the thought. God, how would it feel to have his mouth pressed to hers? Incredible, no doubt. She'd bet he knew how to kiss a woman properly. Probably knew a whole lot more, too.

Then Ben blinked, the connection disappeared, and the air of frustration returned again.

"Good morning, Ben. Did you sleep well?" She'd had a fabulous night of sleep. Just being in Ben's house made her feel more relaxed. In truth, she hadn't felt this safe in weeks.

Unlike the man Kendall remembered from sixteen years earlier, Ben didn't wear the lighthearted smile with the matching dimples in either cheek. Had Jenna's death stripped him of that easy expression or had the years of maturity claimed his fun-loving spirit? Hopefully, her arrival hadn't caused his unpleasant attitude. She never intended to upset him. Actually, the idea of being the one to put that smile on his face appealed to her, although it didn't appear promising at the moment.

"As good as can be expected. I've made coffee." He pointed to the pot in the corner. "I'd say make yourself at home, but from your attire, I see you already have. Breakfast is almost ready." He turned to retrieve the toast when it popped, grumbling something about a hangover and unexpected company. She chose to ignore it.

"You're kind of surly in the morning, Ben. That's something I didn't know about you," she said when he handed her a plate with a stack of buttered toast and pointed in the general direction of the eating area.

Ben followed her with two plates heaped with scrambled eggs and two sausage links each and set one in front of her before he settled onto the seat across from her. "Well, last time you saw me you were eight years old. I'd wager that there are plenty of details about me you don't know."

"Oh, Ben, you'd be surprised what I know." She felt her lips curl into a knowing smile at the secret knowledge she held.

He cocked his head to the side and studied her, seeming to consider her comment. Even without his amused expression and sexy dimples, Ben was an attractive man. His dark brown hair with the slightest wave fell over his left brow, and he pushed it back in an agitated move. His cheek muscles twitched again, but the action showcased his strong jaw line. His straight nose, by no means narrow or small, fit the size and shape of his oval face perfectly. Tiny lines of tension radiated from his eyes, a bit more pronounced at this exact moment, but stress had a tendency to do that.

After a moment of scrutinizing her, he said, "Kendall, I have so many questions for you, I don't even know where to begin. So let's start with a simple one. Don't you have any clothes of your own?" He gestured toward the shirt she wore.

Kendall considered the pile of dirty clothes she'd left lying on the floor in his bedroom. They were so ripe that she'd offend herself if she dared to put them back on. "Obviously I didn't show up here buck naked. I'd have frostbite on my assets." She couldn't help herself, so she flashed him a flirty grin that only made his harsh expression solidify into something more severe. Red. Bloated. As if he might explode. A twinge of guilt hit her in the region of her heart for teasing the poor guy before he'd eaten a good breakfast.

"I brought in my overnight bag with a change of unmentionables, but I left the bulk of my luggage out in my car. If the temperatures dipped like they predicted, it's a solid block of ice by now." She shook her head. "There's no way I'm putting them on my body until they warm up."

Now she wished she would've dragged in all her luggage last night, so she could've at least attempted to make a good first impression on Ben. Actually, naked had been the first impression, and Ben…well, he obviously hadn't been impressed at all. So she really needed clean clothes to bring her A game.

With a loud exhale, Ben shoveled a forkful of scrambled eggs past his lips, probably to prevent the words on his mind from flying out of his mouth. After several scoops, he asked, "Why are you here, Kendall?" He grabbed a slice of toast and gnawed at it, waiting for her to answer.

"I thought I'd visit an old friend in Krysset. Is that so bad?" She took a small bite of eggs.

"That's a load of crap, Kendall, and we both know it. We're hardly friends. Why my house? Why my bed? Why me?"

Waiting for him naked last night had been a big mistake, and peeling back the blankets and inviting him in—that had been a calculated risk. She had no idea what kind of man Benjamin Montgomery had become or if he'd take her up on her offer. All she'd had to go on were her memories and her sister's journal. But if anyone could help her, it was Ben.

"Other than Cameron, you're the only person in town I know. I remember you being brave and kind, funny and sweet, protective and spontaneous. And right now, I could use a friend with those attributes if you're up for the job."

"A friend?" His eyes narrowed in suspicion. God, was her presence in his house that unsettling for him?

"A friend." She nodded.

"Not with benefits, right?"

The fierceness of his question startled her, but then again, she should've expected it. She'd made a huge mess of this entire situation, and that had never been her intention. She was all over the map—with her actions and with her emotions. Hell, even her subconscious was getting in on the act.

Last night she'd had a sex dream about Ben vivid enough to make her blush in the light of day. It was a glorious dream, but that's all it was. Unfortunately, she couldn't get it out of her mind. But then again, his sharp refusal seemed to be stuck in her head, too. Although, she definitely preferred the dream that had ended in an orgasm over the reality that had ended in rejection when he'd headed off to barricade himself inside the guestroom.

"Would you want benefits, Ben?" Kendall asked with a smile, hoping to sound polite.

He sat up straighter and pinned her with a glare that said he didn't appreciate her question. "No, because I could never get involved with you."

Shocked, she sucked in air and blinked twice. His declaration seemed at odds with the palpable connection that filled the space between them when she'd first entered the kitchen. Unexpected. Immediate. Hadn't he sensed it, too? He'd been looking at her lips. He must've recognized the attraction that sizzled in the air while they'd stood inches apart and gazed at each other? The hunger in his eyes had sent a wave of arousal reminiscent of last night's sex dream. Seriously, how could he have not noticed? Or maybe that was precisely why he demanded clarification on her friendship proposal.

"Okay. I didn't expect that answer, but I deserve it. I'm sorry I climbed into your bed last night. I don't know what I was thinking. It's not what I'd planned to do, and all I've managed to accomplish is to confuse everything. So, no. Not with benefits. That type of relationship would never work for me." She shrugged and glanced down at her half-eaten plate of eggs before meeting his eyes. "For me, sex comes with emotional strings. I won't apologize. That's the way I'm wired. And…I sense that you're not interested in getting entwined in my strings. So, no sex. Just friends."

* * *

Liar. No way did Ben believe that "friends only" shit. Not with her shucking off her clothes and slipping into his bed to wait for him. And then the whole "let's cuddle" thing.

And then she had the nerve to ask him if he'd gotten a good night's sleep? Hell, no! There wasn't a guy in town that would've been able to sleep after that invitation, offered up in a sleepy, sultry voice.

He studied Kendall's face, trying to figure her out. While he really didn't know her, he sensed that something wasn't right. "Does Cam know you're in Krysset? At my house?" Of course Ben knew the answer to both. He'd seen Cam's reaction last night after the rumors. He'd heard Cam's frantic attempts to get Kendall to answer her cell phone. Ben had texted the guy at two in the morning to let him know that she was safe and sound, fast asleep at his house, and then Ben had suggested an early morning family reunion at his place.

With a noncommittal shrug, Kendall ignored his question. It figured she'd break into his house, sleep in his bed, and bring fury to his doorstep.

"I'll help you move your stuff into Cam's place after we're done eating. He lives a few miles from here. Then you and I can meet out for dinner and drinks—as friends—sometime before you return to Oregon. Okay?"

"No," she said, standing and moving for more coffee. She carried the pot to the table to refill her cup. "Do you want more?" He nodded, she filled. "I'm not moving in with Cam. I'll stay here with you."

"No." He tossed the word back at her, figuring two could play that game. He stabbed the little brown sausage on his plate with more force than necessary and ripped off a bite with his teeth as the loud rumble of a truck engine rattled the kitchen windows. "Sounds like your ride's here." He pointed with his fork toward the large picture window that gave him a nice view of his backyard and the mammoth black truck that roared up the alleyway and parked in front of his garage.

Kendall winced when she caught sight of her cousin's truck. "Damn. He's up early." The defeated expression on her face almost made him feel sorry for her. Almost.

"You know, Kendall, you were the talk of the town at the bar last night. I texted him, so he'd stop worrying, but I bet he still paced the floors all night waiting for a respectable time to come calling."

Ben watched the giant of a man hop down from the cab of his truck and stride toward the back door. The enraged expression on his face indicated his thorough displeasure at making this house call. Was it simply because of Kendall's arrival in town when she'd failed to gain prior consent from the overbearing oaf? Or was it because she'd landed in Ben's lap?

A solid pounding on the back door screamed of Cam's arrogance and anger. His demand for an immediate response was pretty much par for the course. Most days the man was downright intolerable.

Ben hated the idea of answering the door and inviting the man in, but he stood and headed toward the mudroom, glancing back over his shoulder at the underlying cause of this disruption to what should've been a peaceful Saturday morning. "Kendall, go put on some clothes."

He couldn't remember the sweet little girl in long blonde braids being this difficult. She'd been a precocious child, but he had no recollection of her being outright rebellious.

"Good morning, Cam," Ben said when he opened the door. The right hook hit him in the jaw, and he stumbled back as Cam shouldered his way past Ben and into the house. No doubt the man pulled his punch, or Ben would be pondering life from a horizontal position in the entryway.

"Cam!" Kendall shrieked, racing to meet her older cousin at the door. Or to intervene on Ben's behalf. It wasn't quite clear.

"Damn it, Cam. Why'd you have to do that?" Ben touched his face to check for blood. "I thought we had a truce."

"We did until you decided to take my baby cousin to bed. Kendall, get your ass dressed and get into the truck."

Kendall wrapped her arms around Cam's middle in an exuberant hug. "Cam, Ben and I didn't sleep together. We're friends. That's it," she said, patting her cousin on the back as if she thought she could pacify the guy. She glanced around the hulk of a man and mouthed "Sorry" at Ben.

Pulling out of Cam's arms, Kendall tilted her face upward to smile at her cousin and said, "It's good to see you again. Come on in. You two sit. Cam, I'll get you some toast and coffee. Ben, you should finish your breakfast." Kendall pointed at the table and then scurried into the kitchen.

Had she really just ditched him with her pissed off cousin? Un-fucking-believable.

Ben claimed his seat and glanced at the remains of his now-cold breakfast. "Did you really think I'd take her to bed?" The annoyance of the morning and a sore jaw on top of a nasty hangover gave Ben's voice a sharp edge that caused Cam to glare at him. Ben pitched his voice lower, hoping Kendall wouldn't overhear. "She showed up here and made herself at home. I came in late, you know? She'd already chosen her bed and fallen asleep. I slept in the guestroom. Alone." He shook his head and fixed his eyes on Cameron Aasgaard's icy-blue ones. "She's a baby, Cam. I have absolutely no interest in getting involved with her. You can trust me."

* * *

The tension eased out of Cam's shoulders, but damn, it'd been a long night, worrying about his baby cousin. It felt as if he'd been holding his breath for the past dozen hours or so—ever since that schmuck had walked into the bar and started talking about seeing Kendall around town. Montgomery's open confession helped. At this point, he'd take the guy at his word. Because with Kendall's spirited antics, Cam might need an ally when it came to managing her during her stay in Krysset.

He let out a huge sigh, giving a sharp nod in Ben's direction. "Glad you feel that way. Shit, man. Sorry about that."

"S'all good," Ben said, gingerly touching his jaw. "I'll take it out on you next time we're at the gym."

Cam grunted out a laugh. "Not likely. And thanks for the text. I appreciate that."

He and Ben had been at odds for years, and only recently had they come to an understanding of sorts. But their truce would never last if Ben started making moves on Kendall. For God's sake, the guy was nearly a decade older than her, not to mention the fact that he was a player. Kendall did not need that shit in her life. She had enough problems of her own making without adding Montgomery into the mix.

And quite frankly, the guy seemed to be having his own brand of problems recently. "Listen, I know you staggered home *again* last night. Man, you got to get your shit together. You're dealing with some heavy stuff right now, I get it. But nothing that happened—not with Jenna and not with that gal last summer—was your fault."

"What? You're a psychiatrist now?" Ben asked with a smile. But not the one he usually slapped on his pretty-boy mug. No, this one held undertones of hostility.

"Nope. Just your friendly neighborhood bartender. Go talk to a professional, face the past, and then put it behind you."

Cam eased back in his chair, turning his attention to Kendall, watching her movements across the kitchen. She didn't look happy that he was here. Actually, she looked downright frosty. Probably didn't help that he'd punched Ben. But Cam was on edge. Yesterday, she hadn't even bothered to stop by the bar to let him know that she was in town. And now, her reception was about as cold as this damned arctic snap they'd been suffering through.

What was she doing here? Not that he wasn't glad to see her, because he'd missed her every damned day. But he'd purposely maintained his distance, allowing her to settle into a peaceful life. One that didn't involve him. Or Krysset. Or memories of home.

Kendall delivered him two slices of buttered toast and a cup of coffee, placed them properly in front of him, and then made her way to the breakfast plate she'd abandoned when he'd arrived. She lifted her fork and picked at the eggs, refusing to meet his eyes.

A familiar ache squeezed his heart at her aloof manner, and he wanted to lash out. Instead, he gritted his teeth, dragging in a slow breath, and lowered his voice to an angry growl. "Go pack up your stuff, Kendall. I'm sending you back to Oregon and your boyfriend." His words and tone had the desired response, sparking her angry attention, and she lifted her face to glare at him.

"You have a boyfriend?" Ben asked, sounding rather disappointed.

Cam wanted nothing more than to delve into that inappropriate emotion and the meaning behind it, but he decided he needed to deal with Kendall at the moment. So he ignored the question, as did Kendall, since she appeared to be too busy shooting daggers at him to be worried about anyone else in the room. Her feisty behavior had always made him laugh when it wasn't directed at him. Not the case today.

"He's not my boyfriend, you big jerk. And I'm not going back. You're not the boss of me." The rebellious words spewed from her lips.

"Kendall, you've been saying that since you were eight, and I always get my way. So get moving."

She shook her head and crossed her arms over her chest. Even in her defiance, Cam smiled to himself, admiring the beautiful young woman she'd become, capable and self-confident.

"I already told you, I'm not going back. Krysset is my home, and I've been away too long. I'm staying here."

"So, I've heard," Cam said. No matter how hard he tried, he couldn't seem to keep his irritation out of his words. She'd never once discussed the possibility of moving back to Minnesota, and he couldn't decide if he was more angry or hurt with the fact that she hadn't confided in him. "Pack your bags. I'm driving you to the airport in Minneapolis."

The outrageous mandate with the domineering tone flew from his mouth before he could contain it. Based solely on the expression on Kendall's face, he'd made a tactical error with that statement. But he wasn't backing down. There was no way he'd have Kendall settle in Krysset, and eventually, he'd make her see it was for her own good.

CHAPTER 3

Kendall's blood pressure soared when those controlling words spewed from her cousin's mouth. In typical Cameron Aasgaard fashion. Where to live. Where to go to college. Where to work. Who to date. Ever since the murder of her parents and older siblings, he'd served as the dictator in charge of her life, and she was sick of it.

Enough was enough. This was her life. Her choices. And Cam could either learn to live with it or take a hike. "I'm not going back to Portland. You do know I'm an adult. I'll be twenty-five in less than a month. I believe I can make my own decisions."

"Oh, Dolly, twenty-five's still a baby."

Classic Cam attitude. And he'd thrown in her childhood nickname just to put her in her place. That was the same way her older siblings had wielded the stupid pet name that they'd tagged her with at birth, and she'd hated it. Even Ben had referred to her that way last night when he'd found her in his bed. Probably for the exact same reason.

How could a few moments in Cam's presence cause her to regress to little more than a bratty teenage? Kendall wanted to roll her eyes at his antagonizing words, but that would only provide him with fuel for his argument. So instead she lifted her coffee mug and took a long sip.

The three of them sat in silence for what felt like forever before Ben finally said, "Hey, Cam. I'm headed out to the lake today to help Jackson and Sophie with a renovation project on one of their rentals at the resort. Kendall's welcome to tag along, maybe wield a paintbrush or burp a baby."

Ben paused until Cam gave a slight nod in consent, and then Ben looked in Kendall's direction. He raised his eyebrows in question. She couldn't hide her grin. Anything was better than sitting around arguing with her cousin.

"I'm not sure if we'll make it back into town today or stay at my hunting lodge for the night, but I have a guestroom there as well," Ben said, glancing back toward Kendall again. "Actually, Kendall and I were talking before you arrived, and I invited her to stay here until she found her own place."

Oh, really? It seemed as if Ben wasn't above stretching the truth to help out "a friend." It was exactly the type of behavior she'd expect from the Ben she once knew. Although after the less than friendly welcome he'd showed her earlier, she was surprised that he'd decided to take her side rather than pawn her off on Cam.

* * *

Cam studied Montgomery's face, debating the best way to handle Kendall. Obviously she'd dug in her heels when he'd tried the forceful approach. "Okay," he said, hoping that allowing Kendall to stay with Ben wasn't a colossal mistake. Over the years, his honest attempts to protect her had always been at odds with her bold, live-in-the-moment approach to life. Leaving them both angry with one another more often than in agreement.

"So how's that boyfriend?" With a gentle touch, Cam stroked his fingers over the top of hers before withdrawing his hand again. "Nicholas Cardwell of the Salem Cardwells, if I'm not mistaken."

Kendall gave an unladylike snort, turning to face Ben. "Nick always introduces himself that way. So, of course, the smart ass here"—she jerked her thumb in Cam's direction—"had to introduce himself as Cameron Aasgaard of the Norwegian Vikings, lineage traceable back to the great warrior Thorvald, grandfather to the famous explorer, Leif Ericsson."

Cam chuckled at Kendall's voice, pitched low when she delivered his lines in the same bravado he'd used to piss Nick off. He loved her cheeky spunk and would thoroughly enjoy having her in Krysset on a permanent basis. If it wasn't for the horrific memories of the murders.

"You're related to Leif Ericsson?" Ben's eyebrows rose in disbelief with the question. Cam slanted a haven't-you-been-paying-attention look in the younger guy's direction but remained silent rather than bothering with the pointless explanation. "Great. Assault me, ignore me, and make yourself at home." Ben muttered his complaint and then turned to brew another pot of coffee.

Cam grunted at Ben's irritation and refocused his attention on Kendall when she said, "Cam, Nick doesn't love me. Not as much as he loves himself. It was never going to work between us, so I broke up with him."

Thank God. The guy was a loser, but it seemed as if every boyfriend she introduced him to fell into that category. With the way Kendall whimsically fell in love, his biggest fear was that someday one of losers would stick around permanently. But thankfully, she also fell out of love just as quickly. "Dolly, you can't always leave because things get tough. Are you sure you can't work it out with him?" Please Lord, let her say no.

"First, Cameron Aasgard, don't call me Dolly. Second, it's over. I'm not going back. Besides, you didn't like him anyway. What's the big deal?"

"Yeah, he's an arrogant ass." He cocked his head to the side and surveyed her pretty face. The fact that she resembled her mother—his Aunt Sylvia—stirred the age-old grief he'd suffered at the loss of his aunt, uncle, and two cousins. Time had healed the wounds, but her presence was a reminder of all he'd lost.

All she'd lost.

"Kendall, you asked me to give Nick a chance because you loved him. What's changed?"

"I can't help that I'm slow to judge people. I thought he cared about me." The dejected expression on her face wrenched at his heart. The man had hurt her, Cam knew it with every fiber of his being, and he wanted to hurt the little prick in return.

"Okay." He dragged the word out, ready to change the topic. "Last night at the Brawling Bear, I heard you'd come back to

Krysset. I want you to know, I'm a bit disgruntled that you didn't stop in to say hello, but I'm going to let that go for now." He allowed his lips to curve into a small grin, eager to lighten the words of criticism. "I called your cell phone, but I couldn't reach you."

Guilt flashed across her face. Interesting. And then she stammered for an answer.

* * *

Kendall dug deep for her limited acting skills. "I lost it, Cam." Inwardly, she cringed. Lost indicated that she didn't know where it was or how to find it. She'd guess it was still duct taped to the bottom of a seat on one of the many public transportation buses in Portland. The fact that it had GPS installed and activated meant it could be found if it hadn't run out of batteries yet.

So, lost? Not so much. No longer in her possession was quite accurate.

"I've got a new one with a new number." She rose and dug through her purse for the pay-as-you-go phone she'd purchased a couple days ago. She pecked in his number when he gave it to her and then sent him a text. "Now you can reach me." She smiled, hoping all would be forgiven and the topic of her phone wouldn't come back into play.

"That looks like one of those cheap burner phones, Kendall."

"Yeah, well, I didn't want to travel without a means to call someone if I had car troubles, so I just grabbed one on my way out of Portland."

"I'll pick up a new one for you and bring it by tomorrow."

Kendall tensed at his offer, then gave her head a decisive shake. "No. Don't bother. This will work fine for now, and I'll get my own sometime in the next couple weeks." Never again would she accept the gift of a cell phone from any man. Not even from her overprotective guardian.

She glanced in Ben's direction while he loaded the dirty dishes into the dishwasher. Not all men were bad. Ben had stood up for her today, just like he'd stood up for Jenna years ago. Her younger self had thought Benjamin Montgomery hung the moon and stars. Strong and kind. Dependable and honest. Those were the words she'd used over the years to describe him to her best girlfriends.

And this morning, Ben's actions had proven her descriptive words and long-standing beliefs correct. Just as she'd hoped.

CHAPTER 4

Ben glanced toward the door where the cousins were talking in hushed tones. He had to admit that he found the interaction between those two fascinating. Every time things had grown tense between them this morning, their stance had mirrored one another—arms crossed over the chest with an obstinate glare in the eyes—both refusing to back down or give in. Neither appeared aware of their similarities, and if he dared mention it, both would likely argue until their dying breath that they held nothing in common.

For the most part, Ben had just sat back and watched. But on that one point, he had to side with Kendall. Twenty-five was plenty old enough to make her own decisions. He'd hated to watch while Cam strong-armed Kendall into leaving Krysset. So Ben had decided to intervene on Kendall's behalf, offering up his guestroom. A degree of shock had registered on Kendall's face, and then her lips had curved up into a sweet, shy smile, but surprisingly, she hadn't said a word.

Ben took another quick glance toward the back door where Kendall hugged Cam goodbye, still dressed in nothing but Ben's plaid shirt.

And a skimpy pair of underwear.

His jaw clenched at the memory. He hadn't meant to see them, hadn't been searching, but then she'd twisted just right and white lace had peeked out from underneath the hem of his shirt. The emotion he experienced now wasn't guilt for catching a glimpse of her unmentionables—as she called them—but rather disgust for the way his body had reacted to the sight. Like last night, desire stirred for a young woman he had no business lusting over.

While Ben had agreed that Kendall could stay here, a few ground rules needed to be established. Like wear some damned clothes. Or he'd be a walking erection all day long.

He turned when he heard the back door click closed.

"Thank you." Kendall laughed, and then she raced toward him, picking up speed on the straightaway. Ben knew instinctively what she planned to do before she launched herself at him. Her arms wrapped around his neck, her legs around his waist, and his hands automatically landed on her lace-clad butt cheeks.

Ben held his breath and pinched his eyes closed in a losing battle to ignore the intimate position with her heated core molded against his semi-hard cock, which was growing harder by the second. Kendall on the other hand appeared oblivious to his struggles while she rained kisses across his cheeks and neck.

"Thank you for letting me stay here. Thank you for helping me with Cam. Thank you." She threw her head back and laughed. "We are going to have so much fun together this weekend."

He groaned out loud. Turning around, he set her on the countertop and took a giant step backward. Saving her from Cam's misguided, overbearing dictates stood to cause him a grand case of blue balls if he didn't get his wayward body in line with his more righteous mind. "Yeah, we'll have fun if you don't kill me first."

After Kendall's jeans and sweatshirt had been adequately thawed in a hot dryer cycle, they headed out to Ben's pickup truck. Kendall hustled along the sidewalk beside him, casting a wary glance around the yard and down the street. She seemed almost hyper-vigilant about her surroundings, but it had to be odd for her to be back in this place where her family had been murdered.

Ben drove east out of town in the direction of Jackson and Sophie's resort. "Don't think I've forgotten all those unanswered questions, Kendall. If you're planning to stay with me, I need answers."

"I know, but it's not exactly a short story, so how about tonight over dinner," she said, peeking in the side-view mirror and then out the back window.

"What are you looking for?" Ben asked when Kendall darted a glance over her shoulder for the third time in as many minutes.

"Oh, nothing," Kendall said facing forward again.

"You keep looking out the back window."

"I'm just trying to get my bearings. You know, it's been so many years since I've been here, and things have changed quite a bit," she said by way of explanation. Ben couldn't say that he believed that excuse, but he didn't bother to comment further, and within a few miles, Kendall seemed to relax, taking in the scenery.

They traveled out of town about twenty miles to Lancaster Beach Resort. January on Golden Cougar Lake resembled a frozen tundra landscape. So even though the resort remained open, the Cooper family led a rather solitary existence during the coldest of the winter months.

Ben threw the truck into park outside Jackson and Sophie's house on the resort property and looked at Kendall. Bundled up like Nanook of the North, her long hair spilled out from beneath her beanie cap in a silky cascade over her purple down ski jacket. Her wool mittens and scarf matched her cap, all in a brilliant splash of vibrant colors. The tip of her nose and her cheeks wore a rosy glow from the sharp arctic cold and her lips curved up in an eager grin that warmed his heart.

He had no idea what thoughts danced through her pretty little head, but if he ventured a guess based on her pleased expression alone, she was still basking in the glory of a hard-won fight with her biggest obstacle in returning to Krysset—Cameron Aasgaard.

"Come on. Let's get inside before we freeze to the seats." He rushed her from the truck, letting himself in through the backdoor of the house.

"Hey! Anyone home?" Ben shouted when he stepped inside the kitchen, pushing Kendall in and slamming the door closed behind him.

"Good morning." Sophie came around the corner and into the kitchen with his favorite baby in the world propped on her hip.

"How's my favorite redhead?" He scooped the little girl out of her mom's arms at the same time he pressed a kiss to Sophie's cheek.

"Me, I'm ready for a nap. She needs a diaper change. You volunteering?" She flashed him her usual saucy smile.

"Nope." He held the nine-month-old around her tummy, flying her above his head, airplane style, and giving her a little jiggle. The motion set off a bout of adorably infectious baby giggles. "My sole purpose in life is to make her laugh. Diaper changes aren't funny."

"If I were you, Ben, I'd watch out. She's flying on a full stomach."

"Oh, you'd never do that to your Uncle Ben, would you, little pumpkin?" But to be on the safe side, he shifted the little one into one arm, and she rested her head against his shoulder. Giggling one moment, cuddling the next. About the best disposition a baby could have. He pressed a kiss to the top of her carrot-red curls and breathed in the scent of clean baby.

Ben glanced up from the girl in his arms into Kendall's face. Her blue eyes twinkled as if she was amused by his silly antics with the baby. "Sophie, I want you to meet Kendall Aasgaard."

"Hi, Kendall. It's good to meet you. This is Ryleigh Lynn." Sophie rubbed her daughter's back while the little one played bashful, burying her face in the crook between Ben's neck and shoulder.

"Where's Jackson?" Ben asked.

"Right here." His best friend's voice boomed from the doorway. "I wondered when you'd get your lazy butt out of bed, so we could get to work."

Jackson's eyes settled on Kendall and darted back to Ben's with a *what-the-hell* look. Yeah. Kendall's presence in the Cooper's kitchen was unusual on so many levels it'd take a twelve pack of beer and several hours for the two guys to hash it all out. With no guarantee they'd be able to explain the situation.

"Jackson, you remember Kendall Aasgaard." The expression on Jackson's face would've been priceless if it didn't have potential disaster written all over it. But Ben had to hand it to his friend—the guy covered his shock well.

"Cam's cousin." Not Jenna's baby sister. Thank goodness for Jackson's astute response delivered in a courteous tone. "I thought you lived out on the West Coast."

"Jackson!" Kendall threw her arms around his neck and squeezed, wrapping him in the same exuberant hug that she'd given Ben—except this time she was fully dressed, and she kept both feet planted on the floor. Damn good thing from the look on Sophie's face. She'd have been most unhappy if the other woman had snaked her legs around her husband's waist by way of a friendly greeting.

When Kendall stepped back from Jackson, she flashed a smile Sophie's way. "I was eight years old last time I saw him. All my friends voted Jackson the cutest boy in town."

Stunned at Kendall's blatant confession, Ben felt his mouth gape open. "Hey! What about me?" He frowned at her, ignoring the chuckles from his friends.

"You were second cutest," she said and pressed a reassuring kiss on his cheek.

Jackson laughed. "Come on, runner-up. As a consolation prize, you'll be doing some heavy lifting today."

"Kendall is working as my assistant today, isn't that right?" Ben draped his arm around Kendall's shoulders and herded her back toward the door.

"Oh, no you don't, Benjamin Montgomery," Sophie said. "Kendall and I are going to get to know each other better, aren't we?" Sophie snaked her arm around Kendall, dragging her away from Ben and directing her out of the kitchen. Feminine laughter trailed around the corner into the living room.

Throughout the day as they worked on the renovation, Jackson had the decency to avoid the topic of Kendall, her unexpected presence in Krysset, and more specifically, Ben's part in escorting her around town. Whether Jackson wasn't interested in the details or hoped Ben would openly share, he appreciated his friend's silence on the matter.

Kendall might have landed in his lap, so to speak, but he didn't want her there. Well, his body appeared to like the idea plenty fine, but his brain wasn't on board with it. Even without lengthy details, Jackson would understand the complexities of the situation, and Ben wasn't some whiney woman who needed to consult his BFF for encouragement. And encouragement was precisely what he wanted to avoid. He didn't need anyone suggesting that he take Kendall for a tumble. Without discussion, he was confident that was a bad idea all around.

But, as years of experience could testify, with just the right spin, even the lousiest of ideas could be twisted into a seemingly viable and brilliant plan.

The silence ended as they were wrapping up their work to head back to Jackson's home midafternoon. "So, are you going to tell me or what?" Jackson slammed his toolbox closed. His patience had obviously come to an end.

"I came home from the bar last night, and every light in the house was on. Looked like a fucking party."

A sense of shame unsettled his stomach when he remembered the sight of Kendall stretched out in his bed. He'd been trying to block that image from his mind, because it only drew attention to the fact that Kendall roused his libido in a way that he never would've expected.

"She was waiting for you inside your house? What did she say when you came in? Why did she show up at your place?" Jackson rattled off the questions with a hint of surprise, but he continued walking to the door, snatched up his coat, and pulled it on.

"She didn't say anything. She was asleep. In my bed. Naked."

Jackson stopped mid-zip, his eyes wide. "Kind of like Goldilocks, huh?"

"Yeah, but when she woke up, she didn't scream and go scurrying into the forest. She peeled back the covers and asked me to keep her company."

"And…you climbed into bed with her?" Jackson raised an eyebrow and shook his head. "Sorry, man, I have a hard time not thinking of her as Jenna's baby sister with long blonde braids. Way too young for sex, but I suppose she's got to be in her mid-twenties by now. Better hope Cam doesn't find out."

"He already visited this morning." Ben rubbed his jaw, wincing at the bruise that could've been far worse. "She's going to hang out with me for a few days until she finds her own place."

"I assume from the bruise on your jaw that Cam's not too happy, huh?"

"Nope. He jumped to conclusions. The idiot could've asked first. I didn't sleep with her. You know my criteria. She doesn't fit. Besides, she's like ten years younger than me, and as you said, it's mighty hard not to think of that little girl, no matter how old she is now. If my life had gone as planned, she'd be my sister-in-law."

Jackson slowly nodded. He glanced at the door and then back again, seemingly undecided if he should escape or say whatever the hell was on his mind. Finally, he tugged open the door and stepped outside. Ben followed, and once they'd climbed into the truck, Jackson said, "I didn't realize you guys kept in touch with each other. You've never mentioned it."

"We haven't. I can't even remember our last conversation. Maybe a month or two before the murders. I mean, I didn't even talk to her at the funeral. God, I was such an asshole back then. So wrapped up in my own grief. And then a couple hours later, she was gone."

"What about at the trial?"

Ben closed his eyes and shook his head. He hadn't spoken to her that day either—they'd really had nothing to say to one another—but he'd seen her on the witness stand. Shaken, but bravely telling her side of the story. He couldn't remember her words, really. Just the fierceness with which she spoke. God, he'd respected the hell out of her in that moment.

"You okay?" Jackson asked.

Ben sucked in a deep breath and slowly released it. "I never told you thank you."

"For what?"

"For supporting me through all that. I don't think I'd have made it without you and my folks."

"No problem, man," Jackson said, minimizing the importance of his role in Ben's recovery. But Ben knew that without his friend, he would've crumbled under the weight of depression. Thankfully, he'd come out of that span of time alive and healthy.

Jackson eased the truck into the wide parking spot next to the house. "So what does she want other than a roll in the sack with the second cutest guy in Krysset?"

Ben grunted. "No idea, but I'm not interested." Okay, maybe that was a lie. Especially after his reaction to her this morning when she'd first stepped into the kitchen. At the sight of her, his chest had tightened, and all he'd wanted to do was drink her in. With his eyes and with his mouth. To simply absorb every aspect of her. His hands had wanted in on the action, too, to touch every sweet dip and curve of her body. Until he knew her, and she knew him. It was an instantaneous attraction with the chemistry to ignite into a fiery passion.

And that was so fucking messed up that he hated himself for even going there.

"We'll see," Jackson said, climbing out of the truck.

"What the hell's that supposed to mean?" Ben slammed the truck door harder than necessary and stomped toward the house.

"Nothing." Jackson laughed and pushed into the kitchen.

Before Ben could shuck off his coat, Kendall's excited voice rang through the kitchen "Ben!"

He glanced up as she catapulted herself at him just as she had earlier this morning in his kitchen, arms and legs in a death grip around his body. But this time, he wasn't prepared. While her petite form weighed next to nothing, the surprise attack left him off balance. His open palms landed on her derriere—a region of her anatomy he'd vowed never to touch again—and he stumbled back, colliding with a thud onto the bench near the door. Her heels dug into his back, her core pressed intimately against his hardening erection.

Even with the sudden change of positions, Kendall seemed completely unaware of his shock and discomfort. "I had a great day. The best really. Sophie and I talked and played with the baby. I can't tell you the last time I had this much fun. Thank you for including me in your day." She planted a kiss on his cheek and then unwedged her feet from between the wall and his back.

Jackson stood there, taking in the entire scene with a shit-eating grin on his face—the exact expression that made best friends into mortal enemies. As soon as Kendall exited the room, Jackson roared with laughter. "You need a bodyguard?"

"Probably." Between Cam pounding on Ben's face and Kendall abusing his body, he'd never survive the week.

CHAPTER 5

"Where are we going now?" Kendall asked when Ben gave her a playful smile. This was the most relaxed she'd seen him all day. And his brown eyes—God, she could stare at his beautiful eyes for hours—sparked with mischief like a five-year-old who'd found trouble and intended to share it with a friend.

"We're going to my hunting lodge, darling." She warmed at the term of endearment. Ever since she'd yelled at Cam for calling her Dolly, Ben had started referring to her as darling. Kendall appreciated that Ben had listened to her request and took her feelings to heart.

She gazed out the windshield as they bounced down the road toward Ben's second home. "It's still early. I figured you and Jackson would've worked for a few more hours."

"A couple weeks ago, we did all the demo, so it really was a simple project. We finished the work we'd planned to get done today, and it went off without a hitch. Tomorrow morning we'll go back to install two shower stalls before we head into town in the late afternoon." A bright expression lit up his face, giving him a more youthful appearance. It reminded her of the way he looked a long time ago. When he'd been happy. When everyone in her life had been happy.

She pushed the gloomy thought away and returned his smile. Sitting beside him felt comfortable. Not awkward like strangers, but more like they were friends. As if they'd been friends for forever.

"Besides, I've got plans for you," he said, drawing her attention back to him. He held her gaze for several beats, and the air thickened. God, was it hard to breathe in here or what?

A lick of excitement shuddered down her spine, washing her body with a tingly heat. She knew better than to think his plans were anything other than nonsexual in nature. But for some reason, the idea of making love to Ben had wrapped its claws around her brain and wouldn't let go. Maybe it was fueled by her bold actions last night—inviting him to cuddle with her. What had she been thinking? Or perhaps it was due to that dream she'd had later in the night. The thought of it filled her mind with such vivid images. The gentle caress of his mouth against hers. Two sets of eager hands exploring. Warm flesh pressed against warm flesh. Entwined together, eyes locked as they joined.

Kendall shook her head to clear it. Ben didn't think of her that way. And she shouldn't be thinking of him in that way either. No, she'd had enough guy problems for one day. Damn, she'd probably reached her quota on guy problems for the entire year—and it was only January.

This morning, she'd overheard Ben and Cam's conversation while she'd been puttering around the kitchen getting a small breakfast ready for Cam. Ben had quite honorably expressed his disinterest in her sexually, putting Cam foolishly at ease. Kendall, however, hadn't made that same commitment to her older cousin, and given the right set of circumstances, she could easily see herself trying to sway Ben from his righteous stance.

Now who was the one with the plan to corrupt a friend? Kendall giggled as she pulled her cell phone from her bag and swiped at the black screen. Nothing. No new messages.

She must have voiced her disappointment in some way, because Ben immediately asked, "What's wrong?"

"Nothing. I'm just waiting for a text back from my friend, Dayla. I've texted her half a dozen times, and she hasn't replied. It's not like her."

"You said you got a new phone. Are you sure you entered her number right?"

Kendall sighed and tucked her phone back in her bag. "Positive. I talked to her on my way out of town to give her my new number. I shouldn't be worried, but it's not like her to leave me hanging like this. She knows how worried I get."

Ben touched her arm gently and said, "I'm sure everything's okay. Give her a little longer and then call her again."

Her heart squeezed with his sweet gesture and tender words. Kendall knew she tended to panic when people she cared about were late or didn't answer their phones. It was illogical and often morbid—a throwback to her family's brutal death. Did Ben ever feel that way?

Ben pulled the truck into a long, narrow driveway that sloped upward and curved to the right as a structure big enough to house a half dozen families came into view from between a large stand of majestic pine trees.

"It's beautiful, Ben." She breathed the words on a whispered sigh that sounded way too dreamy and awe-filled compared to her normal tone. But she couldn't seem to help herself. Gigantic golden-hued logs. Grand stonework pillars. And an obscene amount of glass that stretched from the ground up to the highest point of the roof. "It's just like one of those elegant destination photographs in travel magazines," Kendall said while she gazed at the massive structure.

Ben's house left her breathless. Yes, it was beautiful, but it was also masculine and most definitely north woods. Nothing like she'd expected, and yet, it fit Benjamin Montgomery to a T.

"Look at how the sun is filtering through the western windows. It's like the entire place is illuminated from the inside with some mystical deep orange brilliance. It's spectacular. I don't think you could've timed our arrival more perfectly."

"It's nice, isn't it?"

"Nice? Are you kidding?" She laughed. "It's like your own personal ski chalet, warm and inviting. Can we cuddle in front of a roaring fire and sip hot cocoa? There is a fireplace, isn't there?"

He grunted out a small chuckle—most likely due to her breathy, over-the-top description—but then he dipped his head in agreement. "Yeah, there's a fireplace. But ski chalet? Not so much. There's no downhill skiing anywhere in the area. Although, I suppose you could do some cross-country skiing, but it's not my thing." He drove his truck into a long metal outbuilding around back, shifted to park, and shut off the ignition, pausing for a second before he spoke again. His tone lowered, holding a sincere and reverent quality, revealing more of his heart than he probably realized. "I call it my hunting lodge, but I don't hunt or display taxidermied big game inside. It's my retreat, and I love coming out here to get away. I built it about seven years ago."

"You built it yourself?" Her tone of surprise and disbelief hung in the air between them.

"Well, my family owns the largest construction company in northern Minnesota. That helps in projects of this magnitude. It's become our flagship, so to speak. If you visit our website, my hunting lodge is one of the pictures you'll see to advertise the quality of our work."

"So you do pretty good business, huh?" Kendall asked.

"Yup. We have about forty projects in the works right now. Some in the design phase, others in the finishing stages. Some big ones, many small ones."

"Will you give me a tour?" Unable to contain her eagerness, she snatched up her overnight tote that she'd stowed at her feet and jumped down from the cab of his truck.

"Later. Right now, I've got plans for you." Ben repeated the words he'd used earlier, piquing her curiosity further. He plucked her overnight bag from her hand, shouldering it, and then grabbed his small duffle bag from behind the front seat.

They made their way across the yard toward the back entryway and stepped into a huge mudroom. He dropped the bags in the corner. "Wait here." Ben hurried down the steps into the dark depths of the basement.

God, she was glad he didn't expect her to go down there. She stood at the top of the stairs, watching and waiting. Finally, he returned several excruciating moments later, two pairs of bib-overall-style snowpants clutched in his grip.

He handed her the fuchsia pair. "Gear up."

She stripped off her coat and boots before slipping on the pants and adjusting the straps over her shoulders. After yanking up the zipper, she tugged her jacket and boots back on. "Now what?"

"Follow me."

They walked back outside toward the huge outbuilding he'd parked his truck in moments before. "We're going for a ride." He tilted his head in the direction of four sleek snowmobiles lined along the far wall and snatched a key off a small hook near the door.

A few minutes of prep and Kendall was mounted up behind him with her excited expression hidden behind the tinted mask of her shiny black helmet. She couldn't imagine a better excuse to snake her arms around his middle, and she took full advantage of the opportunity, giving him a tight squeeze before he'd even started the engine.

A deep chuckle rumbled through his back. "You won't have to hang on that tight." His words caressed her ear through the Bluetooth speaker hidden within her helmet. "I won't go fast enough to toss you into a snow bank. Well, at least not right away."

"Okay." She eased up a little bit, but the intimacy of his gently teasing words, whispered for her ears alone, spurred her shameless heart into an accelerated cadence that pounded against her chest.

What was wrong with her? She had a reason for being here, and it wasn't to snuggle up close to Ben Montgomery. Even though it felt good. Really good.

Did Ben have any idea where her mind kept wandering? Even with all the layers of winter gear, Kendall figured Ben could sense her heavy heartbeat against his back in the same manner that she noticed the strength of the muscles that ridged his abdomen and stretched the width of his broad shoulders. But when he turned over the engine and gave the machine a bit of gas, all her inappropriate thoughts flew from her mind.

Ben eased the machine down the snow-covered driveway and onto a well-worn, snow-packed path, and then they picked up speed, turning into an open area where he opened the throttle. They sailed across the wide path with the occasional tree on one side or the other, but Ben avoided the obstacles, giving them a wide berth. Together, they raced across his property, and he finally slowed when they reached the edge of a deep gully.

"Wow. What an incredible view." She gazed over the long gouge in the earth, blanketed in fluffy drifts of white with a rocky bank on the far side backed by the setting sun.

"It's a dried-up creek bed. Too many big rocks along this stretch for a snowmobile, but in the spring, we can hike down there." Again, his intimate promise murmured for her alone sent a gentle tingle of arousal through her body.

When was the last time she'd felt this type of attraction to a guy? Maybe her sense of arousal was only due to the huge amount of adrenaline that had been pumping through her body over the past couple weeks. She'd read somewhere that the rush of adrenaline caused by fear often produced a spike in sex drive. Whatever the cause, she intended to enjoy it. But before she could savor the heat settling low in her core, Ben picked up speed and skidded along the icy trail, bouncing over small hills and landing with jaw-rattling jolts on the other side.

The exhilarating, high-speed ride left Kendall laughing while they sped across the open field at the top of the hill, the scenery flying past in a blur. She whooped with excitement when they dipped down a small embankment and bottomed out just as her stomach did.

Now low in the sky, the sun raced to touch the horizon before Ben reached the long, sloped driveway and slowed to enter the garage, parking in line next to three other silver and blue snowmobiles. When he stopped, Kendall jumped from the machine and yanked off her helmet. The ride had definitely taken her mind off her worries for a short while.

"Oh, Ben. That was incredibly intoxicating. I loved going fast. I've never ridden a snowmobile before. Next time can I drive? Please?"

"Sure thing." Laughing, he set his helmet on a shelf next to several others. Perhaps she was a bit too enthusiastic, but she really *had* loved it.

"Tomorrow?" Kendall asked.

"Maybe. I think we're supposed to get a bit of snow tonight and then another arctic blast." He plucked her helmet from her hands and shook his head. "It's not as fun when it's below zero. This afternoon was perfect for a ride."

"I'm glad we had the time." She laughed on her way to the door. "I never imagined those noisy machines could be that much fun." She glanced at his Harley propped in the back corner. "Will you take me on your motorcycle? I've never ridden one of those either."

"Have I turned you into a daredevil or something?" Ben asked, pushing the button to lower the garage door.

She smiled, wiggling her eyebrows, and nodded. "Something."

After they'd stripped off their outer gear and hung it in the mudroom to dry, Ben showed Kendall around his hunting lodge. "This is my favorite space in the entire world." Pride poured from each word when they stepped out of the mudroom into the two-story behemoth of a space.

Kendall gaped first at the kitchen on one end of the open space. "This kitchen is a chef's dream. I love the stainless-steel appliances and all these cabinets." She ran her hand over the smooth stretch of granite countertop. Like an open floor plan on steroids, a long breakfast bar with eight tall stools served as the sole visible divider between the kitchen and the great room.

Next, the wall of windows on the opposite side of the space caught her attention. "Look at those windows," Kendall said, stepping over to the endless wall of windows and gazing out into the darkness. "I'll bet in the full light of day, this would make for a stunning view of your property."

She turned to face him, gazing upward at the high ceiling. "Have you ever been to Yellowstone National Park?" When he shook his head, she continued. "Aunt Rita and Uncle Patrick took me there when I was twelve. The famous Old Faithful Inn has this towering four-story lobby," she said, glancing upward again at the tallest point.

"Well, this isn't much more than two stories," Ben said.

"Sure, but it reminds me of the inn, on a smaller scale. At the time, I was captivated by the sheer size. The inn is massive. And rustic. And masculine. Everything about it exudes strength. It's all dark wood and beautiful stone work." But unlike the century-old inn, Ben's hunting lodge gleamed with shiny golden pine and had a charming, lived-in feel.

Kendall crossed over to the fireplace to get a better look at his eclectic array of pictures arranged along the mantel. Many of the happy faces looked familiar, but she couldn't seem to remember their names. Memories of Jenna slipped into Kendall's mind before she could call them back. This house would've belonged to her sister if she'd lived. And this man—the one that seemed to jumpstart Kendall's libido in all sorts of inappropriate and outrageous ways—would've been Jenna's husband. She slammed the door shut on those thoughts and refocused her attention on the tour and her host. With a deep breath, she finally found her voice and said, "I understand why you like this place so much."

Ben scooped up her overnight bag and his duffle bag and led her down a hallway on the far end of the house. "This wing holds the master bedroom suite and an additional guestroom with an en suite bathroom."

She stepped into the bedroom while he set her bag down next to the door without entering. "I'll be sleeping in the room right across the hall," he said and then pointed to the far side of the bedroom. "Your bathroom. Make yourself at home. Take a soak in the tub if you'd like. I'm going to make dinner."

She spun around to face him, but Ben had already walked away.

Kendall pulled a few things from her overnight tote, set her toiletry bag on the vanity in the bathroom, and then stood in the middle of the room, wondering what to do next. She stared out the window, looking into the darkness. A chill raced up her spine, but she tried to ignore it. She wished she lived somewhere that never saw night. Twenty-four hours of sunshine to fully light her days and nights would suit her just fine.

She had to remind herself over and over that it wasn't the dark that would hurt her. It was Nick. Although, there was no way that sadistic brute could've found her here. Yet. For now, she was safe here, in the middle of nowhere with Ben.

She turned from the window and dug into the bottom of her tote, fingering one of the small leather-bound journals her sister had used to document everything about Ben. Did Ben have any idea that Jenna had written so prolifically about him? Probably not. It wasn't something a teenage guy would be terribly interested in. Although, according to the words penned in those books, Ben was a romantic at heart.

At this point, Kendall wasn't seeing it. Not that she'd call her sister a liar. More like a sappy teenage girl with a fanciful imagination. And to give Ben the benefit of the doubt, he had absolutely no reason to show Kendall his romantic side. They weren't involved. And that wasn't why she'd barged into his life.

Would he find the journals of interest? Perhaps tonight Kendall could tell him about them. And about the reason she'd come to see him. She clutched the small book to her chest and pinched her eyes closed. "Oh, Jenna, I hope this works."

Sinking onto the edge of the bed, Kendall slowly turned the pages of the book, rereading her favorite passages, savoring her sister's sweetly naive words. Jenna had been like a hearty bouquet of flowers and a basket full of puppies all rolled together—beautiful and so damned lovable no one could resist her charm. No wonder Ben had never found anyone to take her place.

Although, the guy seemed content enough, filling his life with things that kept him busy. Projects, family, friends. On the thirty-minute trip from town out to Jackson and Sophie's house, Ben had detailed the long list of improvements he'd helped the Cooper family complete at their resort, as well as his own list of pending projects at the Victorian house in town. Add work to the mix, and it was a wonder the man had any time left to sleep or eat.

But eat, he did. And cook? The guy could do that, too.

Kendall placed her fork down beside her now-empty dinner plate and moaned. "You're really good in the kitchen, aren't you?"

Wineglass halfway to his lips, Ben gave her a sexy grin and said, "A man's got to eat. Besides, spaghetti is one of my favorites, and it's easy." He sipped the wine and then set the glass on the table. "Did you hear back from Dayla? Did you try calling her?"

"I called. It went to voicemail." She took a drink of her wine, trying not to allow those dark thoughts to poke at her mind. "You never answered me about the motorcycle ride. Will you take me?" Kendall cocked her head to the side, waiting for his response.

He tore a bite-size chuck off a slice of garlic toast and popped the bread into his mouth. "Sure. In the spring," he said as he chewed.

A shiver of delight raced up her spine. "Thank you." She eyed Ben across the table, assessing her own reaction to his simple promise, attempting to gage his effortless acceptance of her request. After last night's disappointing rejection, she'd never expected Ben's warm one-eighty in less than twenty-four hours. Waiting in his bed had not been in her original plans when she'd arrived in town yesterday, but in that moment, it had seemed like a good enough idea. Even now, if she were honest with herself, the idea sent a flash of heat to her sex.

But, no. Last night she'd made a poor decision, and judging from his reaction, he was obviously far more mature and far less shallow than the men she'd dated in the past—none of whom would've thought twice before taking what she'd offered. But sex wasn't why she'd come to town. She needed help. Ben's help.

"You never answered me, either. Are you just a daredevil looking for a thrill?" The demand in his tone hinted at the importance he placed on her answer to his question. His eyes narrowed, and she surveyed his face. The usual warmth and amusement were gone, replaced by an unreadable mask.

"No," Kendall said, shaking her head. "But I want to enjoy life. I want to experience new things, sample new foods, and vacation in new places. Whenever I have an opportunity, I wander through art museums and stop at historical markers. I want to live life to the fullest. I don't want to miss out on a single thing. You know what I mean?" She lifted the glass of wine to her lips and took a sip, enjoying the rich, full flavor.

Ben nodded but remained silent, waiting for more.

She swallowed and sucked in a deep breath before pressing on. "Ben, I don't ever want to find myself at the end of my life and look back in regret. When I want something," she said, pausing to reach out and stroke the back of his work-calloused hand, "I go for it. Regardless of the consequences."

A panicked expression crossed his face. She might as well have told him to strip down and assume the position. And while she'd merely been talking in terms of life in general, Ben's mind had gone straight to sex. Poor thing. Her behavior last night and her overtly demonstrative affection today probably hadn't helped matters either. And unfortunately, the more she thought about a sexual relationship with Ben, the more appealing it became. Like something she wanted to grab hold of and try on for size.

Benjamin Montgomery might not realize it yet, but they were a perfect match. Here was a man that would understand her desire to enjoy life to the fullest, a man who exemplified that desire in the way he lived. Everything she'd read about him, and the few things she'd remembered from her childhood had all been true. The additional layers of loss and maturity had added a spicy texture to the rugged teenager she'd known sixteen years ago.

He lifted his wineglass and tipped it back, emptying the contents before reaching for the bottle to refill his glass. Taking another slow sip, he eyed her, seeming to consider her words. Funny, she could almost hear the gears grinding in his head. And then, as if he'd arrived at some monumental decision, his lips curved up into a genuine smile that touched his eyes, and Kendall breathed a sigh of relief.

Ben set down his wineglass and shook his head. "You scare the hell out of me, woman."

"Yeah," she said, nodding in agreement. "I scare myself sometimes, too."

CHAPTER 6

All those conversations with Kendall rattled around in his head like a dozen marbles in an empty wooden box. Over the past twenty-four hours, she'd given him no indication as to why she was here. Even after eating dinner tonight when he'd pressed her for answers, she'd claimed she was exhausted and that they'd talk about all the details in the morning.

However, on several occasions, she'd slipped in a few words that made him think she wanted a relationship with him. Something beyond friendship.

When I want something, I go for it.

What the hell was that supposed to mean?

Even with his unflappable maturity and infinite wisdom, he'd gaped at her, mouth open and eyes wide, while panic had seized his heart and a cold sweat had covered his body. And his damned, traitorous cock had twitched with enthusiasm—proof positive he wasn't mature or wise.

And then, what had the blonde temptress done? She'd grabbed his hand and told him she had every intention of getting what she wanted. Wink. Wink.

Yeah. Talk about instilling the fear of God in him.

But he already knew he was going to hell. A heated desire pulsed through his body whenever Kendall stepped into the room, leaving him hard, ready for action, and feeling like an old pervert. He'd formulated a string of reasons a mile long why he couldn't do what his body so eagerly desired to do.

God, he wanted her. And it made no sense at all. She was young. And blonde. And Jenna's baby sister.

Yeah. That thought made him feel sick with guilt.

But did Kendall really want a relationship with him? Or just sex. He wasn't sure which one, and it really didn't matter. Wasn't happening. Couldn't happen.

Ben rose from his seat in the great room, a half-empty bottle of Johnnie Walker clutched in his fist. He wandered closer to the wall of windows. Just like the weatherman had predicted, the storm was a fierce one. The house creaked and groaned against the stormy gusts like a mighty warrior threatened and battered by an attacking enemy. Ben, along with his best crew, had built his hunting lodge, board by board, piece by piece, and he knew the sturdy structure would withstand the worst storm, but the intensity of the gusting winds and the angry chorus of the torquing timbers declared the awesome power and strength of the impressive winter storm.

Ben flipped on the floodlight to illuminate a wide swatch across the backyard. The thick white flakes dropped from the sky at a frantic pace, blown into frenzied white cyclones by powerful blasts of wind, forming huge drifts around the house and garage. At this rate, they'd have a good six inches or more by morning, and he'd spend the better part of the day digging out of the snowdrifts after the storm ended. He and Kendall might be stuck here, unable to travel the short distance down the road to Jackson's house. And if the snow didn't let up soon, the roads would never be cleared by late afternoon to travel back into Krysset.

When they'd first arrived this afternoon, Kendall had asked him if they could cuddle in front of a roaring fire. The suggestion had made him laugh at the same time fear snaked up his spine. Oddly enough, up to that very moment in his life, hunkering down during a snowstorm with a beautiful and affectionate woman by a roaring fire with a chilled bottle of wine had always held an undeniably romantic appeal. But his self-imposed *Off Limits* sign—complete with flashing lights and warning sirens—had been installed upon Kendall's arrival, and he'd never muster the courage to pass the equivalent of a *Caution, Danger Ahead* warning without pausing and giving it some well-thought-out consideration.

Unfortunately, his little head had been leading the charge, sending images to his big head in an all-out attempt to sway the voice of reason and powers that be, encouraging him to join Kendall in bed. Conserve energy. Share heat. Make love. Its victory cry gained momentum as the midnight hour faded.

Instead of joining Kendall, Ben gritted his teeth and forced his feet to move past the door to where she slept and into his own room. Although, his strongest instincts screamed to turn back. Stake his claim. Fulfill his desire. And of course, the naughty voice in his head reasoned, leave Kendall well satisfied in the process.

Ben climbed into bed. He couldn't wait for morning. For Kendall to detail why she'd come back into his life. He wanted to understand her reasons, and he hoped he could be a supportive friend as she built a new life here in Krysset. Until then, he'd oscillate between self-loathing and mind-numbing lust. But there was no way in hell he'd fall asleep. Not when the conversations continued to replay in his mind while the wind howled outside his window.

At some point, he must have dozed off, because he came awake, intently listening for something that wasn't right in the house. Had he imagined the noise? He listened, attempting to still his racing heart and push aside the sounds of the storm, trying to figure out exactly what he'd heard.

A loud moan and a shrill cry dragged him the final distance out of his dreams.

"No!" A fierce shout followed by deeper moaning and a piercing wail. Kendall.

His heart beat out of his chest. He jumped from his bed, dressed in his flannel pajama bottoms and nothing else. His bare feet touched the cold floor, but the temperature failed to register as he raced out his door and across the hall toward her room. He knocked but didn't wait for her reply, convinced she was in the throes of a nightmare. The bathroom light cast a narrow beam of light across her bed, leaving the corners of the room in deep darkness, but there was enough light to witness her struggles.

Tossing and turning, throwing off her covers as if she fought against an invisible force.

Heart-shattering weeping replaced the sharp wail of moments before. Both sounds of her extreme distress. Both reminders of the nightmare she'd lived through.

Ben couldn't ignore her emotional anguish a moment longer. "Kendall. Wake up now, darling." The mattress dipped when he sat on the edge in order to run his hand over her forehead, pushing back her silky hair. "Kendall. Everything's okay." His hands continued to stroke along her shoulder and upper arm, noting how the odd shadows played across her delicate flesh, painting it with strange discolorations.

She stilled, awareness settling over her. "Ben?" Her whisper sounded uncertain. So different to her usual forthright tone.

"Yes, it's me. I'm here. You're okay." Silent sobs wracked her small body, and she curled into the fetal position while tears streamed down her round cheeks. "Hey. I'm here. It's okay. Only a dream. You're okay."

He brushed at the torrent of tears, but it did little to help. And just like sixteen years ago, her mournful tears shredded his heart. The simple, ridiculous words he whispered to comfort her clogged the back of his throat while he struggled to contain his own sorrow. But unlike his selfish emotions following Jenna's death, when he'd been too wrapped up in his own grief to worry about anyone else, now sadness poured from his wounded heart for Kendall and her continued suffering. Not for what he'd lost, but for everything she'd lost that night long ago.

Ben lifted the covers, slipping into Kendall's bed, well aware that the action might be the stupidest move he'd made in the past decade. His arm snaked around her shoulder and tugged her closer, aligning their bodies together. She curled her petite form against his, their legs entwined. A contented sigh passed her lips when she settled against his chest. Kendall fit beside him as if she'd been designed for him, the intimate position so natural and comfortable. And his fatigued brain accepted that ludicrous notion without argument.

Long moments passed before Kendall's breathing returned to a deep, even pace, and her body sagged in exhaustion. What a blessing that she found relief in sleep after such a horrific nightmare. He speculated it had been about the murder of her family. The murder she'd witnessed and couldn't prevent.

Ben envied her ability to drop off again with little problem; no doubt it was her body's own defensive mechanism. For him, the adrenaline rush caused by her frightened screams wouldn't allow sleep anytime soon. Instead, he listened to Kendall's soft breathing and quiet sighs. With his arms wrapped around her, he caressed the silky skin of her shoulder, savoring the sensation of her small form touching his, all the while vitally aware that the thin fabric of her tank top did little to disguise the press of her firm round breasts against his side.

Once again, his mind raced through the list of reasons to keep his distance. Blue eyes. Blonde hair. Ten years age difference. The little girl with long braids that would've been his sister-in-law. Jenna's baby sister.

Yeah. That thought always seemed to add a heaping dose of disgust and self-loathing on top of his boatload of guilt. Even with all his careful logic and sound reasoning, Ben hated the fact that some miniscule carnal spot in his brain and his unscrupulous body recognized Kendall for what she was—a beautiful, energetic, affectionate woman. One who seemed to sense this attraction between them. The attraction that just shouldn't be there.

Why had she shown up on his doorstep? Or rather, in his bed? Maybe if he knew why, he could enjoy himself a bit more. No.

Ben heaved a weary sigh and squeezed his eyes closed. He might be exhausted—his brain a bit lethargic due to the lack of adequate blood flow since it'd all headed south, pulsing through his painfully hard erection—but he wasn't dead. No, he was a healthy man with a hearty sexual appetite and excellent choice in women, so why did he feel guilty for noticing the alluring woman Kendall had become. Certainly, as a mature, self-controlled adult, he could grant himself permission to appreciate, without touching.

But no way could he fall asleep with her curvy body plastered against his.

After hours of staring at the ceiling and listening to the raging storm, he carefully climbed from Kendall's bed and traipsed across the hall to his own room, tugging on a faded sweatshirt and a pair of heavy wool socks before he snatched up his cell phone to call Jackson after breakfast.

Dawn arrived gray and blustery. The snow had slowed considerably, and a fresh, thick layer of white blanketed the landscape. With his feet propped on the ottoman, Ben slouched into the sofa with his laptop perched in his lap and a travel mug filled with steaming black coffee clutched in his fist. He'd just ended a call to Jackson when Kendall wandered into the great room.

"I thought I heard voices out here," she said. Still half asleep, pillow impressions lined her left cheek, and her hair was a wild jumbled mess. She wore fuzzy fleece pajama bottoms that looked cuddly soft and sexy as hell, and she'd slipped on a matching fleece robe, leaving it gaping open. At least she'd made an attempt to cover up that thin tank top that had held him transfixed for hours while he should've been sleeping.

His libido stirred to life. Damn, it was going to be a long day. "No. Just mine. I was talking to Jackson on the phone."

"How much time do I have to get ready?" She sunk onto the end of the shorter sofa perpendicular to him, stretching her legs out and propping them on the end of the ottoman. Her bare toes played against his sock-clad feet.

He fought the urge to jerk away from her touch. Or participate. "Take a look outside. We're not going anywhere, yet. Maybe later this afternoon. Right now, it'd be too dangerous to travel."

She glanced out the window and shrugged. "It's less than five miles." Kendall tugged her hair back into a sloppy ponytail and secured it with an elastic hair tie that she'd slipped off her wrist. The motion pulled against her bathrobe, opening it farther, and gave him a perfect view of her pert breasts. He forced his eyes back to his laptop.

"Yeah, but the road hasn't been plowed and won't be for a long while. We've had nearly a foot of snow overnight, and the temperature has dropped back below zero. I figure we'll have to stay here again tonight. Hopefully, we can make it back to town tomorrow." He stifled the yawn that threatened to escape. He felt as exhausted as Kendall looked. But at least she'd gotten a few hours of sleep while he'd held her against his chest. Fully awake. Fully aware of everything Kendall. Her velvety smooth skin and her long glossy tresses. Her warm peaches and vanilla scent, touched with a hint of musk. And her occasional sighs when she'd stirred, and then her quiet inhalations when she'd drifted deeper into sleep.

God, she was so sweet, he just wanted to kiss her. Touch her. Best to change the subject. "Tell me about your nightmare," Ben said, watching Kendall's face. She blinked at him several times, clearly surprised that he'd asked.

"Why?"

Trying to keep the conversation light, he playfully brushed his toes against hers. "Because I'm curious, and sometimes talking it out helps."

She gave a disinterested shrug. "You know, I've always hated talking about my nightmares the next day. Or any day for that matter. When I was a kid, I felt like people were just prying for the gory details when they'd failed to protect me in the first place."

"I'm sorry, Kendall. I didn't mean to pry. And I sure as hell don't need the gory details." And that was the God's honest truth, because he'd totally retch up everything in his gut if she started talking about what she saw that night.

"It's the same old dream. I'm trapped in that closet. Helpless. Watching." Ben's stomach twisted at her honest words. He almost regretted asking, but he'd heard all the details before. He really wasn't going to lose it, even though she was staring at him with a look of concern on her face. "I'm sorry, Ben, but I just don't think sharing this with you would be good for either of us."

Ben looked away. Maybe she was right.

Kendall stood and climbed onto the sofa, kneeling beside him. "I never got to tell you how sorry I am that you lost the woman you loved." The shimmer of tears in her eyes gutted him.

"God, Kendall." Ben pulled her into his arms, gently cradling her in his lap. With one hand firmly at her waist, his other hand tilted her face to meet his. "Why would you say that? We both lost her."

"I know. But I thought maybe you needed to hear me say that. To you. For you."

He shook his head. "I'm sorry, too. So very sorry, darling." He held her to his chest for the longest time. Neither of them speaking. Neither of them crying. Just sitting there with their memories.

"I understand, Kendall, if you'd prefer not to discuss your nightmares. That's your right, but know that I'm here if you need me to listen." He pressed a kiss to her temple.

"Thank you," she said quietly, returning to her original spot on the other sofa. "And thanks for holding me. I don't like being alone after one of those bad dreams."

"Do you have them often?" Ben asked.

Sighing, she eased back into her seat and returned to rubbing her toes against his feet again. He admired her feet as they played against his. They were the cutest little feet with pink-tipped toes. "No. Only on occasion, but they seem to be happening more frequently since I started seeing Nick."

Those words gave him a jolt, and he turned to look at her. "Why would that stir up your old nightmares?"

Damn. The expression on her face said she was hiding something. She gave a casual lift of her shoulder and then studied the fingernails on her right hand. Finally, she said, "It's one of the reasons that I had to break up with him. I don't have them every night. I'm sorry I woke you."

He wanted more details, but it was obvious that was all she intended to give him. He smiled as if he accepted her ambiguous answer, but what else could he do? "Don't be. I'm glad I was there for you." Dropping his feet to the floor, he leaned forward and set his laptop on the ottoman in their place. "How about breakfast?" He rose to prepare them something to eat.

"Could we take the snowmobiles over to Sophie and Jackson's place this afternoon?"

"Maybe. We'll see."

"Oh, but I really hoped to drive one today," Kendall said, her disappointment evident in her rather petulant tone. But maybe she was still just tired. Lord knew he was.

"Instead of breakfast, maybe you'd prefer to go back to bed for a few hours."

A shy grin spread across Kendall's face, and she chewed at her lower lip. "Okay, I like the way that sounds, but only if you'll join me."

Ben shook his head. Of course that's where she'd go, since he'd paved the way. "I think we both know that's not a good idea, Kendall."

She stood and approached him. Her slow, stalking steps coupled with the bane of his existence over the past several hours—the perfectly round globes of her breasts, showcased in that snug tank top fully visible beneath her wide-open robe—forced him to fist his hands by his side.

How long could he fight the urge to grab her and drag her back to bed just as she'd suggested?

Ben's eyes remained fixed on her chest, the rise and fall hypnotic as it stretched the fabric tighter against one of the places his hands and mouth longed to explore. He was confident that they'd both be tuckered out by the time he completed his thorough exploration.

Kendall cleared her throat, drawing his gaze back to her face. "What I know is that I slept really well when you held me, Ben."

Now that he'd opened this door, he wanted nothing more than to slam it shut and throw the dead bolt. He weighed each word with caution. "I'm well aware of that, but I found it impossible to sleep with your warm little body wrapped around mine."

She lifted her eyebrows and asked, "Too hot for you, huh?"

Ben felt as if he'd aged two decades overnight, and he heaved a weary sigh, too exhausted to participate in this sexual innuendo game today. Instead, he simply nodded in agreement. "God, yes. Something like that."

CHAPTER 7

After breakfast, Ben showered, and then he built a fire in the fireplace. The hot cocoa was nearly done warming when Kendall wandered into the great room. She, too, had showered and dressed in jeans and a thick sweatshirt, prepared for the snowy winter day.

"Ben, you made a fire. And cocoa? I think I like being snowed in with you."

"Yeah, I've always loved snow days."

Kendall came up behind him, and he was certain she was going to hug him again, but she didn't. She stopped at his side, just shy of touching him. But if he lifted his arm just a fraction of an inch, he'd brush up against her breast.

God, he needed to stop thinking about Kendall's breasts. Or any of her other sexy body parts. But then he breathed in her sweet scent, and he knew he was a goner.

"Come on," he said, handing her a big mug and picking up his own. He led her to the sofa near the fireplace. "You said you wanted to cuddle, so I thought we could do that while we have a little conversation."

"What do you want to talk about?"

Ben grunted at the seemingly purposeful absentminded question. "Why you're here, Kendall. I've been more than patient. So start talking."

Kendall stared at him with an expression that said she'd rather run and hide. He'd laugh if he weren't so confused by her appearance and her resistance to share the truth with him. In his humble opinion, being housebound by a blizzard was the perfect time to tackle whatever it was that had brought Kendall back to

Krysset. Although, judging from the look on her face, Kendall didn't agree. He might even go as far as to say, she found his choice of topics downright repulsive.

After debating her response for several long minutes, Kendall set her mug on the side table and rose. She paced back and forth between where he sat and the fireplace. "My memories. That's why I'm here. In Krysset. And more precisely, in your house."

Ben had known Kendall was going to unearth all those dark days he'd buried years ago. His throat tightened, and he tried to swallow to make it feel better. Didn't help. Memories. God, help him. He didn't like memories.

Ben shook his head. Hell, he couldn't do this. Kendall. Her memories. His memories. He never talked about the past, and he was fairly certain, he couldn't listen to her do it either.

"I'm sorry. You probably don't want to hear this—"

"No, I don't want to hear about the past. I want to know why the hell you've come back—present tense—to Krysset? To my house? To my life? Help me understand."

She paused in her pacing long enough to ask, "Do you remember the fair? I really don't have that many memories of those days, but I remember going to the Wahnata County Fair."

What the hell? Didn't he just say he wasn't interested in the past?

Kendall stared down at him as if she was actually waiting for him to answer that question. What did she think this was, some audience participation event? Damn it. All he'd asked for was a simple explanation, and she wanted to take a stroll down memory lane. Not happening. He stared at her.

"Oh, come on, Ben. You've got to remember. You bought me pink cotton candy, remember?"

He scrubbed a hand down his face, feeling thoroughly put out. "Yes," he said, making the concession even though he didn't want to. "You liked pink."

"Still do."

For some reason, he felt his lips tip up into a small grin as the image of her pink bra and matching panties rolled through his mind.

"I've always remembered you—big, strong Ben. But I especially remember how you protected Jenna from those mean boys that were picking on her. Do you remember?"

"They weren't picking on her, Kendall. They were making lewd suggestions, and then one of them tried to grab at her. She was my gal. Of course I protected her." His voice cracked. He hadn't really protected her. Not when it counted. When Jenna had needed him the most, he hadn't been there to defend her from the worst kind of monster.

Kendall turned away from him and stared into the fire. Probably thinking that exact thing—that he'd failed.

He watched her profile. She wasn't saying anything. Just making him guess. "What's going on, Kendall? Why are you doing this? Why are you bringing up the past like this?"

Kendall nibbled on her lower lip, and finally she said, "Well…I…"

"Are you scared?" Ben waited for her reply. All he could do was extrapolate from her bit about the county fair. "Kendall, are you worried about your safety?" Her eyes were glossy, and her lashes were fluttering up and down like she was fighting to hold back tears. What was she holding back?

And suddenly, those dark shadows he'd noticed on her shoulders and upper arms the past two nights made a whole lot more sense.

"Take off your shirt, Kendall." That got her attention.

Her eyes went wide in panic. "What?" She nearly screeched the words.

"Your sweatshirt. Take it off." Ben said the words quietly, because he didn't want to scare her. But he needed the truth.

"But…" She looked frantic, ready to bolt.

Ben stood and closed the distance between them. "I want to see." The expression on her face gutted him. She knew exactly what he was interested in looking at, and she knew her secret wasn't a secret any longer.

His hands went to the hem of her sweatshirt, and he slowly lifted it. "Lift your arms for me." Holding his breath, he gently pulled the shirt up and over her head. His heart beat a little faster, because God, he wanted to look at the swells of her breasts and her flat little stomach and everything else that was exposed. But instead his eyes immediately fell to the ugly purple bruises on her shoulders, ribcage, and her upper arms.

Ben gently ran the tip of his finger over the discolored skin, slowly moving around to look at her back. There were bruises there, too. Big marks that had to hurt like hell. There was a rainbow of colors, including shades of yellows and greens. This hadn't been a one-time event. He gently traced over the darkest of purple shadows.

Now the accelerated pounding of his heart was for an entirely different reason than lust. The sharp bite of anger beat through him, sending his blood racing through his veins with a deafening whoosh. He fought to keep his anger hidden from Kendall with hands fisted by his side and his jaw clenched to hold back the furious roar that threatened to burst free. In this moment, Ben wanted to rip the man apart. Death would be too good for the bastard who'd hurt Kendall.

"Oh, Kendall," he said. It was just a whisper, because he could hardly breathe. He glanced at her face.

Tears were rolling silently down her cheeks. His memories tried to yank him back to the funeral, but this was different. The expression on her face, the look in her eyes—it was shame. Why the hell would she feel ashamed? He righted the sweatshirt and eased it back over her head, pulling it into place. Then he led her over to the sofa and covered her with a heavy fleece throw.

He settled in close to her, wrapping an arm around her, drawing her nearer at the same time he pushed down his need for vengeance in order to speak in a calm voice. "You need protection. From your ex. That's what this is all about? You've run away from him, because you're scared?"

She sniffled a bit and sucked in a ragged breath as if she wanted to tell him more, but all she did was nod.

"Why me? Cam loves you, Kendall. He'd die for you. You've got to know that. He'd protect you."

With a swift fierceness Ben was coming to expect from Kendall, she said, "Cam doesn't want me. He never did. Not sixteen years ago. Not now. You heard him yesterday morning. He wanted to ship me back to Oregon." Ben doubted that was how Cam actually felt, but that was how Kendall saw it. She seemed to lose some of her heated passion before she said, "Besides, if he gets his hands on Nick, he'd kill him."

"And you think I won't?" Hell, just looking at those bruises made Ben want to kill the son of a bitch. Would he be able to hold himself back if the guy really did show up in Krysset? Ben fisted his hands in his lap. Yeah right, like that was going to prevent the boiling rage from escaping. "If I get my hands on him, I'm going to kill him. Then, after I'm done, that nasty-ass cousin of yours'll kill him all over again."

"I can only imagine," she said on a small laugh while she wiped at the wetness on her face with the sleeve of her sweatshirt.

"Were you living with him?"

"No. Not officially, but he wanted me there all the time. He kept getting more and more demanding, and I don't like that sort of thing."

"Did you break up with him? I mean, did he know it wasn't working for you?"

"I tried, but…" Her words trailed off, and she shook her head. Sadness and more shame.

"The bruises?"

"Some of them. After that, I got a restraining order, but he seemed to follow me everywhere. I just wanted him to leave me alone."

The tiniest flicker of a memory flashed through his mind. A small girl with long blonde braids. That unsure child still lingered on the far edges of Kendall's personality but no longer controlled her destiny. Instead, a courageous, self-assured woman led the way. Kendall had developed into a strong, mature, capable woman. In all the ugliness and pain, one fact outshined all else—Kendall Aasgaard was a survivor. She'd been handed some of the lousiest circumstances possible, and yet, she'd persevered with a brazen attitude that almost dared fate to try to destroy her life again.

Sure, she had her demons. But who was he kidding? So did he.

"Did you report him for being in violation of the restraining order?" he asked. He sensed that the answer was not a simple one by the way she stalled before she answered him.

Hesitantly, she shook her head. "It wouldn't have fixed things. His dad's this big-shot attorney who's gotten him out of quite a few sticky situations in the past. I just wanted it all to disappear. I tried hiding, but no matter where I went, he'd show up. Finally, when I couldn't do it anymore, I packed up my stuff and ran. I came here, because I didn't know where else to turn."

"What about the scratches on your arms? I thought maybe a cat?"

She shook her head. "Nick has a knife collection." She said the words so quietly he could hardly hear them.

Ben swore under his breath. Holy hell. Her ex used a knife on her? That thought made him sick to his stomach. "Great. Then I'll have a good excuse to cut off his balls if he shows up here." Ben took a long deep breath. "What happens when Nick realizes that you've abandoned him for good?"

"He probably won't even come looking for me. I just need someplace to stay for a couple weeks until this entire thing blows over. Then, when I'm sure he won't come around, I'll start searching for my own apartment." Although she tried to give it an optimistic spin, the truth was there in her eyes: fear. "So here I am," she said, somehow pulling herself together enough to put a painful grin on her face. And that pathetic forced expression screamed that, like Ben, she'd graduated from the *fake-it-till-you-make-it* school of thought.

"I'm glad you got away from him. That was smart. And brave. How about we change topics, huh?" Ben asked. Kendall almost seemed to sag in relief. "So why my bed?"

"Oh, umm, I—" She stuttered the words while blushing. Really? Now she blushes? "I'm sorry. I guess I thought that you'd be more willing to help me if…"

"If there was something in it for me?" His words came out far louder than he intended. But God, the only reason she believed that was because she hung around with lowlife assholes. He wasn't one of them though.

Ben couldn't say he was happy with the idea of trouble finding its way to his doorstep, but he was glad that Kendall had trusted him enough to turn to him. He'd do everything in his power to protect her. *Without* becoming involved with her. She obviously was coming off a bad relationship, and he was…well…in no place to get involved. Especially with a woman who didn't fit his criteria and had already warned him that she only did relationships with emotional strings attached.

After Kendall had opened up about her reason for coming back to town, Ben eased her against his body to cuddle just as he'd initially promised. With his back propped on one end and his long legs stretched down the length of the sofa, Kendall wedged herself between his spread thighs and rested her back against his chest. Ben was fairly certain this wasn't a good idea, but Kendall seemed to need the closeness. And to his surprise, it felt as natural as could be.

And of course, the woman fell right asleep. It appeared as if she could drop off to sleep just about anywhere, at any time. He, however, was wide awake, with his cock hard enough to pound nails against her back.

It wasn't long before Kendall sank farther down his body, causing her sweatshirt to rise up just a couple inches to reveal the soft flesh of her abdomen. He tried not to look, but he found himself staring at the narrow band of flesh. He wanted to touch her there to see if he was right. Was it really as silky soft as it looked?

With slow deliberate strokes, he gingerly ran his finger over her abdomen—only where her skin was exposed. Just like he thought, her skin felt like cool, smooth satin, and he could imagine his hands wandering over every inch of her bare flesh. The front of his jeans tightened even more if that was possible. But it was his own damned fault for comforting her in this position.

Giving Kendall a chance to cuddle had been a noble plan, but hadn't fallen anywhere near the category of smart ideas. Kind of like when he'd ridden his bike off the roof of the garage to propel himself toward the moon. Or like the less than wise decision to crawl into her bed to hold her after her nightmare.

It might appear that his decision-making abilities had taken a nosedive since Kendall Aasgaard's startling reappearance into his life Friday night. His close friends or even his brothers might suggest that his poor decisions were the direct result of his emerging emotions toward Jenna's baby sister.

And he'd tell them all to go to hell.

His jaw clenched, biting back that thought. He could hardly tell them off when such a suggestion held a sliver of truth.

Ben cared for Kendall. Always had. However, his concern had never extended beyond the health and wellbeing type of thoughts. Kendall's appearance in his bed late Friday night had annihilated those platonic thoughts and replaced them with ones of pink lace bras and matching thong panties.

Ben tugged Kendall's sweatshirt down where it belonged, dragged the throw blanket off the floor to cover them both, tucking the fleecy fabric around her, and then folded his hands over the top of her covered stomach.

He closed his eyes. See, he could do this. Be the friend she needed without being the creepy old pervert with lewd thoughts. Ben gritted his teeth while he breathed in vanilla and warm peaches, praying she woke up soon.

Kendall shifted, adjusting herself, rubbing against him to get more comfortable.

Okay, his eyes were back open now.

Her blonde tresses gently tumbled across her shoulder. The silky fall of hair spun visions of her naked body straddled over his, her hair a sleek champagne curtain swinging softly with her movements, brushing against her hardened nipples while she rode him.

He shifted to ease his discomfort at the same time he fought to control the rising sexual tension in his body.

"Hmmm, that was so good." Her words were a breathy, sensual moan that didn't do a damn thing to help get his body under control. Thoughts of bringing her to orgasm while she moaned her satisfaction, just like that, nearly had him coming in his jeans. His internal struggle was his sole focus at the moment. "I guess I fell asleep." She yawned and stretched. "Did you sleep, too?"

Not a chance with her body doing all sorts of things to his body. "No."

"I'm sorry that I'm not better company."

"Hush. It's all fine. I was just watching the snow drift. And being pinned beneath your body was all the excuse I needed not to head outside and start digging us out." He gave her a gentle squeeze, now aware of the discomfort she must be suffering due to the bruises on her torso and shoulders.

They sat in silence, simply enjoying the moment, watching the wind pick up the powder-light snow and swirl it into drifts in the yard. Finally, when he thought she'd dozed off again, Kendall said, "I have something else I need to tell you."

"I'm listening," Ben said, hoping it wasn't anything worse than what she'd already shared.

"I'm incredibly attracted to you, Ben." He tensed at her words, but she kept on talking. "I'm sorry if my saying that makes you uncomfortable, but I need to be honest with you. I never intended to feel this way, for this to happen." She was about the boldest, most straightforward person he'd ever meet. What the hell was he supposed to say to her little announcement? "Do you think we could ever be something more than friends?" she asked in the softest voice. "I mean, you are attracted to me, right?"

Ben sighed. "I can't get involved with you. I loved your sister."

Kendall stiffened up in his arms and then swung her feet to the floor, shifting until she was propped on the opposite end of the sofa near his feet, about as far away from him as she could get. An expression of exasperation crossed her face, and she glanced down at the obvious bulge at the front of his pants. The look she gave him called him a liar.

She obviously needed further explanation. "Yes, I'm attracted to you. My boner has been twitching against your back for the past two hours. It's pretty hard to miss. But I don't date blondes. Ever. Because I'm reminded of Jenna. I don't know that I'll ever be able to look at you and not think of her. Add in our age difference and a relationship between the two of us would be impossible."

The pained expression that crossed her face gutted him so thoroughly he couldn't bear to look at her any longer. His gazed dropped to the space she'd been resting in a moment ago. "I'm sorry, Kendall. I just don't think it would be fair to you."

She was silent for so long that after several minutes had passed he looked up. When he met her eyes, she said, "No, it's not fair to you, Benjamin Montgomery. You loved Jenna sixteen years ago, and she's dead." Kendall spoke the words with gentle conviction as if she wanted to rouse him from a deep sleep without startling him too much. "The sister I remember wouldn't want this for you, Ben. She'd have wanted you to go on with your life. It's time to get over her."

What was wrong with him? Why had he shared those thoughts about his great unfailing, never-ending love for her dead sister? Only to put distance between him and Kendall? But as he studied her features, her gaze darted around the room anywhere but at him, and he regretted everything. His words. His actions. His undeniable need to cling to the past.

For some unknown reason, he held this unexplainable faithfulness to Jenna and nobody, regardless of their hair or eye color, had gotten through to his heart. He'd never moved on, and he was certain he never would.

"I care about you, Kendall. More than I want to. We have chemistry, for sure. I've been a walking erection since I found you sleeping in my bed. But I'm afraid it's only lust. Can caring and lusting ever turn into love? Truthfully, my heart's been numb for so many years I don't think I'd even recognize that emotion. You're right, though. I should've moved on years ago. But I couldn't. Or maybe I didn't have a reason."

"Well, Mr. Montgomery, I intend to give you a reason," she said, giving him a smile that said she was dead serious.

After their mutual revelation, they both needed a few moments of privacy. Ben pulled on some cold weather gear and headed out the door to clear the driveway. It wasn't long before Kendall made her way outside, too, bundled up in a similar fashion, searching for a shovel. She cleared the walkway and steps near the lodge while he used the snowplow attachment on the front of his truck. Some of the powdery snow would drift back in overnight, but the task got them up off the sofa and out of the serious conversation for a couple much-needed hours.

For whatever reason, their solemn discussions from earlier in the day were set aside, and they settled in together for a dinner of soup and sandwiches in front of the fire.

"It was a great day, huh?" Kendall asked.

"I had fun. I'm glad we didn't try to rush back to town. You texted Cam, right?"

"Yes."

"You know, he does care about you," Ben said, watching while Kendall seemed to bristle.

She agreed with a long sigh and a reluctant dip of her head. "Yes, I know Cam cares."

"Good. So you need to tell Cam about the situation."

"No way. I'm not telling him." Kendall shook her head.

When Ben had imagined Kendall all grown up, he'd always thought she'd turn out to be quiet and sweet like Jenna or perhaps a peacemaker like their mom, Sylvia. But, no. The real Kendall Aasgaard was her own woman. Outspoken, fun-loving, and strong-willed. Someone who rallied her courage and faced her fears head-on. Someone who forged her own path. "When I think of Cam, I either picture a dictator ruling with an iron fist or a stubborn old mule sinking his heels into the ground."

Ben barked out a laugh. "Well, I'm not Cameron Aasgaard's biggest fan either, but a few months ago, we patched things up in order to support a mutual friend."

"Ben, he punched you yesterday morning." Her indignation on his behalf warmed his heart. And then she reached out and gently touched him, her fingers feathering over his jaw where the bluish tint of a bruise lingered.

"Yeah." He gritted his teeth at the tender caress, extrapolating it in his mind into an intimate gesture. But how could he not? They'd both admitted their attraction for one another. He plucked her small hand from his face and clutched it in his fist to keep her from doing that again. "Cam and I had a small misunderstanding. But he still needs to know what's going on with you."

With her jaw set in a show of resistance, she crossed her arms over her chest. Just like Cam, she'd inherited the stubborn-mule gene. But rather than comment, he laughed out loud.

"Look, Kendall. There's nothing gained by cutting your cousin out. I can't keep this from him, or he'll skin me alive. So, I'm thinking tomorrow night when we get back into town, I'll take you out for pizza at the Brawling Bear, and the two of you can talk. We'll kill two birds with one stone. Otherwise, we'll have to cook dinner ourselves and then call him to come over to my place to tell him. Either way, he's going to find out."

"Fine." Her shoulders sagged in surrender.

"He cares about you and only wants the best for you." When she didn't respond, he decided to switch gears. "How long do you think until Nick comes looking for you? Don't you think you should be prepared? The more people who know of the threat and are ready to act, the better our chances are to let this guy know he can't mess with you anymore."

"I don't know. Maybe Nick will never show up."

Yeah, right. That sounded like wishful thinking. If the guy was as possessive and domineering as the bruises indicated, there was no way that he'd let Kendall go without a fight. Thankfully, he and Cam would be there to defend her if the situation came to that.

Ben grinned as he watched the tenacious woman pick up her empty soup bowl and plate and march into the kitchen, obviously still annoyed that he pressed the issue about notifying her cousin. But Cam would be furious if they withheld this type of information from him. Hell, the man was going to blow a gasket either way. He prayed that Cam could keep his shit together long enough to encourage Kendall in her quest for independence without crushing the progress she'd already made.

CHAPTER 8

Cam's face flushed the color of a ripe tomato while the vein at his temple noticeably pulsated. Both were clearly visible across the booth despite the dim bar lighting. Kendall only hoped he wouldn't stroke out before he processed the news she'd just dumped in his lap. Had it not been for Ben's presence in the seat beside her, she might've been tempted to deliver a sugar-coated version. She glanced at Ben, wondering if he recognized her need for simplicity when it came to her older cousin.

Although a rowdy dinner crowd had filled the bar, their booth had been sucked into a vacuum of awkward silence. Chilled by the empty glare of Cam's unblinking eyes, Kendall reassured herself that the nostril on either side of his nose flared with each intake of oxygen while the muscles in his jaw twitched. Both signs he was indeed alive. Ben's hand rested on her leg, just above the knee, in an unspoken show of support. They both watched Cam digest the unsavory bit of information while he ground his teeth down to tiny useless stubs. All on her behalf.

Okay. Time to soothe the poor guy. "Cam, calm down. I'm okay. He pushed me around a bit, but didn't do any real damage. He's a jerk. And even though it kills me to admit it, you were right."

Even her attempt to lighten the mood fell flat.

After several long moments, Ben broke the silence. "Cam, you have to admit, Kendall did the right thing. She left the asshole after he hurt her and sought out a restraining order. She did well, didn't she?" Okay. Not so subtle, but encouraging all the same. She smiled at Ben in silent appreciation for the positive assessment of her actions.

Cam's head bobbed in agreement. "Ben's right, baby girl." He plucked up both her hands in his big ones and squeezed them tight. "You did everything I'd have wanted you to do in the moment. Except, maybe call me, but I'm not angry at you. The loser ex of yours will find himself in a world of hurt if I ever get my hands on him."

Kendall studied her cousin's face as he and Ben quarreled over who got dibs on Nicholas Cardwell's skinny neck. Cam's coloring had returned to normal, although he had one of those faces that always appeared angry and more than a little threatening. Like both their fathers, his chiseled, strong facial features combined with his sheer size were enough to intimidate the most formidable opponent. His long, dark blond hair, which he secured at the nape of his neck, and his matching well-groomed goatee, completed his Viking persona. Give him an iron helmet, a round shield, and a sword and he'd look like a modern-day Norse god.

Kendall wasn't alone in her assessment of her older cousin. Regardless of his rather harsh features, he attracted women in droves. She'd always considered his rugged face good-looking and often blamed her opinion on the fact that his gait, intonation, and mannerisms subconsciously reminded her of her father.

What little girl didn't think her daddy was the handsomest man in the world?

Although, the passage of time had swept Kendall's memory clean of most of those finer details of her father, so she wasn't certain if the similarities she noted between her male relatives were real or imagined.

* * *

Cam tried to ignore the fact that Ben looked downright comfortable sitting next to Kendall, but it was bugging the hell out of him. The guy had suddenly become important in his little cousin's life, and overall that wasn't a bad thing. Montgomery was steady—well, except for the excessive drinking. But no way could Cam say the things that needed to be said with that guy sitting beside her. "Hey, Montgomery, do you mind giving me and Kendall a few minutes?" Cam asked.

The panicked expression that crossed Kendall's face troubled him. And then Ben leaned over and placed a kiss on Kendall's cheek, whispering something in her ear before sliding out of the booth.

What in the hell was that about?

He reined in his concern over Ben's affection toward his little girl and posed the question. "Kendall, why didn't you tell me about this before? Don't you trust me? I'd do anything to help you, sweetheart."

She gazed into the distance and shrugged. Memories of the sullen teenage girl sitting across from him at Aunt Rita's kitchen table flared into his mind. She'd refused to talk to him back then, too.

When Kendall had told him that she intended to make Krysset her permanent home, Cam had held a brief, personal celebration. A piece of his broken family had returned home. He couldn't wait to get to know the beautiful woman in front of him that had grown from a young child to a mature adult in what seemed like a blink of an eye. "You have no idea how I feel about you, Kendall." Why did she insist on treating him like the enemy? It felt as if someone had planted a stake in his heart and found pleasure in wrenching on it. Not to kill him, but merely to induce pain.

"Oh, I have a fairly good idea, Cameron." She cocked her head in a show of complete sarcasm, and her lips curled into a cynical smirk. "When I'd lost everything, everyone, you didn't want me around. You pawned me off on the first people to show interest in me." Her rant picked up steam and volume, but she didn't stop, and Cam knew better than to suggest it. Besides, maybe an emotional outburst would give him a damn hint as to why she hated his guts.

"You let them haul me to the other side of the country. Strangers. Ancient people, Cam. People who'd already raised their children and didn't want to raise me. You were like my big brother, but you didn't want me."

Her words sliced through his heart, tearing to the depths of his soul. Words that arrested him, convicted him, and left him to rot in the prison of his own making. He'd avoided this topic for too damned long.

Cam shook his head and said, "No, I wanted you to stay with me, Kendall. I wanted you to stay in Krysset." He'd wanted it more than life itself, and she had no clue. No clue how much he'd missed her. No clue how much he'd adored her. Loved her. And she had no idea, because he'd never said the words. It was his fault. And the time had come to right the wrong.

"Peeling your delicate little arms from around my neck and then stuffing you into the back seat of your Aunt Rita and Uncle Patrick's car was the single most difficult thing I've ever done." He could still hear the muffled screams and see the river of tears flowing down her cheeks as she pounded her dainty fists against the rear windows. A little part of his heart had died that day as he'd turned away from her sorrow and puked his guts out in the ornamental shrubbery outside the church.

"That moment, the moment they drove away with you screaming for me from the back seat will go down as one of the worst memories of my life. Right next to your phone call the night of…" The memory of her whispered words from sixteen years ago still sent chills racing down his spine, and they'd haunt his nightmares for as long as he lived.

The phone rang well past midnight. He always hated late night calls. No one called socially after ten o'clock. Only bad news came at that hour. He rolled over, reaching across the bed to snatch the phone off the nightstand.

"Hello." His voice sounded like gravel. A mix of annoyance and exhaustion.

"Cam?" The tiny squeak on the other end of the line allowed him to relax. She'd been playing with the phone again. With two teenage siblings, she'd often voiced her frustration at her lack of phone time.

"Dolly? Is that you? Shouldn't you be in bed, sweetheart? It's too late to call people." He leaned into his pillows, his eyes drifting closed while he listened to her rapid respirations.

"They're dead." A whispered confession. "All. Dead." In a childlike singsong voice. And his blood ran cold. Her tone hollow. Her words emotionless.

* * *

Kendall personally didn't remember that specific detail from the night her family had been murdered, even though Cam had spoken of her phone call many times. But she remembered the blood. Red liquid splattered against the walls. Red gore puddled on the floor. Pools of dark, sticky blood. By her mother's body. By her father's body. By her brother's body.

Unending rivers of blood had been the basis for more than a decade of nightmares.

And she also remembered the eyes. She'd walked from one room to the next, staring into four sets of sightless eyes, certain that dead people pinched their eyes closed. But no. They were all open. Even Jenna's. From Kendall's hiding space inside the closet, she'd witnessed Jenna's body crumple to the ground, while a steady river of red oozed from the gaping wound on her neck. Seeping around her head. Staining her blonde hair. And her open eyes had stared at Kendall.

Other than crimson blood and lifeless eyes, Kendall remembered few things from the bizarre string of days that followed, except being forced to leave with two strangers while Cam turned his back. She'd cried out to him. She'd screamed, and he'd ignored her.

She stared at the man she'd known all her life. Her rock. A firm, non-moving entity during the first eight years of her life. But over the last sixteen years, he'd become the tyrant that arrived in town to set the rules for her, as well as for her aunt and uncle. Didn't they ever become tired of his heavy-handedness?

"Did I ever tell you that I came to the hospital the day you were born?" He leaned back against the hard wooden seat as if he planned to stay a good, long while. She shook her head and stared, annoyed that he'd dragged her from her brooding to answer another one of his stupid questions.

"It was about a year before the car crash." His voice took on a softer, reminiscent tone. He spoke about the crash that had changed the face of his family forever, ripping both his parents away and placing him as guardian of his four younger brothers. After the accident, her five cousins had spent countless hours each week at her family's home.

"My mom dragged me up to the hospital to visit the new baby. I was eighteen and about as interested in seeing a shriveled, smelly baby as I was in going to school to get a diploma. I figured she was hoping to curb my promiscuous behavior."

"Whoa there, cuz. TMI." Kendall cringed behind her outstretched hands, cursing Ben for abandoning her, only to be scarred for life as this little chat veered into forbidden territory. Death and destruction were always valid topics for conversation, but with Cam, she drew the line at discussions about sex.

He rolled his eyes in complete disregard for her sensibility. "Anyway, I held you that day, and it hit me like a wrecking ball. Mom was right. I could've created one of these miniature people with my lack of care. I realized I could be standing right there at that very moment holding my own child. And from that day on, I watched you grow. I reveled in how perfect you were. How sweet."

Cam shrugged off the words as if to minimize their value. "In a weird way, I thought of you as mine. And when your folks died, they named me as their first choice for guardian." He squeezed his eyes closed as if he could block out the distressing memory. Kendall knew from experience that only allowed the vivid pictures to play out on the black screen of the inside of her eyelids. But when Cam's eyes fluttered open again, he gazed at her. Emotions swam in the depths of his eyes. "I was floored, humbled with their trust. The honor of caring for you, their beautiful gift.

"But I knew I wasn't good enough for you. You needed both parents, a woman who could give you all the girly emotional support you'd need as you grew up. Your aunt and uncle were listed as second choice of guardian, and I knew I had to put my selfish desires aside and consider the best thing for you. At the time, I felt they were a better option, so I asked them to raise you. They were kind enough to name me co-guardian and allow me some say in how you were cared for.

"Despite that concession, Kendall, I've regretted my decision for sixteen years. I even flew out one time to bring you home, but Rita urged me to let you settle in. I tried to make the best decisions for you, but my heart has never been the same. Losing you was like another death, piled on all the other ones."

Tears pooled in her eyes. "I'm sorry, Cameron. I didn't know. I thought you hated me." She choked the words out on a sob.

Within seconds, Cam slid out of the booth and slipped in next to her, wrapping his arms around her. His gentle act of comfort reminded her of the caring big brother from her childhood memories.

"I love you, sweet girl. You'll always be my baby girl." He whispered the words near her ear, his strong voice cracking with emotions. "Nothing is more important to me than my family and ensuring that they're safe and happy."

* * *

Ben sat at a stool toward the end of the bar. His attention was divided between the touching reunion unfolding at the table across the room and glaring at the woman talking to Ethan while she ordered up a drink. Mary Sue Prescott. No. She went by the name of Sue Walsh now. Married with a van full of kids. Everyone in town said she'd changed. But Ben still remembered her brother's murder trial and the way she'd stirred up trouble. What was that saying about a leopard not changing her spots?

Warily, Sue slid her gaze to Ben. Must have felt the daggers he was shooting at her back. God, he hated that woman, and the expression on his face must have told her exactly what he was feeling. Sue turned to face front and center—shoulders back and spine straight. When Ethan placed the glass in front of her, she picked up the drink, glanced quickly at the booth where Cam and Kendall were talking, and then raced back to her table and her family.

Ben really ought to make Kendall aware of Sue's presence here. At the Brawling Bear. In Krysset. He let his eyes wander to where the cousins sat and then promptly returned his gaze to his half-empty beer glass. If Ben told Kendall, it would probably only upset her, and she already had more than enough on her plate with her ex.

As Ethan approached, Ben asked, "How could you be so friendly with that woman?" He hadn't bothered to disguise his bitterness.

"Sue?" Ethan, known as Taz Bear by most folks in town, simply shrugged. "She's nice enough."

"You're kidding me. After what she put Cam and Kendall through at her brother's trial?" He grunted out a humorless laugh. "I can't imagine shooting the shit with her. I can hardly stand being in the same zip code."

Apparently not wanting to discuss Ben's issues or Sue's misguided behavior before, during, and after the murder trial, Ethan pointed toward the booth Ben had vacated ten minutes ago. "Looks like they're finally making up. It's about time." The bartender's voice held that wistful quality of a man in love, and Ben fought the urge to roll his eyes. A few months ago, Ethan had discovered the love of his life, Dani, and at the same time, he'd reconciled with his father after a decade-old grudge. Now sickeningly happy, Ethan thought everyone should find their love match or resolve their lifelong feuds, joining him in his disgustingly blissful nirvana.

"Kendall has him wound tighter than a spring. Seldom does he show that much to anyone, but he loves her like a daughter, and I think that's what shakes him up so much." Ben gaped at Ethan and the odd expression of contentment on his face while he gazed at the scene playing out with his lead bartender and Kendall across the room.

"What do you mean?" Ben scowled when Ethan ignored his question, too engrossed in the drama happening in the corner.

Ben gave a quick glace again but had to turn away. From the way Kendall sobbed against Cam's chest, the guy had said something to right all the wrongs of their past, forcing an emotional release that Ben had yet to witness in Kendall since she'd made her reappearance in town.

An odd niggle in the area around his heart caught Ben off guard. Jealousy? Not of their relationship, but maybe because Ben wanted to be the one that Kendall leaned on. However, he had no desire to examine that thought any closer. One thing Ben knew for certain, Ethan had it right. Cam cared for Kendall in a way more like a father.

Ben sucked down a bit more beer, listening while Ethan picked up with his commentary about Cam. "He wanted to claim her as his own child, but now he feels he can't since he sent her away all those years ago. And he doesn't know how to make it up to her. Or how to fix it."

Ben glanced over at the cousins in disbelief and then to the fount of information behind the bar. "Cam said that to you? I didn't know he was capable of stringing more than four words together with lots of grunts in between."

"Yeah. We've known each other for more than a decade. You can't be confined to the small space behind this bar without learning a little bit about a guy. And Cam"—he tilted his head toward the back booth—"he might as well be her father for the protective streak he's got going."

A sweet reconciliation occurred before Ben's eyes. Tears poured down Kendall's cheeks and Cam brushed them aside with gentle fingers, ignoring the wetness on his own face. The sight slammed Ben back to the graveside service sixteen years ago—dark memories painted on a brilliant cerulean canvas sprinkled with perfect autumnal leaves. Similar to the scene playing out in the back corner of the Brawling Bear Bar and Grill, on that day in the cemetery, Cam had grieved on his knees while his little cousin had clung to him. A raw display of emotions publicly exhibited, unashamed, for all to see.

Ben paused to consider his lack of mourning, and Kendall's accusation that he hadn't moved on. Were the two related? He had no idea, but unlike Cam, he wasn't a teary-eyed sentimental type. Ben cringed at the memory of crying at Jenna's graveside service. He'd held back the tears as long as possible, but in the end, he'd lost the battle.

However, when Nikki, a young woman in town, had been murdered six months ago, he hadn't shed a single tear. It wasn't as if he hadn't felt grief, because he had. At the time, he told himself it was because he hadn't been in love with her. Nikki was only a friend. One of the many people, like him, who'd volunteered her time at the food shelf in town. So at her death, rather than crying, he'd drowned his sorrows in one hell of a drunken binge. It hadn't helped a bit.

All the while, Cameron, the angry hulk of a man, grieved or rejoiced in public, allowing tears to fall when he hugged his younger cousin. No sign of embarrassment that anyone might witness it. Although, few would dare comment if they had.

However, today was different. Words had been spoken. Explanations given. A sense of understanding and compassion passed over both their faces. Ben hoped that this moment paved the way to healing for both Kendall and Cam.

Ben picked up the beer he'd been nursing and tossed back what remained, vaguely aware of Ethan's inquiry and his own agreement to another one. Hell yes.

CHAPTER 9

The road to hell is paved with good intentions.

That age-old adage bounced inside his head like his six-year-old nephew ricocheting off the walls after a healthy dose of sugar.

Sure. Ben had good intentions. Provide shelter for Kendall. No touching Kendall. Befriend Kendall. No kissing Kendall. Protect Kendall. No making love with Kendall. Simple. Basic. Attainable for any gentleman.

But all those good intentions had flown out the window the moment he'd learned her ex had hurt her.

Yup. Bye-bye, good intentions.

Hello, possessiveness. He had that in spades. The only problem was, Ben had no right to be possessive. And yet, his misguided brain had been racing at full velocity to rectify that situation.

The fact that his initial, honorable plan had been adiosed was no big surprise. However, his brain's preoccupation was rather unsettling, working overtime to provide viable reasons to disregard his initial good intentions for potentially better intentions.

All of them included Kendall and him, sans clothes, with a fair amount of touching, kissing, and lovemaking.

He never planned to feel this way about Kendall. So now that he did, how was he ever going to fix things? Stepping up behind her where she sat finishing her breakfast, he gently rested his hands on her shoulders. Without a second thought, he leaned over and pressed a kiss to the top of her head.

Shit. Nothing was getting fixed like that.

"Are you ready to go to see Sheriff Ellis?" Ben asked.

"Can I say no?" She gave him a saucy grin and then pushed back her chair. She delivered her dirty dishes to the sink, casting him a quick glance over her shoulder. "Afterward, I'm going to see about getting my name on the substitute teacher list in town. I need to make sure my teaching license is in order here in Minnesota, but even if nothing comes of it until next school year, I'd like to get moving in the right direction."

"Makes sense," he said in agreement while he pulled on his heavy winter coat.

"I still haven't heard from Dayla." Kendall grabbed her coat off the hook above the bench.

"Really? How many days has it been? Do you have any other mutual friends that might be able to check on her?"

"Some. But Dayla's my best friend. I had to let her know I was leaving town. I didn't want to mention it to anyone else."

"Did you tell her you were coming to Krysset?"

"No way. Just that I had a new number and wouldn't be around for a while."

"Let the sheriff know. He might be able to have someone stop by her house or work to check on her," Ben said while Kendall fussed with her scarf and her cap, adjusting it multiple times. If he didn't know any better, he'd say she was stalling. Finally, he gently pulled her in front of him and tucked a tiny strand of hair behind her ear. Then he pressed a light kiss to her temple and hugged her.

Deep in his gut, Ben knew the road he traveled was most definitely the paved path to hell, and yet like a train barreling down the tracks to its preordained destination, he just couldn't seem to stop himself no matter how hard he tried.

Ben pinched his eyes closed and sucked in a breath laced with vanilla and warm peaches, ticking through his long list of reasons to avoid Kendall regardless of their attraction for one another. Unfortunately, none of those excuses seemed quite as weighty as they once had. Why? He couldn't say. He was still a decade older. She was still Jenna's sister. And she still had the most beautiful blonde hair and blue eyes he'd ever seen.

But it wasn't too late to stop the runaway train. They hadn't made love yet. He hadn't even kissed that sweet, sassy mouth of hers. He took strength in the fact that he would never miss what he hadn't experienced. Like donuts and potato chips, he'd add Kendall to his list of forbidden splurges and staunchly ignore the temptation.

With a sensuous smile and slumberous eyes, his newest forbidden fruit gazed up at him. Kendall appeared happy as a dog in a sunbeam as they prepared to step out into the bright Tuesday morning sunshine. His recent flare of attentive behavior expressed as tender concern hadn't disappointed her in the least and only solidified his stance to politely ignore the beautiful temptation.

An arduous undertaking and one, in all likelihood, destined to fail.

"Will you be okay walking to the sheriff's office?" Ben asked.

"Of course. It's not that far, right?" With Kendall's mitten-clad hand engulfed in his larger one, they stepped out onto his porch, and he pulled the door closed behind them.

"No, only about two blocks, and it's warmed up quite a bit."

Kendall made an unappreciative grunt. "It might be above zero, but it's still cold."

Ben laughed. "It's almost February. Spring is coming."

She muttered something about Minnesotans and their warped perception of the weather before asking, "Do you think they can do anything with my court order?"

"I think so, but all we can do is ask."

"I'll ask. You're only along for the refreshing walk. Remember that."

Ben grunted, but decided it was best to not comment. They made their way down the front steps to the small path that led to the sidewalk, piled high on either side with waist-deep snow. Ben's old home stood in the heart of downtown Krysset, across from the city park, and as they walked past, Kendall seemed enthralled by the small group of children playing there. Of course, drifts, knee-high, covered the playground, but that didn't stop them from climbing like little monkeys on the impacted equipment.

"Hi, Mr. Montgomery! Hi, Ms. Aasgaard!" a playful lavender bundle called out.

The shocked expression on Kendall's face and her tentative wave showed just how surprised she was to be recognized in town.

"Good morning!" Ben shouted, taking a moment to survey the group of parents huddled together, clutching to-go cups. His gaze stuttered to a stop on one—Sue Walsh. Twice in less than twenty-four hours.

Damn, that was the type of coincidence he could live without.

He picked up his pace a bit, turning left in front of Juliana's Boutique.

"I should go shopping." Kendall pointed at Juliana's.

"You'd love Jules's store. Very sparkly."

"You shop there often?" Kendall asked in a teasing tone

"No. But I've gotten my sister a gift or two there before. Sarah loves that place."

Ben and Kendall walked down another block, passing the Brawling Bear Bar and Grill on the opposite side until they'd reached the sheriff's department.

With a hand low on her back, he led Kendall up the three steps and tugged the door open, escorting her into the wide front office. A blanket of warmth enveloped them. Ben stomped his booted feet on the entryway mat to knock off all the caked-on snow while Kendall unwound her scarf and pulled off her stocking cap, running a hand over her hair to tame the static electricity.

"Good morning, Ben," Jeanie, the receptionist, said. "And who do you have with you today? Is this Kendall Aasgaard?" she asked all innocent like, but Ben knew that she and every other person in Krysset knew who Kendall was, that she'd returned home, and that she was staying at his place.

Hell, Jeanie probably even knew Kendall's shoe size.

Kendall, on the other hand, appeared downright shocked by the fact the older woman knew her name. "Yes. I'm Kendall." She stepped forward and shook the woman's hand.

"It's nice to meet you. I've always adored your big cousin, Cam. He's such a nice, young man."

Kendall laughed out loud at the woman. Ben wasn't sure what part of that statement tickled her—the nice or the young. At forty-three, Cam wasn't exactly ancient, but definitely not young. And nice? Well, that was questionable.

"I'd like to discuss an issue with the sheriff if he's available."

"Sheriff Ellis is in this morning, and I'm sure he'd have time to chat with you. It'll be just a few minutes," Jeanie said.

Kendall clasped Ben's elbow, directing him to the waiting area, which consisted of a row of four chairs along the wall near the door, and indicated that he should take a seat.

"You can wait here." Not a request.

He'd laugh at her demeanor if the frustrating situation didn't have him tied in knots. With her slight shove against his chest, he caved and took a seat. Kendall towered over him, her eyes narrowed while she surveyed his face, no doubt considering her options.

Might as well make it easy for her. "I'm coming in with you."

Leaning in close with one hand on each armrest of the chair, she shook her head. "No. You've done your duty to deliver me here in one piece. I appreciate that, but I'll take it from this point forward. So, take a break here and wait for me. Friend." She flashed him a syrupy sweet smile, fluttering lashes and all.

CHAPTER 10

If Jim could lock the door to his office, he might actually get something accomplished during the chaos of the workweek. Usually, he struggled to find one hour of quiet each day to tackle the mountain of paperwork on his desk. Sometimes he worked late. But tonight, there was no way in hell he was missing out on dinner. Marcie was cooking him steak, and his stomach couldn't be happier.

His mouth watered at the thought of that thick piece of beef cooked to tender perfection. Medium-well, slightly pink on the inside. Yes, his wife was a superb cook, and he loved her like crazy. And he also loved everything she whipped up in the kitchen—huge dinners, hot breakfasts, and incredible baked goods. Unfortunately, the caloric fast track Marcie had him on had caught up with him when he'd turned fifty-five two years ago, and he'd had to increase his exercise routine to a minimum of an hour a day to keep the slight paunch he'd developed from growing into a full-on beer gut.

A sharp rap at his office door snapped him back to the mountain on his desk and the lack of quiet at the office. A bit of frustration rolled through his brain, and he barked out the one-word command. "Enter."

Jeanie cracked the door and peeked her head in. "A Ms. Kendall Aasgaard would like to speak to you."

"Thank you, Jeanie." He used a more congenial voice, fighting the urge to suggest she pass it on to one of his deputies. Someone else had to be in the office right now. But he had yet to meet the infamous child who'd witnessed the murder of her entire family. He hadn't been sheriff at the time, hadn't even lived in the area, but the story had made the state-wide news and had happened so close to his hometown that he'd paid attention. "Please send her in."

Several minutes later, introductions had been made, and he sat across from the young lady he'd heard so much about. Jim took a moment to survey her face, recalling the case files on her family's murder. He'd perused the old files when he'd taken on the role of sheriff nearly a decade ago. Kendall resembled her mother while the two older children, Carson and Jenna, had favored their father's side of the family with long oval faces and chiseled cheekbones. But even though Kendall lacked the strikingly harsh facial features of the Aasgaard family, she'd inherited the blonde hair and blue eyes just like the rest of the clan.

"Jeanie said you wanted to speak to me, Ms. Aasgaard," Jim said.

She tugged a file folder out of her messenger bag, pulling out a piece of paper and placing it in front of him on his desk. "Please call me Kendall. I have an order of protection against my ex-boyfriend from when I lived in Oregon. Is it valid in Minnesota?" She cocked her head to the side, waiting for an answer.

He nodded. "Yes, it is. Tell me why you needed the court order in the first place."

"Over the course of our three-month relationship, he became aggressive. When he started leaving bruises, I knew I needed to get away," Kendall said. "I got the restraining order, but he followed me everywhere. No matter where I went, he found me like I had a homing beacon attached to my butt."

Jim chuckled at her bluntness. "He'd tracked your cell phone." Not a question. It seemed as if overly possessive boyfriends and stalkers would resort to just about any means available to maintain contact with their victims.

"I ditched it as soon as I figured out how he'd been tracking me, and then I packed my bags and left town."

He exhaled out a loud sigh. "Okay. After he hit you, did you go to the hospital?" She'd glossed over the details. Maybe she'd hoped he wouldn't notice.

With her face tipped downward unwilling to meet his eyes, her body language said it all: the bastard had hurt her badly enough to warrant a trip to the doctor. He hated weak men who felt empowered by a show of strength against the women in their lives. After a moment of silence, she met his eyes and nodded.

"How long after that did you apply for the restraining order?"

She pointed at the document in front of him, dated January second of this year. "More than a month after that first time."

"This happened more than once?"

Kendall sighed. "You see, I just wanted to ignore him and move on. I kept thinking he'd eventually grow tired of the chase, but it only seemed to ratchet up his anger. When he started waiting outside the school building where I was teaching, I feared for the safety of the children with him around. That's when I got the court order, but it didn't seem to make a bit of difference. He'd still show up regardless of the paper. At the school, he'd always stay the required distance away and just watch me. But sometimes, he'd be waiting inside my apartment. It completely freaked me out. I felt paranoid and on guard all the time. I decided to put some distance between us. That's why I quit my job and moved back home. But I'm not willing to deal with him any longer."

He glanced at the court order again. "Ms. Aasgaard, when was the last time you saw this Nicholas Cardwell?"

"On the morning I left Portland."

"Was he violent during that encounter?"

She swallowed and blinked a few times before she straightened in her chair and lifted her chin in a posture of complete defiance. The woman obviously had moxie. "Yes. The night before."

"You should've pressed charges."

"I know, but his father's an attorney in Portland. Highly regarded and well connected. I just wanted to walk away and put it behind me. It was Nick who decided he couldn't live without me. Putting half a continent between us seemed prudent."

Jim leaned back in his chair, picking up a black Bic and tapping out a catchy rhythm. "I heard you're planning on staying here?"

"I am. How did you know that?" A hint of surprise glinted in her eyes, but her tone gave nothing away.

"In Krysset, everyone knows everyone else's business."

"Okay, then." She nodded as if she had no idea how to respond to that. For a moment, he thought she might say something more, but then she stood and headed toward the door. Abruptly she stopped, turning to face him. "There's probably nothing you can do about this, but I can't seem to get a hold of my best friend. She's not responding to my texts, and her phone just rolls to voicemail. I'm beginning to think that Nick…might have hurt her. You know…trying to get to me."

Jim handed her a paper tablet and pen. "Give me her information. Name, address, phone number, and employer. I'll see if the Portland authorities can track her down. Why don't you put your cell number on there, too." After she scribbled the details he'd requested, he rounded his desk and swung the door wide for her exit.

"Thank you for seeing me," she said.

"Kendall, we'll be keeping our eyes open, but I'll need you to call in anything that you think is suspicious. Okay?"

* * *

Kendall stared into Sheriff Ellis's face. Concern and sincerity etched into the fine lines that ringed his eyes and around his lips. She trusted him. Just like she trusted Ben and Cam. After nodding in affirmation, she turned to leave and came face-to-face with Ben. In the hallway. Right outside the office door. He stood waiting, propped against the wall with one knee bent up and the sole of his boot planted flat on the wall.

Nowhere near where she'd placed him.

She stifled the wisecrack and the laughter that wanted to bubble up, because the stern set of his jaw said he wasn't playing her games.

When he pushed off the wall and stepped forward, his eyes went from neutral to intense in a molten minute, making her insides flutter and her core clench. He towered over her, eyes searching, smile nowhere in sight, and she was sure this time he'd claim the kiss she'd reserved solely for him. Instead with his hand low on her back, he directed her toward the door leading outside.

The sheriff's voice stopped their progress. "Ben, keep an eye on her now. I'll let the staff know about the situation and have patrols pay extra attention around your home."

"How did you know I was staying at Ben's?" Kendall asked. It was a rather stupid question with a simple answer: One of the many joys of small town living. But then again, that small town neighborly attitude had gotten Kendall the exact address to Ben's house, and that small town trusting behavior had allowed her to find the hidden key into his house on the first try.

"Nothing remains a secret for long in Krysset." The sheriff turned and disappeared into his office, closing the door with a small *snick*.

"Let's go." The deep rumble of Ben's words near her ear interrupted her thoughts as the firm press of his hand led her toward the door. A little lower and his warm palm would be planted on her bottom. A ridiculous thrill coursed through her body sparking images of his strong hands working the bare skin of her back and butt, grasping her hips when he thrust into her from behind.

Kendall forced those thoughts out of her mind.

Ben had told her that he wasn't interested in pursuing a relationship with her. And while she heard and believed his words of intent, she still noticed the hooded looks he kept giving her and the crackle of heat—an electric charge—that seemed to shimmer in the air between them. Chemistry. That's what Ben had called it. He seemed aware of it but completely able to resist. How could he ignore it?

He must be fighting some kind of internal battle, too. That would explain a lot. Maybe he just needed some time to get used to the idea. And she could give him that, as long as he continued to flash those sizzling gazes in her direction. The ones that glimmered of hope. The ones where the heat in his eyes burned like fire. The ones he thought he hid so well. His gaze was so primal, so feral, like he planned to devour her. And when he locked eyes with hers, everything inside her went weak.

But Ben apparently had no idea of the intensity of his gaze or the promise that seemed to shine within. A promise of earth-shattering, mind-numbing passion. So with each look, Kendall could think of little else besides stripping bare, climbing into Ben's bed again, and rubbing herself against him while he slept.

Not bad. The idea actually had merit.

Completely unaware of the direction of her thoughts, Ben said, "I think I could really use a workout tonight." Exactly what Kendall had been thinking. "I'm going to the gym after work. Do you want me to stop by the house and pick you up on my way?"

Okay, not exactly what she'd been thinking, and definitely not as good as skin-to-skin action. But not a bad way to lose some of this pent-up energy. "A workout sounds like a great idea."

CHAPTER 11

At the firm rap on his open office door, Ben glanced up into his father's grinning face. "Do you have a moment?"

Ben nodded when Thomas Montgomery strolled into his office and relaxed into the chair opposite Ben's desk. All the Montgomery children and their offspring had taken after Tom with his chocolate-colored eyes and dark brown hair. Now he sported a sprinkle of gray at his temples giving him a distinguished look, but overall his father had aged well. Maybe he'd lost a bit of the width across his shoulders and gained some around his stomach, but not much on either count. Tom exercised each day with Ben's mom, Judy, and Ben could only hope he'd be as well preserved as his father in another thirty years.

"Did you stop by to check out the construction site?" The site of an overnight debacle. The site that was going to cost the company thousands to thaw and restore. The site where the front entryway and porch resembled a miniature, frozen Niagara Falls.

"Yeah. It's a damned disaster. Pretty in a hell-freezing-over kind of way, if we didn't have to pay to fix it." Ben leaned back in his chair, wishing the day were over, and it had barely begun.

"Well, what do you want to do?" Tom asked.

Ben stared at the man who'd assumed a similar relaxed position. "Why are you asking me?"

"Not many years from now I'll be retired. I know you make decisions every day, small ones and big ones. But this is one of those disaster control issues that only come around once in a blue moon, so you need some practice." After a quiet beat, his father repeated the initial question. "What do you want to do?"

"Dare I ask who the plumber for the project was?"

Tom grunted out a laugh. "Marc Fullerton, of course."

"Great. My guess is that he's using again. When he's clean and sober, he's a great plumber, one of the best. But last time he messed up it cost the company a significant amount of money, both in labor and product." Leaving the doors unlocked at the two sites he'd worked on that day, followed by a gutting of every inch of copper pipe screamed of lowlife drug users in search of easy money.

"Marc Fullerton is a liability, Dad. I want to fire his sorry ass." Ben stretched his legs, fighting his usual Tuesday restlessness. "But a part of me wants to give him a chance to get clean and sober again. I'm not sure if he'll go for that, but I'd like to offer."

"Seems fair to me, Ben." Like his dad, he reached swift solutions with confidence and decisiveness. This similarity worked in their favor in most situations.

"I'll talk to Marc. Lay out his options for him," Ben said.

His dad stood to leave and paused halfway to the door, his hands shoved into his front pockets. "Don't suppose you heard the news yet?" His dad lifted a brow. "Roland Kearns gave his date of retirement. End of May."

Ben felt his grin go wide, and he laughed. "Good old Rolly is retiring. That's great news!"

"Ben, you know he doesn't like to be called Rolly. I really don't understand this animosity between you two. He's actually a great guy, and he was the first person I hired when I started the company. You know, we graduated high school together. And I'm sure I've told you this before, but he saved my life back in junior high."

"Yeah, I've heard it all before, Dad. The guy pulled you out of the lake before you drowned. Didn't mean you needed to put him on the payroll. I'm sure a simple thank you would've sufficed."

"I fell, hit my head on the dock as I went into the water, and blacked out. If it weren't for Rolly, I wouldn't be around. And neither would you."

Ben laughed. "You just called him Rolly."

Tom rolled his eyes. "Damn it, Ben. You're just about as antagonizing as he is."

"Hey, I didn't call him Rolly until he started referring to me as Young Master Benjamin. And most of the time, I don't call him that to his face. Only to you and mom." Ben chuckled at his father's disapproving glare. "And Jackson when I'm complaining about work."

"Roland's had a tough life, and he sees you as living a life of privilege." Tom shrugged. "But it doesn't matter what he thinks. You're my son, and it was your right to be groomed for a leadership role within the company, regardless of your age. Actually, it's not like you to let something of this nature bother you."

Ben shuffled the papers on his desk unsure what to say to that. Because his dad was right. This wasn't Ben's style, but the guy seriously bugged the hell out of him.

His frustration must've shown on his face, because his dad dropped the topic with a quiet chuckle. "Try to keep your celebrating low key until his final day."

"I think I'll put out some feelers for a new architect."

Tom nodded in agreement and paused as if weighing his words before he spoke. "You coming to Sunday dinner this week?"

"Yeah, I'll swing by for a bit."

"Great," he said with an unashamed grin "Bring Kendall with you. Your mom has been anxious to visit with her."

"News travels, huh? It's not what you think." Ben shook his head, his eyes fixed on his father's face in a feeble effort to read his dad's thoughts.

"Nothing wrong with it. You're both adults. We won't judge."

Yup. That's what he figured. "She's Jenna's sister. I'm not involved with her."

Tom's smile faded at Ben's firm confession. "Remember how you hate being compared to Dan and Joe? Stop doing that to Kendall. Just because she popped out of the same womb doesn't make her a duplicate." With that, his dad walked out of the office, leaving Ben to ponder his words for a moment before he snatched up his cell phone and dialed the number.

Two hours later, Ben's door slammed shut, and he breathed a weary sigh. The sudden silence was almost as deafening as Marc Fullerton's angry voice echoing off the high ceilings while he'd made his choice loud and clear. Enraged by the fact that his drug use had been called into question and indifferent to the documented history of his abuse, the man had denied any problem, citing that he preferred unemployment over random drug testing

Ben fought back a yawn. He couldn't blame someone for slacking on the job when all he wanted to do was curl up on the small sofa in the corner of his office and take a nap. Since Kendall had arrived in town he hadn't slept well, and his focus was shot to hell. Images of the woman who'd kept him tossing and turning with sexual need several nights in a row stood front and center in his mind. It seemed as if his pea-sized brain registered little else.

Now exhausted beyond reason and unable to focus on work, Ben traipsed out of his office and down the hall to the stairwell. When he reached the first floor, he made his way to the small alcove where the vending machines stood. The blessed *thunk* as his Coke landed in the can dispenser had never sounded sweeter. He popped the top and took a long drink before turning the corner into the hallway and almost colliding into Roland Kearns, his retiring architect.

"Congratulations. I hear you're retiring, man. That's great." Ben flashed a wide smile, because really it was excellent news for him, for his company, and hopefully for the architect who didn't seem to want to be here anyway.

"Don't pretend you're happy for me, Master Montgomery." With that snide remark, Roland marched down the hall and out the front door. Ben shook his head, watching old Rolly walk away. Then Ben made his way back to his office and shut the door.

God, he hated Tuesdays. His one full in-office day. He preferred his hard-hat days when he went from jobsite to jobsite, checking on statuses and overseeing construction. He wore his tool belt and helped where necessary. Client meetings also ranked higher than mountains of paperwork. Hearing the dreams of potential customers, bringing in architects and designers to help them achieve their dreams, and then selling them on the quality workmanship that Montgomery Construction could provide them was his area of expertise.

Tuesdays, on the other hand, were just work. Painfully slow. Monotonous. And to add insult to injury, he'd been forced to endure run-ins with two upset and nasty-tempered employees in one day—two more than his usual quota. He didn't appreciate their anger directed at him, but decided he just didn't have the drive to do something about it today.

The only good thing about Tuesdays—going to the gym after work to burn off the pent-up, restless energy caused by being stuck in a ten-by-ten office and forced to do too much paperwork. And now with Kendall sleeping in the next room, not only did he have his usual Tuesday frustrations, he also had plenty of excess tension that needed to be worked out. He could think of much more pleasurable ways to relieve the stress, but sweating and straining through an hour of weight training followed by an hour of cardio was all he was going to get.

And with that sad thought, he dove into the last of his paperwork.

CHAPTER 12

Kendall dropped her gym bag inside the door and kicked off her sneakers. God, Ben was a maniac at the gym. He'd worked out hard for almost two hours, and she couldn't decide if she was more tired from her leisurely three-mile jog on the treadmill or from watching Ben lift weights and then spar with some guy from work. The entire event was thoroughly exhausting.

"I'm going to grab a shower," Ben said while she poured a tall glass of water.

She tipped the glass up and downed the whole thing, finishing it just as her phone began ringing. "Dayla!" Kendall shouted, racing toward the bench in the mudroom where she'd left her bag. She dove for her phone, hoping it was her friend, but when she looked at the number, it wasn't familiar. Her stomach seemed to bottom out.

Oh God, what if it was Nick?

"Here," Ben said, grabbing the phone out of her hand, probably thinking the exact thought that had gone through her mind. Ben connected the call. "Hello."

"I'm trying to reach Kendall," a female voice said.

"May I ask who's calling?" Ben held the phone so Kendall could hear.

"My name is Sadie Johnson, I'm Dayla's sister."

"Oh my God." The words came out on a panicked whisper while Kendall's eyes filled with tears.

"Just one moment, Ms. Johnson, I'll put Kendall on the phone." Ben handed the phone to Kendall and then stood behind her, circling his arms around her waist.

"Hello, Sadie?" God, Kendall hardly recognized her own voice, it was so filled with fear. "Dayla? Is she okay?"

There was a small sob, followed by a weak voice. "She's alive." Kendall felt her knees buckle, but Ben was there holding her. Lifting her. Carrying her to the sofa. He sat down next to her, offering her all his support.

"Tell me what happened, Sadie." Tears slid down Kendall's cheek, and Ben reached over to brush them aside. He was such a good friend. Which was more than she could say for herself. How could she have left Dayla to fend for herself?

"The police believe she was attacked coming home late on Friday night, but it wasn't until early Saturday morning that someone found her, badly beaten, in the parking lot outside her apartment. She hasn't regained consciousness." Another sob.

God, this could not be happening. Not to Dayla. All because Kendall couldn't deal with her creep of a boyfriend. All because she'd ignored the issue and then run like a coward. She should've gone to the cops long ago. She should've told Cam. He'd have helped her take legal action against the guy.

A small sad voice filled the phone line. "The police told me they have a lead, so when Dayla comes around, she can identify the person who did this to her. We're just praying…" Her words trailed off, and all Kendall could do was cry.

"I'm so sorry. I'm so, so sorry." Kendall rocked back and forth repeating those words, and after a moment, Ben took the phone from her hand. She knew he was talking to Sadie in a calm voice, thanking her for calling, asking her to let them know if there was any change in Dayla's condition, assuring Sadie that they'd be in contact again soon.

Ben returned to Kendall's side and held her close while she sobbed on his shoulder. "This is all my fault. I need to go back and see her," Kendall whispered against his shirt.

"We will. You and I will go visit your friend together once they've caught the guy who did this. Until then we need to hang tight here. And, Kendall, it's not your fault. We don't even know for sure that Nick was the one to hurt her."

Kendall glared at him. She knew it, deep in her gut. "But—"

"No. No buts, darling. If it was Nick, what if he's trying to lure you back to Portland, hmm? I'm not letting you walk into more danger. You're going to be brave. You're going to think positive thoughts for your friend. And you're going to pray. The human body is an amazing machine, and she's getting good medical care now."

"But this is my fault."

"No, it's not." Ben was being so sweet. She didn't deserve his kindness right now. "Sadie said they have a lead. Probably from the information that you gave to Sheriff Ellis. I bet the Portland authorities are searching for Nicholas Cardwell at this very moment," Ben said with such conviction Kendall almost believed him.

She gave her head a firm shake. "It's not enough. I need to call the sheriff. I need to make sure he tells them that Nick is definitely the one they're looking for. It's the least I can do for my friend."

CHAPTER 13

Kendall pulled her car along the curb in front of Ben's house. She raced up the sidewalk and onto the front porch, and fumbling with the new key Ben had given her, she unlocked the door. She made her way into the house, flinging her purse and coat on the bench in the entry and dashing up the stairs to get ready.

She'd been Ben's house guest—both here in town and out at his hunting lodge—for not quite a week, and she'd become so comfortable that she hadn't even bothered with the courteous behavior of dragging her sorry ass out of bed before noon. This morning, she'd intended to get up early and visit with Ben before he headed out for work, but she hadn't even heard him get up and leave. It seemed as if she was becoming more and more sluggish as the week wore on.

Hearing about Dayla hadn't helped. Kendall had spent the past two nights tossing and turning while her mind raced with worry over her friend's condition. Of course, Cam had agreed with Ben—a bizarre situation that seemed to be happening with more and more frequency—that Kendall should wait until the situation with Nick was resolved before she traveled back to visit Dayla. Kendall only hoped it wouldn't be too late. That anxiety and heartache had kept her awake into the early hours of the morning until she'd fallen into a fitful sleep. When she had finally climbed out of bed, she'd decided to drive around town.

Being back in Krysset felt right. Like coming home, sort of. An odd sensation since she'd lost her family here, and some might say that the town could only hold bitter memories for her.

But Kendall didn't see it that way. Not even when she found herself meandering the back streets of her old neighborhood.

The house she'd grown up in no longer existed. Cam had it torn down years ago. He'd believed too much blood had been shed there to consider selling the house. At the time, Kendall had hated the idea, accusing Cam of wanting to erase all memories of her family. But now as an adult, she understood his actions and was glad that she'd never have to drive past the old house that haunted her nightmares. A buyer had snatched up the prime piece of property a couple blocks outside of downtown Krysset and had built a new home.

Kendall had sat out front on that familiar street. The houses nearby had all looked familiar; even the yard had looked familiar. But the new house, lovely as it was, had looked oddly out of place.

Visiting the old neighborhood had been a big mistake, leaving her with a morose feeling. She'd continued her drive, stopping at the schools in town, but nothing had seemed to shake that heaviness that had settled over her.

So now, after she freshened up, she planned to head across the park to that store that had caught her attention a couple days ago—Juliana's Boutique. It sat almost directly across the park from Ben's house, and from the street, it looked like the kind of girly shop Kendall could lose herself in.

And at the moment, getting out of her head was exactly what she needed.

Fifteen minutes later, she was out the door and into the brisk January day. She tugged the door closed behind her, checking to make sure it had locked. Kendall hiked her purse up on her shoulder and marched down the porch steps, focused on her destination, through the park and across the street on the opposite side. Regardless of the arctic cold, she planned to walk the short distance.

The flutter of white against her car caught her attention. Kendall let out a delighted giggle, fighting the urge to skip along the icy road. This had to be one of those little advertisements. A pancake breakfast? Or maybe it was for an estate sale? God, she was going to love living in her small town again. She sidestepped to grab the flyer pinned beneath her wiper blade on her windshield and glanced at it.

I'm watching you. Run and I'll chase you. When I catch you, you're dead.

Kendall's heart seemed eager to follow instructions, racing so fast she could hardly think. Blood pounded through her veins, creating a deafening roar in her ears. Her entire body shivered, not from cold but from fear. Was he watching her right now? She glanced over her shoulder at the empty street, the vacant park. Her breath was coming out in fast little puffs, fluffy white clouds rising in front of her face.

Nick had found her. He loved the game of hide and seek. Cat and mouse. Chase. Now he wanted her to run, so he could chase again. And when he tired of the petty game, he'd kill her. That's what he'd said, and she believed it without question.

She darted her gaze around the bleak emptiness. Into the house? The car? Race across the park to Juliana's? There was safety in numbers, right?

She decided on the safety of the house. Tracing her tracks, she ran back up to the front door. Fear and anger, both volatile emotions, swirled in her mind. *Get-in-the-house* and *lock-the-door* waged battle with *how-dare-he-demand-that-I-leave-my-new-life*. When rising panic and indignation joined the fight, Kendall forced back the tears that stung her eyes. She tried to work the key into the lock, wrestling to get the damned thing open. But when the lock snitched, she darted a glance behind her, shouldered her way through the door, and ran into the solid wall of a chest.

Kendall screamed. Two arms caged her in a firm grasp, and she screamed louder.

"Kendall." She heard the familiar tone. Ben.

"Oh, God, thank you." She let herself sag into his arms. "I'm so glad you're here."

"What's wrong?"

She lifted her hand with the note, the sheet of paper rattling in her grasp like the thin wings of a humming bird. He ripped the note from her hand and let out a curse.

Ben didn't release her, but he pulled his cell phone out and dialed a number. He gave some explanation. Kendall didn't bother trying to follow his words. Instead she let him hold her. Leaning her face against this chest, she dragged in his now familiar scent, borrowing his strength and gaining comfort from his closeness.

They say that all good things must come to an end, and in Kendall's life, good things always ended before they'd scarcely begun. Her newfound happiness in Krysset had been premature, apparently a future she wasn't meant to have. Instead, it appeared her destiny was to run and hide from monsters for the rest of her life. Which at the moment promised to be rather abbreviated.

Now with Ben standing by her side, she wanted to voice all her fears and disappointments. Lay them all down at his feet. Beg him to take care of her. Not to leave her. But she knew she couldn't.

She dare not ask him for anything else.

The wail of sirens broke through her foggy thoughts, and Ben carefully directed her to a room on one side of the entryway. It was his media room. Leather and wood. Masculine. Comfortable. He sat beside her for a moment until the rap on the door. He shifted and his warmth disappeared.

She could hear their low voices. "Thanks for coming so quickly."

"No problem."

"She's in here."

"Kendall. Are you getting into trouble already?" Kendall looked up to see the sheriff. He wore a wide confident smile that told her everything would be okay. Ben stepped into the room along with another man and handed Sheriff Ellis the paper she'd found.

"Hi, ma'am. I'm Garrett Reed. Ben, why don't we talk in the kitchen?"

"But—" Kendall tried to protest the separation, but the sheriff rested his hand on her shoulder.

"We're only going to talk, Kendall. Ben will be in the next room." He gestured with a nod of his head, and Ben followed the deputy out of the room just as the front door slammed open again.

"Kendall!" She jumped up from her place on the sofa and flung herself into Cam's arms.

"Cam. I'm so scared."

"Shhh. I know, Dolly. But we've got you. I promise nothing is going to happen."

"Cam, could you give Kendall and me just a few moments to go over things, please?"

After Cam stepped out of the room, the sheriff asked about the threat, her arrival back home, and the timing of her departure. She gave him as much information as she could, but other than the words on the note, she didn't have much to say.

"When you came to my office, I told you most people in Krysset enjoy knowing everything they can about their neighbor," the sheriff said. She remembered his words from Tuesday morning, so she nodded. "Is there anyone other than this Nicholas Cardwell that might want to send these types of notes to scare you, maybe encourage you to leave?"

Kendall snorted out a laugh. She wanted to roll her eyes at him, but decided it was best to be respectful. He was trying to help her after all. "I've been away from Krysset for more than sixteen years, Sheriff, with one short visit for the trial. I don't know anyone here except Cameron and Ben. I have two old aunts that run the Victorian Tea House, but we've never been close. Since I arrived in town several days ago, I've been introduced to a few of Ben's friends."

Sheriff Ellis stared at her with an expression of complete patience, as if he could wait forever for her to figure out whatever he was trying to communicate nonverbally. She cocked her head to the side, studying him with equal composure.

As realization dawned on her, she gave her head a fierce shake. "Are you trying to insinuate that one of the handful of people I've met would want me to leave?"

"Well?"

Seriously? "No. I can't think of anyone."

"What about people you've known forever?"

"Cam or Ben? Are you kidding me?"

The guy didn't say a word. He just sat there and studied her. Did he really think if he gave her the stink eye long enough that she'd change her mind? Wasn't happening.

"I trust Cam and Ben. With my life. If you need to discuss anything with them regarding this, I'm cool with that. They're both good men who'll want to know about anything in regards to my personal safety."

He continued to eye her, seemingly pondering her statement.

"What?" she finally blurted out, knowing she'd just failed Interrogation 101.

He shrugged. "I just find it interesting, Ms. Aasgaard, that you'd relinquish control of information to either Cam or Ben when neither accompanied you into my office a couple days ago. Remember, there aren't any secrets in Krysset."

Meeting his gaze head-on, she said, "I have nothing to hide, Sheriff." She'd shared the worst with Cam already and that had caused a flood of honest communication between them. It seemed that with the truth in the open, nothing could stand between her and Cam and the new twist on their relationship.

The fact that Cam considered Kendall his long-lost daughter ought to have freaked her out. But it hadn't. It simply and completely explained his behavior after all these years. He'd been overly protective and stubbornly demanding in his expectations for her, and yet, he'd remained aloof and uninvolved.

She wished that sixteen years ago he'd have chosen to be selfish—as he'd put it—and kept her in Krysset. Cam's explanation Monday night had put a new spin on everything she'd ever thought about her older cousin, paving the way for a stronger relationship between them from this point forward. After all these years, they had a lot of catching up to do. A lot of healing to do together.

CHAPTER 14

Ben closed and locked the front door behind the sheriff and his deputy. The hushed tones of Cam consoling Kendall in the kitchen came to him, but Ben couldn't focus on words at the moment. Right now, he was at war. With someone he couldn't see. And with himself.

Battling someone who cowardly hid in the shadows, threatening to take something he cared about, was the easy one, because he wasn't alone in the fight. He had the strength of law enforcement and the vigilance of Cameron Aasgaard behind him.

The conflict brewing inside of him, however, he had to face alone. He wanted Kendall. To hold her and love her. And yet, he knew it was wrong to feel this way about her. Ben blamed the current situation—the heightened awareness of the danger her ex posed, and his own need to defend her from that danger. He'd failed twice before—with Jenna and with Nikki—and he refused to fail again.

But Ben knew—to the bottom of his soul—there was something more between him and Kendall. He felt his heart shift in his chest every time she was near, as if it was finally waking up from an extended sleep. Or perhaps that sensation was the initial flutters of his heart coming back to life after sixteen years. To him, Kendall was summer sunshine after a long cold winter. And he just wanted to bask in her presence, soaking in her radiant warmth.

He couldn't avoid her because he needed to protect her, and he couldn't stop touching her because he was so damn attracted to her. And he didn't know how to handle it.

Be her friend. That's what he'd suggest to anyone else in the same situation. Listen to her. Give her a hug or a shoulder to cry on. Watch over her and protect her. But keep your hands and mouth to yourself.

He had every intention of following his own good advice, but the second he stepped into the kitchen, Ben's eyes met hers. Fear, sorrow, grief, frustration were all right there. It gutted him. He couldn't bear to have her go through any of those things alone.

She pushed herself away from Cam and rushed into Ben's arms. God, it felt so good to hold her. Not caring if her cousin was in the room, Ben pulled her close and rested his chin on the top of her head. Pinching his eyes closed, he struggled against the profound wave of emotions that barreled toward him. His body engulfed her smaller one. He ran his fingers through her hair, down her back just to assure himself that she was okay. Finally, he tugged her away, holding her shoulders to steady her. He gazed into her eyes, pushing back the long strands of blonde that fell around her face, tucking some behind her ear.

"I know I scared you at the front door earlier. I'm sorry."

"I didn't expect," she said, pausing for a second, slowly shaking her head. "I didn't know you would be home."

"I stopped by to grab a few files that I'd forgotten in the office here, but then when I came through the back door, I heard the key in the front door. It sounded like you were having problems, so I rushed in there to help you open the door." He touched her cheek. "I had no idea that you were scared, and I'm sure that running into me didn't help the fright factor, did it?"

"No. But I'll be okay. I'm thinking about taking a bubble bath to relax for a while."

"Good idea. Why don't you go on up and use the tub in my bathroom?" Kendall nodded at him. "I have something I need to discuss with Cam before he leaves."

"No. If you're going to talk about me, I'll sit right here."

"Darling, we're not going to talk about you."

"Liar."

He smiled at her spunky tone. "We're going to talk about Nick and which one of us gets first dibs."

"Same old argument, huh?" Kendall asked.

"Yes, but with the threatening note you found, it's revitalized our efforts. Should be a long, heated debate. Nothing you'll find fun. Maybe you'd like a glass of wine?"

"That sounds good."

Always the bartender, Cam moved into action. "White or red, Dolly?" he asked.

Ben escorted Kendall toward the base of the stairs. "You go up and start running your bath, and I'll bring your glass of wine up to you."

Kendall took one hesitant step up and then turned to face him. Nearly eye to eye, she surveyed his face, as if she was trying to crawl inside his mind. He forced a neutral expression and waited rather than doing what he really wanted to do—close the short distance between them and kiss her. The moment seemed to stretch on forever, but then her shoulders sagged a bit. He sensed that she hadn't found whatever it was that she'd been searching for. She gave a stiff nod and raced up the stairs.

After delivering the glass up to Kendall, Ben returned to the kitchen to find an open beer at a spot at the table. Cam sat in the seat across the table and lifted his bottle to Ben.

"I thought we might just need a drink," Cam said.

"God, yes," Ben said, dropping onto the chair and picking up the bottle.

"You wanted to talk to me?" Cam asked.

"I plan to stay home the rest of the day."

"Obviously."

"But tomorrow, I have an important meeting at work, and I just don't think—"

"No problem," Cam cut him off. "I'll be here with Kendall. Actually, it's probably not necessary for her to be confined to the house. As long as one of us is with her, she should be safe to go out to the café or the gym. Maybe even dinner out at the bar. Otherwise our girl is going to go stir crazy in the house."

Our girl? Our girl. Why had Cam used those words? Where had the surly guy gone? The one who'd jumped to conclusions and popped him in the jaw last weekend?

"What do you think?" Cam asked.

"About?"

"I said that I'd pick her up and bring her over to my house for a while."

"That would be good. Anything to keep her from feeling penned up while we keep our eye on her."

"Has there been any change with her friend?"

"Not as of this morning." Ben had personally called Sadie Johnson to check on Dayla's status. "So what's your take on this Nick character? Obviously, he's dangerous."

"I disliked the idiot on sight when she introduced me a couple months ago, and now I have even more reason to hate the guy," Cam said, taking a chug of beer.

Ben grunted, toying with the label on the bottle in front of him. Cam leaned in as if he had something to say, cleared his throat, and then eased back into his seat again. Ben took a slow sip of his beer.

Cam cleared his throat again and said, "I have something I want to talk to you about and this seems as good a time as any."

At the urgent tone in Cam's voice, Ben paused and glanced at the back door.

"It's about Jenna," Cam said more quietly.

Yeah, the door was looking good. Escape. "I don't want to hear it." Not the nicest thing to say considering he and Cam had been getting along fairly well in recent months.

Cam ignored Ben's last comment and rolled right along. "I know you loved my cousin all those years ago. But you have to know it was a young love. An immature love." The guy actually had the nerve to hold up a hand in some kind of pacifying gesture. What the hell? "I don't mean that disrespectfully, but think of the challenges adults face. The pull of career, family, and finances all add a great deal of stress to any relationship. It's working through those stresses that strengthen a loving relationship into something greater."

Ben shifted in his seat and stared out the window, not enjoying this topic in the least. If this weren't his house, he'd leave. But for Kendall, he'd put up with her cousin.

"I'm not saying this to discard your feelings for Jenna, but to remind you that had she lived, your love would've blossomed into far more. You two would've had so much more."

Ben's jaw clenched as he ground his teeth and glared at the other man. The mountainous Viking had some nerve to blabber on about Jenna. Sure, they were related, but Ben knew her as well as, if not better than, Cameron. They'd planned each detail of their lives together, including choosing their wedding date exactly two months after Jenna's intended college graduation, designing their dream home, and selecting the names for their four children.

Ben knew Jenna. And Cam's words were insulting and offensive.

"I mention this for two reasons. First, because it's time for you to move on. You need to pick up the pieces of your life, man. Jenna would want more for you. She'd want you to find someone to spend your life with. Second, I've noticed a change in you where Kendall's concerned." Ben stopped clenching his jaw long enough to open his mouth to correct Cam, but the man held his hand up again to deter the interruption. "Don't deny it, man. You've got feelings for her."

Ben crossed his arms over his chest and rocked back in the chair, tilting it onto two legs. "I promised you I wouldn't sleep with Kendall. I intend to keep my word, so don't bother warning me off by offending me and the feelings I shared with Jenna."

Cam sighed. He rolled his shoulders and gazed at the ceiling as if praying for strength or perhaps the correct words to avoid pissing Ben off any further. Hard to tell.

After a long beat, Cam met him head-on with a fierce look. "In case you haven't noticed, my friend, she's not Jenna. Not in looks. Not in personality."

Ben had no idea where Cam was headed. First the man insulted his love for Jenna, then he questioned Ben's promise to keep out of Kendall's bed, and now he wanted to compare and contrast the two women. Ben remained quiet and waited for more. Why he waited, he couldn't say. Especially when every fiber in his being told him to stand up from the table and walk away.

"Ben, pay attention to the differences. Don't turn Kendall away just because you loved Jenna. Think about it, Ben. Jenna's one thing you both have in common. You both loved her, and you both lost her."

Ben leaned forward, dropping the chair to all four legs. "Almost sounds like you're giving me permission to become romantically involved with your little cousin." Disbelief rang in his voice, and he glared at Cam. Ben's heartbeat kicked up a notch, and he couldn't say whether it was due to fear or excitement.

"Let's say, as long as you treat her well, I wouldn't stand in your way." With those parting words, Cam unfolded himself from his spot at the table and walked out the back door.

CHAPTER 15

I wouldn't stand in your way.

Even an hour later, those words echoed through Ben's mind. Cam's final words seemed to hang in the air as if they were a solid entity that could literally be plucked up, letter by letter, and examined closer. Which would be awesome and much appreciated at the moment. Because what in the hell did it mean?

Ben stared into the depths of the freezer, equally perplexed. What to make for dinner? What to make of Cam's parting statement? One thing was certain—those words put an entirely new spin on things.

With his promise to Cam seemingly no longer in play, not to mention Ben's own traitorous body making impetuous demands and the heat in Kendall's eyes that reflected his own desire, staying away from Kendall and out of her bed were going to be a bigger challenge than Ben had anticipated when he'd suggested she stay with him until this Nick thing blew over.

And while Cam's last words had left Ben in a weird stupefied state, Kendall's cousin had offered an even more bizarre suggestion—to note the differences between the two sisters. Why Ben even bothered to listen to Cam, he had no idea. But at dinner, Ben sat directly across the table from Kendall and was in full-on compare-and-contrast mode.

Damn Cameron Aasgaard for planting ideas in Ben's brain, because at this moment, he couldn't take his eyes off Kendall.

He took a bite of chicken, chewing without thought of the flavor and chasing it down with a gulp of beer. Had he ever truly observed Kendall before? Had he ever noted her beautiful and delicate features? The realization nearly smacked him upside the head. This was exactly what Cam had been trying to tell him. The two sisters were nothing alike. Kendall wasn't a replacement or a consolation prize. She was the grand prize. She was a remarkably strong woman who had been through the worst and yet had come out on the other side, being so thoughtful and sweet, not to mention confident and fun-loving.

Ben poked at the baked potato on his plate without taking a bite. Entranced by Kendall's stories of her day, Ben listened to her, thoroughly captivated by the unique expressions that played across her face. He gazed into her eyes, and for the first time ever, he'd noticed their most delicate crystal-blue color. How could he have missed them before this? They were lighter than blue topaz, and yet, the sparkle and variance in color within her iris reminded him of gemstones with brilliant cut facets glimmering in the sunlight. Framed by her deep brown lashes, Kendall's eyes were the most striking features on her face.

"Your eyes are beautiful. Like aquamarine. Did you know that?" Ben asked her, noting that they were absolutely nothing like Jenna's. A passing flicker of guilt brushed the edges of his consciousness, but he pushed it aside. Following Cam's direction, Ben intended to briefly note the differences between Kendall and her late sister—guilt be damned. Then, he vowed, he'd never do the compare-and-contrast game again. "Your eyes are so large and round. I've never noticed that."

"Okay." She paused and cocked her head to the side, obviously puzzled by his abrupt change in topics. She said nothing more, choosing instead to shovel another forkful of baked potato into her mouth.

Ben set his fork down again. "Your lashes are blond, right? And you coat them with that lash makeup?" He cringed, knowing it was a lame question. But Kendall only laughed.

"Mascara? How could you be thirty-four and not know that it's called mascara?"

He shrugged. "I don't use it, so it's not on my radar." After the words escaped, Ben wondered how many other things fell into that category.

Kendall rolled her beautiful aquamarine eyes in a look of exasperation, turning them a darker stormy color. "Quit staring at me."

"I can't. You're so beautiful. I can't take my eyes off you." That statement made her blush. And shut up.

Throughout the remainder of the evening, Ben took a complete inventory of Kendall's physical attributes and her personality traits. At some point, his visual perusal morphed from simply noting the differences between the sisters to hungrily taking in the subtle shift in Kendall's shoulders when she spoke, the way her hips were full, and the gentle curve of her lower back as it gave way to her sweet little ass.

God, he wanted to touch her there. He wanted to cup her butt cheeks and drag her against him. He wanted to grind his erection against her body just to prove to her what she did to him. Yes, he'd made a vow that first morning to never touch that part of Kendall's anatomy. But at the moment, he could think of little else.

Well, except her breasts. Her breasts were the perfect size for his hands, he was nearly certain, although he'd love a little hands-on experimentation. And her skin looked silky soft. Again, an up-close-and-personal would prove that.

"Are you okay?" Kendall's quiet inquiry caught his attention.

"Yes," he said in a husky tone.

"You hardly touched your dinner earlier, and now you just seem off. Do you feel okay?"

"I'm fine. Just thinking."

Kendall gave him a wicked smile as though she knew exactly where his thoughts had taken him. Maybe, but most likely not. With his adamant insistence that they keep their relationship platonic, would she ever expect him to be contemplating his own personal review of every inch of her flesh? Would she be surprised that it was Cam's little announcement as he'd walked out the door this afternoon that had prompted Ben's perusal? Kendall would probably be just as shocked as Ben had been.

Hours later when Kendall headed up the stairs to bed—that sweet ass swaying with each step—Ben was so turned-on and his dick was so fucking hard, all he could think about was following her upstairs and joining her in bed to find some mutual relief.

CHAPTER 16

Last night when Kendall had climbed the steps to go to her room, the final words out of Ben's mouth had been that Cam would be here tomorrow to hang out with her for the day. More like babysit, but whatever. She knew it was a losing battle to argue, so she ignored it. Instead she decided to look at the situation as an opportunity. An opportunity to get to know her older cousin better. As an adult.

So she wasn't surprised when she wandered into the kitchen Friday morning and found Cam kicked back on one of the kitchen chairs with his laptop in front of him.

"Good morning, Dolly," he said.

Kendall noted two things. First, he sounded wide awake as if he'd been up for hours. And second, even with all the requests not to call her Dolly, he'd done it again. Although, for some reason, this time it didn't bother her. Maybe because it held an affectionate tone of family and belonging, reminding her that Krysset was indeed home.

"Morning. I thought you worked last night." She reached for a large mug and filled it with coffee.

"Until two."

"And you're up? Already?"

He laughed. "Yes. I'm up. I thought I'd keep you company today."

"Babysit. Call it what it is." Even though she was giving him a hard time over it, Kendall was comforted by the company. She hated being alone for long stretches of time. Once this all blew over, she'd probably need to find someone in search of a roommate.

"Then we'd be calling it security detail, now wouldn't we? Until we catch this guy, someone will be with you at all times."

"God, Cam, I hate this. Now I'm just pissed at myself for being so bad at choosing men."

"It's not your fault for not seeing it. Some people are real good at hiding their cruel side. Especially when they have the looks and money to back it all up."

Kendall stared at her cousin. "You remember when you accused me of falling in and out of love more often than most people change their underwear?" The little smirk on his face said he remembered quite well, but she didn't give him a chance to speak up. "I think I might be falling in love with Ben," she said the words in little more than a whisper. Damn. She'd wanted to be bold. Stand firm. Be independent. But she—

"I know you are." His words interrupted her thoughts.

"What?"

"I know that you have feelings for Ben, and I think he's pretty sweet on you, too. Now grab some breakfast and pull yourself together. We're taking a little drive today."

Kendall stared at Cam, unsure what to think. His words surprised her. Somehow Cam seemed to have read the directions of her emotions regarding Ben and wasn't startled in the least when she told him she was falling in love. And then he'd suggested that Ben might be having similar feelings toward her. Was it possible?

She had no idea where Cam intended to take her, because her mind was too stuck on the her-and-Ben bits of the conversation to question anything else. But she finished a second cup of coffee with a slice of toast before making her way back upstairs to prepare for the day.

Last night, Kendall had noticed a subtle change in Ben's demeanor, and her heart had twisted and flipped like an enthusiastic pintsized gymnast. His tender interest had bordered on intimate, and her weak brain skittered between their defined role of good friends and her sudden desire to redefine that role into something more along the lines of passionate lovers.

Ben had been attentive and touchy in a focused way. Not in an arm playfully draped around her shoulder way. No, this had been purposeful. Holding her hand, touching her cheek, brushing her hair back behind her ear. As if reassuring himself that she was okay.

Each time he reached out to touch her, the teasing grin fell from his face and that playful glint in his eyes went molten and intense. A mutual response flared to life within her body like a sparkler ready to ignite an explosive string of fireworks given the right encouragement. The air between them shimmered with energy, or maybe it was only wishful thinking. But the way her breath hitched in her chest followed by her inability to drag in a lungful of oxygen might indicate that some sort of scientific phenomenon occurred when they came in contact with one another. Perhaps their nearness resulted in a chemical imbalance, leaving the room oxygen-less and the occupants panting.

Who was she fooling? Definitely not the academic community. The explanation was far less scientific and far more plebeian. Kendall desired Benjamin Montgomery with every fiber of her being. Her body reacted to his closeness and almost exploded with his gentle touches. Imagine what would happen when he finally kissed her. When those lips she'd been dreaming about pressed against hers, she'd devour him whole.

She vibrated at the delicious thought, although it wouldn't be their first kiss. She'd kissed him as often as she could, but only on the cheek. And yes. Several nights ago, he'd given her a peck on the cheek when he'd slipped out of the booth at the Brawling Bear. A sweet kiss. A non-intimate kiss. The kind of smooch one might plant on their mother or an aged grandmother.

Kendall smiled, remembering the slight panic and bewilderment that had crossed Cam's face in that moment. She wanted more of Ben's kisses in a far more intimate way, and if she'd read Cam's expression correctly several nights ago, he wanted to lock her away in the tower room until she turned forty.

And yet this morning, he'd seemed accepting of the fact that there was an attraction between her and Ben.

Less than an hour later, Kendall sat in the front seat of Cam's enormous pickup truck, bouncing along a gravel road a couple miles outside town. Branchy trees on either side. The occasional evergreen tree. Lots and lots of white snow. She had an idea where they were headed, but it had been so long that she couldn't be sure. But then they turned into a narrow driveway, almost claustrophobic, and she was certain.

"We're at your house."

"Yes. I thought you could use a change of scenery."

The tight woods gave way to an open yard and an old two-story house with a large front porch and two dormer windows on the upper floor.

"It looks just like I remember. Except it's got new siding, doesn't it?"

"And a new roof. Come on." Cam came around to her side of the truck and helped her down. He led the way up the stairs and through the back door.

Stripping off her winter gear, she glanced around, eager to wander through the house. Cam gave her a quick tour, and although he'd renovated the kitchen and bath with modern touches and everything inside had recently received a fresh coat of paint, the tour brought back old memories of a sweeter time. A time before her family had been murdered. So much tragedy had touched both of their lives. Just like her, Cam and his four younger brothers had lost their parents. Her aunt and uncle had been killed by a drunk driver, and although Cam was only nineteen at the time, he'd immediately stepped into the role of caretaker for his siblings.

"Have I ever told you how proud I am of you?" Kendall asked.

"For what?"

"For taking care of your brothers when your parents died."

"You were barely a year old, so you have no idea how much I sucked at being a parent. That's why I hauled them to your house all the time. Aunt Sylvia made it look easy."

Kendall glowed at the memory. "She was a good mom. And I remember enough. But I never understood just how life-changing it would be until I turned nineteen and imagined myself with four kids, ranging in age from eleven to seventeen. That's when I really admired you."

He gave a little snort and shook his head. "I wasn't doing a damned thing with my life. God, Kendall, I was a complete fuck-up."

"But you pulled it together and did what you had to do."

He ground his teeth, seeming to consider her words. She could almost guess he was thinking about his brother, Everett. Her least favorite cousin. The cousin that had been her brother's closest friend. The cousin who had introduced her brother, Carson, to Ryan Prescott, the drug dealer who had brutally murdered her family.

"I see you're still waging that battle, huh? It's not your fault." Kendall repeated those words that he'd said to her earlier in the day, and he just glared at her. But really? How many years was he going to blame himself for the deaths of her parents and siblings, and then his own brother's death shortly after? "I know it seems like Everett's bad choices snowballed into an avalanche that crushed a majority of our family. But it wasn't your fault any more than it was my parents' fault for being overindulgent with my brother. They knew about his drug use, and yet they chose not to send him to rehab. I always wonder if they had some god complex, because they personally wanted to help him get better. And the addict in Carson took advantage of their generosity with his own disingenuous behavior."

"If I'd have raised him better, Everett wouldn't have gotten mixed up with drugs, and he wouldn't have gotten Carson into it either. And Ryan Prescott never would've had the opportunity to touch our lives." Hindsight might be twenty-twenty, but it sure did suck.

"Maybe. Maybe not. You know, sometimes I wonder what would've happened if my dad hadn't fallen asleep in his recliner that night," Kendall said, meeting Cam's gaze. "I mean, I read the police report. It said that Carson was murdered first in the basement. He was high or drunk—didn't fight back. Then Ryan went to the main level. Maybe he just would've left if my dad hadn't been such an easy target, right there in the living room."

"Maybe," Cam said.

"I know it sounds like some childish fantasy to think that my dad could've fought Ryan off, but I've always wondered. If he'd been awake…maybe things would've turned out differently."

They sat in silence for a few moments. It felt comfortable. She didn't feel as if she had to fill every second with words when she was with Cam. She could be in her thoughts and let him be in his.

"Have you seen or talked to your brothers recently?" She hated to ask. It was another sore spot for Cam. There'd been some sort of friction between them in the past several years—something she wasn't privy to—and she doubted he'd share now.

"Nope." He crossed his arms over his chest and glared at her.

The brooding expression made her want to laugh, but instead a little grin that she couldn't suppress tugged at the corner of her lips. It might've been inappropriate, given the seriousness of the rift between her older cousin and his remaining three younger brothers, but she couldn't help thinking she could tease him into a better mood. "If I was bolder, I'd ask you how that makes you feel."

Cam laughed, and his bad mood disintegrated like dust. "If you were bolder, we'd all be in a lot more trouble. And if I told you how I felt, you'd have to bleach your ears."

"That bad, huh?"

"That bad." He gave a sharp nod.

But damn that made her all the more curious what this long-standing battle had been about. He never gave an inch on the topic. She could guess it was related to Everett's death, but it had seemed to develop after that, so she really had no idea. And Dalton, Finn, and Graham had never reached out to her in the sixteen long years she'd been exiled to Oregon, so as far as she was concerned, Cam was in the right, and they were in the wrong. End of story.

"You know, Kendall, even though I didn't sound happy when you first came to town, I really am glad you're here."

"Me, too."

"I just don't want your bad memories to drag you into a dark place."

"That was the exact reason you didn't want me to be at the trial, but I want to live in Krysset, just like I wanted to testify."

"You made yourself very clear. Then and now. Actually, you were a complete brat back then."

"No. I'd just had enough of you telling me I was too young, and I was putting my foot down." A small laugh bubbled out at the memory of her younger self giving a decisive stomp of her right foot as she'd emphatically said those words years ago.

"I remember how you insisted on being part of locking Ryan Prescott away for life."

"It was my tiny bid to take back control of my life, although I didn't realize it at the time. But I'll tell you, I've never regretted the decision. It wasn't fun to relive those painful moments in the courtroom, but the pleasure of putting a murderer behind bars was all worth it to me."

"Blood hungry?"

Kendall tipped her head in acceptance. "Back then I was. When I heard that Ryan had died, I couldn't have been more thrilled." Five years after the trial, Ryan had been shanked in a brawl at Stillwater Correctional Facility. He'd bled out before the correctional officers gained control of the rioting inmates. Eager for Ryan's spilt blood, Kendall had reveled in his fitting demise. "I took me another five or six years before I realized that neither his imprisonment nor his violent death had fixed the damage he'd inflicted on my life."

They sat in silence for a moment before Kendall asked, "Do you ever see the Prescott family around town?"

"Sure. Ryan's parents are still around. They keep to themselves pretty much. And Mary Sue moved away after the trial. A few years ago, she moved back with her husband and a bunch of kids. Actually, she goes by the name Sue now."

"For me, she was the worst part of the trial. She seriously believed I was lying. That I was railroading her little brother because I came from a wealthy family. So much anger. Do you remember that?"

Cam nodded. "Misplaced loyalty, maybe. The first time she and her family came into the bar for pizza, she apologized for her behavior at Ryan's trial. She's been nothing but polite ever since."

"Imagine knowing that your own child or your own sibling had killed four people. What a nightmare." She shook her head, trying to wrap her mind around it. "I feel bad for them, you know?"

"I do. Three more lives ruined."

Kendall couldn't remember another occasion when she'd spent so much focused time with her cousin. It had been good. Some of their choices of conversation had been a bit emotional, and she'd needed to hold back the tears. And some had been light, fluffy topics that had left them both laughing. Through it all, she'd discovered a side to her cousin she hadn't known existed before. He was kind and thoughtful. He rarely put others down. And he was damned hard on himself.

CHAPTER 17

Ben dropped his phone into the cup holder and carefully picked up the cellophane wrapper from the seat beside him before climbing from his truck. Releasing a weary sigh, he pinched his eyes closed for a brief moment and allowed himself to breathe.

"It's time," he said out loud, even though there wasn't another soul around to hear him.

He made his way along the path, soaking up the noontime sunshine. The packed snow crunching under his work boots was the only sound in the vast open space that had been set aside from the rest of society by a thick fence of evergreens and a mix of deciduous offerings, which now stood completely barren of leaves.

Ben followed the path leading to an enormous gray granite monument that rose above all others, marking the family plot for four generations of Aasgaards. Each individual grave was distinguished with a more modest marker in the same gray stone, making it easy, even in the snow, for Ben to find the place where Jenna had been laid to rest.

But then again, it seemed as if he came out here so often—trampling down the snow in the winter or wearing a dirt trail into the green grass of summer—that finding the exact spot had never been a problem.

Head bowed, he read the gravestone. Jenna Marie. The date of her birth and death. And then the words: *Forever in our hearts.* Cam had picked out two epithets and asked Ben to choose the one he thought Jenna would like most. It was a consideration that Cam wouldn't have had to give Ben, and he'd always appreciated being included in the decision.

God, he'd read those words over and over. Each and every time he'd come here. How many times had he stood right here, gazing out at the field of jutting stones? More than one hundred times, at least. Some people thought it was creepy to stand alone in a cemetery, but the comfort Ben found here, at Jenna's grave, was so complete he couldn't stop himself from visiting.

He always updated her on the comings and goings in town, like when Jackson had discovered his love, Sophie, and then again when their baby had been born. He even told her about his friend, Nikki, who'd been murdered toward the end of summer, and how her death had dredged up some of the old feelings of failure to protect an innocent woman. Opening up to Jenna, here where no one else could hear him, was a therapy of sorts. And it gave him a sense of connection to her. Because he couldn't seem to let that go.

"Oh, Jenna. I am so…I'm…" He exhaled deeply, feeling that familiar choked-up sensation. But he wasn't going to cry. Not here. Not today. "I've come to realize that when I come here the first words out of my mouth are always an apology. I've spent so much time and energy shouldering this guilt for not being there to defend you that night, for not seeing the potential bad ending that your brother's drug addiction might cause, for not running away with you so we could marry on our own terms the moment I graduated from high school. I know you still had one year of high school left and a college degree to get. I know it's a stupid thought, but you see, I've spent sixteen years searching for a way around what happened to you. And I've found hundreds of reasons to cling to my guilt. A day doesn't go by without my mind churning up some new way I could've saved you.

"Today, I'm not going to apologize to you." Ben swallowed hard. "Because I was at college two hours away. And what happened wasn't my fault." Why was that so hard to say? "You see, Jenna, I needed to say those words out loud. They are the same words I've heard repeated, over and over, by well-meaning people for the past sixteen years. People who love me and want to see me stop grieving your death. But you were my life, and I hated them for asking me to set aside my grief.

"In the past week, two people—people you knew and loved—actually had the nerve to tell me that you wouldn't be impressed with the way I've been managing my life since you left me. They both suggested that I move on. And now I've found someone. I'm pretty certain I'm falling in love with her. I haven't felt this way about anyone. Except you.

"You know I love you, and I probably always will. But I came here today to say goodbye. The time has come to let you go. It hurts me, but I know now that it's the right thing to do. I won't be visiting you here again, but that doesn't mean the great memories we had together will fade."

Gently, he withdrew the single, long-stemmed rose from the cellophane sleeve and stooped to place it at the base of her grave marker. He ran his fingers over the indentation of her name just as he'd done every time he'd visited.

"Goodbye, Jenna," Ben whispered.

CHAPTER 18

As they raced back toward town at the end of the workday, Kendall decided she had her work cut out for her. Both Ben and Cam had a lot of healing left to do. And this guilt thing? Guys, let it go. She was definitely going to have to work on that with Cam. He wasn't responsible for every bad thing that touched his family's life, regardless of what he thought. Now she just needed him to realize that.

Kendall's heart beat a little faster when they rounded the corner near Ben's house. Although she'd had an awesome day reconnecting with Cam, she missed seeing Ben. She wanted to hear all about his day, and if she dared dream, she'd really like another hug. Or better yet, a kiss.

Cam parked his truck at the back of Ben's house and escorted her to the door. Before they'd reached the bottom of the step, Cam came to an abrupt halt.

"Stay." What, did he think she was a dog?

"Why?"

He flipped out his phone and dialed. "Jeanie, this is Cameron Aasgaard. Send someone out to Ben Montgomery's house. Back door."

"What's going on?"

He ignored her questions and punched in another contact. Kendall cocked her head to the side and stared at the back door. Along the doorjamb was a white sheet of paper, folded in half.

"She got another threat. Posted on your door." Cam paused, probably because it wouldn't do any good to talk over all the swearing that was coming from the other end of the phone line. Sounded like Ben. "See you soon."

Kendall took a step forward to see it better, and Cam grabbed her arm and pulled her against him, wrapping her up. Protecting her. From what?

"Cam. Knock it off. I want to see." She peeked around his shoulder.

Yes, there was a note—held in place with a wicked-looking switchblade. Kendall peeled her eyes from the glinting blade that speared the paper and sank into the wooden frame around the door.

How could she have thought Nick Cardwell had ever truly loved her? How had she managed to find a monster cut from the same cloth as the man who'd murdered her family? She shivered at the thought. Nick had known about her past, about her family's violent death, about the fact that Ryan Prescott had slit each of their throats and would've killed her in the same manner if he'd found her hiding place.

Nick, the man who'd professed his all-consuming love for her and insisted he'd die without her, had taken that knowledge—her own personal nightmare—and twisted it into a daily threat. Each morning, he'd palmed a knife from his vast collection, displayed it for her viewing before closing it, and then slipped it into his hip pocket. "For your protection," he'd said. However, anytime she'd voiced an opinion contrary to his, he'd remove the knife from his pocket and finger the closed handle while he'd waited for her to humbly reconsider.

To any outsider, the action appeared a nervous habit, but to Kendall it had served as a threat, plain and simple. And yet it'd taken a brutal beating for her to get it through her thick skull that Nick Cardwell didn't love her.

Ben, on the other hand, hadn't spouted words of love yet, but he'd told her that he cared about her. His cautious touches and tender devotion supported those words. Now she realized how wrong she'd been to instantly accept Nick's declaration of love when his harsh actions contradicted his syrupy vows.

For the second time in as many days, Kendall heard the sirens and answered the questions. Even now, sitting at the kitchen table, she felt numb—from the cold and from the shock of it all.

Cam had draped a blanket around her shoulders and heated some hot cocoa for her. But it was Ben that she wanted.

"When will Ben be here?" she asked Cam. Again. It seemed as if it had been forever since he'd dialed Ben, and she just wanted him home with her. Funny that she thought of his house as her home now.

"I'm right here." She heard his voice before she saw him elbowing his way through the contingent of law enforcement gathered around the back door.

Kendall surged out of the chair at Cam's side and stumbled across the room. The simple sight of Ben had the power to turn her day around, so she lifted her face to his with an optimistic expression that felt as unsteady as her knees. When his strong arms encircled her, drawing her up against his chest, she wanted to cry with relief. Ben was here, and he'd take care of everything.

She had no idea how long he held her like that, rubbing his hand up and down her back. He talked in quiet tones to Cam and the sheriff's guys who were working around her. Finally, Ben extracted himself from her grasp, and Cam was there to hold her.

"I've got to go to work, Dolly. Ben's going to take care of you. Okay?" Cam asked.

Kendall nodded. While Cam probably hadn't meant that to sound suggestive, the idea popped into Kendall's head and sounded plenty good right now. Yes, she'd like Ben to take care of *all* her needs. Why had that thought surfaced? In the midst of all the other life-and-death stuff, it seemed rather warped.

"Thank you, Cam. For everything. I really enjoyed spending the day together at your house." She forced a smile. Probably looked pathetic. But she'd tried. Cam gave her a kiss on the cheek and headed for the door.

"Hey, Ben," Cam said. "Don't forget what we talked about yesterday." And then Cam was gone.

"What exactly did you guys talk about yesterday?" Kendall asked.

"You." The one word answer was all she got.

CHAPTER 19

It was half the truth, but Ben had no intention of telling Kendall that Cam had asked him to see past his love for Jenna and consider Kendall as a—what?—replacement. No, that's not what Cam was suggesting. Ben had to be fair. Cam had accurately read both Ben's attraction to Kendall and his personal fight to maintain a respectable distance from her.

Ben would admit he'd tried hard to hide both his attraction and his fight, but as a bartender, Cam was just too good at reading people.

And then he'd all but given Ben a green light. Which was damn odd, all things considered.

"*Let's say, as long as you treat her well, I wouldn't stand in your way.*" Ben had spent plenty of time since yesterday, mulling over Cam's declaration.

Now an entire weekend lay before Ben and Kendall. Where to begin?

Once law enforcement completed their work—snapping photos, bagging and tagging the fancy switchblade and threatening note, and asking a shitload of useless questions—they'd offered their reassurance that they'd have eyes on the house and then finally departed. After locking up the door, Ben drew Kendall into the media room. He sat on the sofa with her on his lap and her legs stretched out across the length. To cuddle. Which was about all she seemed up to at the moment. She'd barely spoken since he'd returned home.

"Talk to me, Ben. I need to hear your voice." Her tone worried him. It was so flat and lifeless. Was it shock? Or exhaustion? He'd give her a bit of time and see if he could distract her and coax out the Kendall he was so used to seeing.

"Last night, I noticed your eyes because of something Cam had mentioned." Kendall didn't respond to his words but sat still as stone and waited.

"When I was growing up, everybody knew I was Tom Montgomery's son and that Sarah, Dan, and Joe were my older siblings. Not because of our last name, but on looks alone. If you put us into a stadium filled with people and asked a complete stranger to sort out who belonged in which family, we'd have always been sorted together, we look that much alike. It bothered me, you know?"

Kendall lifted her head from his shoulder to look into his eyes. A huge grin lit up her face. "I've always loved when I see a family together with a pile of kids that all look alike. It's like belonging to a club just by the arbitrary arrangement of DNA. Nothing you can choose or not choose. Nothing that others can force you into or out of."

"Yeah, well, it's not all that it's cracked up to be. Maybe if I'd been the oldest, but I was compared to Sarah academically and Joe athletically, and in both cases, found sorely lacking. Dan, well, they'd compare us, and I was a well-behaved angel." Ben chuckled at the memory, then stilled and darted a look at Kendall. Perhaps he'd said too much.

Kendall gazed at him with a tender expression, and she stroked her thumb over his cheek and along the length of his jaw. Her touch was cool and gentle, and immediately he wanted her hands all over his flesh, wrapped around his erection. Which was getting harder under her behind. He shifted her, adjusting himself, although she didn't seem to notice.

"You have good memories of your childhood, Ben. I don't begrudge you for having your original family around to create memories with. I have family memories, too, both with my biological family and then my surrogate one in Portland. It wasn't the life I'd have chosen for myself, but I've learned to make the best of it."

"Yesterday, Cam reminded me that you didn't look anything like your siblings, which I'd known on some level to be true. I've lumped you, as well as all other blonde-haired, blue-eyed women, into one category to be avoided at all costs for fear I'd think of Jenna."

Kendall met his eyes. "To protect yourself."

Ben broke from her scrutiny and stared across the room for a moment, pondering Kendall's statement before he nodded. "Yes. To protect myself." Funny, he'd thought he'd spent the entire sixteen years looking for some way he could've protected Jenna, but perhaps all along he'd been trying to protect his own heart.

"Just as I'm not a carbon copy of my siblings, no matter how much we look alike, I know you are a unique individual. I wanted to tell you that."

Kendall smiled, seeming to accept his assessment.

Ben lifted a hand to toy with the buttery fall of hair across her shoulder. Silky soft, the locks slipped over his fingers like a crystal-clear waterfall. A frenzied need swept through him. A need to kiss her. To taste her. To bury his fingers in her satin tresses and devour her sweet mouth. "Kendall, I'm going to focus on discovering the real you. The one who arrived in Krysset searching for someone to protect her. I want to be that man for you. I want to be the one to defend you and the one to hold you whenever you're scared."

* * *

Kendall's heart fluttered in her chest. No one had ever said something like that to her before. And no one had ever made her feel that tingly urgent need like Ben's declaration had. She was just attempting to digest the heartfelt words and the barrage of sensations springing from all her erogenous zones when his large hand snaked around the nape of her neck, drawing her closer. Her body hummed with anticipation. Her heart tapped out a wild rhythm. Quick puffs of air burst from her lungs.

Finally, after what seemed like years of waiting, Ben was going to kiss her. She'd dreamed of this exact moment. What would his lips feel like pressed against hers? How would his mouth taste as their tongues played together? At last, she'd see if the chemistry that sizzled between them actually exploded when their lips met. Her body responded with the simple thought of intimacy. Her nipples tightened while a damp heat pooled low in her core.

After several long heartbeats where time stood still, he closed the distance between them. The lightest caress of his lips crossed hers, feather soft, gentler than she'd expected from this strong, virile man. And yet, the exact type of kiss she needed from him, cautious and tender, almost coaxing. One meant to set her at ease at the same time it set her on fire.

She opened her mouth on a soft sigh while pleasure pulsed through her body, and he took the invitation, darting his tongue into her mouth in a tentative search for hers. His kiss ranked well above any of her previous kisses and far better than her wildest dreams. It was a kiss a woman could lose herself in, one that ought to go on forever and ever. The kind of kiss at the end of a movie with a huge heart drawn around the loving couple with the words *The End* scripted across it.

But all too soon, he lightened the kiss, easing away from her lips. He pressed his forehead to hers and stared into her eyes. There was no grin on his face, just an intense expression that sent pulses of energy to all her sensitive regions. He lifted her off his lap, putting her on her feet, and then stood, reaching for her hand.

"Time to eat," he said, leading her toward the kitchen.

She trailed behind, rubbing her fingers across her kiss-swollen lips. The disappointment of abruptly ending their kiss by no means overshadowed the immense pleasure of finally savoring his lips against hers. However, she'd be lying to herself if she didn't admit she wanted more. Oh, so much more.

Time to eat, indeed. She'd be more than happy to straddle his lap and devour him.

CHAPTER 20

"I'll have a diet Coke," Jim said, settling onto the barstool across from Ethan. The place was loud and crowded, but he shouldn't have expected different on a Friday night. "How's Danielle doing? I saw an advertisement for her photography studio."

At the simple mention of his wife's name, Ethan grinned from ear to ear. He set the glass down in front of Jim. "Danielle's great. She purchased the storefront between Swenson's Ice Cream Parlor and Ferris Steakhouse. She won't be open for business for another month, but she hopes to get a few spring weddings on her calendar."

"Glad to hear it. Is Cam around?" Jim asked eager to be done with his last task of the day, which had dragged on longer than he'd planned.

"In the backroom. I'll get him." Ethan turned, opening the door behind the bar far enough to poke his head in and say something to Cam. "He'll be out in a moment, Sheriff. Have a good night." Ethan meandered down the length of the wooden bar to serve another patron at the same time Cam stepped out of the backroom.

Although Jim had learned to school his emotions, the look on his face must've broadcasted his worry, because the moment Cam caught sight of him, his expression went from sociable to guarded.

"Sheriff Ellis." Cam reached out to shake his hand, attempting a congenial tone, which Jim appreciated. The conversation had the potential to be difficult enough without

Kendall's cousin flying off the handle. "Didn't expect to see you again today."

"Wondering if I could have a moment with you."

Cam gave a tight nod, looking about ready to grind nails with his teeth. He said something to Ethan and then rounded the bar. "We'll go back into Ethan's office. Quieter there." Cam led the way to the corner office at the back of the bar.

Once inside, Cam shut the door, closing out the barroom noise, and then crossed his arms over his wide chest. He gestured with his head toward the small sofa and chair combo, so Jim took a seat and watched while Cam sank onto the seat across from him.

Kendall had been fiercely certain that she could trust Cam and Ben with her safety. Overall, Jim's gut told him the same. He'd known her cousin since he'd moved to Krysset and taken up the post of sheriff about ten years ago. A protector at heart, Cam concerned himself with the wellbeing and safety of those around him and, above all, his family. The idea that he might send threatening messages as a means to scare Kendall didn't fit the picture.

While Jim didn't know Ben Montgomery as well, the smattering of interactions he'd had with the co-owner of the construction company hadn't set off any warning bells at the time. He appeared to be a standup kind of guy, honest and hardworking. Ben's involvement with Kendall, on the other hand, left Jim questioning his initial assessment. Oddly, Ben had been involved with the eldest Aasgaard daughter before she was murdered, and at the moment, Kendall resided at Ben's home—although, according to the rumor mill, not in his bed.

However, Jim would wager that their roommate status wouldn't be platonic for long. On Tuesday morning when they'd stopped by his office, Jim had noted Ben's intense gaze—hot enough to melt the three-foot snowdrifts that lined both sides of Main Street. It wasn't the kind of look a man gave a woman he hoped to send scurrying away in terror. Jim had witnessed the same interested glint in the eyes of many young men who'd come to date his three daughters, and he'd made a point of answering the door in uniform with his weapon handy to dissuade the weak-minded and weed out the riffraff.

This afternoon when he'd been called to the scene at Ben Montgomery's house, Jim had watched Ben and Kendall's interaction. Kendall had been all over the guy, clinging to him as if she couldn't live without him. That embrace alone left little question as to her intentions.

Yeah, Ben didn't stand a chance.

* * *

"What's this about?" Cam asked, eyeing the sheriff across from him.

"Let me preface this conversation with the fact that I've put more patrols around Ben's house." Jim lifted his glass to his lips and took a long sip before proceeding. "When Kendall and I spoke yesterday at the Montgomery residence after she'd found that note pinned to her windshield, she commented that you and Ben Montgomery were the only two people in town she knew and trusted. She also gave me permission to discuss any aspect about her situation and protection with either of you."

Cam searched the sheriff's face for some sneak preview of where the conversation was headed, but the guy wasn't giving anything away. "Of course, I want her safe. It's all that matters to me."

Sheriff Ellis sucked in a deep breath and released a long, slow exhale. The bracing action caused Cam's agitation to spike from apprehension up to alarm. Whatever details the sheriff had collected required a healthy dose of fortitude to share. Not a good sign. Probably not good news.

"We've got an arrest warrant for Nicholas Cardwell, and we've sent out a BOLO for the guy. It took a while to gather enough evidence."

Cam could scarcely contain his aggravation with the situation. "Yesterday's note on Kendall's windshield alone—the one where he threatens to kill her—should've been enough for you people."

"It was for me," the sheriff said in an unruffled tone.

"And the guy assaulted her best friend. Dayla still hasn't regained consciousness." How the sheriff managed that tranquil attitude, Cam had no idea. At the moment, he couldn't find a calm tone to save his life. "What the hell has to happen before you take this seriously?"

"We need to follow the law, Cameron, so when we finally catch the coward, it sticks. And as far as the attack on Ms. Johnson goes, there were no security cameras in the area. Right now, they're waiting for her to wake up or hoping a witness will come forward with information. Until then, it's considered an unrelated incident."

Cam couldn't stop the growl that rumbled within his chest.

"I did some poking around and found several instances where the more senior Mr. Cardwell, a prominent attorney and Nick's father, managed to miraculously sweep away some unsavory situations for his son with a boatload of cash before the criminal justice system caught wind of them. If they had, charges would've been filed against Nick. That detail, along with the order of protection and the two threats Kendall has received in conjunction with her hospital record—"

"What the hell? Hospital record?"

"I figured that would be your response. You know, I can't help but wonder if Kendall didn't grant me permission to discuss all aspects of her safety with you because she was too afraid to talk to you about this herself."

"What's that supposed to mean?" Cam's frustration escaped in a growl of words as the conversation veered toward topics guaranteed to ignite his rage.

The sheriff gave him a pointed look. "Don't shoot the messenger."

Cam grunted. "Depends on what you tell me."

"At first, Kendall glossed over the fact that Nick had attacked her. When I asked if she'd visited the local emergency room, she reluctantly indicated she had. I reviewed the dates and background that she gave me with the protective order issued by the court and things didn't add up. I called a few friends and did a little digging. Something went terribly wrong in this case. At the very least, her injuries should've prompted an investigation. In my opinion, the guy should be behind bars, Cam."

Jim polished off his Coke and deposited the glass on the small table to the side of the chair. He leaned forward in his seat, resting his elbows on his knees, his hands dangling loosely. "I received an unofficial overview of the hospital reports. She actually visited the emergency room twice between Thanksgiving and New Year's."

A vicious curse slipped from Cam's lips. His chest tightened with anger, and his breath exploded in sharp bursts. How could someone be so very cruel? To Kendall? His baby girl, hurt by some asshole with a death wish. "Damn bastard. I'll kill him if I ever catch him around here."

"I'll pretend I didn't hear that, Cam." Jim eased back in the chair and tugged a folded slip of paper out of his inside jacket pocket. "The first incident report indicates a variety of bruises and two cracked ribs. Also states that she was accompanied by her significant other who was attentive and affectionate toward her. The second report indicates much of the same except that she arrived at the hospital alone."

"Son of a bitch," Cam muttered under his breath. His gaze shifted away from the hospital report clutched in the sheriff's hands back up to the guy's grim face. "Didn't she press charges?" Cam wanted to rip the coward's balls off and shove them down his throat. Fury roared through his veins, the pounding beat of his heart was so intense he could scarcely make out the sheriff's words as they droned on. He took a deep breath and focused on the sheriff's explanation.

"Kendall insisted that she'd fallen in both cases. Although, her injuries weren't consistent with a fall such as she explained at the hospital. The hospital staff was required to report this to the authorities to ensure that a follow-up investigation occurred. Their failure to follow that procedure is being looked into as we speak."

"God, I could tear someone apart for allowing this to happen," Cam said, trying to tamp down the blinding rage that churned through him.

"Although my source wasn't able to locate any additional medical records for Kendall in the Portland region, she did mention at our first meeting that Nick had been violent with her the night before she left for Minnesota."

"You've got to be joking? Three times? She made it sound like a one-time occurrence." Frustrated and gut sick, Cam wanted to punch something.

"From what she told me, she had to work to separate herself from him. That's why she came back home. Remember, Kendall refused to be a victim in this situation. Don't turn her into one. Don't coddle her. I guarantee you she'll rebel. Protect her, but don't smother her."

"He hurt her. I'd never do that." Cam threw the words at Jim, disgusted that he'd even dare to compare Cam's actions to those of the abusive asshole Kendall had been involved with.

"I know. But Kendall's tenacious. She's been controlled, abused, and stalked. She needs to have power over of her life. Don't strip her of that control." Cam dipped his head in silent agreement, watching while the sheriff stuffed the paper back into his pocket. "All of this information helped us solidify that arrest warrant, as well as a warrant to access all of Nick's financial information. That's actually what I wanted to speak to you about."

"You can track him? Using his credit card?"

"That would be the idea. Except, it seems as if our guy withdrew a large sum of cash Monday morning and then went off radar."

"What? You're telling me you lost him?"

The sheriff lifted his shoulders in a casual gesture. "Law enforcement in the Portland area stopped at his place of residence and at his employer. Nick hasn't been home, nor has he been at work. According to the police officers that made the inquiry with Nick's employer, no one seemed particularly concerned that Nick hadn't put in any time at the office yet this week. Sounded as if it's a common occurrence. I guess that's one of the perks of working for the old man."

"Of course, he's not in Portland. He's here. In Krysset. Leaving threats for Kendall." It didn't take Sherlock Holmes to come to that conclusion.

"True, but since we can't track a credit card unless he uses it, we're out of luck, other than to drive up and down the streets looking for cars with Oregon plates." Sheriff Ellis stood and walked to the door.

"So that's all you have? What about his cell phone?" Cam didn't bother to hide his disappointment and disgust with how slow this investigation was moving. He wanted the asshole arrested and jailed. That was the only way Kendall would be safe.

Sheriff Ellis shook his head. "GPS on the cell phone places it inside his home. Must have a burner phone on him. So for now, that's what we have. We'll watch for something to pop on his credit cards or for him to show his pretty face in town, but until then, we wait." With that, the sheriff walked out of the office, leaving Cam to sit and stare at the empty room.

Cam's mind was a tornado of thoughts. The investigation. The waiting around. The cowardly actions of the son of a bitch, hiding behind pansy-ass notes and getting off on the fear he stirred. And then Kendall. His sweet baby girl. God, she didn't trust him. He'd thought they'd gotten beyond this petty behavior of keeping each other at arm's length. It killed him to know that she didn't trust him enough to share that she'd gone to the emergency room. Not once, but twice.

Now he had to wonder how her ribs were healing up. Just about every time he saw her, he'd crushed her in his eagerness to hug her. Had he caused her more pain? Why wouldn't she tell him about it? Probably worried about his response. Over the years, he'd given her more than enough examples of his extreme, over-the-top reactions to the smallest of situations involving her wellbeing.

But damn it, they'd spent the entire day together today, talking over some pretty heavy topics, and she hadn't bothered to mention it. And a trip to the emergency room wasn't small. He had every right to rage.

That was exactly what Kendall would expect, and probably why she'd avoided the topic altogether. Cam let out a frustrated growl.

Could he do it? Could he let Kendall know that he was now aware of her trips to the emergency room while at the same time keeping his shit together? He wasn't sure. But he needed to talk about it, because he had to know if her cracked ribs had healed completely. More than anything, Cam needed her to understand that she could trust him—with the big stuff, as well as the little stuff—without him going off half-cocked, itching for a fight.

The best way to prove that to her would be to calmly discuss the situation.

Cam laughed out loud in the empty office. Now there was a first. The words "calmly discuss" had never been paired in his conscious stream of thought before this moment. Perhaps he actually had some hope of proving himself worthy of Kendall's trust.

CHAPTER 21

"You've got paint in your hair," Ben said, looking down on the top of Kendall's head where she knelt, trimming the edges of the wall along the wide baseboard. The call about an hour ago from Sadie Johnson had turned Kendall's mood around. Dayla had opened her eyes this morning and announced that she was hungry. She'd also been awake enough to confirm that Nicholas Cardwell had attacked her.

Relieved by her friend's improved health, Kendall had been relaxed, playful, and absolutely giddy ever since.

"Where?" Kendall brushed her fingers across the top of her head, smearing what was there or adding more to it. Basically, the girl was a hot mess.

He laughed. "You're making it worse. Stop touching yourself." Kendall cocked her head upward to catch his eyes, her brows raised in amusement. "And get your mind out of the gutter."

"I will if you come down here and kiss me." She turned around completely and tipped her face up to his. Apparently, she wanted to make the process as simple for him as possible.

He stood over her, shaking his head. "We won't get anything done if I start kissing you. How about, we finish this room, and then I'll give you a kiss."

"My labor is worth at least two kisses," she said in a pouty tone.

"Deal," Ben said, rolling the paint down the wall in even strokes. "I can't believe you've never painted before."

"I'm doing pretty good, huh?" she asked, leaning back to inspect her work.

"Didn't your aunt and uncle ever do this kind of thing?"

"No, they wallpapered the entire house back in the '80s and have never felt the need to mess with perfection." She scrunched up her nose. "They even have the ceiling papered in one of the bedrooms," she said with a little laugh.

"Not a fan of wallpaper. I've stripped off too many layers of the stuff in just about every room in this house. Swore I'd never do that to a wall again." Ben bent down and dipped the roller into the paint pan again. With wide strokes, he covered the wall with the rich sage color.

"So you've torn down wallpaper, and you can obviously paint. What else are you responsible for around here?"

"Pretty much everything you see. Floors, walls, woodwork."

"You're kidding."

"No. The place was a disaster, but I've always loved this house. When I was a kid, I'd play at the park across the street and think, 'Someday that house will be mine.' So when it came on the market, I decided I wanted to tackle it."

"Tackle? You knew it needed a lot of work?"

"The outside was in rough shape. I had guys from work come out and help me with the new roof and the siding."

"What's your favorite project?"

"The foyer." He paused to glance at Kendall. She had given up on the edging project and now sat cross-legged in the middle of the floor. That was okay. At least she was keeping him company. "It's such a grand old space. A room unto itself, you know."

"I love all the woodwork. And that wide sweeping staircase in the center. Someday I'm going to dress in my evening gown and wait at the top of the staircase for you to announce my grand entrance." He laughed at the haughty tone she'd put on.

"I refurbished all the trim work."

"Around the doors?"

"Yes. And the ornate molding at the baseboards and the crown moldings along the ceiling. The banisters on either side of the stairway and each and every spindle. All of it had to be stripped of multiple coats of paint. And then I stained it all a deep rich mahogany."

He knew he wore a proud smile, but he couldn't help it. The elegant, two-story foyer screamed of excess, and now that it had been returned to its original grandeur, Ben couldn't have been prouder. Every time he climbed those steps, he admired the shiny luster and the smooth finish of polished wood against his palm while a warm sense of satisfaction filled his chest at a job well done. Of course, a fresh coat of paint on all the walls and refinishing the hardwood floors throughout the first floor had added the finishing touches to the yearlong project.

"I've noticed the furnishings you've added. Period appropriate," she said, turning her attention back to edging.

"I go to auctions and estate sales when I have time. It's not my favorite thing to do, but I wanted to have a couple rooms that looked as they should. Unfortunately, it's…" Ben lifted his shoulders. "It's not me. I feel like the front parlor is a museum."

Something about the old home restored to its flawless original beauty, or perhaps better, reminded him of an old woman who'd undergone a facelift, nose job, and cheek implants all in an effort to appear decades younger. Polished to perfection, the look no longer fit the nature of the owner. In the same manner, Ben no longer felt as though he fit the furnished, decorated Victorian and its formal style, rigid and harsh like a strict mother. He preferred the warm comfortable surroundings of his hunting lodge.

Kendall bobbed her head in agreement. "I can understand that."

"It's been a labor of love. Fun. Educational. And far more expensive than I would've ever imagined. And that's saying something since I'm in the construction business. But now, I've had enough. I'm tired of walking into a room only to face another project that needs to be completed. Every unfinished task is a glaring reminder of the enormous undertaking I started when I bought the house six years ago. There are a handful of smaller projects I'd like to wrap up, and then I'm considering putting it on the market."

She stood up and glanced around the room. "Done with my part. Kiss me."

"Bossy little thing, aren't you?"

"You owe me."

He wasn't anywhere near done with the room, but he just couldn't deny her the kiss she'd been asking for a moment longer. Setting the roller against the side of the paint pan, he grabbed a rag and wiped his hands. Then he approached her. She was breathing fast, anticipating. So was he.

She didn't even bother to wait for him. Nope. She closed the distance and flung her arms around his neck, planting her palms at his nape and dragging his head down for a soul-shattering kiss. God, he'd have thought she was starving the way she devoured his mouth. Her open lips moved over his. Her tongue played against his, coaxing and encouraging his participation. She nipped and sucked, licking at his lips. And when he finally thrust his tongue into her mouth, she clamped down, sucking on it hard.

Her mouth was so hot, he groaned at the thought of her sucking on another part of him. He grabbed her ass and pulled her up against him, rubbing himself against her. He was primed and ready to be buried inside of her. It was a kiss meant to annihilate all his thoughts and inhibitions. All his good plans to wait until they got better acquainted.

Of course, right now his libido liked Kendall's plan a whole lot better than his.

Why was he holding out again?

Oh, yeah. Ben wanted his first encounter with Kendall to be special. Over the past six months, he'd had so many hookups he'd lost count. Taking Kendall to bed now, without allowing whatever it was between them to grow and develop into something more, would only make this event blend into the countless others.

That was why he believed that waiting was for the best. To make sure that this was right for both of them. Something in his gut told him there was too much at stake, too much to lose by making love too soon.

Even though the little minx was doing her damnedest to get him into her bed.

The heavy chime of the doorbell rang from downstairs, causing them to pause midstroke. Still lip to lip. Both breathing way too hard. Talk about piss-poor timing? Probably for the best. He pulled away from Kendall and headed to the door.

"That was kiss number one, mister. You still owe me," she said from the room while he descended the steps.

Ben threw open the door to find Cam on his front porch. "Hey. I need to talk to Kendall for just a few minutes," Cam said.

"Kendall, Cam's here."

Within seconds, she raced down the steps and threw herself into Cam's arms. Neither one of the cousins appeared to be worried about the paint splatter decorating Kendall—pretty much everywhere. Like always, she hugged with abandon. Cam, on the other hand, seemed a little stiff today, almost as if he feared that he might break her. Or then again, maybe he wasn't so keen on being smeared with second-hand sage-green paint.

"Hi," Kendall said, pressing up on tiptoe and placing a kiss on Cam's cheek.

"I only have a few minutes, but I wanted to talk to you. Can we sit?" He gestured to the media room. Kendall led the way, and Ben turned toward the kitchen to scrounge up something to eat. "Ben, why don't you join us? I think you should hear this, too."

The three of them found spots to sit, Kendall leaning up against Ben's side—nothing subtle about her position—so Ben went all in, snaking his arm around her shoulder. He wondered if Cam was having second thoughts about the whole *I wouldn't stand in your way* thing right about now.

Cam said, "Kendall, I know about the ER."

ER? Holy hell. That bastard had hurt Kendall badly enough for a visit to a doctor? Why hadn't she said anything about it? Ben sensed Kendall stiffening up beside him. Or maybe it was just him, preparing to beat the living shit out of the guy when he finally showed his ugly mug around town. But either way, Cam simply held up his hand to stave off any objections or questions and plowed right along. "Have your ribs healed?"

Ribs? Kendall never mentioned any of this to Ben. He could feel himself coiling tighter by the second.

"Yes. My ribs feel fine." Kendall paused, and if Ben guessed correctly, she was holding her breath, debating her next words. "Thank you for asking." She added with such courtesy he'd have thought she and Cam were nothing more than acquaintances. Ben would've laughed out loud if the situation weren't so damned serious.

"Good." Cam seemed to sag with relief. "When I heard, I worried that I might have hurt you more when I hugged you."

"No." Kendall pulled away from Ben's side and moved to where Cam sat, placing her hand on his knee. "You didn't hurt me. But I'm guessing from the expression on your face that I hurt you."

Those words caught Ben off guard, but judging from Cam's grim look, Kendall was probably right. Cam gazed across the room, shaking his head. "I just want you to trust me enough to come to me with anything, Kendall. But I understand that sometimes I can overreact a bit."

"Ya think?" Kendall teased, patting his knee. "I didn't tell you, because I didn't think it was a big deal. I wasn't trying to keep secrets. I took care of it. I broke up with Nick after the first event. The second time…I shouldn't have opened my door when he knocked. I got the restraining order after that."

Questions were pouring through Ben's mind, and he could hardly contain them. But he did his best to observe silently, because Cam had already redirected the discussion to information Sheriff Ellis had shared with him the night before about Nick being off the grid. Several minutes later, with a warning to be on the lookout, Cam left.

Ben hated the weird rush of emotions he was dealing with at the moment. Although he was pissed off at her asshole ex for what he'd done to Kendall, Ben also felt a little bent out of shape that Kendall hadn't shared the truth with him. Was he entitled to feel disappointed or hurt that she'd failed to share very specific details with him? No, not really.

Cam had obviously been in that same boat—completely unaware of the seriousness of the situation. Surprisingly, Cam seemed to contain his anger at Nick and his sadness over being excluded from those certain details of Kendall's life.

Ben needed to at least try to do the same.

He'd acknowledge his rage over what happened to Kendall, but beyond that, Ben had no right to feel more or demand more. Yet.

CHAPTER 22

"Should I be scared?" Kendall asked, allowing her teasing intentions to ring clear in her tone. They'd settled into this comfortable banter since their kiss Friday evening. They'd joked and laughed, and occasionally found their way back to the sofa to watch a movie and make out a bit more. But it was all above the waist. Unfortunately.

Ben stood on the opposite side of the kitchen, frying up four sausage links—two for her and two for him—a side dish to the oatmeal he'd cooked. Regardless of Ben's choice of breakfast entrées, sausage links seemed to be a constant, and Kendall figured he bought them by the caseful.

"Scared? No," he said, reassuring her with a slight shake of his head. "It's just Sunday dinner with my folks. Now if my brothers were there—or worse yet, my sister, Sarah, and her big mouth—well then, I'd be the one scared. But it'll be fine." He darted a glance at her over his shoulder, a toothy smile pasted on his face.

She laughed, imagining all the secrets a handful of older siblings would unearth for her. Family gatherings exploding with animated whoops and hollers as one and all fell victim to tales of youthful foolishness, unrequited love, and misbehaviors—those both punished and overlooked. She dreamed of being immersed in such chaos, being teased at the same time she doled it out to her loved ones. That type of camaraderie required countless, unguarded hours spent together over the course of weeks, months, years, through the best and worst of times. It required family.

Although she longed for those kinds of cherished interactions, she'd never begrudge others for having sisters, brothers, or parents just because hers had been ripped from her life. Especially not Ben.

Forcing the wistful thoughts from her mind before a hint of sadness flickered across her face, she asked, "Your sister likes to meddle in your life, I take it?" She held out her hands for the bowl of oatmeal he offered her and set it on the table.

"Understatement of the year." His words huffed out like a petulant youngest child when he delivered two small plates with the sausage links to the table.

"Tell me about your parents. I don't remember them. Actually, I'm not sure that I've ever met them before." She sprinkled a healthy scoop of brown sugar into her oatmeal and stirred the gooey, warm mixture before sampling a small bite to assess the sweetness.

"Probably not," he said, slipping into his chair across from her. "But my mom has been looking forward to meeting the woman who's sleeping in her son's bed." A wolfish grin curled his lips.

Kendall's jaw dropped in momentary speechlessness. With her elbows perched on the table, she buried her face in her hands. Why that thought bothered her she couldn't say. Sleeping with Ben appealed to her, the attraction sizzled between them, and she intended to make her dream a reality. Her best and current plan: weaken his resistance, maneuver around whatever self-imposed obstacles he'd set up, and then blow his mind with hot sex. However, his mother unabashedly discussing their living arrangement, regardless of its status, somehow disconcerted her.

After several long moments, she found her tongue and stammered out a response. "Please. Tell me she didn't say that."

"No, she didn't." Ben waited for her to meet his eyes for confirmation, and when she breathed a relieved sigh, he added, "That's what my dad said."

"Ugh!" A mortified groan erupted from her throat.

He chuckled while she squirmed in her seat. She couldn't explain why the fact his parents thought they were having sex rattled her. But then Ben's amusement touched his eyes and a pleased expression crossed his face. The tease took pleasure in her discomfort.

Time for a little payback.

She breathed an over exaggerated sigh. In a slow delicious movement, she stroked her tongue over her lower lip before she drew it into her mouth to nibble. "We wouldn't want your parents to be wrong, Ben. I think after breakfast you should take me upstairs to that king-size bed of yours and let me put you through your paces."

Desire and control warred across his face, and his devious grin fell. "Not yet."

Shoveling a spoonful of oatmeal into her mouth, she nodded at his statement. Interesting. He had some timeframe she wasn't privy to. Sounded like someday, just not now. She could work with that.

"Okay, then. Tell me about them." The salacious tone of moments earlier was replaced by her sincere need to know what she'd agreed to with an invitation to lunch at his parents' home today.

He finished chewing his final bite of sausage. "Tom and Judy are good people. I know a lot of adult children who can't tolerate their parents, but mine are cool. I'm the only one of the four kids that stayed in Krysset." He chuckled, pinning her with his warm brown eyes. "I'm the only one who stayed in Minnesota. That means I'm the one nearby to help the folks out at the same time they meddle in my business. But for the most part, they give me the space I need. Of course, I work with my dad. If our personalities clashed, we'd have problems, but overall we get along well."

Kendall nibbled on a sausage link, imagining what it would be like to work with one of her own parents, day in and day out. It sounded idyllic. Something she'd never have a chance to experience. But perhaps the situation wasn't all roses for Ben. Although with his easygoing demeanor, she'd guess he'd have no troubles working side-by-side with his father. That thought gave her pause. Were the workload and managerial responsibilities divided evenly? Did his father bark out orders while Ben obeyed? Or did Ben get to play big-boss-man fifty percent of the time?

Ben interrupted Kendall's quiet deliberation. "My mom runs a tight ship, always has. I think she won the award for the strictest mom on the block when I was growing up, and that's saying something since I'm the youngest. You know how parents get more indulgent as the years go by? Not the case here." He shook his head to emphasize his point. "Everything has a place. Everyone has a chore. Responsibility for the efficient and systematic functioning of a home falls on everyone's shoulders who find refuge there."

Her jaw hung open at his recitation of the bizarre string of words, and he grinned at her puzzlement. "Mom said that a lot."

Kendall didn't know what to say, so she returned his smile and nodded.

"When you step in her front door, she'll expect you to hang your coat on a hook along the front wall, remove your boots, and slide them under the bench on one of the drip pans."

"Wow. I'm glad I asked, or I might have just flung my coat into the corner, and then kicked my boots off and left them in front of the door. Talk about an embarrassing faux pas."

He laughed. "You're my guest. I'd have hung up your coat and placed your boots neatly where they belong."

"You've been trained well." Kendall teased him.

"Yes. But beyond her need for order in a house with four children, she's a great mom. Loving. Warm. Attentive. Once you're inside, she'll greet you with a ferocious hug. She loves family gatherings."

Kendall's good humor evaporated, replaced by wariness. "I'm not family, Ben."

"She doesn't discriminate, Dolly."

"Don't call me that, Benjamin." She scowled at his grinning face, but she felt her expression slowly morph into a smile. No way could she remain annoyed with him and his teasing words.

She scooped the final spoonful of oatmeal, poised to load it into her mouth. "Do you bring lots of women home for her to hug?"

"No. Never." Not since Jenna. His unspoken words hung heavy between them.

"Anything else I need to know about your mom?"

"If you step foot into her kitchen, she'll put you to work." A grim expression crossed his face. "I avoid it at all costs."

"Good to know."

Several hours later, she realized how thorough and spot-on Ben's description of his mother had been. After they stored their winter gear near the doorway, Judy Montgomery stretched up on tiptoes and wrapped her arms around her son, planting a loud kiss on his cheek, and then she turned her attention to Kendall.

With deep brown hair cut in a classic shoulder-length style and brilliant green eyes that none of her children had inherited, she exuded warm, motherly kindness. Just a bit shorter than Kendall, she held Kendall's gaze for several moments, searching her face, maybe mentally making comparisons to the big sister that had held her youngest son's heart. Maybe still held his heart, Kendall couldn't be sure.

Kendall cringed knowing she was being measured. Compared. Would Judy Montgomery accept her as a unique individual, or just the next Aasgaard sister in line, struggling to undo the damage that Jenna and her death had done to Ben's heart?

Kendall's anxiety ratcheted up a notch. Her stomach tightened. As a general rule, she paid little attention to whether others accepted her or not. But this was different. Mrs. Montgomery's opinion mattered to her, because Ben mattered to her. The accelerated beat of her heart pounded loud enough for Ben's mom to notice and comment. But instead, she inventoried each feature on Kendall's face.

Kendall wished she'd have worn her pretty light blue sweater today. It brought out the color of her eyes, which at this moment held the older woman transfixed. She stared into Kendall's eyes as if she were sucking out every dream, downloading every detail, and hand plucking every memory that Kendall had ever stored within her gray matter. Then when Kendall thought she couldn't bear a second more scrutiny without disintegrating into a sobbing puddle of insecurity, Ben's mom hugged her, and Kendall hugged her back.

Just like Ben had told her, Judy Montgomery didn't discriminate.

When she pulled away, she maintained contact with Kendall's upper arms. "It's a pleasure to meet you after all these years, Kendall. You've grown into a beautiful young woman."

"Thank you." The words rushed out as she attempted to stop the pink that slid up her neck and across her cheeks. No time to blush now. "Thank you for having me for dinner, Mrs. Montgomery."

"Oh, please, call me Judy. I'm glad you're here." Judy released her and gestured around with open arms. "Please, make yourself at home."

The Montgomery home was a modest-sized two-story on a large lot about six blocks south of downtown Krysset. On the left of the entryway, Kendall noted the immaculate formal living room with pristine white carpet and uncomfortable-looking furniture. Without a doubt, the room had never had a human being settle in and *make themselves at home* there.

On the right of the entry stood a steep staircase leading to the second story. And as if on cue, a deep voice rumbled from above. "I thought I heard someone come in." A set of feet pounded down the staircase.

"Kendall, I presume." An older version of Ben—one with a touch of gray at his temples and deep crinkles around his eyes—stopped in front of her to introduce himself. "I'm Tom Montgomery."

"It's nice to meet you, Tom." She held out her hand, but learned that Ben's dad didn't discriminate either when he wrapped her in a welcoming embrace.

After a brief moment, he released her. "I'm glad that Ben dragged you along for lunch today, Kendall. We've been looking forward to meeting you." Tom's grin slipped just a little, and his eyes sparkled with moisture instead of merriment.

"Thank you for having me," she said, hoping that his rush of emotions was due to seeing her after all these years and not his memory of how special Jenna had been to his youngest son.

Ben's dad covered his show of emotion with words. "It always catches me off guard when I meet up with someone after many years. I've gotten older, my children and grandchildren have gotten older, and yet for some stupid reason, I expected you to still be that short little kid with the blonde braids. But you've grown up, and you're as pretty as your mom, Sylvia."

"Thank you." She appreciated his thoughtful explanation, although she breathed a sigh of relief when Judy broke the silence.

"I need some help in the kitchen, Kendall."

Ben leaned over her shoulder, the stage whisper loud enough for all to hear. "That's code for interrogation time."

"Benjamin. Behave yourself." Judy playfully swatted at her son's shoulder before turning toward the kitchen. He chuckled, looking thoroughly amused.

Kendall glanced at Ben one last time before she followed Judy down the hallway that led into the kitchen at the back of the house.

"You'll find the items for the salad on top of the center island. The cutting board is in the lower cabinet on your left, and the knives are in the top drawer on your right." Efficient. Everything in its place, exactly as Ben had said. "Now, I've heard that before you left Oregon, you'd been working as an elementary schoolteacher. Third grade, right?"

Ah, yes. The joys of living in a small town with an even smaller gossip network.

"Yes. Exactly. I love teaching third graders. The kids are still enthusiastic about learning, and yet, they don't need help tying shoes and zipping up jackets. Makes my job a lot easier. Do you work outside the home, Judy?"

"Oh no, dear. I'd never find time to be employed. I take care of our home. Well, except I don't do garbage or lawn care." She scrunched up her nose, making a face. "Those are Tom's responsibilities. Ben got me involved at the local community food shelf where I volunteer several times each week."

Judy directed the conversation with a warm, easygoing manner through the latest novel at book club, her plans for the gardening projects in the spring, the latest happenings at Bible study, and their neighborhood's monthly gaming night. The conversation ebbed and flowed between them as if they'd known each other for years, putting Kendall at ease. She credited that to the relaxed atmosphere in the Montgomery kitchen. With the effortless skill of a master chef, Judy moved from one task to the next with purpose, each motion measured and exact. No franticness. No chaos.

Kendall relaxed, her previous worries put to bed by the menial task of chopping vegetables for the salad and the easy banter with Ben's mom. Until Judy blindsided her with the jumbo stumbling block purchased from Protective-Mom's-R-Us.

"So, you're shacked up with my son. Are you in love with him?" The direct words were punctuated by the metal tip of the meat thermometer she pointed in Kendall's direction. With its long thin steel stem, the simple kitchen implement clasped in her fist could inflict severe damage in the wrong hands.

She stared at Judy, and her apprehension returned. Kendall could barely squeak out the words. "Yes, Mrs. Montgomery. I'm in love with Ben."

It wasn't her voice or her demeanor. It reminded her of Jenna. Timid and shy. Afraid to speak her mind. Fearful of what others thought. Her accommodating big sister would've shrunk at Judy Montgomery's accusatory and demanding tone.

But Kendall wouldn't. Not a chance. She was no one's punching bag and no one's welcome mat. She'd stand up and speak her mind boldly. "Yes. I love him," she said again with her normal confidence.

Judy swung wide to the right, and with a wild motion, she stabbed the ham dead center. Then with her free hands, she gave a gleeful clap. "I'm so glad. He needs someone like you in his life, Kendall." She turned back to the ham then glanced over her shoulder. "Anything you need to get him to the altar, Kendall, you call me." A wicked grin curled her lips. "His sister, Sarah, might help in that matter, too."

CHAPTER 23

Tuesday evening Ben sagged into the front seat of his truck, put the key into the ignition, and headed for home. Could this week get any worse? He knew better than to test Fate by asking the question.

The weekend had been so perfect. Sure, it had started out badly on Friday afternoon with that second threat toward Kendall knifed to his doorjamb, but for some reason, the reality of the situation had settled in and had forced a closeness between him and Kendall—like being stuck in the blizzard together. All they could do was hunker down and wait. Okay, he'd admit that the whole waiting-on-pins-and-needles gig was going to get old really fast, but for one weekend, it had been kind of fun.

Kendall seemed to take it all in stride, remaining fairly upbeat. Only twice during the entire weekend, did she comment on anything negative. Once, she'd blamed herself for choosing to date a violent lunatic, and later in the weekend, she'd become apologetic for forcing him to remain shuttered in his home for the long stretch of days. He'd pointed out that being locked up with a beautiful woman was no sacrifice on his part. That had put an end to the crazy self-recrimination, but he wondered how many more days until her frustration about being confined would start to show through.

Lunch at his folks' house on Sunday had given them a brief change of scenery. Which was good, because Kendall wasn't getting the reprieve of going to work. Nope. Just the changing of the guard. Cam would keep her company for the day. And one of the deputies from the sheriff's department would spend the day circling the block or parked outside Ben's house, vigilantly watching for Nicholas Cardwell to show his scrawny, soon-to-be-incarcerated ass. And then once they'd found him, life could return to normal.

Ben wanted to laugh. With Kendall in his life, in his house, eager to climb into his bed, there was no returning to his normal, pre-Kendall days. Nope. That sweet woman had single handedly twisted his regular old life around and filled it with something far more exciting. Funny how he'd never considered his life dull before, but now he couldn't imagine going back. He couldn't imagine Kendall not being with him every single day.

Yes, the weekend had been absolutely perfect—like a flawless crystal bubble that had encapsulated him and Kendall. A woman he never would've paired himself with, but a woman he could now see creating a future with.

And then that pristine, hope-filled weekend shattered, ushering in the week from hell.

Or at least that was what Ben and his dad had dubbed it.

On Monday, Ben had pulled up to Montgomery Construction headquarters, two miles south of town, to find his dad standing outside in the biting cold wind, staring up at the front of the building.

"Good morning, Dad. What are you doing out here? You're going to freeze." His shouted words were nearly lost in the gusting arctic wind.

"Take a look." His dad jerked his head toward the building as he typed a text on his cell phone.

Ben's gaze traveled upward the height of the two-story cement building until his eyes settled on the spider-webbed design on the upper left window. Cracked. With a quick survey of the other seven windows on this side of the building, he noted that each one had a least one hole, some several. The damage purposeful.

"Damn. I'd guess BB gun." Ben jammed his hands into his coat pockets and hunched his shoulders against the wind.

"Yup. Whoever did it, took out every window in the building. I've texted all the construction-site managers, and I'm waiting for status reports to come in. So far, two sites received the same treatment." His father delivered the bad news in his standard calm tone.

The remainder of Ben's day had been spent doing damage control, filing police reports, and insurance claims. The grueling day might as well have been a monotonous, in-office Tuesday for all the endless paperwork he'd done.

But no, Tuesday had dawned bright and early with its own set of problems, spiraling into comparable chaos. A new home on the edge of town built for the Jacobson family—a project nearing the end of construction—had sustained severe water damage, similar to the fiasco while Marc Fullerton had worked as their plumber. However, this situation screamed vandalism rather than sloppy workmanship. Each sink had been stopped and every spigot turned on, overflowing throughout the house. The locked doors did nothing to hold back the flood of water that oozed between the minute cracks, creating beautiful and costly ice sculptures.

Montgomery Construction had suffered vandalism on occasion over the years, but the unfortunate and expensive events had always been staggered and, in general, had usually equated to small-scale damage.

These incidents were not.

And Ben's list of viable suspects had shrunk to one: Marc Fullerton.

"Don't point your finger too fast," his father had said to him in that fatherly wisdom-filled tone when he'd picked up the phone to dial Sheriff Ellis. "Keep your mind open to all possibilities."

Ben had rolled his eyes like an irritable teenager. "We both know it's Fullerton." His harsh words held more bite than he'd planned. "Sorry, Dad."

Ah, hell. He'd been on edge all day, and he'd snapped at more people than just his father. Between bitching at people and doing paperwork, he'd spent a fair amount of time apologizing to the ones he'd been short with. If he thought he could behave better, he'd wish for a do-over. But he knew his frustration level would still spike, and he'd undoubtedly still grouse at his employees, his father, or anyone else in earshot. He dragged his weary body from the cab of his truck and headed toward the backdoor of his house.

The fact that he'd tossed and turned the past two nights hadn't helped his less-than calm behavior at work. But it seemed that no matter how tired he was when he climbed the stairs to go to bed, once he slipped between the sheets his thoughts turned to Kendall. He couldn't help but relive those delicious kisses they'd shared over the past few days. The feel of her skin. The light pressure of her lips against his. The tentative touch of her tongue. And that's about all it had taken. His vivid imagination had spun out of control with the notion of kissing her again and digressed with little trouble into fantasies of making love with her. His lack of sleep in collaboration with the monumental stress level at work had left him mentally and physically exhausted.

This afternoon, Kendall had texted him that dinner would be ready at six thirty. She'd promised to keep a plate warm if he returned home late. Now at six twenty-seven, he was grumpy, famished, and ready for the week from hell to come to an end.

God, he could use a relaxing weekend. Yeah, right. That wasn't going to happen for three long days. And it was probably a bit optimistic. The most he could hope for at this point was a less destructive Wednesday.

The moment he stepped into the house, the delicious aroma of garlic and tomatoes wafted through the air to greet him. And if he wasn't mistaken, there was a sweet scent mixed in, too. Chocolate cake?

Within a heartbeat, Kendall stood in front of him, unzipping his jacket, dragging it off his shoulders, and then smothering him in an excited hug. He wrapped his arms around her and hugged her back.

"I missed you today," she said, whispering the words into his ear.

"I missed you, too. I wish I'd stayed home. It was a horrible day," he said against the top of her head. He held her flush against his body, and his cock hardened with the closeness. "And I missed your mouth. I've got to kiss you."

"I think I'll just leave now." Cam's voice rumbled from the kitchen.

Ben separated himself from Kendall without a kiss. "Hey, Cam. How did it go today?"

"Good. Non-eventful, but good." Cam gave him a dark look that said he was eager to extract a pound of flesh from Mr. Cardwell. "Can't wait for that arrogant jackass to show his face. I'm going to beat it to a bloody pulp. Unless one of those deputies outside gets to him first. That would be a shame since I've been sitting around plotting exactly how much I'm going to enjoy it." The guy looked dead serious.

"Okay, then. I hope you get a shot. After I'm done with him." Ben opened the door, so Cam could leave. He was kind of enjoying needling the big guy.

"The food is ready, Ben. Come and eat."

"It smells heavenly, Kendall. I noticed it the moment I opened the door. Spaghetti?" Kendall nodded with a little smile on her face. She looked as if she was trying to please him with her meal. "It's my favorite, you know." Again, she bobbed her head up and down but didn't say anything. So unlike Kendall. "And chocolate cake?"

"Brownies."

"Sounds good. I will most definitely save room for dessert."

With the first bit of pasta, he groaned. He obviously didn't know how to make spaghetti because Kendall's meal was incredible. Far better than any pasta dish he'd ever whipped up. "This is delicious, Kendall."

"Thank you. I'm glad you like it."

"I didn't know you cooked like this."

She blinked at him with a duh expression on her face. "I've got nothing better to do. You're probably going to put on a little weight if Nick doesn't show up soon." He wanted to tell her that was unlikely, but then she said, "I prepped caramel rolls for breakfast, and there are chocolate chip cookies. I made two batches, so you can take some to share at work."

She looked perturbed, so he decided not to tease her. "I'm surprised you found the ingredients to bake all that."

"Cam arranged for a delivery from the grocery store." Kendall sighed. "So, your day was bad. Does that mean you won't have time to watch a movie with me?"

"Hmm, is that code for making out with you on the sofa?"

At least that got her to smile. He'd missed that smile. And her voice. But now she was quiet. Too quiet.

"How was your day with Cam?"

"Boring." She took a sip of the red wine she'd poured herself. "I'm sorry. I brought this on myself. I just want it to be over, you know?"

"I understand. And I'm sorry that all this crap is happening at work and taking my attention away from you in the evenings. I don't have enough time to watch a movie, but I definitely have time to kiss you."

"Well, I have a better idea," Kendall said. Was her voice huskier than normal?

"Oh?" he asked cautiously, fairly certain he knew where this was leading.

"Maybe we could delay the kissing time until later. And you could hurry through your work. And then we could enjoy our kissing time in bed together."

He tried not to grin. It *was* a better idea than a few kisses. But he wasn't sure he wanted to encourage her that way. "While I think that's a great plan, I'm not sure that I can kiss you and then sleep in the same bed with you without making love to you."

"Great. That sounds about right."

"I was thinking that we should wait until your birthday. Wouldn't that be a great way to celebrate your birthday—our first time together?"

"That's like…ten days away. Are you kidding?" She sounded as if she was in agony.

He chuckled. At least he wasn't the only one hurting right now. "I want our first time together to be special, and with work right now, I can't give you the attention you deserve."

She let out a whimpered moan and sagged back in her chair, snatching up the wineglass as she went. Her expression was, well, sulky, and the pillow of her lower lip was more pronounced by the pouting set of her mouth. "Are you sure you don't want to?" she asked with such seriousness he wanted to laugh.

"I absolutely want to. We've had this conversation before. I've pointed out my hard cock multiple times—entirely your fault," he said in a teasing lilt. He cocked his head to the side, waiting for the next words out of her mouth.

"And I've offered to make it all better for you."

"And I appreciate that. Really I do."

"It's okay, Ben." With a look of complete understanding, she stood to clear the table. But instead of picking up dishes, she moved toward him. She pushed him back in his seat, straddling his lap, barely wedging herself between his torso and the table.

Wrapping her arms around his neck, she combed her fingers through the hair at the back of his neck. She held that pose—her core pressed against his obvious erection—and gazed at him. Her lips were slightly parted and those pretty aquamarine eyes had a sexy half-closed thing going as they darted a glance at his lips. He couldn't help himself. He licked his lips, anticipating what she'd taste like.

His hands slid under her shirt and found the silky soft skin on her side just above her waistband. He let his hands wander that small stretch from below the band of her bra down to the top of her jeans. Back and forth. Up and down.

God, he wanted to touch her everywhere. Wanted to bare every sweet inch of her flesh and kiss and nibble and stroke until they were both mindless with need. And then he wanted to take her. Slow and sweet. But he wasn't fooling himself. The first time they joined, it was going to be hard and fast. He had a feeling Kendall wouldn't have it any other way.

She continued to stare at him from her perch on his lap. He could feel the heat of her core through her jeans and his pants. He could hardly wait to get rid of all these barriers. But for now, they provided at least a little obstacle to keep them from going at it right here at the kitchen table.

"I'll wait another day or two, and then I'm going to ask you again," she said as if she was making a great concession. And then she tried to move off his lap. Not happening. He held on tight.

"You haven't even kissed me, Kendall."

She crushed herself to his erection, rubbing against him, driving him crazy. She kissed him. Gentle strokes of her lips, her tongue. She licked her way into his mouth, nibbling on his lip, kissing his cheek, his jaw, his neck.

"I could come this way." Her whispered confession had his cock kicking under her crotch. Oh, God, so could he. "But instead, I'm going to serve you a brownie, so you can get to all that work you have. I just wanted to let you know how much I missed you today."

"Thank you for supper and for brownies and for being patient. I don't want our first time cheapened by rushing it. It's too important to me. You're too important to me."

CHAPTER 24

At nine thirty, Kendall padded into the media room where Ben was working, leaned over the back of the sofa, bracing one hand on each of his shoulders, and pressed a small kiss to his cheek. "Good night, Ben."

"Good night." He reached up, squeezing her arm right above her wrist, and dragged her down again so he could brush his lips across hers. "Thank you again for making spaghetti tonight. It's my favorite, and the meal was delicious." With that, he released her arm and returned his attention back to his work.

Kendall climbed the steps to her room, wishing Ben had more time tonight. But she couldn't fault him, considering his work week had been rolling along like a cart with four square wheels. Frustrated and exhausted, he was pouring over dollar figures, as well as a list of possible vandals, and probably would continue into the wee hours of the morning.

She pulled her sister's diary from the box in the closet and clutched it to her chest. Kendall had yet to share the journals with Ben or even tell him of their existence. Her initial plan had been to show him, knowing they'd have some emotional significance to him. But during their discussion at his hunting lodge, when he'd admitted to still holding strong feelings for Jenna, Kendall had decided he probably didn't need any more emotional connections to a woman who'd died years ago. Some might argue that it wasn't Kendall's call to make, but the journals belonged to her now, so it seemed logical that she could choose who and who not to share them with.

Those journals were Kendall's most precious possession, and she'd treated them with reverence for the past sixteen years.

Jenna had filled three leather-bound books with verbose descriptions of Ben. Sometime the words made Kendall laugh, and sometimes they made her cry. The third, and final one had always been her favorite. Jenna had developed quite the active imagination by journal number three and had graphically described what she envisioned her first time with Ben might be like. Her sister had painted pictures of a sweet lovemaking session, including exacting details of who kissed what and when. It was charmingly innocent.

Kendall, of course, had more experience in this arena, now eight years older than her sister had been when she'd penned the flowery text. But the wide-eyed words and the affectionate thoughts that had served as the source for the fanciful descriptions permeated Kendall's heart with an odd sorrowful love that she couldn't set aside.

A silent tear slipped down her face. Resting the journal against her chest, Kendall pinched her eyes closed, holding back the sadness that leaked from the corners of her eyes, attempting to draw some memory from the dark recesses of her mind.

She brushed away the tears and lifted the treasured book again. As a young child, Kendall had watched Jenna document her teenage life within the pages of the books, and over time, they'd become a symbol of the perfect love. Perhaps an unattainable love. A one-sided, inexperienced infatuation with no real standing in reality. One that reeked of flowery prose and whimsical dreams. But to Kendall, Jenna's heartfelt words were so pure and innocent, filled with anticipation for a future with a man she loved, that Kendall couldn't help but read them over and over again. She wasn't sure whether it was the inspiration she gleaned from pouring over the hope-filled words, or perhaps the warm memories of a happier time in her life.

Memories of her dearly loved family and of the old home they'd shared. And memories of the secret door deep within Kendall's walk-in closet. At the age of eight, a walk-in closet was little more than a secret hideout rather than a treasure trove filled with shoes, clothes, and purses. Kendall had spent countless hours playing within and sneaking through the miniature door that led into a similar closet—Jenna's closet. Only four feet high and narrower than most doors, its purpose had been the topic of much speculation between the two of them. The ongoing debate raged for years, and they'd always fallen back on their favorite excuse: the two girls who'd originally inhabited these rooms must have shared a beloved dog called Lucky. That small door had allowed Lucky to go from one room to the other with ease.

Kendall smiled at the memory of the dog that had served as the source of hours of childhood chatter between her and her big sister. A dog that had never really existed. And yet, had saved Kendall's life.

Unlike Kendall's closet, her big sister's closet had been utilized for its intended purpose—packed to overflowing with clothes and accessories. But the filled-to-capacity space hadn't stopped Kendall from being a nosy little sister, creeping from her own closet into her sister's to spy through the slatted louvered closet door. Mostly Jenna hadn't done anything interesting, just homework or writing in her journal. On occasion, she'd lounge on her bed and talk on the phone. Jenna had been a great big sister, far more tolerant and nurturing than Kendall ever would've been. The intrusion of her little sister had never bothered Jenna, and she'd often said, *"Hi, sweet puppy, Lucky."* or *"I know I'm being stalked by Lucky today."*

But on that night with the terrified screams and the sticky-wet puddles of blood, Jenna had said, *"Stay safe, my sweet puppy, Lucky."* And then the man had moved the red knife fast.

With a wall-coating splatter of red, Jenna's body slumped to the ground. Her head thudded against the hardwood floor while her sightless eyes stared at the closet door Kendall hid behind. A pool of blood stained the floorboards under Jenna's face and neck.

Kendall screamed and screamed until her throat ached, but she was alone.

"Kendall. Wake up." The concern in Ben's voice pulled her out of her nightmare. The bed dipped low when he sat on the edge and stroked the hair away from her face. "It's okay. It's a bad dream. You've only been in bed for a little more than an hour."

She clamped her eyes shut, but it didn't prevent the silent tears from flowing down her cheeks while her breath came in fast gulps.

"Shhh. Oh, Kendall, don't cry. You're breaking my heart."

Kendall felt the bed shift, followed by the rustling of fabric like clothing being removed. Then the covers lifted, and Ben slipped in beside her. "Scoot over, darling. I'm going to hold you for a while."

* * *

Warm peaches and vanilla, the scent Ben would forever identify with Kendall, assailed him the moment he lifted the sheets and hugged Kendall close to his body. As she curled into him, pressing her tear-dampened cheek against his chest, a sharp pain pressed into his rib cage. Ben shifted around and extracted a small book clutched in Kendall's hand. She must've fallen asleep reading. He pried the book from her fingers and dropped it over the edge of the bed. It fell with a thump onto the floor.

"My book." A half-asleep whisper, tinged with panic.

"I set it on the floor. No reading now. Let's sleep." No need to ask her twice. Her body went limp in his arms. How this woman could drop off to sleep with such ease, even after an upsetting nightmare, was a mystery to him.

If only he could drift off to sleep so effortlessly, but with the stress of work and the scent of peaches and vanilla tickling his nose, it wasn't happening anytime soon. He pressed his lips to her forehead, fighting the desire that grew in his boxers. He'd been sporting a semi most of the day. The conversation over dinner had stiffened matters entirely, so he'd been hard as steel by the time she'd climbed onto his lap. Straddling him and rubbing her heat against his boner had nearly done him in.

What had been the logic behind waiting until the night of her birthday? He couldn't remember. But when the time came, it was going to be fucking awesome.

"Ben?" He immediately heard Kendall's voice, even though he was pretty certain that he'd actually been asleep. At some point, they'd shifted, so now her soft body was spooned in front of his. His hand rested possessively over her breast and her curvy bottom pressed against his steel-hard erection. If death by exhaustion was a possibility, he might as well be wrapped around the lush curves of a sweet woman when he went.

"Why aren't you sleeping?" he asked.

"Make love to me. Please."

He rolled her onto her back and came up on one elbow beside her. His other hand gently slid up beneath the long T-shirt she'd worn to bed until his fingers brushed along the curls between her legs. No panties. Nice. And then his searching hand continued northward until it found one breast. A firm globe with a perfectly puckered tip that fit in his hand as if she'd been made specifically for him. It seemed as if he'd waited forever for this one moment. Now all he could think about was sinking into her lush body.

"Are you sure?" Well, at least he had the decency to ask.

"Yes, I need you." She boldly grabbed his cock through the flimsy fabric of his boxers and gave him a slow stroke. "Tonight."

She shoved at his underwear, and he assisted by pushing them off one leg and then lifting her nightshirt up to expose both of her breasts. It wasn't exactly classy, but she didn't complain. Then he settled between her thighs, keeping most of his weight off of her body, and wedged the length of his cock against her core. She was all warm and soft and wet.

God, he was dying to be inside her. He kissed her. Greedily taking her lips. Urgently cupping her breasts, toying with her nipples. This wasn't what he'd planned. Not fast. Not frantic. Not half clothed and half asleep. But this was for Kendall. What she wanted. What she needed. And he needed to make it good for her.

"You are so incredibly beautiful."

She lifted herself, stroking her clit against his erection. "Now, Ben," she said against his lips.

He notched the tip of his cock to her entrance, pausing only to savor the sweet moment he entered her for the first time, when an annoying chirp squawked from the vicinity of the floor. He moaned into Kendall's mouth and then took a quick glance at the clock on the nightstand. Shortly after three. Not a good sign.

"Sorry, Kendall," he said. He dove for the pile of clothes and snagged his jeans on the first attempt. Flopping back onto the bed, he answered the persistent ringtone that belonged to his father's cell phone.

"What's going on, Dad?" His voice sounded gravelly and annoyed. If his dad noticed, he didn't comment on it.

"Ben, sorry to wake you. We have a fire at one of the sites. The fire department's on the scene. I'm headed over now. Should I swing past to pick you up?" That was his efficient dad. Succinct and straight to the heart of the matter. Even in the middle of the night.

Kendall sat up in bed, readjusting her nightshirt, and then wrapped the blankets around her. Her lips were swollen from his kisses, and her hair was a beautiful, messy tumble. God, she was sexy. Gazing at her just made him want to climb back into bed and finish what they'd started. Best not to look at all.

He turned away, digging through the pile of clothes. "I'll be ready in five minutes," Ben said and disconnected the call, tugging his jeans on along with the thermal shirt he'd stripped off only a short while before when he'd climbed into Kendall's cozy bed.

He glanced at Kendall again. "There's a fire at one of the sites. I'm going to call Cam, and I'll let dispatch know that you're alone and ask that one of the deputies stay right out front. Okay?" He snatched up the heavy flannel shirt he'd also discarded onto the pile. "Will you be able to go back to sleep?"

She let out a laugh that sounded like a cross between a whimper and a growl. "I'm exhausted, I'm horny, and now due to my great request that you make love to me, I'm wound so tight I think I might explode."

"I feel your pain, babe." He stooped to kiss her cheeks, and then because he couldn't help himself, he kissed her sweet mouth. "I have to go, but I'll lock up and make those calls.

You're safe." He caressed her cheek and forehead while he spoke, brushing her hair back from her face.

"Thank you. You be safe, too," she said. Her voice was sleepy, and her words were followed by a throaty sigh. And then she curled up in a tight ball, hugging the pillow he'd abandoned.

He straightened and stepped away from the bed, fisting his hands at his sides before he touched her again, or he might never get out the front door to meet up with his father.

CHAPTER 25

It seemed to Ben that thirty-seven active projects, all in some stage of renovation or construction, provided an imaginative vandal with far too many targets for destruction, as well as a plethora of ways to wreak havoc.

For the Montgomery's construction business, November and the beginning of December had been blessedly warm, lacking the usual snowy precipitation common in northern Minnesota. Their construction teams had forged ahead on a variety of projects, keeping an eye on the weather forecast until the week before Christmas when they'd received a walloping blizzard followed by a mighty arctic blast that ensured the snow would hang around until the late spring thaw. As the storm had approached, teams had hurried to enclose any structure that still stood open to the elements.

The latest vandalism site, sparked by an arsonist's compulsion or a vandal's ambition, had been the sole project that hadn't been sufficiently enclosed at the time of the intense snowfall. After that storm had passed, one crew had shoveled out the majority of the heavy white stuff while another team had installed windows to keep out any future moisture. Montgomery Construction had gotten lucky today. Damp wood had hampered the fire's destruction, slowing the damage that could've easily spread to the entire structure. That fact, paired with the quick response of the Krysset Fire Department, had left the vast majority of the building still intact. According to the fire chief, an overturned space heater surrounded by garbage was the most probable source of the blaze; however, the investigators hadn't yet ruled it arson.

Ben had. His gut said an arsonist had hauled in the trash, tipped the space heater, and ignited the blaze. Nothing would convince him otherwise, especially not accusations that his crew had behaved in an unprofessional or sloppy manner.

Montgomery Construction had a zero tolerance for employee trash littering the jobsite. Large metal dumpsters were always available, and all employees were expected to clean up after themselves. Ben's dad had initiated the policy years ago, and Ben figured his mother's everything-has-its-place mentality had rubbed off on his dad.

His project manager, Trent Davis, had locked up last night after the last workers had gone for the day. Honest, diligent, and responsible, Trent had held the position for more than seven years, working his way up through the ranks at Montgomery Construction. If he said he'd turned off the heater, Ben believed him. End of discussion.

Unfortunately, that wasn't the end of the problem. Someone had deliberately upended the space heater to cause the fire. But who? This event, along with the destruction at other properties over the past two nights, screamed of sabotage—one person or one group of people intent on taking down Montgomery Construction.

The cluster of events felt personal, aimed at damaging his family's business, or perhaps him personally. Maybe a disgruntled employee? A dissatisfied customer? Another construction company hoping to step over the writhing body of Montgomery Construction as it gasped its final breath on the way to bankruptcy heaven?

Who would do this? Ben racked his sleep-deprived brain, attempting to make sense of the chaos. He'd already rattled off the names of several people who might take pleasure in inflicting a little pain on him or his business. Marc Fullerton, the druggie plumber. Roland Kearns, the soon-to-be retiree. Northern Lakeland Construction, an up-and-coming builder a few towns over that wanted to change the landscape in the construction scene—perhaps by wiping Montgomery Construction off the map. He chuckled to himself, remembering the conversation with Saul Okerstrom, his surly competition. Now on second thought, maybe old Saul had enough reason to help Ben's business along the road to oblivion.

The only other name that had popped up as a possible suspect was Travis Johnson and his wife, Jill, who were less than pleased with the results of their kitchen remodel and more than vocal about it. Still, resorting to arson seemed drastic, even for the hypercritical Johnson family.

Back in his office in the same clothes he'd worn yesterday, Ben wandered down the hall toward the dark aroma of freshly brewed caffeine, and his mind wandered back to Kendall. When he'd first joined her in bed last night, her soft body had curved around his and her tiny hand had pressed on his bare chest. She'd returned to sleep like a lazy old hunting hound by a roaring fire, too comfortably cushioned against his body to be bothered by the fright of a scary dream. For him, the need to claim her had raged through his mind, and he'd resigned himself to the fact that he would lie there like that—awake for the rest of the night. Thankfully, he'd dozed off while he'd fought the desire to touch her, to smooth his hands up and down her body, to strip her of the T-shirt she'd been wearing.

But then when she'd stirred and called his name, he'd been the one wrapped around her body with his hand holding her luscious breast, her beaded nipple pressed against his palm. And then she'd whispered her sweet request, and the battle had been lost.

They'd almost made love. Almost. Against his better judgment. And without a condom. And only because she'd asked him so prettily. They'd both been half asleep, moving against one another. The entire event had that hazy, dreamlike quality. And if he didn't know better, he'd swear it had all been just that—a dream. A very, vivid dream.

So now he was operating on little sleep, stressed out due to all the shit going on at work, and horny as hell.

As he leaned against the wall beside the coffeemaker sipping the hot elixir of the gods, waiting for the caffeine rush to kick in, the obnoxious ring tone for one of his site managers began screeching from Ben's phone. Damn, he needed to change that.

"Hey, Trent." He answered with faux gusto, hoping the old adage, *fake it 'til you make it*, was based in truth. He wasn't feeling it yet.

"Ben, I have something here you need to see. I'm out at the building site for the new medical facility near the highway."

Ben sighed, rubbing at the tension that seemed to be growing in his forehead. "You want to text me a picture?"

"No." Trent stalled. "I think you'll want to look at it in person."

* * *

Jim Ellis stood shoulder to shoulder with Ben Montgomery at a construction site on the edge of town, staring at the sheet-rocked wall. The guy had been having a rough couple weeks. First the threats to his houseguest, followed by the rash of vandalism to the corporate office and several construction sites. Target practice. Water damage. And as of last night, a fire. And now this latest act of vandalism.

Scrawled on one of the unfinished walls in dripping blood-red spray paint, they stared at the lettering. *"Ben, the bitch is mine."*

"Kendall's ex-boyfriend?" Ben stared blankly at the wall.

"That'd be my guess."

"The rest of the vandalism's related?" A question, but from the tone he'd already figured out that nothing this obvious turned out to be a fluke.

"A coincidence? No. I'd say the same person did it all."

Ben turned and faced him, strain and fatigue etched in the lines around his face. "Has anyone spotted Nick around town? The locals like to talk. Maybe a rental car or one with Oregon plates? What about local hotels? Or any of the resorts in the area with winterized cabins?"

Jim smiled at the young man. "I've got the job under control, Ben. We haven't found him yet, but he can't hide from us forever." He followed Ben out the door toward his squad car. "Do you know if Kendall told Nick Cardwell about you during their relationship?"

Ben shrugged. "I don't know. I guess that'd be something you'd have to ask Kendall."

"Do you have a website that lists your current projects?" An easy access list for the general public or a hardy to-do list for an enterprising vandal.

"No." He shook his head, a look of defeat crossed the young man's face, and he didn't bother masking it.

"How many construction and renovation sites are you involved in right now?"

"Thirty-seven in eight counties." He released a weary breath.

"Only the ones in close proximity to town have been hit. Makes me think someone's driving around, looking for signage with Montgomery Construction outside." Jim paused for a moment to let that detail sink in before he continued. "I want all the signage taken down at each construction site." That simple action wouldn't stop anyone with an axe to grind, but it might slow them down a bit.

The shocked expression on Ben's face disappeared within seconds, replaced by purposefulness. He pulled out his cell phone and keyed in a text. "I'll send something out right away. All the signs will be down before lunch."

CHAPTER 26

"Almost? What the hell is that supposed to mean?" Dayla sounded better today, stronger. She still refused to Skype, insisting that she couldn't be seen without makeup. But come on, they'd been roommates for years and had seen each other in the worst of circumstances. Kendall hated to think about how badly her friend had been hurt by the bastard Kendall had dated.

"Tell this Ben character to strip down, get back to bed, and finish the deed. Doesn't he know it's not polite to make a lady wait?" Dayla asked, completely incensed on Kendall's behalf. It was kind of how Kendall felt when Ben had picked up the phone rather than make love to her.

"There was a fire at one of the jobsites. He needed to go out there to meet up with the fire department."

"Hmmm? I've never done a construction worker before. Does he wear his tool belt to bed?" Clearly Dayla was feeling better.

"The lights were out, but I don't think so." Kendall giggled, knowing that was only the first of many questions her friend was going to ask now.

"I want all the deets, girl. Spill." A teasing demand, but Dayla knew better. Kendall wasn't much for sharing the details of intimate encounters. Not even now when she was feeling totally guilty about the dangerous situation she'd put her friend in. "For God's sake, Kendall. I'm not going to be hooking up for a very long time. I need to live vicariously through you."

"I'm having those nightmares again."

"Oh, sweetie, I'm sorry." Dayla, better than anyone else, knew how debilitating those bad dreams could be for Kendall.

"I guess I was screaming and crying. Ben came in to wake me, but I was really upset. So, he took off most of his clothes and climbed into bed with me. He held me, and I fell right back to sleep."

"Figures. I don't know how you do that."

"Me either," Kendall said, considering the lost time she could've savored, pressed up against Ben's rock-hard abs. She shrugged. "I don't know what happened. A few hours later, we shifted around, and I asked him to make love to me." She'd whispered those words, pleading with him to make love to her. In her sleepy fog, it had seemed like the right thing to do. To use their bodies to ease the ache of their bad memories. To relegate those sorrows and fears to the deepest, darkest corners, so those bad things didn't stand in their way of living life a moment longer.

And with her quiet request, he'd kissed her. Caressed her. Wedged himself between her thighs. Told her she was beautiful.

Kendall sighed at that dreamlike memory. "Our bodies moved like we were on autopilot. It felt as if we'd been together forever. But then the phone rang, and it was over before it started."

"Ugh! That's all I'm going to get out of you, isn't it?"

"Yes." The fine details about what happened between her and Ben were private. "I'm glad you're feeling better. When are they sending you home?"

"Tomorrow, maybe," Dayla said in a sad voice. "I'm going to stay with Sadie for a while. Until I'm…" The words trailed off.

"I'm planning to come back to Portland to visit soon. Ben said he'd travel with me."

"You sound really content, Kendall. I'm happy for you. You deserve a good guy, for once. But wait till I'm feeling better, okay?"

CHAPTER 27

Kendall jammed her arms into her coat and zipped the thing up while Ben laced up his hiking boots. Thank God it was Friday afternoon. Kendall had never been so happy to see the end of a work week in her entire life—not even when she'd been gainfully employed.

"You okay?" Ben asked.

"Of course. Why?"

"Because you sighed about four times in the last minute. Are you tired?"

"No. I was just thinking that going to work had been easy compared to this sitting-around-and-waiting thing. It's getting old. You know? Waiting for Nick to leave another threatening note. Waiting for you or Cam to escort me out of the house or into town."

Ben gave her such a tender look she felt ungrateful for complaining. "I know this is hard for you, but it's for the best," he said.

She quickly said, "I know what Nick can be like—so proper in public and so aggressive in private." She really couldn't argue with Cam and Ben about being able to deal with him on her own. Nick had shown that he had no remorse about hurting her or her friend, so it was best to stay at home with the doors locked until they arrested the jerk.

It was just that this week had dragged on forever, with only one prominent shiny spot—Ben's hard body snuggled up next to hers for those couple hours after her nightmare. The memory had kept her hot and bothered for the past few days. And at night? Well, the slight lingering scent of wood and musk on the pillow had fueled her fantasies.

"Kendall," Ben said, his expression filled with concern. He was all bundled and prepared to step out the door. She must have ignored him. Not purposefully, just too deep in thought. "You're acting strange. You okay?"

"Sorry. I was just thinking how glad I am that it's Friday." She gave him a smile. It probably looked guilty.

"You're doing a lot of thinking today. Are you sure you want to go out? I know it's been a hell of a week."

"No way. I have to get out of this house. Besides, I can't wait to see Cam," she said just as Ben's phone rang. He checked the screen.

"I'm sorry, Kendall, I've got to take this. It'll only be a few minutes," he said.

"No problem." She sat on the bench near the door to wait, watching while he paced down the hallway to his home office where he'd spent the entire day working so she wouldn't be home alone.

All week both Ben and Cam had rearranged their schedules for her. How would she ever repay them for all the kindness they'd shown her? Well, she could definitely think of some ways to compensate Ben.

Yeah, her overactive libido was ripe with some mighty graphic mental imagery.

And that was about all Kendall had these days—her overly creative thoughts—because the stars and planets hadn't yet aligned, and Ben hadn't given in again. Frankly, it was maddening. The guy wanted it as much as she did, but he was stubborn, dedicated, and committed to sharing their first time on her birthday.

Kendall was not on board with the whole waiting gig, and she'd told him as much. Multiple times. It seemed that rolling over on top of her had been done in a moment of weakness, like sleepwalking—sleep sexing. Or maybe it was simply muscle memory. He was so familiar with the procedure that he could do it without thinking or without even being awake. Whatever.

Of course, her sister had never written anything like that in her journal.

Jenna's journal.

Recollection slammed her, followed by a brutal tidal wave of heart-stopping panic. She'd fallen asleep on Tuesday night, clutching the leather-bound book to her chest, and then there was a vague memory of Ben tossing the book toward the floor when he'd climbed into bed with her after her nightmare. How could she have forgotten about it until now? Where was it?

Since Ben was still immersed in his phone conversation, she muttered a few words in his direction and raced out of the mudroom, dashing up the flight of stairs to her room. She had to find her sister's journal.

Could Ben have picked it up? Read it? If he had, it'd be the equivalent of hitting the refresh button, or reinstalling the old version of the operating system that Kendall had labored so hard to update.

Okay, that was selfish. But what if instead of rekindling his love for a dead woman, he spiraled into a dark pit of despair and grief, never to climb out again? She'd never considered that reliving the memories of Jenna might flat-out defeat the poor guy.

Kendall couldn't imagine finding pain within those poignant words. When she read them, her sister's voice echoed through her mind as if Jenna stood before her speaking the words aloud and, for some reason, that had always comforted her. While Jenna's journals were among the most treasured possessions Kendall owned, those three small books had the potential to rip Ben's life apart.

Damn. Why had she been this careless?

Like a mad woman in search of gold, she threw herself on the floor and peered under the bed, noting the lack of dust bunnies as she reached out and grabbed her prized journal. It must have been pushed under the bed when Ben had scrambled to dress in the dark after his father's late night phone call. She breathed a sigh of relief, clutching the small brown leather book to her chest.

"You look goofy, swimming under the bed like that."

She sat upright, shoving the book behind her back. Cool, real cool, Kendall.

"You scared the crap out of me, Benjamin. Don't you know it's rude to sneak up on people?" Indignation rolled from her lips. "I told you that I'd be right back," she said in a grumbling voice. Shoving the book under the bed again, she climbed to her feet.

"You dropped your book again." He wiggled his finger toward the space beneath the bed. "I finished my call just as you raced up the steps. What's going on?"

"Nothing." She shrugged, feigning indifference. "I just remembered my favorite book slipping onto the floor last night, and I wanted to retrieve it." Stooping, she snatched up the book and shoved it under her pillow, cringing at her poor choice of hiding places. Maybe she should inquire about a safety deposit box at the bank. Or maybe she should just burn the damned books that promised to offer more heartache than comfort to the man who had loved the author.

"Come on. Time for some fun." Ben led the way, and less than ten minutes later, Kendall was engulfed in Cam's all-consuming bear hug.

The second she'd stepped foot inside the Brawling Bear, she'd sought him out and raced toward him, throwing herself into his embrace, savoring the safety of his muscular arms and his massive frame. He'd always held her like this, as if his life depended on it. And she'd always tolerated it.

Not today. Today she was all in. Kendall squeezed Cam with the same intensity he always showed her. She breathed in his scent, musky and masculine with a hint of something purely wild, a scent unique to Cam.

He pulled back with his hands clutching her shoulders and studied her face. Concern tightened the creases around his eyes, hardening his already unforgiving features. Prior to last week's revelation and their many discussions since then, she'd have taken one look at his face and assumed he was furious. But now that she understood he loved her like a father loved a daughter, their entire relationship felt different. Natural. Real.

"Oh, baby girl. I missed you today. You're okay, right? No more threats? You haven't spotted Nick lurking around, have you?"

"I'm fine." She rose up on tiptoe and pressed a kiss to his cheek. "You wouldn't believe how many times the sheriff's car has circled Ben's house. Those poor guys must be dizzy by now."

"Good. Sheriff Ellis said he'd step up security until we flushed out the little prick."

"I've been on guard, you know. Watching. Waiting. I'm kind of surprised he hasn't made himself known yet."

"Well, he hasn't stopped by the bar. Since this is one of the first businesses along the county road that dumps onto Main Street, we tend to get lots of strangers wandering in looking for directions. Although, if he'd stepped foot in here while I was behind the bar, he'd recognize me from my not-so-friendly visit a couple months ago."

"Yeah, you both acted like a couple brutes," Kendall said, sensing Ben's presence behind her even before he touched her. Her body tingled with excitement like the static-filled air before an electrical storm. Then he draped his left arm around her shoulder, drawing her closer, and her heart soared.

Ben reached out his right hand to shake hands with Cam while Kendall eased into Ben's embrace. Her cousin nodded at Ben and grinned in the weirdest display of acceptance Kendall had ever witnessed. It was as if Cam had just given Ben permission to take her home and have wild monkey sex with her. What a contrast to the interaction between Cam and Nick a couple months ago.

"Let's grab a booth. Do you want pizza or a burger tonight?" he asked, tugging her a bit closer and rubbing his hand up and down her arm. She loved the way she felt when she was near him. Warm, safe, and cherished.

"Pizza sounds great." Kendall couldn't stop the visible shiver that raced through her body at his words and his touch. Perhaps Ben hadn't noticed.

"We'll take a large, five-meat pizza, two garden salads, and a pitcher of beer." Ben placed his order with Cam, and then he maneuvered Kendall into one of the giant wooden booths. The high sides surrounding the booth gave a sense of privacy and yet afforded them a nice view of the stage.

"I'm glad you ordered a salad to balance out the veggie-less pizza." She flashed him a teasing smile.

"Did you want a vegetarian pizza? You eat anything I put in front of you without complaining so I figured you weren't too picky." He snatched up her hands and stroked small circles with the pad of his thumbs across the back of them.

"I'm not, but you haven't put asparagus in front of me yet." She scrunched up her face in a show of disgust. "What about you? I've cooked dinner without asking you for food choices, and you didn't seem too put out by what I served."

"You haven't served me Brussels sprouts or Jell-O." His distain toward the offensive vegetable and the congealed fruity liquid couldn't be disguised.

Kendall laughed. "Good to know."

"I overheard Cam talking about an unfriendly visit. What was that about?"

Kendall shook her head. "God, Ben, it was bad. Cam came out to Portland for a short visit at the beginning of November. I never intended to introduce him to Nick. We really hadn't been dating that long, and it felt like it was too soon. Anyways, it turned ugly really fast when Nick showed up at my apartment. He was mad as hell to find another man in my living room, and it didn't matter to him that Cam was a family member."

Kendall paused when the waitress delivered the beer and two glasses. Ben poured Kendall a glass and set it on the table in front of her and then filled his own and took a long drink. "I know you've got more, so go ahead. Keep talking."

She heaved a sigh. "Cameron threatened to rip Nick's balls off if he hurt me. As you might guess, the conversation following that lovely little warning was a bit strained. Nick refused to leave with Cam there, and Cam refused to talk with Nick there. Both of them just glared at one another." The complete show of dominance had been primal, almost animalistic, and yet in the end, neither had whipped it out to mark his territory, namely her. Thank goodness. However at one point, she'd worried that she'd have to step in to soothe their massive egos, both unwilling to give in or to back down. But then Cam had growled and bared his teeth—a behavior beneath Nicholas Cardwell—and the self-appointed title of supremacy had been erroneously established—in both their minds.

* * *

Ben watched while Kendall toyed with the glass in front of her, seemingly lost in thought. "I'm surprised that Cam didn't take out the guy on the spot." Ben's words seemed to bring Kendall out of her memories and back to the conversation.

"I always thought Nick's need to oversee every aspect of my life was charming, like he cared enough to be involved. He made it clear he wanted to protect me. But after Cameron left that day, it seemed like some sort of switch was flipped and Nick's true character surfaced. He became verbally abusive, and that escalated to physical abuse within a few short weeks."

"You think that Cam's visit set him off?"

Kendall eyed Ben as if she was debating her next words. Finally, she bobbed her head in slow agreement. "Maybe. But I'd never tell Cam that. He isn't at fault for what's happened. That's all on Nick. At some point in the future he'd have shown his violent side." She wore such a dejected expression as she shook her head and asked, "How could I have ever thought I was falling in love with him?"

Ben held her hand across the table, unsure what to say to that. Unsure where their relationship stood. Without a doubt, he was falling in love with Kendall, because what he felt for her wasn't simply a physical attraction. Kendall had made it thoroughly clear that she was attracted to Ben. But would she ever fall in love with him? Or would she be too cautious with her heart to let her guard down long enough to find love again.

They sat in silence for a long while, both lost in their thoughts. Finally, Kendall said, "You said Sophie and Jackson were going to be here tonight."

He tossed back the rest of his beer. "Jackson's singing, but I wanted to get here early to let you visit with Cam and eat before the place gets so crowded we can't find a table."

"Why's it going to be that crowded?" Kendall stared at him.

Ben shrugged. "Jackson's singing. Once women find out, they text all their friends, and before you know it, the place's mobbed."

"He's that good, huh?" She raised her eyebrows at him in disbelief.

"You just wait and see."

CHAPTER 28

Kendall had to agree. Good didn't begin to cover Jackson's skills. The guy was fabulous. With his body gently swaying to the music, he sang about making love. Sexy as hell.

"Sophie, how can you stand having him sing like that in front of all these horny women?"

Sophie giggled at Ben's loud groan. "Kendall, you have to work on your bluntness."

"She knows what I mean." Kendall reassured him with a gentle touch of her hand on his upper thigh.

"Yeah, I do. Most of them have gotten a lot better. Still, I like to be here when he sings. Maybe it's a bit of jealousy, but it makes me incredibly hot for him. I can barely wait to drag him out of here to have my wicked way with him in his truck." Both girls laughed at Sophie's admission.

Ben groaned again. "Remind me to never follow the two of you out to the parking lot. I'll be back." He slid from the bench he shared with Kendall. He turned back, flashing her a sexy smile that sent her stomach flipping in excitement just like a rollercoaster ride.

* * *

Ben stepped from the men's restroom into the dark, claustrophobic hallway at the back of the Brawling Bear, heading for the bar and another beer. From behind, someone gave him a slight shove attempting to force their way past him—obviously eager to get back to their own drink of choice. More shocked that anything, he glanced over his left shoulder. Sue Walsh. What the hell was up with this woman? He shifted sideways and allowed her to pass.

"I see you're fucking the other Aasgaard sister now," she said under her breath and then scurried down the hallway.

He couldn't bring himself to respond to her crude comment. Didn't see the value in attempting to correct her inaccuracies. Instead, Ben made his way to the bar and found a seat, fighting the urge to march over to the table where Sue and her husband sat with another couple. He wanted to set the record straight. Wanted to tell her it wasn't any of her damn business. But it would only draw attention to Sue Walsh's presence and potentially upset Kendall.

Maybe he was the one with the problem. Maybe he was the one who couldn't change, refusing to leave the past in the past. But then again, he wasn't the one slinging lies and hateful statement. Just like at the trial sixteen years ago. Proof that the only thing Mary Sue Prescott had changed was her name.

"Do you want another beer?" Cam asked.

"Sure."

"I got the text you sent with the picture of the latest vandalism. Thanks for keeping me in the loop," Cam said as he set the glass of tap beer in front of Ben.

"No problem."

"Talk about fucked up. Red spray paint dripping down the wall like that. Looked like blood. A threat, pure and simple."

"Yes. Apparently, Nick wants me and everyone else to know that he's responsible for all the damage to Montgomery Construction properties over the past week. Ties all the problems at work together with the threat to Kendall. I can't wait until they catch the son of a bitch."

"Me, too," Cam said, moving down the bar to pour another drink.

* * *

Kendall watched as Sophie ripped her gaze from her husband on stage and turned her attention back to the conversation. "Yeah. Jackson's getting lucky tonight." Sophie wiggled her eyebrows in Kendall's direction. "Is Ben getting lucky, too?"

Kendall laughed at Sophie's bold question. "If I had my way, you bet. But Ben's calling the shots here, and he has some grand plan to wait until I'm too old to enjoy it." They both giggled.

"Oh, look. Ethan's wife, Dani, is here." Sophie waved toward the bar at a tall, slender brunette. "Dani, come join us!" she shouted.

A model-thin beauty made her way from behind the bar and slid into the booth beside Sophie. She stretched out her hand to Kendall. "Hi, Kendall. I'm Dani Bearbower."

Now Sophie, with her red curls, her bright green eyes, and a dusting of freckles, was cute. But Dani was exotic. Her lovely olive complexion—enviable to pasty-complected Minnesotans at the end of January—gave her a Mediterranean appeal, as did her perfectly sculpted face and her dark brown hair.

"It's nice to meet you, Dani. We were just discussing Sophie's lusty and uncontrollable appreciation for her husband's voice."

"Yeah. Her and every other woman in the bar." Kendall couldn't help but laugh along with the two women across from her.

Within minutes, Kendall felt as if she'd known Dani her entire life. How long had it been since she'd gone out with girlfriends? Before Nick had started controlling her every movement. No. She wouldn't allow thoughts of Nicholas Cardwell to ruin her night out with friends. Kendall focused on the women across the booth from her, but every few minutes she'd let her gaze wander to Ben. Mostly he seemed to be listening to Jackson, but occasionally he'd speak to Cam.

"It amazes me how many woman show up to drool over your husband," Dani said.

"I know. No way would Jackson allow a bunch of horndogs to behave that way around me," Sophie said, with a shake of her head. Although she'd kept her tone light, Kendall sensed that it bothered Sophie.

"Ethan would never go for it, either," Dani agreed, patting the back of Sophie's hand. "What about Ben? Is Ben the jealous type?"

"We're so new, it's hard to say. If I had to guess, I'd say yes. Extremely jealous. But then again, isn't everyone when they see their special someone being appreciated by someone of the opposite gender?" They both nodded their agreement as a man approached their table.

"Hey, ladies. I'm sorry to interrupt." The guy gave them a playful grin but seemed to be focusing his attention on Kendall.

"Hi, Jake," Dani said. "How are you tonight? Do you know Sophie Cooper and Kendall Aasgaard?"

"No," he said, extending his hand across the table, shaking each woman's hand in turn. "Jake Nolan. Well, actually, I stopped over to say welcome back to Kendall."

Kendall cocked her head to the side. When people said that to her, it usually meant they knew her when she was kid. "Thank you, Jake."

"You and I were in the same first grade class. I was a bit shorter back then, so you probably don't remember me."

Kendall laughed. "You're right. I don't. But sit down, and tell me what you've been up to."

Jake took the spot that Ben had just left and gave them a brief rundown of his current job, speaking to all three of them. When he'd finished he turned to Sophie. "So you're Jackson's wife, right?"

A slow grin spread across Sophie's lips. Her eyes took on a mischievous glint when she asked, "So, Jake, do you enjoy listening to Jackson sing?"

"You know it." He leaned back in the booth, obviously making himself comfortable. "When Jackson's singing, the place is mobbed with single women." His playful expression made its reappearance.

"I guess that explains the excessive amount of men maneuvering through the sea of women," Kendall said.

"Yup. Jackson's voice draws the women here like cattle to slaughter."

Kendall landed a playful punch on Jake's shoulder. "Oh my God, that's pathetic, Mr. Nolan." They all laughed, and Dani added. "I think flies to honey is a better analogy."

"I guess." He shrugged, but had the decency to look adequately shamed before a devious smile curled his lips. "Some of us guys need all the help we can get."

Kendall threw back her head and laughed. Happiness welled from her heart. For the past month since Nick's brutal attack, she'd resembled a tender seedling struggling to take root, afraid she'd wither and die before she found fertile soil. Now back in her hometown with budding connections in the community, not to mention her relationships with Cam and Ben, Kendall felt grounded and strong as if she'd taken root at last.

* * *

Ben hated sitting at the bar when he could be tucked into the cozy booth beside Kendall. Actually, being tucked into bed with her sounded even better. One week from tonight, Kendall would celebrate her twenty-fifth birthday, and he intended to do it up right. A nice dinner out, perhaps at Ferris Steakhouse, and then bring her home to make love with her. What better way to mark a major milestone in one's life than with another great milestone for their relationship? Certainly, the two of them could hold out for one more week.

Although, he had noticed the shiver race through Kendall's body while he'd gently caressed her arm. Maybe a week *would* be too long.

Cam stopped in front of him. "You've got competition, man." He tilted his head toward the table that Kendall, Sophie, and Dani now shared.

Ben turned as Kendall burst into laughter, tossing her head back and presenting the slender column of her neck. If he were next to her, that simple move would accentuate the scent of peaches in the air, or perhaps he'd merely be tempted to shift closer, dragging in a deep breath of her fruity fragrance. A giddy smile plastered across Kendall's face while she listened to the high-maintenance gangly guy, eating up his every word. Unimpressed, Ben couldn't imagine Kendall being attracted to someone who used more styling products than she did. The guy probably moisturized his face twice a day, too.

"You think she's interested in that Nolan guy?" Ben turned his attention back to Cam, not sure if he should cut in or allow it to play out. Overall, it might be best for Kendall to move on and forget about him.

Cam shrugged. "If you're interested in her, you might need to get moving on that."

Ben slammed the beer he'd been nursing for the past fifteen minutes, giving the ladies time to discuss whatever the hell topics girlfriends chattered on about. The hysterical laughter within the first five minutes of his absence led him to believe that they hadn't progressed beyond the topic of sex. But now, the time had come to stake his claim.

He stomped his way back to the table just as Mr. Hair Gel departed, but not before rubbing the back of Kendall's hand and planting a kiss on her cheek. At least Ben wouldn't need to make an embarrassing scene to ask the bozo to move along.

"What did he want?" Ben didn't bother to hide the gnarly attitude in his voice.

"Jake and I were in first grade together," Kendall said, bumping shoulders with Ben when he slid in closer along the polished wooden bench.

"Yeah, great. What did he want?"

Kendall smiled. "To say hi. Why? Are you jealous?"

"Maybe." He glared at her, daring her to comment, and then draped a protective arm around her shoulder. Even though he hadn't said or done anything funny, all three women burst into laughter. Ben sulked, but kept Kendall tucked against his side as he turned his attention toward Jackson and the rowdy crowd of oversexed women.

* * *

Kendall should've figured as much. She already knew that Ben was the protective type, and jealous wasn't that far removed. But he had nothing to be jealous of. She wasn't interested in anyone else. And even though she was having fun with the girls, it was Ben she really wanted to spend time with.

Leaning into his embrace, Kendall relaxed against his side. She sighed, realizing just how comfortable she felt in Ben's presence. She cuddled up as close to him as she could while Jackson belted out the final words of the song.

"I'm taking a little break," Jackson said to the crowd. "But I promise to come back to sing a few more songs before I take my beautiful wife home for the night."

"That's my cue," Dani said, sliding out of the booth and standing beside the table. Within moments Jackson was by her side. "Great set, Jackson."

"Thanks, Dani," he said, taking Dani's place in the booth, crowding against Sophie while she all but melted into his side. They made a cute couple.

"Can I get you guys anything else?" Ethan Bearbower's deep voice drew their attention. He stepped up to their table, slung an arm around Dani's shoulder, and kissed her cheek.

"Hi, Taz." The greeting went around the table while Jackson and Ben both shook hands with him. "How are you doing tonight?" Ben asked.

"I'm great. Look at this crowd." He jerked his thumb over his shoulder toward the swarming sea of bodies. "So, what'll it be?"

"Why don't you bring us another pitcher, Taz," Ben said.

"No problem," Taz said, making his way back up to the bar.

"It was nice to meet you, Kendall. Have a great night." Dani wiggled her fingers in a little wave and then followed her husband toward the bar.

"So, did you ask her yet?" Jackson asked Sophie, but his eyes landed on Kendall.

"No, I was waiting for you," Sophie said. "Kendall, we were wondering if you'd be available to watch Ryleigh Lynn tomorrow night. Ted, Jackson's dad, and Lydia are always great about watching her, but we hate to ask them two nights in a row."

"Oh, wow. I'd love to watch your sweet little girl, but—" Kendall glanced up at Ben. The grave expression on his face suggested he was thinking along the same lines as her. "But I don't think it's safe right now. Not with my ex making threats against me." Ben tugged Kendall closer, clearly agreeing yet knowing she'd feel horrible about turning Jackson and Sophie down.

Sophie gazed up at her husband when he said, "Ben has kept us up to date on the threats, Kendall. Ben will be with you, and you have a sheriff's car right outside the house. Sophie and I have discussed it, and we aren't terribly concerned. Life is full of risks, and there are no guarantees for tomorrow. But one thing Sophie and I agree on is that we need to keep living our lives and keep our worrying to a minimum. That being said, we're completely confident leaving our daughter in your capable hands."

Usually Kendall found she was the one in the crowd pushing the envelope, willing to take the greatest risk. Now with Jackson and Sophie's little girl, this seemed like more risk than even Kendall was willing to take. "I don't know, guys."

"Please, Kendall. We're just planning to go out to Ferris Steakhouse and then stop over here so Jackson can sing a set or two. We'll be less than five minutes from Ben's house the entire night. Everything will be fine." Sophie made the statement with such conviction it brought tears to Kendall's eyes. She'd only recently met Ben's friends, and yet, they had complete faith in her to care for their daughter. Even with all the crap going on in her life.

"Okay. I'd loved to watch Ryleigh Lynn for you," Kendall said, laughing as Sophie cast her husband a naughty grin.

CHAPTER 29

Ben was positive that Ryleigh Lynn lived and breathed the old adage *misery loves company*. Could she scream any louder?

The little tike wound up yet again for another scream. Earsplitting. Yes. Apparently she could scream louder.

He and Kendall had tried everything to improve the baby's mood: rattly toys, her favorite blanket, a rousing game of peek-a-boo, even a bottle. But it seemed that the only thing the inconsolable baby wanted was her pacifier. His babysitting cohort plastered a sunny expression on her face, no doubt wishing she hadn't agreed to the child-care duty for tonight, while he upended the diaper bag in search of the beloved Nuk.

Kendall had helped him earlier today while he'd taken on the grouting project that had stalled out several weeks ago. So now in a show of camaraderie, he was assisting her in the baby project. And failing thoroughly. He loved Ryleigh Lynn like crazy, but the whole soothing-an-ornery-baby thing was way out of his scope of expertise. In the past, this was the point in time when he'd have unceremoniously tossed the cranky kid back into her parents' loving arms and escaped to another quieter room.

Hell, who was he kidding? He'd passed the abandon-and-escape point more than twenty minutes ago.

With an exaggerated bounce, Kendall belted out the lyrics to "The Itsy Bitsy Spider" off key and at the top of her lungs, all to appease the little bundle in her arms. The girl's unceasing cries grew in volume as if she'd been tricked by the singing act before and refused to be suckered again.

With his own increased agitation, Ben breathed a frustrated sigh. And then there was silence—for like five blessed seconds—

while Ryleigh Lynn gulped a lungful of air. Too short. Too damned short. It was as if the silence and the gulping had only prepared the kid to up her raging high-pitched racket to the next level.

Through it all, Kendall looked relaxed and capable, as if babies screeching in her ear happened all the time. Someday she'd make an awesome mother.

Where had that thought come from? He eyed her suspiciously. He had no idea, but it seemed like a fair assessment.

Ben's eyes lingered on her natural movements. The way she brushed back the sweaty locks on the baby's forehead and placed kisses on the top of her little head, all the while Kendall's hips swayed to the rhythm she heard in her own head.

Oh, yeah. He could easily envision her bouncing a brown haired, chocolate-eyed baby—his son—while her stomach swelled with baby number two. He shifted, adjusting the front of his jeans to accommodate his arousal. Damn, he was falling hard. He should stop staring at her, but she was so natural. Beautiful. Loving. Tender. So caring with a child that belonged to someone else.

Due to the prolonged, painful decibel Ben hadn't even noticed that Kendall had stopped her out of tune singing and now stood glaring at him. "What?" he asked.

She forced a smile. "Have you found it, or are you conjuring one from your mind?"

He shook his head and said, "I hate to call Sophie, because she'll want to come rescue us, but I can't find the damn thing anywhere."

"Go in the kitchen and make the call."

"You want me to take the baby, and you can call?"

She shook her head. "I'll be fine. Maybe deaf, but fine."

"Hang in there. Between the two of us we can conquer one fussy little kid," he said, attempting to give her some measure of reassurance at the same time he tamped down the feelings of elation over his reprieve in the silent kitchen. He pressed a kiss to Kendall's temple and then one to Ryleigh Lynn's, and then he hit the speed dial for Sophie.

The noise coming through his cell phone gave him a pretty good idea of the commotion at the Brawling Bear when Sophie answered his call. Funny how bar noise had never seemed as bothersome as the ear-piercing wail of an unhappy baby. "Sophie," he said, shouting into the phone. "Where's Ryleigh Lynn's pacifier?"

A loud rustling noise filled his ear before Sophie's voice yelled over the phone line. "It's probably by her coat and blanket in her car seat. I piled it all by your front door. Do you need me to come back?"

"No, we've got this. Have fun." Ben disconnected the call on his way to the entryway before he begged the woman to come back and relieve him of the horrible noise. He plucked up the pacifier that had been buried in the blanket and headed back to the parlor. "Found it," he said. Kendall looked as relieved as he felt.

"Thank God," Kendall said, giving the baby the thing she'd been crying for. "Funny how much noise one of these little creatures can make, huh?"

Ben grunted. "Not funny. Makes you realize why they use that sound to torture people." He watched as Kendall danced with that bouncing, swaying motion again, her hips rocking to some inner rhythm. "Now that we've got her settled, would you mind if I run upstairs and grab a quick shower? It'll only take me ten minutes."

"No problem." Kendall smiled down at the baby in her arms. "Right, Ryleigh Lynn?"

* * *

Ben disappeared up the steps, and Ryleigh Lynn voiced her disapproval. She plucked her pacifier out of her mouth and tossed it on the floor at Kendall's feet. "Really?" Kendall asked, stooping to pick it up. She offered it to the baby again, but all Ryleigh Lynn did was shake her head and cry. "Oh, baby," Kendall said with a sigh.

So, she paced the first floor of the monstrous Victorian with the little girl in her arms. Through the kitchen and casual dining area, then down the hallway into the formal sitting room on the right and around the fancy furniture in the center—two straight-backed chairs, an equally uncomfortable-looking sofa, and an elegant coffee table. The entire setup screamed stuffy old women sipping tea. Not down-to-earth Ben enjoying a bottle of beer.

While it was all lovely, she didn't care for the room in the least. In the far corner stood the single modern piece of furniture—Ryleigh Lynn's pack-and-play—where, if she ever calmed down, she might take a cry-induced snooze.

Kendall crossed the mammoth entryway near the front door into the media room—a space that seemed more Ben's style. A leather sofa and two over-sized upholstered chairs were arranged around a sturdy coffee table that no doubt hosted more beer bottles and socked feet than tea cups and Royal Worcester porcelain vases. A huge flat screen TV hung on the end wall above a long credenza-style cabinet that housed all the electronics and gaming systems a guy could possibly want. Yes, this room personified Ben—fun, inviting, and unpretentious.

Kendall belted out "Yellow Submarine" at the top of her lungs. Her repertoire of children's songs was woefully lacking. As was her ability to pull a single song out of her brain that had clean lyrics and of which she could remember more than three words. Perhaps listening to sustained crying caused memory loss. Who'd have guessed?

She made the circuit again, down the foyer hall through the dining area, kitchen, and into a hallway with a bathroom on the right and a bedroom on the left that served as Ben's home office. Today they'd grouted the bathroom walls and then the floor. Well, more like Ben had grouted while Kendall had watched in fascination. When her patience had worn thin, she'd begged for a turn with the trowel, but her request had been denied as he explained how much he loved to grout tile. He'd babbled on about the immense fun the job of grouting walls could be, although he admitted that he preferred working on the tile floors. After several failed requests, he'd finally relented and handed her the trowel to smear on the thick, goopy substance. It was fun in a messy sort of way. She'd wondered if Ben's resistance hadn't been his own personal version of Tom Sawyer white washing a fence, but in all her enjoyment, she'd been uneager to surrender the trowel to demand an answer.

Kendall switched to "Jingle Bells" as she rounded the corner into the stuffy sitting room again, anxious for Ben to get done with his shower. She could hear the water running upstairs, so it was going to be a while. The singing didn't seem to calm the baby in the least, but it settled Kendall's rattled nerves a bit, so she sang on. Perhaps she was just on edge with all that prolonged crying. Ben had said it was a form of torture. Or maybe it was the odd loneliness she'd felt when Ben climbed the stairs for his shower. Either way, a heightened awareness of her surroundings had her twitchier than normal. Not surprising. But in due time they'd catch Nick, and she knew her life would return to normal.

* * *

"Hey, Cam." Chaz hopped onto a barstool in front of him.

"What can I get you, Chaz?" In all likelihood a beer, but Cam's job meant asking that question. Over and over.

"Beer. So, where ya gonna stack all your out of town guests, Cam?"

"What?" Most times the conversation ebbed and flowed in a particular pattern. *Hey. How ya doing? What can I get you? What's new?* None of which took great brainpower or concentration. Then once in a while those statements, like the one that Chaz just threw down, popped out of nowhere, making no sense at all. Cam grunted in disgust. He worked in a bar, and inebriated bar-goers rarely made sense. But Chaz didn't appear drunk.

"Your relatives from Oregon. I saw their red SUV, Lexus, I think. Fancy with lots of chrome and shiny clean like it just rolled out of the wash. Ya know what I mean?"

Cam stopped pouring mid-glass and slammed it down. "When? Did you catch the plates?" Just like Chaz's old man who owned the local repair shop and the lone tow truck in a thirty-mile radius, the young guy ate, slept, and breathed cars.

Chaz blinked and gave his head a shake like an electric shock had jumpstarted his brain. "Two minutes ago. A slow cruise down Main Street. Oregon plates. NCRDWL. I figured he's a fishing enthusiast since he has night crawler on his plates."

Now Cam blinked at Chaz, but he didn't have time to explain to his favorite auto mechanic that crawler didn't contain the letter D. "Thanks, Chaz. I've got an emergency, Ethan. I'm leaving." He rounded the bar, abandoning his boss to deal with serving up the drinks.

Cam attempted to skirt around Sophia Cooper, who stood blocking the door, but he nearly plowed her over. Quickly he grabbed her arm to steady her. "You seen Kendall tonight?"

"She's at Ben's. Watching Ryleigh Lynn."

"Someone spotted Nick Cardwell's car two minutes ago on Main. Call the sheriff's office." Without a backward glance, Cam raced out the front door to his pickup truck parked along the curb. The engine roared to life, and he executed a hasty U-turn in front of the sheriff's office and accelerated down Main Street toward the park as he hatched his plan.

* * *

The sound of running water stopped and the doorbell rang.

"Looks like your momma got worried after Uncle Ben's call," Kendall said to the sweet, inconsolable girl in her arms as she rushed toward the front entry. She swung the door open. "That didn't take you long." The words were barely out of her mouth when the door was shoved farther open, knocking Kendall backward.

It all happened so quickly. The wind whooshed from her lungs, and a jolt of panic blasted through her. The door clicked closed. And there stood Nick. Larger than life inside Ben's front entry.

"Nick." She backpedaled into the sitting room. "What're you doing here?"

"I'm here to bring you home where you belong." He stepped forward, an aggressive move that conflicted with the pleasant smile on his face. The dimples that bookended either side of his mouth had served as false advertising last autumn when they'd met, just as they did now. The only difference, with pain and heartache, she'd grown wiser over the past couple months and knew without a doubt that the brute didn't possess an ounce of kindness.

Keeping a watchful eye on Nick, Kendall took another step away from the biggest threat of her life while he continued his slow stalking strides toward her. She pivoted to the side, holding Ryleigh Lynn snug in the arm farthest away from Nick, shielding the baby with her body while she extended her other palm out in a silent request for him to stop.

In true Nicholas Cardwell fashion, he used that simple gesture to his advantage, grabbing her arm and wrenching it behind her back, shoving her deeper into the room. Kendall cried out in pain, stumbling, but righting herself before she fell. She clasped the still-crying baby closer to her chest.

Ryleigh Lynn seemed to sense the rising tension in the room and shoved her thumb into her mouth, sucking the digit viciously and stopping only to release a hiccupped breath. Red-rimmed and teary, her big green orbs blinked as if she could somehow digest the actions of this man and understand the why of it all.

Kendall knew better.

Blessed with great genetics, Nick flaunted his assets like a model on a runway. His chiseled facial features, Caribbean-blue eyes, and trim, athletic build coupled with his neatly tousled wavy brown hair turned heads wherever he went. But beneath the beautiful facade and expensive clothing, the man was pure evil. Nick wanted. Nick took. That simple.

Kendall needed to put her brain together and think. Fast.

First priority: protect Ryleigh Lynn.

Oh, God. Kendall's stomach rolled at the thought, and she hugged the girl tighter against her body. The Coopers had entrusted their sweet baby girl to her care, and she'd failed them. Not fully acknowledging the true danger Nicholas Cardwell posed had endangered not simply her life, but anyone in close proximity. She should've known better than to agree to watch Jackson and Sophie's daughter while this threat hung over her head. Foolish. Stupid.

Second priority, escape. Or maybe she should wait for Ben to come down. It'd only be a matter of minutes. But if he barreled into the fray without any thought, he'd surely get hurt. She needed to give him a warning of some sort. God, she hoped he grabbed a weapon.

No. That thought was crazy. Waiting for Ben would put him in danger, and she'd never forgive herself if anything happened to him.

Escape. With the baby in her arms, certainly Nick would allow her to walk out. He couldn't be that cruel that he'd harm a young child.

That thought fled when Nick pulled a black object with silver trim from his hip pocket. Throughout their relationship, Nick always carried a pocketknife of one kind or another. Some quite benign-looking. Others threatening and probably illegal.

He held out his hand toward her with a dramatic flourish and pressed the button along the edge. A metal-on-metal *snick* sliced the air, exposing a long, pointed switchblade. The polished four-inch length of sharpened steel reflected the lamplight like a sparkling bauble or bangle, a mere decorative accessory. On the surface, it functioned as an innocuous showpiece, a select item from a vast collection of antique to modern weapons, and yet in the wrong situation, it could be dangerous. Deadly. Just like the man who wielded it.

God, when would Ben come down?

She glanced at the elegant clock on the wooden mantel. How many minutes had it been since Ben had shut off the shower? It felt like forever. How much time until he made his way down those steps? Five more minutes? Ten? She knew with Nick's agitation she wouldn't be able to stall much longer.

Thankfully, he seemed more than eager to ask stupid questions.

"Why did you run away from me, Kendall?" Nick cocked his head to the side. An expression of complete puzzlement crossed his face as if the beating he'd dealt her wouldn't be enough to send her scurrying away from him.

"Nick," Kendall said, projecting her voice. Loudly. Clearly. For Ben to hear. "I didn't run away. I came to visit my cousin, Cameron." The lie fell from her lips with ease.

"Why would you want to visit him?" Incredulity replaced the confusion on his face.

What had she ever seen in this guy? "Well, Cam *is* my family, and sometimes I miss him." Her wistful words and tone were the honest truth. She'd missed Cam desperately for sixteen years.

"I love you, Kendall. I'm your family now. You don't need anyone else. Don't you miss me?"

"Of course, I miss you, Nick. You're my world." She called on her paltry acting skills, hoping her expression looked genuine as she spewed her lies. "I intended to call you as soon as I got home to Portland."

He grunted, a very un-Nick-like behavior. "I checked with your aunt and uncle. They kindly shared the fact that you had moved back to Krysset. Permanently. If you'd have brought your cell phone on your journey, it would've made my life much easier, and I never would've needed to bother your ancient relatives."

"Did you hurt them?" The question blurted out before Kendall had time to process the ramifications of her criticism.

"What the hell kind of question is that?" he roared, startling Ryleigh Lynn who had finally calmed down against Kendall's shoulder.

"Well, you're holding that knife like you plan to hurt me." She flung the words back in his face, knowing the inconsistency of his words and behavior was lost on him.

"I'd never hurt them. They like me, and they're always kind to me." Because they had no idea how cruel and abusive Nick could be. "I repaid their kindness with my own. You, on the other hand…" He shook his head, his expression grim. "You're a frustrating woman, but I forgive you for all those times you've made me angry. And I'll eventually forgive you for running away from me."

Kendall's mouth gaped at the audacity of his words. In his mind, he'd been justified in his violent action. He'd voiced his opinion before. Each occurrence had been her fault for failing to capitulate to whatever Nick had wanted.

"Grab your coat and bundle up the kid. She's coming with us."

"No. I promised her mommy that I'd watch her. She's at work, but she'll be back in an hour or so. Then after they're gone, the two of us can leave." Kendall darted a glance at the mantel clock again. "Put the switchblade down now, Nick. You're scaring the baby."

"She doesn't look scared to me. I think she's curious, like maybe she wants to touch the pretty, shiny knife." With the blade held out sideways, he moved closer, twisting the handle so the metal glinted, catching the light and Ryleigh Lynn's attention.

"Nick, quit being such a jerk." She wrapped her arms around the baby, turning her out of Nick's reach.

"She's not my kid, Kendall. I don't need to be nice to her. Now pack her up."

"Then why do you want to bring her along? She cries a lot. Let's wait till her mom picks her up, then we can leave." She held her breath waiting for Nick to make another move. "Where are we going? Back to Portland or somewhere else?"

"Home."

"Okay. It'll be nice to get back home, where I know people." She forced the muscles in her face to form a smile. Believable? Probably not, although that strained expression didn't appear to bother Nick in the least. Kendall picked up the tune she'd been singing before Nick had come to the door, and prayed that Ben hurried.

CHAPTER 30

With an open phone line between them to sync their movements, Ben waited at the top of the stairs for Cam to make his way around to the back of the house. Cam had called—just as Ben had been pulling on his clothes—to inform him of Nick's appearance in town. Ben had heard an outraged male voice downstairs, confirming Nick's arrival at the house, and together, Ben and Cam had sketched out a rough course of action while Cam had made the short drive from the bar.

Thankfully, Ben had removed the spare key from its not-so-hidden hiding spot under the welcome mat when he'd first become aware of the threats aimed at Kendall and then given it to Cam since he'd been coming and going from the house nearly every day.

"Ready." Cam's low voice came over the cell phone.

Ben killed the call and pocketed the phone. He didn't try for stealth, thundering his way down the steps to cover for the noise of Cam keying the back door and making his way inside the house.

"Hey, darling, how's our baby girl!" he shouted, hoping to alert Kendall to his presence, as well as to cover any ruckus coming from the back of the house. His responsibility was to get to Kendall's side, ensure she and the baby were out of Nick's slimy grasp, and maneuver Nick's back to the doorway, giving Cam the element of surprise.

The plan, however, hadn't contained provisions for the nasty-looking switchblade at Kendall's throat.

"Whoa." Ben put both hands out in a signal of surrender, sizing up the man Kendall had once dated. Late twenties, maybe thirty. Well-dressed in an expensive-looking wool coat, black dress pants, and shiny black dress shoes. Pretty-boy face with striking blue eyes, the kind that drew attention from the opposite sex if they could ignore the crazed expression on his sweet mug. And chunky rings on two fingers of his knife hand that would hurt like hell if he started swinging.

The man stood about the same height as Ben, but Nick had a trimmer athletic build, like a runner, with a lot less upper body bulk. Ben could take the guy in a knock-down brawl with little trouble, but with Cam on the scene Ben knew he wouldn't get an opportunity.

Nicholas Cardwell didn't stand a chance.

However, at the moment, Nick's left arm was clamped around Ryleigh Lynn and Kendall, while his right hand held the point of a blade to the soft, vulnerable flesh under Kendall's chin. Ben took another tentative step closer.

"Ben. Please take the baby from me."

He walked toward Kendall, his hands out in front in a gesture meant to placate the idiot with a knife. Ben reached out and plucked Ryleigh Lynn from Kendall's hold. Thankfully, Nick loosened his grip on the kid. And then Ben popped the pacifier into Ryleigh Lynn's mouth and gently set the babe into the port-a-crib they'd erected in the far corner.

Damn. Most times Ben loved the rush of adrenaline that powered through his body during high-risk, high-stress activities. Give him race car speeds and skyscraper heights any day of the week over the imminent threat to someone he cared about. He sure hoped the sheriff hurried. Cam said that Sophie had promised to dial 911. Without a doubt, she and Jackson would arrive on the front stoop in about two minutes.

Ben shuffled around the room, attempting to maneuver Nick into position. "Put the damned knife down, Nick." He propped his hip against the straight back chair in feigned boredom. "I know you two are involved, so you don't have to do this possessive show for me. I know she's your woman."

"Then why is she sleeping in your house?"

Ben grunted. "It's not like that, man. Now set the knife down. You don't want to accidently hurt her."

Nick pondered that but tightened his hold. Kendall squeaked.

Ben gave an exaggerated sigh as if the act of explaining himself was a monumental inconvenience. "I was engaged to her big sister about a hundred years ago. That's how we know each other. We're pals, not lovers. Never have been. Never will be." Harsh and absolute. Without an ounce of remorse.

Ben knew better than to glance in Kendall's direction. Knew the look on her face would be filled with a combination of disbelief and pain. Knew he'd never be able to resist taking the words back and sweeping her into his arms to kiss away the hurt he'd painted on her face.

With Nick's arm wrapped around Kendall's chest, his hand in a firm grasp at her shoulder, he jerked Kendall back against him, causing her to whimper. The steel tip of the knife was poised at the tender skin of her throat.

The scene played out like an ugly do-over yanked from the dark recesses of Ben's worst nightmares. For years, he'd wrestled with the what-ifs over Jenna's death. What if he hadn't been away at college? What if he'd been there to protect her? To fight for her? To save her?

This time, losing the gal he cared about wasn't an option. With a plan in place and the element of surprise—an angry Cameron Aasgaard—Ben reminded himself he wasn't a one-man show. Forcing indifference, Ben fisted his hands to avoid lashing out against Nick in an attempt to tear Kendall from his grasp.

"Kendall. Is that true?" Nick demanded.

"Yes. It's true. He's nothing to me." She sounded defeated, and she stared across the room refusing to meet his eyes. "I'm renting a room here, and I've been helping with household chores as a way to earn my keep. Today, I grouted the bathroom off the kitchen."

Ben wanted to laugh. Damn, the girl was good. She could play act with the best of them. She hadn't grouted, she'd sat in the hallway outside the bathroom, laughing and talking while he'd slaved. He hadn't expected her to help, but she'd asked several times, and so he'd finally relented and handed her the trowel to give it a try. After about two minutes, she'd graciously handed it back to him and took up her post as CEO—chief entertainment officer—outside the bathroom door.

"Is that so?" Nick asked.

"Yeah, man. I think it's important for everyone to chip in, and she's plenty capable. I make her work for it. Cooking, cleaning, watching babies." Ben shrugged like a natural-born chauvinist. If his mom or sister heard him, they'd kick his ass from here to Sunday for spouting that sexist nonsense.

Nick loosened his grip on Kendall but didn't let go. He eyed Ben tentatively, searching for something. Proof of Ben's words? Reassurance, perhaps? Finally, after what seemed like forever, Nick allowed his knife hand to fall to his side, and he shoved Kendall away from him. "Glad to hear it," he said, directing his attention to Ben and all but ignoring Kendall. He pocketed the knife and grunted out a laugh. "I think we're more like-minded than that damned cousin she traipsed halfway across the continent to visit."

The words had barely left his mouth when Cam lunged through the doorway into the sitting room and dove onto Nick's back. The flying tackle crashed them to the floor but not before taking out the antique coffee table that wasn't able to withstand the sheer force of four hundred pounds slamming upon its delicate surface.

Kendall screeched her surprise and stumbled backward to avoid the scuffle. With the way her ragged breathing sawed in and out, Ben guessed that she was teetering on the brink of a panic attack. She had one hand gripped at her throat while the other clutched at her stomach, but Ben saw no sign of blood from where he stood on the opposite side of the room. He didn't dare leave the baby or haul her through the ruckus that had exploded in between his post and Kendall's.

With movements practiced and efficient, Cam used plastic ties he'd concealed somewhere in his T-shirt and jean ensemble and trussed up Nick faster than he'd tackled him to the ground. The entire tussle, all a fraction of a minute, caused minimal effort for Cam, but as he stood, his internal struggle was evident. Muscles clenched. Hands fisted. His entire body rigid with unspent and scarcely controlled fury. Rage radiated from him while he tamped back his obvious desire to pulverize the man to a bloody pulp.

The tackle had knocked the wind out of Nick, but as soon as he regained his breath, he struggled to free his arms. Cam growled, bending toward the man laid out, facedown, hands bound behind his back. He grabbed Nick's wrists and yanked him upright to his feet, giving little concern to wrenching the man's arms from his shoulder sockets or breaking bones. Served him right after the treatment he'd shown Kendall.

"Let me go," Nick roared in pain.

The sudden outburst startled Ryleigh Lynn, her pacifier dropped from her mouth, and she set up an outrageous wail. Ben scooped up the little tike with one arm, attempting to pop the pacifier back into her open mouth while she howled. He crossed to where Kendall stood, quiet and shaking, no doubt reflecting on how tragically tonight might have ended. The calm moments after a life-threatening event tended to do that to a person. Ben wrapped his free arm around Kendall, drawing her closer to him.

Nick threw out a string of expletives and another demand to be released.

"If I'm going to do anything to you, it won't be let you go." Cam's deep tone, steady and unwavering, belied the anger radiating from his body. "I'd rather rip your balls off and shove them down your throat."

"No need for that, Cameron." Deputy Jason Amato came from the entryway, gun drawn, with several other deputies on his heels. "I think we'll take it from here."

Kendall clung to Ben's side, her face buried against his chest, her body trembling while she allowed quiet sobs to escape. He could've lost her tonight. The thought made him want to cry, too. Since the baby and Kendall were both sobbing, he could easily join in. Lifting her face from his chest, she brushed the tears from her cheeks and gazed up at him through watery eyes.

"It's over," she said.

"God. Kendall." The words choked in his throat.

He gazed at her beautiful face. Even in the aftermath of her fear, a fierce strength and determined resilience glowed from within her, a survivor in the truest sense of the word. He shook his head, fighting the tears that stung the back of his eyes, and pressed her face against his chest again, but not soon enough. She must've noticed the embarrassing glossy look in his eyes while he struggled to control his own emotions. He kissed the top of her head, leaning his cheek there, and inhaled the glorious scent of Kendall, breathing a prayer of thanksgiving for her and the baby's safety.

Over the next several minutes, they watched from their little huddle in the corner while a controlled chaos overtook the sitting room. The team from the sheriff's department tossed out questions as Nick protested and Ryleigh Lynn cried. Both at full volume as if neither wanted to be bested by the other. Sophie and Jackson arrived after Nick had been read his rights and was being escorted through the front door out to the waiting squad car.

"Baby girl," Sophie said, leading the charge. The Coopers pushed their way around the crowd and grabbed Ryleigh Lynn from Ben's arms. "Shhh. Mama's got you now." She cooed to her distraught daughter while Jackson enveloped both of his women in a big group hug.

Kendall shrugged out of Ben's hold, and he allowed her the freedom, but he retained his grasp of her right hand. She boldly stepped forward to stand in front of Jackson and Sophie. Although sadness and shame covered her face, her stiff posture indicated that she'd steeled her spine against the inevitable onset of criticism and ridicule from the baby's parents, and she was prepared to take whatever came her way, head-on. Ben knew better. He and Jackson had been friends forever, and although the man had a protective streak for the two women in his life, never would he blame Kendall for the events that had escalated out of her control.

"I'm sorry, Sophie, Jackson. I never meant for Ryleigh Lynn to get caught in the middle of all my ugliness." Kendall kept her eyes fixed on the couple in front of her while huge tears rolled down her face.

Jackson shook his head and stepped forward. "We're the ones who pushed you into babysitting tonight. You tried to warn us. Everything's fine. You're safe. Our daughter's safe." He wrapped Kendall in an affectionate embrace. His relief-filled eyes met Ben's over Kendall's shoulder.

After a long moment, Ben tugged Kendall from Jackson's arms, clutching her in another fierce hug. Ben knew from the way his friend stared at him that he hadn't fooled Jackson with his calm veneer, so Ben didn't even bother to hide the fact his hands shook.

"I'm sorry I left you alone. I shouldn't have done that, Kendall."

"You didn't leave me alone. You were taking a shower."

"Yes, but I was a fool to think that Nick couldn't get in here." He pressed another kiss to her forehead and then one to both temples before hugging her close again. He didn't want to let her go. Ever.

Actually, he wanted to kick everyone out of his house and haul Kendall upstairs, strip her bare, ensuring each and every inch of her delicate flesh was unharmed, and then make love with her. No way in hell was he waiting another week.

Ben held on to Kendall while his best friend in the entire world stood by and smirked at him. At least Sophie had the decency to pretend to be focused on the baby almost asleep in her arms.

"Kendall. Ben. Cam. We need you to come down to the office to make a statement." Deputy Amato rounded the pile of toothpicks in the center of the room that used to be a coffee table. Ben turned when the sheriff's deputy and Cam sidled up beside him.

"Can we do that in the morning? Kendall's pretty shaken up right now." Ben hoped the deputy accepted his request. At this point, he couldn't bear the idea of having Kendall out of his arms. Actually after what they'd just been though, Ben couldn't imagine a moment in the near future when he'd happily leave her side.

An odd sensation tightened his chest. Was this what it felt like to be in love? Ben couldn't be sure and refused to name it. And while a month ago, that simple notion would've scared the crap out of him, he realized the thought of losing Kendall to some lunatic was far more terrifying.

"Yes. We'll expect to see you by ten tomorrow morning. Cam? What'll it be? Tonight or tomorrow?"

"I'll be there in a few minutes, Jason." Ben wanted to chuckle. Only Cam was arrogant enough to use the officer's first name. But the deputy nodded and headed toward the door.

Ben released his hold on Kendall and took a step back, allowing Cam to properly hug his little cousin. "I hate that man, Dolly. I'd like to castrate him and then beat the hell out of him."

"I know." She breathed out a weak laugh at her cousin's fierce confession. "You did good not hurting him."

"Gee, thanks for the vote of confidence, baby doll. I feel better now, knowing that he's locked up."

"Me too," Kendall said. A strained smile flitted over her lips but didn't touch her red-rimmed eyes. Cam cupped her cheek in the palm of his giant hand while she gazed up into his face with a loving expression. Ben looked away, feeling like a voyeur just as he always did when the cousins were having a private moment.

"I need to have a few words with Ben before I go down to the office to talk to Jason," Cam said, casting a glance in Ben's direction.

Ben gave a single nod of his head and walked out of the room toward the kitchen in search of a couple beers.

* * *

Lacking the energy required to argue with her cousin, Kendall watched Ben stalk from the room. She figured Cam had nothing more than angry accusations to fling at Ben for leaving her unguarded, and she hated the idea of that conversation especially after the night they'd all had. But men will be men, and hopefully with a little chest thumping, they'd get it out of their systems.

"Go talk to Ben, but be nice," she said, giving Cam's chest a quick pat. She tried to pull out of his embrace, but he wasn't lightening his hold. "I need to go apologize again to Sophie and Jackson before they leave." Kendall fought the tightness in her throat and chest. How would she ever get out from under the heavy weight of guilt that seemed to be sitting on her heart? First Dayla and now the Cooper family. How many people would be impacted by Kendall's poor choice to become involved with Nick?

"Kendall," Cam said. His tone was so vehement he might just as well have growled at her. "What Nick did wasn't your fault. Not tonight and not before. You don't need to apologize for his actions. Everything turned out okay." She nodded and slipped from his arms.

Kendall stood in silence while the Coopers bundled up their baby into her snow gear and snapped her into the infant car seat. When they finished, Jackson led them toward the front door with Sophie on his heels. Kendall trailed behind, brushing away the tears that refused to stop leaking from her eyes. At the front door, Jackson stopped and turned to face Kendall.

"I'm sorry for all the trouble I've caused you," Kendall said.

Sophie ignored the apology and crushed Kendall in a hug. "Thank you."

"For what?"

"For keeping our little one safe. You did good." Sophie released her and stepped back to include Jackson in her words. "Bad things happen in the midst of life, things that can change everything in the blink of an eye. We need to trust those around us to keep their wits. And we need to have faith that God will provide the strength required to get through the roughest of patches. Don't worry, my friend, we'll be calling on you again to watch Ryleigh Lynn."

Kendall choked back a sob. Her fingers covered her lips to prevent the flood of emotionally sloppy words from pouring out. "Thank you," she said in a whisper.

Jackson placed a hand on her shoulder. "I'm glad you're okay. If anything had happened to you, I think it might've pushed Ben over the edge. He's in love with you, even though he hasn't admitted it to himself. Take care of him, Kendall." At a loss for words, Kendall pressed her lips together, unable to stop the tears as the Cooper family walked out the door.

Finally, it was over. Nick's threats hadn't felt real until she'd cracked open the door and he'd forced his way into the house tonight. Perhaps in Krysset, surrounded by friends and family, she hadn't really believed that he'd be able to get to her, or maybe because she'd already suffered through her fair share of violence in her twenty-five years of living that she just couldn't bring herself to imagine more.

But when he'd pressed that sharpened length of steel against her throat, fear had overtaken her. Not for herself, but for the friends she'd come to care about. For Ben. For the Coopers. And for their daughter.

Cam might've jumped on Nick's back, but Ben was her hero, and now she wanted to bask in Ben's strength and presence. Kendall followed the sound of Cam's deep voice drifting from the kitchen. He'd commented that he needed to have words with Ben, but she had no idea what he'd actually want to discuss after a night like tonight. She didn't want to interfere, and yet she didn't want Cam to be the legendary bully he so often was, or for him to blame the course of tonight's events on Ben.

But what she found was nothing like she'd expected.

The two men she cared for most in the world, one as her protector guardian and one as something more, stood in the kitchen, leaning against the countertop, each with a bottle of beer in his hand and a smile affixed to his face as if this night had been nothing more than a casual gathering of friends and family. Both men were serious about the topic of conversation, but in good spirits, and neither appeared offended or angry in their tone or stance.

She cleared her throat politely to let them know they were no longer engaged in a private discussion, which no doubt revolved around her.

With a quick gulp, Cam downed the remainder of his beer, set the bottle down, and walked toward her. "See me to the door,

Kendall," he said when his big hand grasped hers. The contradiction in size left her feeling like the little girl he'd always considered her to be.

When they reached the privacy of the entryway, he pulled her into another fierce embrace. "I'm so damn relieved, I can hardly think straight. I love you, Kendall."

She nodded her head, her action constrained against the great wall of his chest and the tightness of his arms surrounding her. "I love you, too, Cam." He released her, pressed a kiss to her cheek, and slipped out the front door.

Kendall sagged against the door, resting her forehead against the wooden surface. She was so weary. The adrenaline rush she'd experienced while she'd faced off against Nick had plummeted once Cam had tackled him to the ground, leaving behind an overall fatigue and annoying tremors that coursed through her body. The cool touch of wood against her forehead eased some of the aftereffects, but nothing would wipe away the memory of Nick holding out his switchblade to entice the young child in her arms. She pinched her eyes closed to force the image from her mind.

When she'd first met him, she never would've guessed he could be so cold and cruel, and she never would've expected these brutal attacks. The entire experience left her questioning her own sound judgment, because at one point not long ago, she'd believed that she'd loved that monster. How was that even possible?

She released a sigh. Like Cam, she, too, felt relieved. The anxiety and strain of watching and waiting, being on guard and on edge had taken its toll. She'd closed this chapter of her life, sealed it up tight and locked it in the memory vault with all the other gruesome memories only to be revisited in the dead of night in her darkest of nightmares.

A small shiver raced over her body. Not from the thought of nightmares, but with the thrill of excitement. Ben was near.

* * *

From the darkened dining room, Ben watched Kendall lock the door behind her cousin and crumble against it, no doubt the side effects of the adrenaline rush. As he approached her, a visible shiver quaked through her body as if she sensed his presence behind her.

The sexual tension had increased over the past week, but today the tension had been over the top. Every look. Every casual touch had ramped up the intensity of his attraction for Kendall. It seemed as if every thought that passed through Ben's head revolved around the woman—her naked body, her sweet mouth, her wet, welcoming pussy. In his bed. On the table. Against the wall.

Once Cam had trussed up Nick and the sheriff's department was on site, an overwhelming need had possessed Ben. He'd wanted to press Kendall's back against the wall and take her hard and fast to celebrate life with her. Another one of those pesky side effects of adrenaline.

He stopped mere inches from her, close enough to feel the heat radiating from her body, and he gathered the long locks of flaxen silk from the back of her neck. Her familiar scent wafted up to greet him. She smelled so damned good, he couldn't deny himself the pleasure of pressing his lips to the curve where her neck met her shoulder. Her smooth skin and luscious scent intoxicated his senses while his lips played across the flesh he found there.

At the touch of his lips, Kendall's breathing hitched and she tilted her head to the side to give him better access to the column of her slender neck. One hand lingered on her opposite shoulder where he clasped her rope of hair that would fall into a champagne cascade across her back if he released it; his other hand clutched to the curve of her waist just above her hipbone. He resisted the temptation to tug her back against him, knowing if he did, she'd easily notice the hardened length of his desire pressed against her backside.

"Ben." His name slipped past her lips on a sexy sigh, and he imagined her shouting his name as she orgasmed, pinned beneath him. Her breathy words fueled his mental imagery, and he hardened further, lost in his fantasy of taking her right now.

All of a sudden, she stiffened, apparently waiting for him to respond. He rewound the conversation, searching for the appropriate answer to the question he'd ignored. Something along the lines of the topic of conversation between him and Cam.

"He wanted to discuss a little matter with me." Kendall's body relaxed into his with the simple answer.

"What matter?" she asked, seemingly oblivious to the fact that he was ready to move on to more speechless forms of communication.

Yeah, there was no way Ben was telling her that he and Cam had been discussing the possibility of her taking a job at the Brawling Bear. It seemed that Ethan was looking for another server for the late-night shift, and Cam wanted to run it past Ben before he approached Kendall. The woman would be thoroughly pissed off if she knew they'd been talking about her like that.

He lifted his head from the spot of flesh he'd been kissing and spoke near her ear in a low whisper. "Nothing important. I took care of it."

"Was he mad at you?" Ben got the distinct impression Kendall had a never-ending supply of questions if he allowed her free rein tonight.

"No." His firm word was spoken in a husky tone that left no question about his plans for her, and then he spun her around to face him. With one hand at the back of her neck and the other hand at her waist, he tugged her against the length of his body and devoured her mouth before another question escaped.

CHAPTER 31

Kendall gasped when Ben's lips sealed over hers in a greedy kiss. It was demanding, almost harsh, as if he'd held himself in check too long and now couldn't control the sexual need, urgent and intense, that had grown between them over the past several weeks.

Her lips parted on a lusty sigh while she reveled in the glorious moment she'd longed for, in the heady sensation of his mouth on hers. And he used that to his full advantage, as his tongue plunged into her mouth with surprising urgency. She closed her lips and sucked on his tongue, eliciting a low guttural groan from him, and he jerked her tighter against his body. The hard plane of his chest and the thick arousal at the front of his jeans gave her an entirely new sensation to bask in, the intimate nearness ramping up her own hunger. He wanted her, just as she wanted him. That knowledge sent a personal thrill zipping through her mind and a matching ache pulsing between her legs.

With her back pressed against the cold, hard surface of the door, cooling her backside, his wide chest radiated enough heat to warm her front side. And yet, it wasn't enough. She wanted more, and she wanted to give him everything she had. Kendall wrapped her arms around his neck, plunging her fingers through the hair at the nape.

By the time Ben concluded the assault on her lips, they both struggled for air. He rested his forehead against hers. "I could've lost you tonight." He dragged a ragged breath through his parted lips and squeezed his eyes shut as if that alone would put an end to the bad rerun looping in his mind. "I'd hoped our first time together would be special. But now all I can think about is ripping your clothes off and inspecting every inch of your body. Right here in the entryway."

"I'm okay." She caressed his jaw, his slight shadow beard rasping under her fingertips. "In case I haven't made myself clear enough, I'm ready to make love. I want to be with you." She waited, hoping he'd take her words as truth. All systems were a go, in her opinion. Without another word between them, she'd divest him of his clothes, especially his jeans, for an up-close inspection of her own. But instead, she waited. Her chest heaved slightly from the aggressive kiss and the anticipation of more.

Finally, as if he'd made some monumental decision, troubled Ben disappeared, replaced by a man ready to do battle, serious in his current undertaking. With frightening intensity, his gaze latched onto hers. The potent heat she found in his eyes was empowering, sexy, and utterly delicious.

His fingers found the zipper of her hoodie. Slowly he worked it downward, allowing the backs of his fingers to brush her aching breasts. Her quick intake of air—a natural reaction, but one she couldn't hide from him—gave away just how turned on she was. She held his gaze while her sweatshirt slipped from her shoulders, landing on the floor by their feet with a gentle thud.

In just her tight-fitting tank top, cut low to reveal a flirty glimpse of cleavage, she felt naked next to Ben's fully clothed body. Although, he didn't seem to notice, because his intense gaze never left her face. Kendall took the narrow space of separation as an invitation and placed her hands low on his abdomen. Beneath that shirt, she could feel the bands of muscle—the same ones she'd felt those nights he'd climbed into bed with her after her nightmares. Now she wanted to see them. Her hands roamed up his abs and chest to slip the first button free of its hole and then the next.

When she'd completed the long string of buttons, Ben let the flannel shirt slip from his arms and, without further coaching, jerked the second layer of clothing, a thermal knit shirt, up and over his head, leaving him to stand before her bare-chested. Just as she'd suspected, the guy was ripped. With fingers that itched to explore, she stroked the dark brown hair that sprinkled over his chest and around the flat dark discs of his nipples. A narrow path of hair, beginning just below his bellybutton, disappeared into his waistband, begging her fingers to follow. Kendall reached for the button on his jeans only to have both hands snatched up by his larger ones.

"Uh uh. You're next." Whether his fingers were more nimble or her inhibitions were less, within a few short seconds she stood bare to him except for her bra and panties, a matched set of snowy white lace. "You're beautiful, Kendall." He exhaled the words on a whispered breath.

He lingered, taking a moment to appreciate her body instead of impatiently stripping her bare and thrusting inside her. Kendall loved the expression on his face while he surveyed her. Not an ounce of lewdness or comparison was visible in his concentrated inspection, but rather a look of complete adoration. His tone reverent, his eyes worshipping. Each action and word meshed together and ignited a fire deep in her womb.

He traced the lacy fabric of her bra—the demi cup hardly contained her nipples—and as he brushed his forefinger across the delicate skin, it puckered and popped from beneath the lace.

"Nice." He smiled.

He gently pinched the eager pearl now on display for him and then dipped his head, tracing his wet tongue around the dark pink flesh before drawing it into the heat of his mouth. After he'd given thorough attention to the first nipple, he lifted his head to watch the other breast, teasing the nipple out of its lacy hiding spot as well.

As if on command, the second one poked out from the edge of her bra, and he showered it with equal attention. With her bra still in place cupping the lower half of her firm breasts, Ben seemed content to play with her exposed nipples. He transferred his ministration to her lips and neck. "I think I'm going to leave that on you. I like the way your perky little nipples came out to play with me. Very sexy."

His hands wandered lower, running the distance along the curve of her waist to her hip. With a tender caress, he traced the lace band of her panties before slipping his fingers inside to cup her mound. Her pulsing clit begged for his finger's direct attention, and she pressed her hips upward in a not-so-subtle invitation.

"Impatient, are we?" His eyebrows lifted in question.

"Yes, we are."

Ben stripped off her panties and gave her a taste of what she'd been asking for by sliding two fingers into her. She clenched her inner muscles, tightening them around his digits and making him groan.

"Damn, you're tight, darling. The thought of those muscles squeezing my hard dick as you orgasm around me makes me so fucking hot, I could totally lose it right now." He pumped inside her a few more times, but then his fingers disappeared.

And she was the one to groan. "Tease."

But with the way Ben yanked the condom package out of his pocket, Kendall knew she wasn't the only impatient one around here. She unbuttoned his jeans, lowered the zipper, and eased him out of his confinement. Within seconds, he'd stripped off his jeans, underwear, and socks, and then tore open the condom wrapper, covering his erection.

"How many times will you orgasm before I can come?"

"Huh?" How was she supposed to answer that? "Hopefully once."

"How about twice?" He stated it like a foregone conclusion, so she hated to burst his bubble, but once might not even happen. Although, she *had* been thinking about this moment a lot lately. Maybe she would orgasm. Just once.

But there was no time to analyze, because he was there kissing her, sinking his tongue deep into her mouth with a slow thrusting motion that imitated their lovemaking to come. And then he lifted one of her legs and wrapped it around his hip. He cupped her bottom, and as if she weighed nothing at all, lifted her fully off the ground. She didn't need any encouragement to wrap her legs around his waist, and he took a step forward to press her back against the front door.

Ben notched the tip of his erection at her entrance, but just waited. She was so ready for him, anxious to feel him inside her. But he took his sweet time, leisurely kissing her until she was so needy she didn't think she could wait a moment longer. Then he powered in, balls deep, on one upward thrust while they mutually moaned their pleasure at the joining.

"Oh, Ben. Oh, that feels good."

"Damn right, it's good." Ben pumped deeper while her ankles, locked at the base of his back, propelled her, moving them in unison. He continued the pounding rhythm, and she felt her inner muscles tighten and coil inside her. That hard-to-come-by orgasm was within her grasp, and Kendall allowed herself to relax into the sensations as they washed over her.

"Oh, yes. Ben!" she shouted, feeling herself clench down around the thick length of his erection. Her body shuddered, and the final spasms of release gradually faded, but Ben continued to stroke his still-hard cock inside her. She opened her eyes and found him staring at her, his jaw tight. He kissed her lips, gentle brushes at first and then harder, more demanding, and her core opened to him, heating with fresh excitement that built from out of nowhere.

No matter what he'd suggested at the get-go, she was not a two-orgasm gal. One, about fifty percent of the time. But never two. Then again, she'd never had sex with a guy who'd maintained control through her orgasm rather than letting go and finding his own release.

The thought that Ben had held back for her was sexy as hell and sent a tingling wave of arousal through her. The sensitive, tender flesh between her legs swelled, prepared to explode all over again. Releasing her hold around his neck, she leaned back onto the cold door. With her freed hands, she cupped her breasts, still partially covered by her bra, and caressed her thumbs over the pearled peaks, and then tweaked them between her thumb and forefinger. Clamping down on her inner core muscles, she squeezed her eyes shut, searching for that illusive ledge to hurtle herself over.

"Look at me, Kendall," Ben said.

She whimpered as she hung near the edge of a second orgasm. How had he done that? So close. She didn't want to lose it, but as he requested, she forced her eyes to open to mere slits while she reveled in her growing pleasure.

"Kendall, I'm going to come, and I want you to watch me. Don't shut your eyes. Okay?"

"Yes." The word came out sounding like a moan, but she forced her wide-eyed gaze to focus on his face. Her own release hovered just beyond her reach when he picked up his pace, thrusting into her. Over and over again. Her legs, locked at his lower back, countered the motions while her fingers toyed across her nipples.

His eyes never left hers when his pounding rhythm increased. Ben powered in and out, and then, with a jerking thrust, he shouted out her name. Stunned by the rapture on his face and the pleasure in the depths of his dazed eyes, Kendall felt herself let go, too. Together, they rode out their climax in perfect, pulsing unison.

CHAPTER 32

The woman was definitely going to kill him.

Ben groaned while Kendall freed her legs from around his waist, disconnecting where they were joined as her feet found the slick tiled floor. Based on the way his own legs shook, like two wet noodles propping up his incredibly relaxed torso, he held tight to her upper arms until she could steady herself against the wall. A slip in the wet shower could be dangerous. True. But with the events of the evening, he also knew he didn't want her far from his reach.

After making love in the entryway, they'd climbed the steps to the master suite, and she'd excused herself into the bathroom. When he'd heard the gentle cascade of water falling in the shower, he couldn't resist. He'd opened the door and entered the bathroom. She'd looked delicious, with her eyes closed and her head thrown back, water sluicing across her shoulders, off the sharp peaks of her breasts, down her abdomen into the soft layer of blonde curls between her thighs.

"Do you need any help?" His question had been sincere. What kind of host would he be if he didn't offer to fulfill his guest's basic needs?

His hospitable query had led to her suggestive response, which had led to another round of against-the-wall sex in the shower.

He plucked the bottle of body wash off the shelf and squeezed a large blob onto a washcloth, working the soap into a thick lather of bubbles. Ben worked the suds over her arms and shoulders, across her breasts and down her tummy, paying special attention to her more delicate areas that might be tender now after round two of lovemaking. Without moving since she'd slid from off his body, she drooped against the wall, eyes closed.

"Next time, my bed," Ben whispered in her ear. While Kendall seemed to like the down and dirty version, hard and fast against the wall, it hadn't been his plan for their first time together. Their next time would be slow and easy, a gentle lovemaking in the comfort of his bed—after he discussed favorite positions, favorite foreplay, and favorite time of day. He hoped she'd be open to sharing all her favs with him, because while he loved a vocal woman in bed—Kendall's lusty moans and satisfied shouts had definitely spurred him on—he preferred to work with a blueprint. He wasn't a mind reader and never wanted to be. Hell, whatever thoughts rattled around in most women's brains would probably scare the shit out of him.

When he spun her around to lather her back, Kendall's eyes cracked open to narrow slits and she cast him a sleepy look over her shoulder. "I think I might need a few minutes."

He laughed. "Yeah. Me too." Who was he kidding? He was done for the night. But the memory of her muscles squeezing his dick while he fought the urge for release blasted him with another wild rush of arousal. He'd always loved a good physical challenge, sexual or otherwise, and Kendall had given him one hell of a challenge. Especially when she'd sounded as if it might be hit or miss on the one-and-only to begin with. But selfish, he was not, and he couldn't imagine orgasming himself without allowing her the pleasure she deserved.

Grabbing the hand-held nozzle, he rinsed the lather from her body, then gave himself a good once-over before shutting the water off and stepping out. He snatched a couple towels off the shelf, seeing to Kendall before himself. After drying off, he brushed out Kendall's thick hair and braided it into one long rope.

"Where'd you learn how to braid?"

"Around," he said, not wanting to talk about the disappointment on his little niece's face when she'd discovered her Uncle Ben didn't know how to braid hair. Ben tugged Kendall toward the bed. "Let's rest."

She curled against him, one leg thrown over his, one hand on his chest just above his heart. Kendall gave a hearty sigh. "I enjoyed that."

Ben laughed at her whispered confession. "Going by the loud shouts in my ear, I figured you liked it."

* * *

Kendall slapped at his chest in a teasing manner, barely able to lift her hand. The man was going to kill her if they kept this up. Four orgasms in less than an hour. But damn, it would be a sweet death. The man knew how to make love. He had the stamina of a race horse, and the skill of a sex god. She hadn't expected that of him. Fun, playful, yes. But the man was serious about his sex.

Curled against his body, she relaxed to the sound of his steady, deep breathing and the solid thud of his heartbeat. Kendall released a heavy breath, allowing a wave of contentment to wash over her.

"So, you don't always come during sex?"

What? Clearly, he hadn't drifted off to sleep like she'd suspected, but why launch an investigative probe into a rather embarrassing line of questioning now? His timing was lousy, in her opinion. A better time for this topic? Hmm, how about never?

She sighed again. But not from blissful, post-orgasmic satisfaction. No, it was something more akin to awkwardness over his choice of pillow talk. "No, not always. Never twice." Simple. True. End of discussion.

"Why not?" Okay, obviously not the end of the discussion. And after what she'd just experienced with Ben, a freaking good question.

"Well…" she said, dragging out the word while she searched for an answer. "I need a bit of prep time. Although tonight I climaxed quickly, I'm not always that responsive. Some guys don't wait." Enough with the details already.

"What's the best way to stimulate you? What do you like?"

She gasped. "Why would you ask that?"

"Because I don't lack patience when it comes to making love. I want it good for you. Every time."

With her head pillowed on his chest, embarrassed and on the spot, she pondered her answer. She'd never put into words what she needed to get off during sex, but the question was a valid one. If she didn't know, how the hell would he?

Ben remained silent and still, but she sensed him coiled like a snake, waiting to strike. "Kendall. I can't read your mind." His gentle words reiterated her thoughts.

Ugh. He actually expected her to come up with an answer. While she talked a good game beforehand, verbalizing her needs seemed illusive. Almost like her orgasms fifty percent of the time.

"Well, I'm not good at one-night stands, because for me, sex starts before I get in the bedroom. I need kisses, sexy words whispered over the phone at lunch, a casual touch, or holding hands. I need the emotional connection that comes from a relationship. Beyond that, my breasts are extremely sensitive, and I'll absolutely shatter if you suck on my clit."

"Excellent," he said. His voice filled with praise. He rolled over on top of her, supporting his weight on his elbows. He kissed the tip of her nose and then gave her a rather loud kiss on her lips. "All very useful pieces of information. Thank you. That wasn't so difficult, was it? For a second there, I thought maybe you'd clammed up on me."

She shook her head. "No. It's just not something I've put into words before."

"Yeah. But think about it. If every person in a relationship told their partner what made them happy in the sack, imagine the amount of satisfied sex acts that would occur daily. People would be walking around a whole lot more relaxed with a smile on their face, right?"

"True." She had to agree, although she never would've considered it for the entire populace at large.

"Okay. So, let's say that on a smaller scale that could make a huge difference in our lives. You tell me what you like, what you don't like. I do the same."

"Hmmm," she said wearily. "Could we start tomorrow?" She didn't think she could carry on a logical conversation much longer.

"We've already started, and starting is the worst, right? You've shared with me. I've told you I need to hear what you like and what you don't like. Now we're headed down relaxed road to smiles-ville." He rolled over again, situating her with her head pillowed against his shoulder.

"I liked orgasming twice each time. I liked that a lot." She mumbled the words against his chest, exhausted beyond measure and unsure if her words were even coherent. But his response let her know he'd understood and agreed.

"Twice is nice. It should be a standard, don't you think?" She grunted her approval and felt his chuckle rumbling through his chest. "Good night, Kendall." He pressed a kiss to the top of her head and held her close.

Definitely a good night. Probably the best night of her entire life, she decided as she drifted off to sleep.

CHAPTER 33

This had to go down as the best string of days he'd ever lived. Ben searched his memory bank for an equivalent or greater. Nope. Nada. Nothing better.

And he gave every ounce of credit to Kendall Aasgaard.

The woman had crept into what he'd deemed his perfect life, she'd rattled his cage while she'd pointed out that he needed to get over himself and move on, and then had suggested the unimaginable—a sexual relationship between the two of them. Man, she made him smile.

Ben settled into his desk chair in his home office and flipped open his laptop. Why had he even bothered bringing work home? No way would he get it done tonight. Lately, he couldn't focus for shit. Except maybe when his mind wandered to Kendall.

Never in a million years would he have considered dating a blond-haired, blue-eyed woman for two reasons. First and foremost, fear that a fresh face with fair hair and sky-hued eyes might channel the memories of all things Jenna. Second, worry that a flood of emotions and guilt would drown him at the most inconvenient moment if he moved on with a permanent blonde companion. With the logic of a mule, he'd believed avoidance of the golden-haired portion of the female population was his only alternative.

And yet, he hadn't given a passing thought to Jenna while he and Kendall had made love that first night. Not until the following morning over breakfast had he realized his fears and worries hadn't come to fruition. Memories of Jenna hadn't danced through his mind, and guilt hadn't incapacitated him.

Without reason, he'd worried and evaded an entire quadrant of women over something that had never happened. But that was the way of worry.

The one thing he appreciated most about Kendall was her bold, in your face attitude. She was a real-life walking, talking billboard for the motto "*live life to the fullest.*" And when Ben sat down to seriously consider things, including all she'd overcome in her lifetime, Kendall put his lingering grief and failure to move on to shame.

Kendall's exuberance for life followed her to bed at night. Energetic and creative. Eager to touch and be touched. After her hesitant response when he'd asked for her sexual preferences that first night, he'd never expected the level of detail that followed over the next twenty-four hours. Ben had learned an abundance of incredible information—a lifetime supply of tips and helpful hints—and a fair quantity of things he'd been warned to avoid. The details had poured from her lips at a frantic pace, the vast magnitude enough to fill a book, and he cursed himself for failing to take notes.

Ben's phone vibrated with an incoming call, startling him out of his thoughts. "Hi, Cam," he said when he connected the call.

"Hey. Just heard from the sheriff. Nicholas Cardwell insists that he didn't pin threatening notes to Kendall's windshield or your back door."

"He's lying."

"I agree. I'm sure you or your dad will be getting a call from Ellis, too, because Cardwell also says he didn't vandalize any Montgomery Construction worksite."

"What? What about the red spray paint? He wrote, 'Ben, the bitch is mine.' Who else would write that?"

"That was exactly what I asked Ellis. He suggested someone with an axe to grind against your business—"

"But there isn't anyone."

"—and someone that knows you're seeing Kendall."

"So, the whole fucking town." God, Ben wanted to rage. To hit something. To rip his office apart. Just to gain some bit of control.

"Nick claims he rolled into town right before he stopped at your house—the address Kendall's aunt and uncle gave him. But without a credit card trail, there's no easy proof either way."

"I don't believe it."

"Neither do I, and I think Sheriff Ellis agrees. But he says due diligence requires that he explore Nick's claims. Even though they already have enough to charge him with, including failure to comply with an order of protection, forcible entry, attempted kidnapping, and assault with a deadly weapon."

After thanking Cam for the update, Ben rang off, slammed his laptop closed, and headed upstairs, making his way to the room Kendall had claimed as her own. While she'd slept in his bed for the past four nights, all her gear was strewn in the guest room from one end to the other. A vast array of books, papers, and clothes lay across her unmade bed, huge piles of discards and countless shoes littered the floor, a rainbow of unmentionables dangled from dresser drawers propped opened like a grand staircase ascending to a treasure trove of jars and bottles while the wide-open closet doors belched up the remaining wardrobe of fabrics.

"You want a sandwich or something before you go?" Ben asked when he came to a halt at her open door. If the way she jumped at his simple query was any indication, he had a backup job as a ninja if the whole construction gig didn't pan out.

"Uh." She fumbled with something in her hands, shoving it behind her back when she turned toward him.

Okay, maybe he wasn't so ninja, and she was just totally engrossed in something she didn't want him to see.

She met his gaze, but the faulty smile she'd plastered on didn't light her face or touch her eyes. "Yes, I'd love a sandwich. I'll be right down." She maintained eye contact and held her stupid fake grin, waiting for him to take a hike.

Dismissed. No need to tell him twice. He turned and trudged down the steps.

What was she trying to hide? She'd held a book, maybe the same one he'd tossed out of bed after it'd jabbed him in the ribs. The same one she'd tried to hide that day he'd found her searching under the bed. The book, small and leather-bound, looked worn but of good quality. Maybe a family Bible; however, it seemed too thin for that.

Ben let his thoughts churn while he pulled out the makings for a couple sandwiches. He might as well eat, too, and then he'd walk Kendall down the block, so she could work a shift at the Brawling Bear.

He wasn't excited about her temporary job working three nights a week at the bar. Okay, he'd admit his attitude on the topic sucked. He'd spouted something stupid about needing to protect her, which had gotten Kendall's hackles up. Definitely the wrong approach. She'd simply sicced Cam on him, who'd guaranteed that Kendall would only work shifts with him and that he'd see her safely home after they closed up for the night.

Ben should've just told her the real reason—that he wanted her with him every evening when he got home, not out working until the early hours of the morning. But real or not, it was a selfish reason, so he'd kept his mouth shut. He consoled himself with the fact that it was only until she secured her teaching license in Minnesota and established herself as an elementary schoolteacher again. Then they could work the same shift.

While he stacked slices of ham and cheese on whole wheat, his mind rolled back to Kendall and her odd behavior. Why had his presence startled her? Why didn't she want him to see that book? Was it filled with some kind of secrets? Hell, after all their dirty talk over the past few days, Ben figured nothing stood between them. But obviously, some things still did. He had to admit it hurt a bit, her clandestine behavior, as if she'd slammed the door on the candid rapport they'd been building. Whatever secrets that little book held were apparently important enough to hide from him.

Ben breathed out a loud sigh as he plated each sandwich. Maybe if he asked, she'd come clean. He hated the idea of secrets lingering between the two of them. When she'd turned to face him, hands behind her back, he'd behaved like a polite gentleman and ignored her evasive actions and her guarded behavior. But it piqued his curiosity. What the hell was she hiding?

Perhaps he should take a little peek for himself. After all, this was his house.

No. Regardless of how inquisitive Kendall's lack of disclosure made him, he wasn't that much of an ass. Kendall deserved privacy on any matter she wished to maintain. Besides, the simplest explanation was most often the truth. She'd been engrossed in a damned book. He'd startled her, at which point her unusual behavior had been nothing more than her surprised response to his abrupt appearance in her doorway. Nothing more.

* * *

"Are we celebrating something special tonight, ladies?" Kendall asked the group of four women sitting around the table. They all looked to be in their mid-thirties.

"Just girls' night out. We're getting away from our kids," one of them said.

"And our husbands." They all seemed to chime in at once.

The one closest to Kendall cocked her head to the side. "Are you Cam's cousin, Kendall?"

"I am." The words had barely passed her lips when the other three women glared at the one who'd asked. Apparently, some silent communication between friends. The woman shot all the others a pained look and then focused on Kendall. She had a familiarity about her, but Kendall couldn't place her. Her light brown hair shimmered with gorgeous, artfully done caramel highlights.

"Hi. This is Chelsea, Cheryl, and Amy, and I'm Sue," she said, sticking out her hand to Kendall.

Kendall politely shook each woman's hand, although Sue seemed to be the friendliest of the group. Kendall felt almost required to say something—anything—to Sue since she'd been so welcoming. "How many children do you have, Sue?"

"Six."

"Oh. Wow. You do know what's causing that, don't you?" Kendall asked with a teasing grin.

All four women laughed. "Yes, but I just can't seem to control myself," Sue said.

"If I were in your shoes, I think I'd need to get away, too. So, what can I get you ladies tonight?"

Once Kendall had taken several orders, she stepped up to the bar for Cam to pour her drinks. "I see you met Sue," Cam said, tipping his head to the table of women.

Kendall nodded at her cousin. "And Chelsea, Cheryl, and Amy," she said, ticking off the names on her fingers and wondering how she'd remember all the names she'd learned tonight. She glanced over her shoulder at the Wednesday evening crowd. The Brawling Bear seemed to buzz with energy. It wasn't as crazy as she'd seen it that night when Jackson had sung, but it was still hopping.

Working as a server was a perfect fit to Kendall's personality. She'd worked a similar job during her college days, loving the exciting, fast-paced atmosphere. The tips were usually good, and she could talk her way through her workday. Overall, she was stoked about the opportunity.

But if Ben's grumpy disposition and brooding manner tonight were any indication, he was less than thrill with her new temporary job. During the short walk from his house to the Brawling Bear, he hadn't said a word.

Finally, right before they'd reached the door, she'd asked, "Are you coming in for a drink?"

"I'm not. I need to get home. Big meeting in the morning. Cam's going to escort you home, okay?"

"Okay."

"And make sure you kiss me when you climb into bed. Yes, I want you in my bed tonight."

"But I'll just wake—"

"No, I sleep better when you're by my side," Ben had said with a firmness that left little question in her mind, and then he'd put his hand on the nape of her neck and pulled her in for a breathtaking kiss that wiped out any remaining question.

She sighed at the memory of that kiss and the touch of loneliness she'd experienced as he'd walked away into the dark night. In that moment, she'd realized just how much she'd come to rely on Ben's nearness.

While she delivered her drink orders, she considered the developing relationship between her and Ben. This week had rushed by in a contented blur. When she'd first considered becoming involved sexually with Ben, she'd never imagined the intense demands he'd place on her. They usually made love a couple times every evening and once in the morning. Each time, he'd coaxed one and sometimes even two orgasms from her before he found his release. He asked that she voice her pleasure, before, during, and after, and he lapped up her constructive criticism and enthusiastic praise while he doled out his own. Kendall was certain the open, honest conversations helped fuel her endless orgasms.

One of Ben's personal requirements was an eyes-wide-open policy. He expected her to look at him while they made love, which was a change from any experience she'd had prior where she'd pinched her eyes tight and participated in her own little fantasy world. But not with Ben. He wanted her to know and acknowledge who was loving her. And she'd admit, she loved every minute of it. She felt as if she'd never get enough of him.

Although, earlier today he'd scared the crap out of her while she'd been reading one of Jenna's journals and the words of love her sister had written. Stupidly, Kendall had fumbled the entire thing. Attempting to hide the book—the equivalent of waving a red flag at a charging bull—had brought unwanted attention to its existence. A foolish mistake. One she'd never make again, she promised herself. If she had a chance to go back and re-do the entire scene, she would've pretended that she held nothing more than a book of prose to inspire her.

After Ben had gone downstairs, she'd buried the journals deep within the folds of her summer clothing at the back of her closet. She didn't believe he'd search through her belongings, since invading her privacy stood in direct contrast to his bent on open communication. Kendall figured Ben would ask before he snooped, which would give her ample opportunity to evade.

What would she say if he asked? Not the truth.

The words in those books had the potential to ruin everything. Not only their budding romance—although that'd be the first thing to explode in her face. No, Ben's emotional state would certainly take a hit. Like the razor-sharp edge of a sword, Jenna's sweet words held the power to slice open his wounded soul, eradicating any progress he'd made in the letting-go and moving-on process. The commitment and love Jenna had felt toward Ben leaked out of every flowery word on every damn page of three entire journals dedicated to nothing other than Benjamin Montgomery.

No. She could save Ben the pain at this point. Someday in the future, when he'd put the past behind him and moved miles down the road, then maybe she'd share with him.

Kendall had to force herself to get back to work. Getting fired for daydreaming on her first day on the job would be pretty pathetic. She made her rounds through the barroom, stopping at tables and taking orders. When she came to Sue's table again, the four women easily drew her into their conversation.

"What's the most romantic thing your husband's ever done?" the one named Cheryl asked the group at large.

"Romantic? Since I've married him? Nothing," Amy, the thin brunette with the sour expression, said.

"Oh, come on. There has to be something? Like, just the other night, Steve planned a candlelit dinner for two. He even dropped the kids off at his mom's house, so we could have some privacy."

"Wow, Steve sounds like a good catch," Kendall chimed in. Amy still looked put out by the question on the table. Kendall couldn't help but wonder why they were talking about romance when one of their friends was obviously having such a hard time. It seemed a bit insensitive of her friends if the woman was having relationship troubles. "Interesting choice of topics, ladies."

"Cheryl and Steve are celebrating their fifteenth wedding anniversary on Friday. And she's still blissfully in love, even after all these years."

"Congratulations, Cheryl," Kendall said to the beaming woman. "I guess Friday is a special day. It's also my birthday. I'll be twenty-five." Everyone called out happy birthday.

Everyone except Sue. Her sullen expression seemed at odds after her friendly introduction moments ago. With a faraway look in her eyes, it was obvious that she was completely lost in her own thoughts. Finally, she said, "I just discovered that Jeff has kept every love note I've ever written him." Her cheeks turned a deep shade of red. Embarrassed? Because she hadn't meant to reveal that aloud? Or possibly because the conversation had moved on, and it seemed rather random? But Sue smiled, giving a small apologetic shrug. "I thought it was romantic."

Kendall and the other women at the table agreed. Even Amy.

And while Kendall agreed, her mind turned over Sue's admission, examining it from all sides. Sue wrote love notes. Jeff adored the love notes enough to secret them away. And Sue considered that romantic.

How would Ben feel about Jenna's journals? They were filled with nothing more than love notes really. They weren't exactly written from her to him, but they explained—in great detail—Jenna's love for the man. If someday in the future Ben learned that the three journals existed, would he want to read them? It didn't seem like a healthy activity for him, but who was Kendall to stand in his way? Would there ever be a time in Ben's future that those words would provide comfort? Or would they just tear him apart?

The remainder of the night Kendall played with those questions, and by the end of her shift, she'd decided two things. First, there was no expiration date on words of love. And second, the three books she'd treasured for the past sixteen years had to be destroyed.

CHAPTER 34

Ben slammed the door shut and started his engine. He was exhausted from too little sleep, and it wasn't because he'd spent last night engaged in marathon sex, either. It was from staring at the ceiling, worried about Kendall. Hating the fact that she wasn't by his side. After one night of her new job, he was so thoroughly done with it.

Last night when he'd left Kendall behind at the bar to work her shift, the silence of the house had pressed in on him the second he'd stepped through the mudroom and into the kitchen. In the few short weeks that Kendall had lived with him, she'd wheedled her way into his mornings, noons, and nights, and the simple act of walking through his own empty house—one he'd occupied alone for more than six years—had seemed wrong. Lonesome even.

But thankfully for the next couple nights, Kendall didn't have to work, so when he got home Kendall would be there. He gave his Chevy Silverado a little more gas.

When he'd returned last night to the empty house, curiosity over the leather-bound book had gnawed at him, distracting him from the pile of paperwork he'd brought home. He'd wanted to know. What could be worth such effort to hide? What could be that private? His thoughts had run in circles while he'd puzzled out potential stories to explain Kendall's behavior, and not a single one sounded plausible. In all likelihood, once he heard the truth, he'd realize it had been staring him in the face the whole time. But until then, frustration and curiosity were his enemies. For a split second, he'd considered searching through her room. But he knew in the end he'd regret it. So instead, he'd gone into his own room, closed the door, and waited for Kendall to come home. And once she'd returned, her enthusiasm had taken over, keeping his body, mind, and soul happily occupied.

Ben stepped foot into the house, and immediately his stomach growled in anticipation. The aroma—some garlicky goodness—was roasting in the oven. His lunch, hours ago, had consisted of a ham and Swiss sandwich, a can of Coke, and a candy bar, followed by several cups of stronger than average office sludge. Now he was jittery and beyond hungry.

And much to his disappointment, Kendall wasn't waiting for him in the kitchen. Rather than calling out to her, Ben went in search, hoping to catch up on his Kendall withdrawal with a kiss or two. He warmed at the thought of her sweet mouth locked with his in a kiss passionate enough to delay dinner. Potentially in front of a roaring fire, if his sense of smell was correct.

His stocking feet made no noise, padding along the wooden floor toward the scent of smoke and the crackle of dry wood. He came to a discreet stop at the doorway into the formal parlor.

Kendall. On the floor near the hearth. Sitting with her legs crisscrossed. A silky curtain of hair fell forward, obscuring her face and her view of him. Thoroughly absorbed in the mysterious leather-bound book in her lap.

The familiar scene slammed into his memory—keen and unmistakable—dragging him back to his past.

Jenna.

Like a right hook to the jaw, the image permeated his brain. Non-solicited, the memory of Jenna—a near replica of his Kendall—caught him off guard. He shook his head to dislodge the wayward thought at the same time a sickening wave of nausea rolled through his gut.

This had been his fear for sixteen years. That he'd glance at a blonde woman and think of Jenna. Yet this was different somehow. This was a memory, forgotten with the passage of time, but as brilliant and real as the day it had happened.

Sylvia Aasgaard had greeted him at the door. "Hello, Benjamin. How are you today?" She stepped aside, allowing him to enter.

"I'm fine. Thanks. Is Jenna around?" He glanced down at his scuffed-up sneakers. Mrs. Aasgaard never spoke a mean word to anyone, but he always felt awkward and underdressed whenever he stopped for a social visit with her daughter.

"Jenna is in the family room. Go on in." She smiled as if she knew his discomfort.

He toed off his shoes and wandered into their family room where Jenna sat, pretzel style on the floor near the fireplace, engrossed in the book propped in her lap.

"Jenna's journal." The words fell from Ben's lips before the thought formulated in his brain. Kendall held Jenna's journal. The small leather-bound book. The secret book that she'd tried to hide from him. Why? Why bother secreting away her sister's journal?

Startled by his presence or by his declaration, Kendall slammed the book closed and hugged it to her chest. And then she snatched up two identical books stacked on the floor.

"How did you know?" Her gaze darted toward the crackling fire in the fireplace as if debating the merits of tossing them into the blaze. Her eyes grew wide in disbelief. Hurt contorted her face. "You snooped through my things. I can't believe you'd do that, Ben. Why didn't you ask?" She glanced back at the fire again.

"Oh, my God, Kendall. You're planning to burn them. Don't. They're Jenna's. Don't you dare burn them!" His voice cracked, and he swallowed hard, trying to fight the hollow sensation in his chest. The thought of Kendall destroying Jenna's personal belongings felt as if the love of his life were being ripped from this earth for a second time.

Tears pooled in her eyes, and she blinked them back. "Why shouldn't I? So you can read them? So you can fall in love with her all over again?" Kendall choked out the words on a frustrated whisper, allowing fat tears to roll down her cheeks as if she'd given up on the floodgates that contained them. As if she'd given up on him.

Ben's entire body shook with anger. Or maybe anguish was a better word, because he felt so incredibly hurt by Kendall's intended actions that he could hardly stand to look at her. How could she? The question made him crazy, and his temper flared. "How could you ever consider destroying them?" His voice was anything but calm and understanding, because he deserved a fucking answer.

"How could you invade my privacy?" Her accusing glare called him an absolute jackass.

Ben pinched his eyes together to block out the expression plastered on Kendall's face and he counted to ten. God, he wanted to rage, but it wouldn't do a bit of good. Ben knew he needed to pull himself together, so he dragged in a breath. Searching for a way to defuse the situation. Sensing it was useless. He sucked in another deep breath and held it, and then he opened his eyes to stare at the blonde across from him who'd stolen his heart, plucking it right out of his chest.

And now she intended to toss his still-beating, bloody hunk of flesh into the blazing fire.

He lowered his volume, choosing his words cautiously and with purpose. "I didn't. I didn't rummage through your things. I remember Jenna writing in those books years ago."

Without a sound, Kendall's tears traced a wet path down her cheeks, dripping off her chin, and she did nothing to stop them. Put there by his abrupt behavior. Ben wanted to reach out to wipe them away, but he knew she'd never allow it.

She stood and said, "I made dinner. It should be ready now."

Ben fought the temptation to grab her when she walked past him to the door, but before he could reach out to her, Kendall shoved the three small books against his gut. He let them topple to the floor at his feet.

Kendall stumbled toward the staircase, her feet thudding on each riser. The slam of the bedroom door echoed his uncontrolled shouts rather than the whispers of her choked-up words.

Damn. He was an idiot. He snatched up the poker, separating the logs, and then with the small shovel, he scooped ash and sprinkled it over the flames, suffocating the fire. Tending a fire wasn't in his plans for the night. He wanted food and Kendall. Not necessarily in that order. But he'd cope.

He stooped to pick up the journals and carried them out to the kitchen. His stomach rumbled, reminding him of his hunger, and so he pulled the casserole from the oven. He appreciated the effort Kendall had gone to in order to make him a meal, and he intended to eat it. It'd give both of them time to process.

With a plate of food in front of him, he stared at the stack of three leather-bound books on the kitchen table. Kendall hadn't wanted him to read the words penned by Jenna. Why? He couldn't imagine what had been written in those books more than a dozen years ago that would cause her to become that upset or to go to such lengths to keep them away from him.

Hell, she'd planned to throw them into the fire.

Last night, he'd deliberated over the most prudent action to take: to search or not to search. He'd settled on allowing her privacy. Now he was glad he'd chosen that path. The pain on her face when she'd accused him of invading her space had sent a dagger through his heart and enraged him all the more.

Now he waffled between cracking open the books to read Jenna's words or leaving them closed. Kendall had all but given him permission when she'd shoved the books into his chest, but for whatever reason, she'd prefer that he not read them.

He cautiously stretched out his hand and smoothed his fingers across the soft leather. Jenna. His sweet gal. The love of his life. God, her death was so unfair. She'd been ripped from this world far too young. He wanted to breathe in the words she'd written, bask in their healing sentiment, and revel in the memory of her soft voice. If he opened the books, he'd hear her words pour over him like soothing waters. His Jenna. The woman he'd loved.

Had loved.

The words struck him, and he stopped in his thoughts, considering the past tense of his words and the direction of his future. He *had* loved Jenna with all his heart. Years ago. And no matter how much it had hurt, the pain had dissipated. He'd feared loving again, but he'd been living. Sort of. Now he had

Kendall. And he loved her. Present tense. And he suspected that he'd love her in the future, too.

Would opening the books to read the words ease the ache of loss? In all likelihood, no. It might even make it worse.

Maybe Kendall's act of tossing the books into the blaze had been unselfish, noble even. Burning those journals to prevent Ben from reading her sister's words certainly ensured he wouldn't suffer any additional emotional pain. But at what cost? That drastic action was a huge, unnecessary sacrifice for Kendall. The way she'd returned to those books over and over, keeping them all these years, spoke to the importance of the words written within.

An hour later, Ben rapped on Kendall's bedroom door. When he received no response, he turned the knob and peered inside. The dim lamplight illuminated the emotional damage he'd caused. Unlike her usual sleep position—arms thrown out in utter abandon—she'd curled onto her side in the fetal position, facing away from the door. His heart clenched in his chest at the sight of her. He watched and waited, wondering if she'd cried herself to sleep, or if she played possum to avoid speaking with him.

After several long moments, he reached for a quilt folded on a chair in the corner and covered her before he spooned against her back. She stiffened when he tugged her closer.

"Shhh. I'm sorry I yelled, Kendall. I was wrong. I was just so stunned that you had those journals… And the pain that Jenna had been taken from me… And you were going to take something else. I'm sorry. I lost it."

In silence he waited for a response but nothing came. So, he continued. "I didn't open them. Now. Downstairs. And I didn't dig through your stuff. I promise. I won't deny that I wanted to know what you were hiding from me, but I would've asked instead of invading your privacy. You have to believe me on that. Jenna's my past, Kendall. You're my future."

A loud sob escaped her chest, her entire body shuddered as if she might break into a million pieces, and he wanted to cry right along with her. His unfair, knee-jerk response had caused her sadness. His brash words had hurt her. And that was the last thing in the world he wanted to do.

Ben lay awake for hours, staring at the ceiling in Kendall's bed after she'd stopped crying. He'd whispered gentle words in a stupid-ass way to soothe her while her breathing hiccupped, and her tears dried. All the while, she hadn't uttered a single word to him. Now he had no idea if she'd forgiven him. Or if his confession about her being his future had come too late.

He hoped they could put their first fight behind them to celebrate tomorrow, Friday, Kendall's twenty-fifth birthday. Ben still planned to take her out to a fancy dinner at Ferris Steakhouse.

If she'd let him.

CHAPTER 35

Kendall wanted to make love to him. If he'd let her.

After he'd yelled, and she'd stormed out. After she'd shut down and cried herself to sleep. After he'd apologized and called her his future. After all that, the only thing she'd been capable of doing was to sob while he'd held her in his arms. The strength and comfort she found there confused her, mixing with the odd combination of joy and relief, as well as sorrow for their mutual loss and desire for a future together. With a man who never should've been hers.

In the dark before dawn, she slipped from his embrace and ventured down the hall to the bathroom. After using the toilet and brushing her teeth, she assessed her reflection. Swollen eyelids, blotchy skin, and a red nose. Lovely. What every man envisions for his future. She splashed cold water on her face and blotted it dry. Because that minimal corrective action alone couldn't possibly have reversed the damage of a good long cry, she avoided another glance at the mirror and tiptoed back down the hall to her room.

Ben's alarm clock on his cell phone would ring in a little more than an hour, so she stripped off her clothes and slipped back under the quilt that he'd draped over them. Kendall curled up against Ben, her head nestled on his bare chest, soaking in the warmth that poured off of him. At some point, he'd stood and stripped off his clothes and now slept in nothing at all. She forced her eyes shut, willing herself to doze again, but her mind refused to turn off, rehashing their first official fight.

Last night her heart had ached, and she'd been too emotionally wiped out to discuss more with him. She'd absorbed the words of his apology and cried until she'd fallen into an exhausted sleep. Now, removed from the situation, she understood his immediate reaction to the sight of Jenna's journal. A definite surprise and not the good type. Their reactions had snowballed, and she'd stormed off in sorrow, worried she'd lose him to the memory of her blonde-haired, blue-eyed sister.

When she'd first arrived in Krysset, hoping for Ben's protection, it had been glaringly obvious that Ben had never moved on after Jenna's death. Thinking that she and Ben might somehow become involved seemed like an uphill battle. But this past week, the pieces had fallen into place, and the thought that Kendall's prized possessions—Jenna's journals—might be the stumbling block to her own happiness screamed of injustice.

She shoved the thought away. No way would negative thinking drag her back down today. Not on her birthday. While Ben had spooned against her back, his words had filled her heart with hope. He'd admitted she was his future. She had to accept his statement and move forward. Together they'd determine if they had a permanent future regardless of their connection to Jenna.

Kendall couldn't wait a minute longer. She stroked her finger across his chest, down the firm wall of his abs until she rested her hand on his heavy erection. Like most mornings, his body was primed and ready for action even in sleep, and she took advantage of the moment to enjoy the silky soft skin stretched over his thick steel length. Little by little her fingers drifted lower, cupping and gently massaging the sac below.

She knew the exact moment he awoke. His breath caught in his chest, and his hand reached for the back of her neck, tilting her face upward to steal a kiss.

"Happy birthday." His husky tone broke the silence.

"You remembered." Her words escaped on an airy breath, filled with obvious surprise. She figured their fight last night had probably wiped clear any memory of her birthday, putting his plans on permanent hold.

"Of course, I remembered." He grinned and his dimples peeked through his rough, day-old whisker growth. His sleep-droopy eyes and his tousled hair, jutting out at all sorts of odd angles, gave him that sexy morning look. He kissed the tip of her nose. "Now, birthday girl, how would you like to celebrate the dawning of your special day?"

"I'm going to ride you, if you don't mind."

He chuckled at the suggestion. "Have at it, darling."

Moments later, panting and senseless, she straddled his hips, pressing her hands against his pecs when she leaned in to ravage his kiss-swollen lips again. The man looked sexy as sin laid out below her. His arms rested above his head, his cock twitched against the slick folds of her skin, and she reached between them and guided him toward her hungry, wet opening. She dragged the head of his penis through the damp arousal at the apex of her thighs, circling it around her engorged nub before slowly levering herself onto him.

"Mmm." She paused to adjust to the spectacular sense of fullness when he entered her. Her inner muscles spasmed in protest, and she squeezed them tight, eliciting a groan from Ben.

His hands skimmed over her breasts, fingering her nipples. The sensitive flesh puckered at his touch, and Kendall murmured her approval while electric tingles sparked across her skin. She loved the way her body ached for the touch of his hands, and she whimpered when they left her breasts and skated lower down her sides, gripping her hips.

Ben helped her set a luxuriously slow tempo that did nothing to prolong the rush to completion. As she slid up and down along his hard shaft, each muscled ridge in her core sensitized, pressing her closer to the edge. She threw her head back, toying with her own nipples and grinding herself against him. The exquisite sensation of pure euphoria swelled beyond anything she'd expected this morning when she'd instigated this round of lovemaking. Now she balanced on the sharp edge of orgasm, needing just a bit more.

"Eyes, Kendall." Ben's ragged voice snapped her from her own private race to climax back to the joint effort occurring in her bed, one he insisted be a shared journey, run together toward a common goal.

She opened her eyes, gazing at the tenderness and desire written on his face. The muscles deep within her tightened while she rode him up and down in a steady motion, angling her pelvis to roll her most crucial bundle of nerves against his body. With her eyes fixed on Ben's, her core clamped down on him. She came apart, shattering into a million sparkling pieces, knowing that he trailed behind her by a millisecond.

He groaned, and then his expression of dazed blissfulness morphed into horrified panic. Ben lifted her off his body, disengaging from the place they'd been connected, and Kendall landed on her knees beside him.

"Did I hurt you?" she asked, panting while she fought the urge to groan at the abrupt end to her birthday orgasm.

"Condom." His forearm covered his eyes. His jaw clenched. His erection seemed to be pulsing, but he obviously hadn't finished.

"I'm on the pill. Don't worry. I had all the standard tests run last month. No STDs. It's okay." He sagged, relief washing over his face. She gave him a gentle kiss, and he slowly lifted his arm, so she could look into his eyes. "I'm sorry I forgot. It just felt so good."

"It felt fucking awesome." He groaned, and his jaw clenched again. "God, woman, the things you do to me. After all these years, I've never forgotten a condom. Not once. I'm clean, too."

"So, you liked going bareback, huh?" He simply nodded as if he were in pain. "But you stopped yourself. Come on," she said, patting him on the shoulder. "Mount up, cowboy."

"Are you sure?" Ben asked.

She leaned into him and gently brushed her lips to his. "Yes."

Without warning, Ben flipped her onto her back and rose up on his knees between her thighs, lifting her legs over his arms. "I'm going to come inside you, Kendall. You're going to feel every last inch of me as I lose myself there."

Eyes latched with hers, he thrust his stiff erection into her still-throbbing channel. Powering in and out. Over and over again. The pleasure climbed, building as he rocked against her. Until they both soared together.

* * *

Nothing better than sex in the morning. Ben was certain of it. He stood over the stovetop making Kendall breakfast. She loved blueberry pancakes, and for her special day, he'd planned her favorite breakfast meal.

"I'm taking you to Ferris Steakhouse tonight for dinner. We have reservations at six." He glanced over his shoulder when Kendall made her way into the kitchen and wrapped her arms around his middle, nuzzling her nose against his shoulder blades as though she were inhaling him.

"You don't have to make a big deal. We could have a quiet night at home, and I could cook something for us." Her insistence made him want to laugh.

Ben twisted in her arms until her cheek nestled against his chest, and she dragged in another devouring breath.

"Mmm. You smell so good, kind of like spicy, woodsy man," Kendall said, burrowing her face into his shirt again.

He laughed. Damn, he was in a good mood today. Better than good. Fucking awesome. Enough so that he might just laugh the whole day through.

After last night when his anger had spiraled out of control, he'd messed up the entire situation, leaving him to question whether he'd ever partake in true laughter again. But here he stood, a new day dawning with a beautiful, loving woman in his arms while his emotions soared lighter than air. Like the sensation of dangling five stories above the city sidewalk, harnessed to the steel grid of a skeleton building. Like nothing bad could ever touch him again. Individually and together, he and Kendall had endured the worst life threw at people. And now, all that lay on the horizon promised the best. For both of them.

"If I allowed you to lift a finger on your birthday, my mom would show up on my doorstep, in person, to shoot me," Ben said. Now it was Kendall's turn to chuckle, no doubt imagining Judy Montgomery doing just that.

But Ben wasn't joking. His mother expected him and his older brothers to behave as gentlemen in all circumstances, observing all important days such as anniversaries, birthdays, and Valentine's Day. And no matter what Kendall said, Ben wasn't interested in dealing with the wrath of mom.

"Any plans for your day?" Ben asked Kendall when they'd finished up their breakfast.

"I'm not sure, but if I head out somewhere, I'll be back home by four, which should give me plenty of time to get ready," Kendall said, sipping at her second cup of coffee.

"Great. I should be home around that time, too. I'll see you later then." He kissed her lips before he shrugged into his winter jacket and headed out the back door.

The morning passed in a blur of meetings with various site managers, followed by a business lunch at the Brawling Bear Bar and Grill that dragged on longer than planned. Ben leaned back in his chair and eyed the man across from him, Tony Maxwell, a potential client he'd been working with over the past month.

"I have to admit, Tony, I think your idea for a year-round entertainment complex is brilliant."

"I can't take the credit. After waiting for years to purchase another resort on Golden Cougar Lake, my dad decided to pursue another route to enlarge the family business. He announced that he intended to build a hotel with a restaurant." Tony chuckled, shaking his head at some distant memory. "But you know my sister. She sank her teeth into the idea, and before my dad could take another breath, we had a one hundred eighty-seven thousand square foot entertainment complex, complete with a hotel, two restaurants, and a variety of shops run by local artisans along with a themed indoor water park, an indoor mini-golf course and a three-screen movie theater. Conveniently located right off the state highway."

Ben laughed. "She's the visionary in the family, huh?"

Tony grunted. "She likes to think so."

"Montgomery Construction wants this project. We believe it'll draw tourists to Krysset year-round, which will be a huge boon for this town's economy."

"Both my dad and I believe this development will rival those in Wisconsin Dells, and we hope to draw some of their winter business to Krysset. It's a strategic and prudent business decision."

"Tony, I hope you'll consider the bid and call me with your approval to go ahead on the project." Ben stood, reaching to shake the man's hand, confident that his offer was competitive and that he'd sold the project. Besides, who else in the eight-county area had the connections that Montgomery Construction had?

"You'll be hearing from me."

"Excellent. We'll be speaking soon, then." Ben exuded confidence, the best way to conclude a business deal. Once Tony Maxwell had exited, Ben grabbed the cushioned black folder containing his luncheon tab and walked up to the front of the bar to chat with Cam.

"Business lunch?" Cam asked.

"A huge project if it goes through. Not only would Montgomery Construction profit in the short run, but the town of Krysset would benefit in the long run."

"I guess business is good then. How's our birthday girl?" Cam beamed when he mentioned his cousin.

"I'm taking Kendall to Ferris Steakhouse for dinner, and then we'll stop by. That's still the plan, right?"

Cam nodded. "I've been quietly spreading the word that it's her birthday, and people should stop by between eight and ten. Jackson and Sophie, Danielle, your mom and dad, and a few other folks from around town that wanted to wish her well. I ordered a couple sheet cakes."

Ben laughed, passing Cam the check presenter and his credit card. "How much cake do you expect Kendall to eat?"

"It's Friday night, and Jackson's singing."

Ben held up his hand to indicate he'd heard enough. "Say no more. I get it. The guy is my best friend, and until Sophie, I benefitted from his abilities to vocally charm the opposite sex."

Rolling his eyes, Cam swiped Ben's credit card through the machine. "I don't even want to think of you with all his extras now that you're with Kendall."

"Yeah, probably for the best." Ben signed the receipt Cam handed him and changed topics. "How did Kendall's first night on the job go? She sounded excited about it."

"She was great. It was fairly slow, so that gave her time to get her bearings and visit with people. Lots of folks introduced themselves. Even Sue Walsh."

"Really?" Ben cringed at the name. "Was Kendall okay with that?"

"Of course."

"What's that supposed to mean? I hate seeing the Prescotts around town. Especially Mary Sue."

"Sue. It's Sue now. And they keep to themselves, so I leave them be." Cam sighed. "They all deserve a new life, man. It was my family that was destroyed, but what Ryan put his family through sucked. They were convicted in the court of public opinion and exiled in their own town, all for something they didn't do. I don't hold it against them."

Ben gaped at the giant of a man behind the bar and then shook his head. "What the hell, dude? You're usually an overprotective ogre. And now you have this pansy-ass attitude over Sue Walsh. I don't get it. You seem completely detached about the fact that Kendall and Ryan Prescott's bitter older sister just came face-to-face after all that nasty shit she spouted at the trial. What happened to Cameron Aasgaard—the great protector and guardian of all? Why the hell aren't you freaked out?"

The big guy just gave a callous lift of his shoulders. "I don't hold it against her." He repeated his earlier excuse.

One thing Ben knew for certain, Cam was right about Ryan Prescott. The guy had put his parents and older sister through the wringer all those years ago. For any parent to suffer through the pain and humiliation after their child brutally murdered four people was unthinkable. Unfortunately, Mary Sue had compounded the horrific situation by spouting her own brand of hatred and slinging a fair amount of slander to muddy the waters.

"I remember Mary Sue being ornery about her baby brother going to jail," Ben said. "She blamed the entire event on the Aasgaard family. I remember her rant being completely ludicrous. A cover-up of some sort. Planting ideas in the mind of an impressionable child. Manipulating a child to testify against an upstanding young man. God, everyone knew Ryan was a low-end drug dealer who couldn't keep his hands off the merchandise."

Ben hadn't spent many brain cells pondering Ryan's parents and how they'd managed during that time or since. Mary Sue's hateful words had raged for all to hear daily, forcing Ben to tune out as much as possible. He and his own parents had attended the trial and waited with Cam and three of his brothers, Dalton, Finn, and Graham, for the final verdict to come down. And then Mary Sue had left town.

Too bad she hadn't just stayed gone.

"Hell, you're a better person than I am. Mostly I don't think about it," Ben finally said with a small grunt.

"Maybe you should."

"Why?"

"Lots of baggage to haul around. Why not cope with it and move on?"

Ben grunted again, tired of hearing those words. But what if Cam was right? Maybe if Ben dealt with his feelings, events like the little run-in with Sue Walsh outside the restroom wouldn't bother him so much. Maybe he wouldn't be so annoyed when he saw her around town—at the park or café or gym. Perhaps he'd even be able to forget. Just like Cam had.

CHAPTER 36

Kendall found things to keep her busy all morning, but by lunchtime she was mind-numbingly bored. Working the evening shift at the bar was probably not going to be the solution long term. She needed to work while Ben worked, or she was going to die of boredom.

After she had a bite to eat, she settled into Ben's media room to watch one of the few romantic comedies he owned. She'd seen it several times, but it was a good one that would hold her attention for a little bit while she painted her nails. Kendall didn't make it to the end of the movie before she opted to take a relaxing soak in Ben's large bathtub.

Except, her brain raced rather than relaxed, so soaking meant thinking.

Nick refused to take responsibility for the threats or the construction accidents, which everyone was certain he'd been causing. She didn't believe Nick's story for a moment. The guy might be a complete asshole, but using only cash had been smart. There was no trail of him anywhere between here and Oregon. Not a single slip-up. Although, from what she'd heard from Ben and Cam, she had nothing to worry about, because Nick wouldn't be getting out of jail anytime soon.

Unfortunately, there was this tiny corner of her brain that wouldn't stop asking, *"What if there's someone else?"* But who? Who else would want to run her out of town? The only person who'd been unhappy about her being in Krysset was Cam. But only in the beginning. Since then, they'd patched things up, and now, Cam seemed genuinely pleased that she was here. Besides, if he really wanted her to leave town, he'd get all bossy and demanding. He'd never threaten to kill her.

With all the mental gyrations, there'd be no relaxing today. Kendall climbed out of the tub, wrapped one towel around her body, cinching it just above her breasts, and then grabbed a second towel to contain her dripping hair. After rubbing lotion on her arms and legs, she exited Ben's bathroom and padded down the hallway toward the guest bedroom she'd appropriated. When she passed the top of the staircase, she heard the back door click closed.

Kendall smiled to herself. Maybe Ben had managed to duck out of work a little early this afternoon to surprise her for her birthday. That would be just like him to plan something special. She quickly stepped into her room, tugged the towel from around her head, and worked a pick through her hair.

She stifled the little giggle that threatened to bubble out. She felt powerfully wicked at the thought of tempting Ben in nothing but a towel. The guy would go wild, which just about guaranteed her a round of sex somewhere in the kitchen.

Sex on the kitchen table would definitely break up the monotony of the day.

Hoping to catch Ben by surprise, Kendall tiptoed down the stairs. At each step, she was certain that a loud creaking noise would give her away, but each tread was quiet. Come to think about it, there wasn't any sound coming from downstairs at all. If Ben hadn't come in, what had she heard? She was certain it had been the sound of the back door clicking closed. But then again, maybe it was only wishful thinking.

Pausing at the bottom of the steps, Kendall listened for Ben in the kitchen or maybe in his home office. But the house stood eerily quiet. "Ben?" Tentatively she made her way through the entry into the casual dining space. "Huh?" What had she heard? Kendall took a few more steps and then peeked into the mudroom on the right. No Ben.

She laughed at herself. Damn, but Ben had spoiled her with his attention over the past week. Now she just expected him to be here all day long to keep her company. Taking comfort in the fact that it'd only be an hour or so longer before he came home, and then they'd have the entire weekend to spend together, she turned to go back up to her room.

But before she could move, an arm snaked around her neck. The sudden and violent action startled her. Panic coursed through her veins. Kendall tried to scream. It was weak and would never attract attention outside the house.

Nick had escaped.

He'd come back to get her. And this time, he'd kill her. Guaranteed. If her frenzied heartbeat didn't kill her first.

With both hands, she tugged at the unyielding vise cutting off her air supply, hoping to dislodge it. Or at the very least, loosen it enough to draw in a deep breath. But the arm she connected with wasn't the arm she'd expected. Her brain stumbled over the incongruent signals her body sent.

Confused, her world tilted on its axis. Reality and nightmare collided.

The appendage she gripped was that of a slender woman.

The body pressed against her back nothing like Nick's hard muscular chest.

Who? Someone with a lot of upper body strength, because whoever it was, was dragging her away from the mudroom door, around the dining table, and into the corner of the kitchen. She tried to fight, but all she could do was stumble backward.

"Bet you don't even know who I am," a hateful voice taunted into her ear.

CHAPTER 37

Kendall's heart pounded so loud she could barely hear the taunting words whispered in the snidest tone. *"Bet you don't even know who I am."* Her mind raced with possible answers. None logical. Most sarcastic.

Kendall caught her own panicked reflection in the glass of the china hutch across the room. And the rage-warped expression of the woman behind her.

"Sue?" Her frightened tone was no more than a squeak. What the hell was she doing here? Kendall fought the arm that pressed against her throat.

Last time she'd been attacked, Nick had overpowered her with little trouble, but that shouldn't be the case now. Kendall should be able to best a woman who'd given birth six times, for heaven's sake. The woman ought to be hauling kids to hockey practice or piano lessons. She ought to be at home baking cookies or shoe shopping for her horde of children. At the very least, she ought to be exhausted.

"Of course, the simple answer. Like always, you're so wrapped up in yourself that you pay no attention to what's going on around you." Sue's arm squeezed as if to punctuate her statement with a little physical punishment.

Kendall tugged at Sue's forearm, leaning back to lessen the strangled feeling of the limb wrenched around her throat. The entire position put Kendall at a disadvantage, throwing off her center of balance.

"Who?" She had no idea. The violent struggle and the lack of air were not conducive to deep contemplation.

"Come on, Kendall. We've met before."

Kendall remained silent, unwilling to waste any more oxygen on words. A flicker of doubt raced through her mind before she could squash it. The odds of this ending well were shrinking.

Her only hope—Ben. In due time, he'd return home. In all likelihood, too late, but her body would be discovered. And he might even help the officials put the pieces together. But who would guess that Sue was responsible?

"You were a foolish eight-year-old who sent the wrong man to prison. You gave the simple answer then, too." Her volume increased while cynicism dripped from her words. "Blame the man who escaped with his life. Someone overpowered Ryan. But when he regained consciousness, the real killer had already vanished, leaving an innocent man to take the fall. I'll admit Ryan used, but he told me the truth. Someone else was in your house that night, and Ryan was too high to fight them off. But you accused him anyway."

Kendall shook her head. Puzzle-piece memories hurtled through her mind in a jumble of disjointed thoughts: Ryan slicing his knife through the air, connecting with Jenna's throat. A red spray of liquid splashing the front of his shirt and dripping down the wall. His bloody hands raking through his disheveled hair when he leaned over her sister, watching the blood stream from Jenna's body. The hysterical, insolent noise spouting from his grinning lips as he tossed his head back and laughed. And in each snippet of memory, Ryan Prescott's maniacal face remained front and center.

"And all of Wahnata County believed you, because you're a member of the honorable, invincible, delightful Aasgaard family. You think you're above the law, don't you?"

"No. You're wrong," Kendall whispered. The hold around her neck had loosened to allow oxygen into her lungs. The iron grip was surprisingly strong for a woman.

"Do you know who I am now?" Sue repeated the question

"Mary Sue," Kendall said, not disguising the fear in her voice. Perhaps Ben would return home before four o'clock.

"Because of your lies, Ryan died in prison. You. All dolled up in a frilly dress with shiny Mary Jane's and lacy anklets, your hair in two long braids looking like pure innocence. No wonder the jury believed your pathetic story. You put him behind bars, bitch."

"He killed my family." Maybe she could buy some time for Ben to arrive. Could she talk like this for more than an hour? Probably not.

"Lies. Lies. All lies!" Sue screamed, her voice rising to a shrill, uncontrolled tone.

Kendall decided less was more at the moment, so she pinched her lips closed, refusing to refute Sue's words.

"Did you know my brother died on his twenty-fifth birthday?" Sue paused as if waiting for a response but jerked her arm tight against Kendall's airway, not giving her an opportunity to answer. "No. Probably not. All the same, you're at fault. You might as well have jammed the shiv into his back yourself. He bled out on the floor. Alone."

Kendall shook her head frantically, yanking at the arm that strangled her, unable to squeak out a single word. She should've screamed for help when she'd had the chance. She should've fought as if her life hung in the balance from the second the arm had snaked around her neck. Now she knew. Death was a serious possibility.

Here.

Today.

Alone.

The knowledge gave her a surge of strength, and she tugged harder to free herself.

"You took his life. And now I'm going to take yours."

A searing pain pierced through Kendall's right side. With a whoosh, her lungs emptied. Her knees buckled beneath her, and she sagged against the arm holding her upright. A warm gush of liquid dampened her side. A hot burning sensation followed by a second intense stab. Pain blasted into her.

Sue released her hold. Kendall dropped to her knees, and then her face thudded onto the tile floor. Black spots formed in front of her eyes even though the bright sunlight poured through the windows. She fought to hold on to consciousness, but the room around her blurred. Somehow, she knew death had found her.

A flurry of movement. Followed by the swish and click of the closing door.

Alone.

On the floor with her cheek pressed against the hard tile, Kendall's mind jumbled and swirled while she struggled to remain conscious. Sue Walsh was really Mary Sue Prescott. At the bar the other night, the older woman had seemed familiar, but beyond that, Kendall would've never recognized her as Ryan's big sister. Just like all those years ago at the trial, Sue accused Kendall of lying to send Ryan Prescott to prison. Which wasn't true at all. Why wouldn't Sue believe her?

Kendall knew she had to contain her rambling thoughts and act before she lost too much blood. A strong possibility. She'd lost her towel somewhere along the battle, so when she reached behind her to where the pain originated, her fingers slid along her skin. Wet. Thick. Slippery. She drew her hand back, and it was covered in blood.

How long did it take to die from a stab wound? She had no idea. A more urgent concern, however, seemed to be her inability to draw in a full breath of air, even without the arm of steel constricting her airway. The entire process of breathing hurt like hell. If it wasn't a necessary evil, she'd stop right now. But in this predicament, she needed to do more than just breathe in and out. She needed to get her sorry ass off the floor and dial 911. She needed help. She needed Ben.

She was certain each arm weighed a couple tons when she struggled to drag them upward to prop them under her body and push herself up onto her knees. Standing wasn't happening, but maybe if she could crawl, she'd have a chance at getting to her cell phone. With a rush of adrenaline, she maximized the small dose of extra energy and pushed her arms underneath her. The dead weight of her torso felt like lifting a boulder, heavy and immovable.

Even through her pain-filled haze, Kendall recognized the seriousness of the situation. She had to make the move now, or she might die. Here. Alone on the floor in Ben's kitchen.

Using every ounce of strength she possessed, she forced herself to her hands and knees. Her cell phone was inside her purse, which she'd left dangling on the back of the chair on the far side of the table. She could see it from where she was. Now she just needed to get to it. She shifted her palms an inch forward and then her knees. And then another. And then again.

She could do this, she cheered herself on. She could save herself. With a glance down at the floor beneath her, she knew she had little choice, or she wouldn't live. Blood dripped onto the cold tile floor with a splat, one fat drop falling into the next, leaving a growing puddle of her precious life source.

The progress was slow, and each time Kendall sucked in air, a wheezing sound whistled from her mouth. Her achy arms shook from exertion. And the red pool beneath her expanded one droplet at a time, seeming to grow at an alarming rate. She'd moved almost three feet when her arms gave out, and she collapsed onto the floor again. The warm liquid squished beneath her, sticky against her skin.

The reality of the situation slowly seeped into her awareness. She'd never make it to the table to reach her cell phone. There was no way for her to call Ben. Or Cam. Or anyone else who might help.

Tears of frustration and disappointment slid across the bridge of her nose and dripped onto the floor faster than she could blink them away. She'd cheated death sixteen years ago when she'd hidden from Ryan Prescott while he'd slaughtered her family. He'd sliced each of their throats, and they'd all bled out. Each in a different room of the house. Each alone in their silent suffering during the final moments of their lives.

But Fate had planned that Kendall would die in the same vicious, violent way. Now it was her turn. Murdered. Not by the same man who'd killed her family, but by his older sister who sought revenge for his death behind bars.

Oh how different life might've been if her brother, Carson, hadn't been introduced to drugs. If he and Cam's little brother, Everett, had steered clear of Ryan Prescott. If her parents had handled Carson with a firm hand and kicked him out of the house or sent him to rehab.

Now Kendall, too, would die.

Alone.

Her darkest nightmares come to life.

CHAPTER 38

Ben was late.

He'd planned to be home almost thirty minutes ago. But like the rest of his day, this last meeting, a conference call, had stretched beyond its scheduled end time with no easy way to politely wrap it up. Once it was over, he'd rushed out of the office with his cell phone in his fist. He glanced at the screen as he raced down the stairs. Nothing from Kendall, but his mom had called three times.

Ben punched the speed dial for Kendall and waited while her phone rang to voicemail. "Hey, Kendall. I'm running behind. I have one quick stop to make, and then I'll be home." He hit the end button and pocketed his phone. It was odd that she hadn't picked up, and she hadn't responded to his text an hour ago either. Napping wasn't really her thing, but perhaps she was just preparing for their night out and had left her phone in the kitchen.

Ben sprinted across the parking lot to his truck. He'd just gotten into the driver's seat when his cell phone chimed, indicating an incoming call. Kendall. It had been hours since he'd talked to her. "Darling, how are you?"

"I'm very good, Benjamin, but you can call me mom," his mother said. He could hear the smile in her voice.

"Hi, Mom. I thought it was Kendall." He shoved aside the touch of embarrassment. No sense in hiding, because his parents knew him too well. He started the engine and backed out of the parking spot. "Sorry to be rude, but I'm in a bit of a hurry."

"Oh, that's okay. I won't keep you long. I've actually tried to call you multiple times, but your phone just kept rolling to voicemail."

"What do you need, Mom?" he asked, his impatience showing in his voice. But she really would talk his ear off if he let her.

"I was in town this afternoon, and I don't mean to be nosy, but..."

"Spill it, Mom."

"I saw Sue Walsh coming out of your house."

"Sue? Why would she be there? I don't even like the woman."

"I know. And it seemed a bit off. She didn't exit like a guest, you know. She turned and tugged the door closed, and then she tested it to make sure it had locked. Like she owned the place. It's been bugging me, so I just wanted you to know."

"Thanks, Mom. I've got to go." He went to disconnect and then backpedaled. "Hey, Mom, what time was that?"

"About an hour ago."

Ben's mind raced in a thousand directions at once while he struggled to formulate a cohesive thought. Mary Sue or just Sue, didn't matter to him, she was still the same person. And he wasn't on friendly terms with her. Cam said that she'd been at the bar when Kendall had worked, but Kendall hadn't mentioned anything to him. Perhaps Kendall had invited Sue over, but he just couldn't wrap his head around that. A wave of panic seized Ben's heart. This could be nothing, or it could be something huge. He needed to get back home to Kendall.

Ben hit the blinker with more force than necessary and turned out of the parking lot. That was the last rule of the road he followed as he sped toward downtown Krysset and Kendall. Two miles stretched on like two hundred even though Ben broke every speed limit in his path. The uneasy feeling in the pit of Ben's stomach worsened as he passed the *Welcome to Krysset* sign at the edge of town. He couldn't shake the sensation that something was wrong.

Ben whipped onto his street, slowing enough to ensure all four wheels remained in contact with the pavement. He made a sharp turn into his driveway and slammed the truck into park. Racing to the door, he hoped that Kendall would be happily preparing for her birthday dinner out.

Ben barreled through the back door. "Kendall!" Nothing but silence. He raced into the dining room, but Kendall wasn't there or in the kitchen. Ben headed toward the front of the house, but his peripheral vision caught something, halting him in his tracks. Horror gripped his heart, and his knees tried to buckle on him.

Kendall. On the floor near the table. Unmoving.

Bright red stained the fair skin on her back and smudged her ashen face and hands.

With a punch of adrenaline, Ben lunged forward to kneel beside her lifeless body. He had no idea why she wasn't wearing any clothing, but he grabbed for the discarded bath towel near her feet and pressed it firmly on Kendall's wounded back.

"Oww." Kendall's soft moan was the sweetest sound he'd ever heard. She was alive.

"I've got you, darling," he said close to her ear as he tugged his phone from his pocket and dialed 911.

"This is 911. What's your emergency?"

"This is Ben Montgomery. I need an ambulance at my house." He rattled off his street address, punched the speakerphone button, and then set it aside without disconnecting the call.

"Kendall. The ambulance is on the way. It's going to be okay." He brushed her hair back from her face. Her skin was cold to the touch. Ben wanted to pick her up and hold her against his body to warm her, but instead he slipped his jacket from his arms and draped it over her torso. Whipping his old flannel shirt over his head instead of unbuttoning it, he covered her legs.

"Ben?"

His heart broke at the pain in her voice, and he choked on his own sob. "Yeah, darling, it's me. I'm right here."

"Good." Her weak voice hardly broke the silence of the room.

"You're going to be okay. I've got you." His useless reassurance seemed like too little too late. Where had he been when she'd needed him?

"Hate being alone."

"I know. I've got you, and I'm never going to leave you. I love you." The declaration of love bubbled right out of his mouth as if he'd been saying those words forever. They felt right. Damned perfect, actually. Why had he waited this long? He'd behaved like some idiot afraid of commitment or afraid of his own feelings, waiting until now, the moment when he feared he might lose her.

He shoved the thought from his mind. Kendall would be okay. "I love you, Kendall."

Ben applied pressure to the wound with one hand, using the other to stroke her long hair away from her beautiful face. His caress across her forehead lessened the anguish that pinched her expression. Most likely the human contact alone comforted her. He wasn't fool enough to believe that he eased the horrific pain she must be suffering from a gunshot wound. Or a knife stab. He wasn't sure which, and he had no intention of easing up on the pressure to figure it out.

She moaned and her eyelids flickered open and closed in an effort to remain conscious. Right now she lay on her stomach with one cheek pressed to the hard tile floor and her arms stretched above her head as if she'd collapsed in the effort to drag herself from the place of the brutal attack toward the table. A dark trail of smeared blood marked her path and the growing puddle on her right side completed a bloody exclamation point. She'd obviously lost a great deal of blood, but it was her labored breathing that concerned him.

God, would Sue Walsh really hurt Kendall like this?

"I'm right here. Can you tell me who hurt you, Kendall?" Ben whispered near her ear. Had Sue Walsh actually come into his house and attacked Kendall with the hope of killing her? It seemed crazy. What would she have to gain?

"Sue. Ryan's sister." Her words came out breathy in a pained whisper, and he knew each word she spoke came at a tremendous cost.

The wail of the approaching first responders gained volume, and he stroked his hand over her hair, brushing it back from her face. "God, I'm sorry, Kendall. I should've been here earlier. The ambulance is on its way. If you listen real hard, you can hear the sirens."

The tender sensation of love that filled his heart just about destroyed him. He hadn't felt this emotion for so long that he'd often wondered if his heart hadn't broken beyond repair sixteen years ago. He traced his finger across the pale skin of her cheek. It was smudged with blood, and she looked incredibly fragile right now. But his Kendall was beautiful and strong, and she'd been through more in her short lifetime than anyone should be forced to bear.

If anyone else had suffered through the endless hell of pain and grief that Kendall had endured, they'd never believe that loving, thoughtful, and selfless people existed in the world. And yet through all the violence directed into her life, Kendall had survived. She had a bold and carefree attitude, she tried to live each day to the fullest, and above all she sought out the best in each person she met.

"Hang on a little longer, Kendall."

"Don't want to die alone." The words whispered out, the pain of speaking those few words caused deep lines across her forehead.

"Whoa. You're not alone, and no one's dying today. You got that?" With his hand pressed against the wound on her lower back, he noted her shallow, labored breaths along with the wheezing inhales and exhales each time she struggled to fill her lungs with oxygen.

"Kendall. Are you with me?" At his prompting, her eyelids opened but fluttered closed again. "You're not alone, and I promise you, you'll never be alone again. I love you, Kendall."

CHAPTER 39

Beep. Beep. Beep. The monotonous sound reassured Ben that Kendall had survived. The doctors had confirmed as much a couple hours ago. He grabbed her icy cold hand and watched her chest rise and fall along with the annoying beeping.

Dear Lord, he'd almost lost her today. He forced that horrific thought from his mind, a mental action he knew he'd perform a million times in the next day or two. But if he allowed his brain to wander down dark and grisly paths, playing out all the other less than positive outcomes, he'd go crazy before the night was over. He needed to stay in the here and now, focused on Kendall and her recovery.

"I'll turn the volume down." He glanced up into the excessively cheerful face of Nurse Maggie. Or Megan. He couldn't remember and didn't care. "You don't need to listen to that incessant noise any longer. You know, the doctors say she'll make a full recovery, but she probably won't grace you with her twinkling eyes or bright smile for another four to six hours. Maybe more. You're welcome to rest in the recliner if you'd like. I'll bring you a pillow and a blanket. And if you need something to drink, coffee, tea, soda, water, it's all around the corner to your left. If she wakes up and you'd like to call me, push the button on her bed." Talk about incessant noise. Ben nodded, but nothing more.

He turned his attention back to Kendall, tucking her arms under the blankets and grabbing for another blanket to drape over her body. She looked tiny and fragile lying in the bed. Her face was still pale, nearly translucent. The nurse had assured him—with an overexuberant amount of words—that Kendall's color would return to normal in a day or two. He knew he'd feel a hell of a lot better when she opened her eyes and whispered his name.

Ben glanced up at the clock. Almost midnight. Less than an hour left of her birthday. He snaked his hand under the covers to clasp her chilled fingers, willing the heat from his own body to seep into hers. He needed this time with her, a few moments alone before her cousin returned to the room.

He'd hoped to make her birthday a memorable night. It definitely fell into the unforgettable category. Like the kind of memory permanently etched into the brain, the kind that could never be removed no matter how much bleach was poured across it. The image of Kendall's unmoving body, covered in blood, would forever be imprinted in his mind.

But the surgeon who'd patched her up had insisted she'd be okay. Ben clung to that memory, too. Along with the other kinder, gentler memories of the evening. Like his mom and dad rushing into the waiting room. Tears had streamed down his mom's face while emotions glimmered in his dad's brown eyes. Together their loving embrace engulfed him in a huge group hug he'd never forget.

Jackson and Sophie had arrived shortly afterward with the baby in tow. Ryleigh Lynn had stretched her arms out wide, asking Ben to take her, and then he swore she'd said, "Unka Ben" when she'd cuddled against him. Within moments, Jackson's dad, Ted, and his lady friend, Lydia, had arrived to collect the little one, leaving Jackson and Sophie free to remain at the hospital with Ben while he waited for word on Kendall's condition.

Sitting with Jackson in that waiting room had brought back memories of a time not long ago when Sophie had been fighting for her life, and Ben had gone to support a distraught Jackson. Today, the three of them had sat in companionable silence on the sofa, Sophie on one end and Jackson on the other with Ben sandwiched in the middle. Ben hadn't bothered to hide his emotions from his best friend. They'd been through too much together to be shy about that kind of crap. Jackson's presence during the tense, long hours of Kendall's surgery had comforted him more than any other.

However, Cam's arrival had been the most poignant. As always when dealing with his little cousin, Cam's surprisingly candid behavior contrasted with his usual harsh demeanor.

Ben had traveled by ambulance with Kendall to the hospital, and while she'd been whisked off to God only knew where, he'd been relegated to the emergency room waiting area. Cameron, a man known to be difficult in the best of circumstances, plowed through the doors, roaring like a madman and demanding to speak to the doctor treating Kendall.

"Cam," Ben shouted to get his attention, and Cam turned toward his name.

Ben stood, his body shaking from the earlier adrenaline rush, dressed in a white thermal long-sleeve shirt with dark red bloodstains smudged on the sleeves and smeared across the front from when he'd tended to Kendall before help had arrived. His faded blue jeans had fared no better. In five seconds flat, Cam's face went from blow-a-gasket red to weaving-on-his-feet white, his angry tirade washed away and replaced by mind-numbing, fear-induced panic.

"Oh hell, Ben. Tell me she's alive." Tears gathered in the man's blue eyes. They lacked their common icy glare, but instead possessed the warmth of love and worry any concerned parent would hold toward their child. Like the other touching scenes Ben had been privy to involving Cameron and his cousin Kendall, the man held nothing back.

"She's alive. They're stabilizing her and prepping for surgery."

Cam sunk into the nearest chair, and Ben found one nearby in the empty room.

Cam leaned forward, resting his elbows on his knees and burying his face in his hands. His entire body shook from a release of emotions, and when he lifted his head, unconcerned about the wetness on his cheeks, he said. "I can't lose her, too, Ben. She's all I have left."

After that brief show of emotions, Cam had pulled himself together and had returned to his usual gruffness. And now that

Kendall had come out of surgery and looked as if she'd make a full recovery, the big oaf had gone in search of food, no doubt stalking the halls of the hospital like an angry mountain lion.

While they'd waited, Cam had admitted that he blamed himself for the attack on Kendall, because he'd trusted Sue Walsh and had believed that she no longer held a grudge. And while he and Kendall had discussed Sue's presence in town, Cam feared that Kendall hadn't connected the name with the face when she'd served Sue at the Brawling Bear a few nights prior, leaving her unprepared.

Of course, news of Kendall's attack and Sue Walsh's arrest had spread through town like wildfire. So over the past seven hours, Ben had visited with a wide range of folks within the hospital walls who all voiced their shock over Sue's actions. None had suspected that she'd behave in such a violent manner. And like Cam, all had felt inclined to live and let live.

Ben, on the other hand, felt like an ostrich with his head buried in the sand. Oh, he'd known who she was and had always suspected she was still angry over the fact that her brother had been sent to prison. But Ben had flat-out ignored her when he should've been paying close attention to her actions. His apathy left him with a hearty dose of self-loathing and guilt. He figured that between him and Cam, they had the full gamut of self-recrimination covered.

"I'm sorry, Kendall," he said in just a whisper. "I should've been there to protect you." The stark realization broke him. Too similar. Too unimaginable to bear. A flashback to a past decade, a past love.

Had cruel and merciless Fate expected him to pick up the pieces a second time around? Another loved one lost, yanked from this earth by a brutal murderer? Fate should know a man's heart could only take so much. Ben would've never moved on or gotten over another personal tragedy of this nature. He shuddered at the morbid thought and gave Kendall's hand a gentle squeeze.

Tears pricked at the back of his eyes, and he swallowed around the rock-like lump that formed in his throat.

Overwhelming pressure built within his chest nearly choking him, but like a warrior he fought against the wretched pain. Stoically, he held back the emotions of sorrow mixed with profound relief.

Until a guttural sob burst from his lips.

Then, as if an explosion had struck the bedrock of his fortitude, shattering his fragile control, a tear slipped from his eye. Followed by another. And then another.

Adrift in the sea of emotions, Ben allowed the sixteen years of bottled up grief to pour free at the same time he rejoiced, thankful for his second chance with Kendall.

Alone, huddled near her bed, Ben granted himself permission for a moment of sadness, complete with an embarrassing display of tears. But after he cried himself out, he lingered in quiet reflection, grateful for the incredible gift he'd received in his friendship with Kendall.

He'd almost lost her. Not once, but twice. This blond-haired, blue-eyed beauty. The one who'd crept into his home and life, stealing his heart without warning.

No. She'd given him ample warning of her intentions, and she hadn't stolen it. Kendall had jump-started it in a way he'd never known possible. A heart he wasn't even sure he still possessed.

And tonight she'd almost died. The woman he loved.

The thought sent a fierce pain through his chest in the region of his now-beating heart. He loved Kendall. While he had suspected that he was falling in love, he'd foolishly refused to speak of it, process it, or acknowledge it. But slammed with the real possibility of losing her, his heart had twisted in agony, allowing those emotions to pour right out.

And damn, it felt good.

He loved Kendall. With his entire, functioning heart. And he planned to prove it to her each day for the rest of their lives.

Kendall was special. The kind of woman a man grabbed hold of and kept for all time. She'd pulled his sorry ass out of the deep rut he'd been wallowing in and set him back on the path to life. Kendall's harsh words had been right when she'd insisted that

Jenna would've hated the man he'd become. The bitter allegation had hurt, especially coming from her little sister, but truer words had never been spoken, and they'd provided him with the long overdue, swift kick he'd needed.

A part of Ben wished Kendall had come back to Krysset sooner, or maybe, had never left. But then their relationship might never have made it to this juncture. No. The timing had been perfect for Kendall to arrive on the scene.

He gazed at the flashing lights of the now-silent machinery, and a gentle sense of peace washed over him. He loved Kendall beyond reason and couldn't bear to live without her. And rather than fighting the feelings a moment longer, he accepted them.

Ben smiled, stroking the hair back from her face, wondering how she'd ever managed to turn his life around like this. "I love you, Kendall."

CHAPTER 40

"I love you, Kendall." Although she'd lost count, it seemed Ben had spoken those same four words to her more than a thousand times over the past three weeks. As she'd surfed in and out of her drug-induced fog while he lingered by her hospital bed. As he'd helped her walk to the bathroom. As he'd tugged her fuzzy pink slippers onto her feet, which had seemed a hundred miles away from her outstretched hands. Even as he'd helped pull her shirt over her head.

Sheesh, talk about helpless.

And through it all, Ben had approached the most mundane of tasks with the patience of a saint and the gentleness of a skilled nurse. His kindness and attentiveness had been punctuated with words of love and adoration the entire time she'd recouped from her stab wounds. She still had weeks to go before she'd be back to one hundred percent, but she'd been discharged from the hospital and now moved around unassisted, albeit slowly.

She'd been lucky. The doctors had informed her of that morbid fact multiple times. The ice pick, Sue Walsh's weapon of choice, had punctured her right lung on the first stab and had merely hit flesh on the second stab. Any further south and her kidney would've been compromised, changing the entire scenario and maybe even the blissfully positive outcome called being alive.

So yeah, she considered herself lucky, too.

Even after all these weeks, the fact that Mary Sue Prescott had come close enough to do damage sent an arctic shudder through Kendall's body each time she thought about it. It seemed that the news of Kendall's arrival in town had stirred Mary Sue's deep feelings of resentment again, uncovering the rage that lay buried for years. Hearing that Kendall would be celebrating her twenty-fifth birthday had been the catalyst that caused Sue to snap—without a single thought for her husband or six children.

The woman had been arrested and held without bail. But keeping with the rant-inspired persona that Mary Sue Prescott had mastered, Sue Walsh boldly professed to planning each vengeful act and stabbing Kendall. The woman was responsible for the threatening notes on Kendall's windshield and Ben's back door, as well as all the random acts of vandalism directed at Ben and Montgomery Construction. After she'd confessed, she'd quickly been sentenced and moved to the women's prison facility in the Twin Cities.

"I love you, Kendall." The beautiful words fell from Ben's lips again, dragging her back to the present and spurring her heart to beat a little faster. He gifted her with the words of his love over and over, and like a starved baby bird, she greedily ate it all up.

Together, they'd found a common ground—her sister, Jenna. At Cam's suggestion, they'd redefined their mutual loss as the common thread that bound them together forever, a cornerstone to build their relationship upon.

Kendall fingered the diamond pendent around her neck and gazed at Ben. Even in the low lights of the crowded bar his chocolate-colored eyes seemed to dance with happiness while he watched her. He appeared to take great pleasure in helping her celebrate her twenty-fifth birthday in style.

"Thank you again for the necklace. It's beautiful. You didn't need to buy such an extravagant gift." Tears sprung to her eyes again, and she blinked them back. Even happy tears didn't belong on a night like tonight.

"I know I didn't have to. I wanted to. Sorry it's a bit late for a birthday gift, but I'd hoped you'd be well enough to enjoy a full evening of celebrating."

Thus far, it'd been a spectacular evening. They'd shared a quiet dinner at Ferris Steakhouse, complete with the flicker of candlelight on the table between them while quiet music played in the background. Strings of miniature white lights twinkled around the entire restaurant, interwoven with the variegated greens of ivy, the hopeful white puffs of calla lilies, and the sunshine yellow petals of daffodils. All were imported signs of spring in mid-March, but Kendall would take the promise of spring any way she could get it.

Hinting that Cam had planned a birthday surprise for her, Ben had suggested they stop at the Brawling Bear after dinner. Kendall had cringed on the inside, hoping the surprise didn't involve people jumping out from hidden locations, screaming at the top of their lungs. She wasn't sure she'd recovered enough for that much of a jolt. She loved celebrating her birthday, but surprises she could live without. Gritting her teeth, she'd agreed to a short stop at the bar, acknowledging Cam's potential disappointment if she failed to make an appearance.

"Promise me you'll take me home after a little while." Kendall begged when Ben opened the passenger-side door of his truck, helping her down.

"I promise we'll leave after cake. Okay?" His words soothed her uneasiness. Cake as a surprise she could handle.

But Cam's surprise consisted of more than a tiny birthday cake. Nearly everyone she'd met upon her return to Krysset had congregated at the bar along with dozens of people she'd never been introduced to, all prepared to help her celebrate her belated birthday.

Kendall glanced at her cousin behind the long wooden bar. He, too, wore a pleased expression as he gazed her way. From the immense crowd gathered, Cam had done his part to spread the word that they'd be celebrating tonight, although in the small town of Krysset the dissemination of gossip seemed to be effortless, no matter what the topic.

"Kendall, that pendent looks real nice on you. Montgomery managed to pull off a decent gift, huh?" Unaffected by Cam's verbal jab, Ben chuckled while a huge, satisfied grin curved her cousin's lips. Actually, tonight both of their moods appeared downright jovial.

Perched on the end barstool in the front corner of the bar, Kendall surveyed the entire room as the crowd ebbed and flowed around her. More than a hundred people had come out tonight to wish her a happy birthday, and a good portion of them she didn't recognize. But Cam helped her with names and relationships, making the appropriate introductions when necessary. It seemed as if her cousin knew everyone in town, not to mention their significant other, their children, their grandchildren, their coworkers, and pets.

"Happy birthday, Doll." Jackson spoke near her ear, and then he slung his arm around Kendall's shoulders, giving her a small one-armed hug.

Sophie wrapped her into a gentle hug. "Happy birthday! It's nice to see you up and around again," she said. "Maybe we can have lunch out sometime this week."

"I'd like that," Kendall said, agreeing with a smile and a firm nod, certain that the boisterous crowd drowned out her every word.

Ben vacated his barstool, indicating Sophie should take his place. Then, Jackson gave his wife's shoulder a gentle squeeze and kissed her cheek before walking away. Ben wedged himself between her and Sophie while Cam huddled close on her other side with his elbows propped on the shiny surface of the bar. Kendall expected a conversation to ensue, but all eyes were riveted on Jackson's back while he maneuvered his way across the room, down the three steps to the lower level, and then onto the raised dais. He snatched up a microphone stand, adjusted its height, and set it in the center of the stage. Several guys joined him, taking up positions on guitar, keyboard, and drums.

"Attention, people." The crowd hushed when Jackson's deep voice reverberated across the room. "As you all know, we have a birthday girl in our midst tonight." A small cheer went up throughout the bar. Kendall rolled her eyes.

"Well actually, her birthday was three weeks ago, but due to unforeseen circumstances, she wasn't able to hang out with us that night. I think we should invite Kendall to the stage, so we can all sing her a little song. And then I've heard that Cam ordered up three sheet cakes to share. So, please don't leave tonight without having a slice. Come on, Kendall. Ben, why don't you escort her up here?"

Kendall glared at Ben. "You've got to be kidding me."

"Oh, come on, Kendall. You're not shy." Ben prodded, clasping hands with her, and tugging a little on their entwined fingers.

With Ben leading the way, Kendall squeezed through the crowd, responding to the occasional greeting, waving to those who shouted her name. At least cake followed public embarrassment on this evening's agenda, because she'd definitely had enough action for one night. Home, Ben, and then bed sounded mighty appealing at the moment.

Kendall followed Ben down the few steps to the lower dining area, which served as an extension to the main floor, divided only by a combination of railings and half walls. The open floor plan allowed the action on stage to be viewed from anywhere in the establishment. Kendall spotted Ben's parents at a small table in front of the raised platform, and she waved in their direction while Ben led her up the two short steps on the right side of the stage.

"Just a moment, guys," Ben said. He stepped up to the microphone, dragging Kendall front and center. "I need to say a few words to Kendall before we sing 'Happy Birthday.'"

Kendall peeked out over the crowd of happy faces. Ben's words were true. Shy wasn't often an adjective used to describe her. However, standing on stage, with all attention directed her way, wasn't exactly her style either. Kendall averted her eyes, but not before she spotted Cam. He'd followed her and Ben down the steps into the lower dining area and now stood leaning against the railing that divided the upper and lower levels. He wore a small grin that brightened when their eyes met. She held his gaze a moment longer before turning her attention to the man in front of her.

With both of her hands clasped firmly in his, Ben gazed at her as if not another soul existed. And his smile? Well, it wasn't that practiced grin he pasted on for the entire world to see—the one where he looked as if he alone knew the punch line to the world's most hilarious joke. No. That smile, Kendall had learned, had masked years of sorrow, and according to Ben, it had helped him get through some of the darker times. He called it his *fake-it-till-you-make-it* smile.

But the smile he shared with Kendall now appeared somehow different. More relaxed and natural. Like he'd let his guard down and allowed the true Benjamin Montgomery airtime. Slight dimples still showed on his smoothly shaven cheeks, and his eyes still held a spark of playfulness. But an extra flicker of intense, sensual heat, meant for her alone, morphed his standard amused expression. With little effort, his smile resulted in Kendall's knees quivering like jelly while a tingly anxious sensation swirled low in her abdomen.

"Kendall, I made a promise to you on your birthday. Now you might not remember it, but I promised that you would never be alone again. Kendall, I love you."

The weight of every eye in the bar pressed in on her and Ben. Not a single sound broke the thick silence as if they collectively held their breath, waiting for Ben to continue his speech or for her to respond to his words of adoration. Before she opened her mouth to declare her reciprocating love, Ben dropped to one knee. Still clutching both of her hands, he pressed one to his lips.

"Kendall, will you marry me?" Ben released one hand, palming a velvet jeweler's box.

Kendall gasped when he popped the box open, revealing a round solitary diamond set in platinum. The simple setting held an enormous diamond, larger than she'd ever dreamed of, which perfectly matched the pendent he'd given her earlier in the evening as a birthday gift.

Tiny spots twinkled in front of her eyes. Tightness gripped her chest. Dizziness twisted on the edges of her brain. Breathe. Releasing a loud rush of air that she'd been holding since Ben had dropped to one knee, she sucked in a lungful of oxygen. She darted a glance around the room at the sea of faces. It seemed as if everyone held their breath with her, caught up in the excitement of the moment.

With a quick scan of the crowd, she glimpsed Ben's parents almost right in front of where she stood. Ben's mom's trembling fingers pressed against her lips and tears glimmered in her eyes as she waited on Kendall's reply. Kendall gazed down into Ben's upturned face where he knelt before her. He, too, waited on her answer.

"Are you asking me to marry you?" Kendall asked. Ben chuckled at her sincere question while a hushed rumble of laughter rolled through the room. "Oh, I mean, yes. If that's the question, yes. Yes, I'll marry you, Ben." She threw her arms around his neck and kissed him. The bar broke out into a chorus of cheers and applause.

And then Ben pulled back to slip the extravagant ring on her finger. "I love you, Kendall." He mouthed over the roar of the excited crowd.

"I love you, too." Kendall's words were drowned out by the down beat of the band as Jackson led an energetic version of "Happy Birthday."

Cam's booming voice rang above the multitude, drawing Kendall's attention. His lips curled into a genuine heartfelt smile. Even his eyes shown bright and clear just like the brilliant azure sky on a spring day, promising new beginnings. Something Cam deserved as much as she and Ben did.

A commotion out of the corner of her eye caught her attention. Ethan and Dani wheeled a metal cart up the short ramp between the kitchen door and the stage. On top of the cart sat a huge rectangular cake, decorated in bold pink flowers and a rainbow of colored sprinkles. Complete with twenty-five blazing candles. When the rolling cart stopped in the center of the stage, Dani pulled Kendall into a quick hug and whispered into her ear. "Congratulations." Then the bartender and his wife disappeared into the crowd.

As the final words rang out, Kendall sucked in a deep breath and blew out the flickering candles to the cheers of friends and family. Twenty-four candles extinguished in one breath. Not bad for a girl recovering from a punctured lung.

Only one candle remained, and every woman in the packed bar whooped their approval. Their shrill, energetic appreciation grew in intensity until the building seemed to vibrate around them.

Kendall laughed, knowing she couldn't have planned it if she'd tried. Yes, indeed, if junior high folklore could be believed, she had one boyfriend.

No. Make that one husband-to-be.

To my reader,

Thank you for taking the time to read ***Chased***. I hope you've enjoyed Ben and Kendall's story. Please take a moment to leave a review at Amazon or Goodreads. It doesn't have to be anything elaborate, just honest.

If you haven't had a chance to read the first two books of the Changing Krysset series, ***Challenged*** and ***Consumed***, I urge you to go out to Amazon and get yourself a copy. In book 1 you'll meet Jackson and Sophie. Book 2 is all about Ethan and Danielle. I know you're going to love them. Just like ***Chased***, these two stories have a sweet romance with a twist of suspense and steamy-hot sex.

Happy reading & welcome to Krysset,

Kate

Visit my website for more information: KateCarley.com

Turn the page for a peek at Kate Carley's romantic suspense novel.

Challenged

One devastating lie set the course for Sophie Lancaster's life. Can one earth-shattering phone call change it?

Jackson Cooper certainly hopes it won't—at least not permanently. For the past twenty-one years, Sophie has avoided coming home and now has the nerve to show her face, purely for the reading of her grandfather's will—that thought alone is enough to have Jackson grinding his teeth in molar-cracking frustration.

But Grandpa Ray's final request, a life-changing challenge to save the family's resort, pairs Jackson with this woman who makes his blood boil—in more ways than one.

With Jackson's vow to honor his dear friend and Sophie's promise to prove her worthiness to a grandfather she barely remembers, they set off on a yearlong adventure.

Can they learn to work and live together, forging a new bond built on respect and a common goal? Can they rely on each other without giving into their growing desires?

Just as the sizzle of attraction between them heats up, the challenge becomes a dangerous and deadly game when outside forces threaten their resort, their budding relationship, and their very lives.

With their future hanging in the balance, will they survive the challenge?

CHAPTER 1

Swirling red and blue lights always accompanied the most unpleasant events of life—death, destruction, the occasional speeding ticket. Tonight, five police cars and two ambulances lit up the darkness to announce death. As usual, curious neighbors lined the street, dressed in a variety of bedtime apparel, some more revealing than others, to witness the carnage firsthand.

Sophia's booted heels clicked out a confident cadence, steady and strong, masking her inner terror and her thudding heartbeat. She made her way past the gawkers and the rescue workers, up the driveway, and onto the porch of the small white house. Her stomach rolled at the thought of stepping through the front door. No matter how often these events occurred, she always arrived nauseated and light-headed with tingling hands and feet.

"Hello, Ms. Lancaster. How are you tonight?" The detective in charge greeted her, the same one she'd seen at her last two calls. She'd never forget his face—harsh indifference softened by caring eyes.

"Hi, Detective. I'm fine." A nervous sigh escaped louder than she'd expected, and his eyebrows rose in concern.

"I'll warn you now—it's gruesome in there." He jerked his

head toward the door and gave her an apologetic look, perhaps remembering the last time he'd called her to a murder scene to take three children into protective custody. That night the stench of blood had slammed into her the moment she'd stepped through the door. Fighting her stomach's strong objection to the horrific sight and odor, she'd held back the gag reflex as long as possible before rushing to the door and the nearby bushes where her evening meal had made its reappearance.

His sincere blue eyes searched her face, probably for early warning signs of retching, before he said, "Mom's boyfriend stabbed her at least a dozen times and then blew his brains out. Little girl, neighbors say her name is Jessie, is sitting by her mom's body."

Why did she have to be the one on call tonight? "Thanks." Sophia stepped through the doorway, immediately noting the coppery tang of blood. Her stomach rolled in protest. Would she ever become immune to the wretched smell of spilt blood? Or to the sight of it? She cast a fleeting look around the room. After three years of collecting children at scenes like this, she knew in her heart of hearts the answer to both questions was a resounding no. Yet this vital aspect of her job, finding immediate and safe housing for a child at risk, spoke to her soul on such a fundamental level she couldn't imagine throwing away her career simply for a queasy gut.

Watching where she stepped, Sophia approached the little girl and knelt down, well out of the pool of blood. Small red handprints stained the front of Jessie's pink pajamas. Her blond curls rumpled from sleep, her big sky-blue eyes stared up at Sophia.

As part of her job, Sophia often looked into the eyes of abandoned, neglected, or mistreated children, speaking words of promise, of kindness, weaving tales of princesses and knights to encourage their trust. Trust she knew she didn't deserve and hadn't earned. Trust she knew had been destroyed by the adults that should've treasured these beautiful children.

And each night those innocent eyes haunted her dreams.

"Hi, Princess Jessie. My name is Sophia. When I was your age I loved reading fairy tales. Do you like fairy tales?" Wide eyed, the girl focused on Sophia's face but remained silent.

"Whenever the princess in the tale finds herself in trouble, what happens?" Sophia paused, more for effect than an expected response, but a tiny squeak of noise broke the silence.

"Prince Charming comes to her rescue." One large tear slid down Jessie's cheek, and she brushed it aside with blood-smeared fingers.

The sight of that single tear wrenched at Sophia's heart. Every protective instinct within her rose to the surface. She wanted to scoop Jessie up and run from this ugly nightmare. She wanted to rock her, let the child cry on her shoulder, assure her that things would be okay.

But that was a lie. Jessie's life had changed forever, just as Sophia's life had changed in a heartbeat when her father had died. Nothing had ever been the same after that.

"Yes, that's right," Sophia said, blinking back her own tears. She oscillated between the desire to be violently sick and the desire to sob like a baby. She needed to get out of this house and away from the stench of blood. Gathering her wits, she assumed a chipper attitude and continued. "Well, I'm not sure if you're aware of this, but the dress code for Prince Charming has changed over the last few years. When he comes out to rescue the princess, he's often dressed in a uniform, like a police or paramedic uniform or even firefighter gear."

Jessie's brow furrowed in contemplation. She glanced toward the door and then back to Sophia. "He's Prince Charming?"

Sophia peeked over her shoulder at the stoic detective. A small grin tugged at the corner of his mouth before the ever-present emotionless mask slipped back into place.

Nodding, she said, "Yes, he's Prince Charming. He and his friends are here to take care of your mom, but we're in their way."

"My mom is dead." Huge blue eyes stared at Sophia, waiting for confirmation.

"Yes. I'm sorry, Princess Jessie." Her voice cracked. "I'd like to take you someplace safe tonight, okay?"

The girl slowly bobbed her head in acceptance. Rising, Sophia stretched out her gloved hand to take Jessie's blood-covered fingers. Leading the way, Sophia stepped out into the fresh air.

Two steps outside the door she stopped, her fingers still gripped around Jessie's little hand. Sophia closed her eyes and breathed through her nose, attempting to calm her stomach. A deep cleansing breath in, hold for two, and release. And again.

"Ms. Lancaster?" The detective's deep voice startled her out of her calming meditation. "Are you okay? You'll find bushes off to your left."

Sophia waited for the snickers to rise up from the rescue workers gathered nearby. Surely, they knew of her past transgressions. But when she opened her eyes, she was met with a half dozen pairs of concerned eyes blinking back at her.

She turned to address him. "Thank you, Detective, but I'm fine." She looked down at the golden mass of curls and then met the detective's gaze. "How do you do this?" She pitched her voice low, searching his kind eyes for a clue to solve all her problems.

He glanced back at the door and shook his head. "Too many years of practice. Some people get used to it. Others don't."

"The ones who don't get used to it, what do they do?"

"They find a new career." His quiet words were spoken in a nonjudgmental tone.

Sophia nodded. She'd heard that before. Every day from Roxy and last week from her boss. "Thank you, Detective." Sophia turned, escorting the child away from the house and the morbid spectacle that held the neighbors in awe.

Halfway down the driveway, Jessie's hushed words reached Sophia's ears. "Good night, Prince Charming."

* * *

"Good morning, sunshine!" Roxy said with faux cheerfulness when Sophia stepped into the kitchen and poured herself a cup of coffee.

"Good morning," Sophia said, sitting down at the table across from her best friend.

Roxy's long fingers wrapped around her coffee mug. "I heard you leave last night. Bootie call or work?" Her black eyebrows arched in poised anticipation of the answer she already knew.

Sophia restrained herself from rolling her eyes. "Work, of course. I need a quick shower before I go into the office for the day." She sipped her coffee and silently waited for Roxy's impending lecture. Friends since their freshman year of college, they'd proven that opposites attract. Roxy's olive complexion, silky raven hair, and almond-shaped eyes set her apart as an exotic beauty, while her bold and outgoing demeanor captivated everyone she met. Sophia's five-foot-three frame, wild red hair, and quiet disposition left people thinking "little sister." At best she might be called cute, but next to her friend, Sophia was simply average.

During college, she'd wished for Roxy's model-like figure and her enthusiastic and sociable personality, but it was Roxy's large family that had made Sophia's heart twinge with jealousy on more than one occasion. A dad and mom, eight siblings, grandparents, and countless aunts, uncles, and cousins. She couldn't help but feel envious of this huge, loving clan.

"I've decided to create a petition to have the dress code changed at work. All the good- looking men should be required to work shirtless."

Sophia's head snapped up in time to watch a lazy grin spread across her friend's face. "I thought that would get your attention," Roxy said, easing back into her chair and assuming a bored pose. "You do know what I'm going to say, don't you, Soph?"

"Yes, and I don't want to hear it today. I don't stick my nose into your business. I don't tell you to quit your job." Her voice shook, and she clamped her jaw shut to halt the flow of useless words before she crossed the line and made a mess of her friendship, too.

"That's true." Roxy agreed with a nod. "Because you're the kindest person I know. You believe you can turn everyone's life into a fairy tale with a happy ending. And by the end of the day, you have nothing left. Between your job that sucks the life out of you and your insane volunteer activities, you have no time left for yourself. You can't keep this up."

"But I like what I'm doing. Every day I help people who need a little extra to get by. I can do it, and I want to. I'm not hurting anyone."

"Except yourself. Over the last six months you've lost weight, and look at your nails. You've chewed them down to nothing. You're stressed, you're burning the candle at both ends, and you're not taking care of yourself."

Sophia released a weary breath and plunged into the only logical explanation that she could formulate, hoping her words conveyed her passion and the importance of her efforts. Efforts she knew Roxy viewed as obsessive. "I feel like a juggler. If I slip up, bad things will happen. Someone will go hungry. Someone will fall between the cracks or even die. I can't stop juggling or everything will collapse. People are counting on me."

Roxy gazed at her, concern showing in her electric-blue eyes. "I understand and value your desire to help people in need. But you can't help everyone. That's all I'm saying. I care about you and want the best for you, my friend," she said, polishing off her final gulp of coffee. She rose and headed to the door. "I have to get to work. Please consider scaling back." Roxy picked up her purse and keys off the small table by the back door. "And maybe you could find a job that doesn't induce vomiting." She wrinkled her nose. "I hate waking up to that sound."

With the quiet click of the door, Sophia was alone. She sipped at her coffee, putting off the inevitable. No doubt her boss would want to speak with her regarding her newest case.

And if she didn't keep a steady voice and dry eyes, he'd likely reiterate his condemning words from last week—that she lacked the emotional fortitude for the job—followed by his recommendation that she grow thicker skin or find new employment.

The unexpected ring of her cell phone drew her attention and she checked the caller ID. Usually she'd let an unfamiliar number roll to voicemail, but at the moment, a mindless distraction was just what she needed. "Hello."

"Hello. May I please speak with Sophia Elizabeth Lancaster?" The official tone pushed her current problems far from her mind.

"This is Sophia."

"My name is Jake Rutgers, and I'm a private investigator. I've been hired by Mr. James Thompson, Esquire, to find you, Ms. Lancaster."

"An attorney?"

"Yes, ma'am. Mr. Thompson has asked me to inform you that you have been named in the Last Will and Testament of a Mr. Raymond Lancaster, who passed away two weeks ago."

Her throat tightened on a sob and tears filled her eyes. She blinked in a hopeless effort to control them. Family? Was it even possible? She'd been on her own for so many years, always longing for a family and a home to call her own.

"Ma'am? Are you still there?"

"Yes." She forced the word past the lump in her throat.

"I apologize for calling you with bad news. I understand this isn't the way a person should learn about the death of a family member. I'm sorry for your loss." He sounded sincere.

"Mr. Rutgers, I'm afraid there's been a horrible mistake. My grandfather's name was Raymond Lancaster, but he died more than twenty years ago. I'm obviously not the Sophia Lancaster you've been searching for. Have a good day." Her finger reached to disconnect the call, but then his deep voice rumbled through the phone.

"Please, Ms. Lancaster, just a moment. I have additional information here."

All she could hear through the phone line was the frantic shuffling of paper while he probably searched for one convincing piece of data. She doubted he'd find it and prepared to end the call when he spoke again.

"Are you the daughter of Jonathan and Bridget Lancaster?"

"Yes." Sophia barely choked the word out before the tears fell.

In the right circumstances, that one simple, agreeable word could've held the ability to restore families, to provide shelter in the storms of life, and to inspire hope. But today, affirming her relationship to her deceased parents, and by default, her recently departed grandfather—had he truly been alive until two weeks ago?—only solidified her loneliness in the world. That one simple word reminded her of all the things she'd lost over the course of her life and at the same time it exposed a heartbreaking reality: she'd missed out on the one thing she'd longed for in the past twenty-one years—family.

CHAPTER 2

Jackson Cooper sped down the single-lane paved road, the windows rolled down and the country music blaring. He belted out the lyrics as he maneuvered his black Ford F150 toward town. The light breeze swayed the branches of the birch trees and kicked up the sweet scent of wildflowers that bloomed along the side of the road. Warm spring days with clear blue skies and brilliant sunshine brightened his mood, but the hole in his heart left by Ray's death lingered.

He did his best to ignore the tightness in his throat and chest that seemed ever-present over the last three weeks. Each morning he'd pulled himself out of bed, attacked the never-ending list of tasks Ray had created, blasted his favorite tunes, and sang at the top of his lungs. The physical labor and catchy lyrics kept him focused on the here and now, instead of buried in memories of the past.

Jackson slowed his truck to a twenty-mile-per-hour crawl and clicked off the radio when he turned onto First Street, entering historical downtown Krysset, where time stood still. One-, two-, and three-story brick buildings lined the streets. Visually appealing storefronts and unique shops lured tourists in droves. Antiques and rare book vendors, distinctive boutiques and gift stores all thrived, as did a variety of small restaurants.

The majority of the town had been erected in the late 1800s and early 1900s. Restoration and preservation of those original structures was paramount to the good folks at Krysset's historical society. Over the past twenty years, only two new buildings had been created to harmonize with the already existing structures and provide continuity to the old town facade. All in all, few things had changed in the original four-square-block expanse.

One concession made to the forward march of progress had been the installation of stoplights at three of the busier corners in town. During the off-season the old fashioned stop sign would've been plenty for the twelve hundred permanent residents, but during the summer months when the population swelled to thousands, the modern method of traffic control had become mandatory. The proximity to Itasca State Park and the abundance of lake resorts and private cabins nearby had kept the small town of Krysset booming.

Jackson lifted his hand in acknowledgment to Charlie and Old Sam. They eyed his slow-moving truck with curiosity. A major source of gossip, those two old geezers staked their claim on the bench outside the barbershop in the early spring and remained permanent fixtures until late autumn. Nothing happened in Krysset that escaped their scrutiny and speculation. Providing the community with a valuable public service, they passed along every juicy tidbit, many with added artificial color and flavoring. Now all who made their way along this stretch of road and paused to greet the two old men would know that Jackson Cooper had been in town today.

Jackson released a sigh, feeling the weight of their eyes on his tailgate as if they could determine his exact purpose in town by watching where he turned next. He glanced in the rearview mirror, confirming their gawking stares. He shook his head in silent resignation. The overactive gossip mill, accepted as a mainstay of small town living, was the one thing Jackson didn't appreciate about the quaint resort town.

He waved when he passed Annie writing on the sandwich board sign in front of her bakery. Before he returned to the resort today, he intended to stop in and buy a loaf of bread and perhaps one of her famous apple pies or a chocolate cake. Maybe both. He only traveled the twenty-mile stretch of road once or twice each week so he planned to stock up on supplies while he was in town.

Jackson turned the corner at First and Main and spotted Juliana Ferris sweeping the sidewalk in front of her boutique. As vigilant as Charlie and Old Sam, Juliana noticed his truck at once and stopped her cleaning routine to acknowledge him. Straightening herself, she sucked in her gut and pushed out her breasts. Well-endowed but seemingly proportional to the rest of her curvy, statuesque body, she always took great pains to accentuate her abundance.

Acquaintances from their school days, he and Juliana were among a small handful of students from their graduating class that had remained in Krysset. They always shared a friendly greeting when they bumped into one another around town, even though they rarely ran in the same circles.

Truth be told, Juliana had become a bit of a recluse over the past several years with her head down focused on her business. She owned and operated a thriving clothing boutique, designing and creating a large portion of her merchandise. Her store was a huge success due to her savvy marketing skills and her own personal creations. The rare moments when her head popped up and her attention wandered beyond her boutique, she fixated on the husband hunt.

Those were the moments that Jackson avoided her like the plague.

However, he knew Jules would be more than annoyed if he drove past with only a wave. Since time was short before his meeting, he'd need to make the conversation a quick one. Jackson pulled his truck to the curb near her storefront.

"Hey, Jackson!" She waved and bounced up and down, behaving as if her girls might be overlooked if she didn't jiggle them. He fought an overwhelming urge to reassure her that every guy who came along not only noticed but also appreciated her double Ds.

Jackson pasted on his appreciative smile. "Hi there, Jules. How's business?"

"A bit slow today," she said, leaning into the open passenger-side window of his truck and offering him a lovely peek at her ample cleavage. He'd seen the view before. Still not interested.

Jackson glued his eyes to hers and chose the most harmless topic of conversation he could think of. "Is the website still working for you?" As owner and sole employee of Cooper Software Design, he'd created dozens of websites for small business owners in the area, including Juliana. For a reasonable fee, he'd make modifications as their business needs changed.

Juliana gave him a distracted nod. "Well, look at you, Jackson, all dressed up today. You look great." Her smile faltered, and her brow furrowed. "You're not getting married today, are you?"

He made a concentrated effort not to roll his eyes at her blunt question. Leave it to Juliana to notice the suit and tie and think wedding.

Oddly enough, he'd never wear his lone suit again without thinking funeral.

"No, Jules. I've told you many times—I'm not the marrying type. I have a meeting with James Thompson today."

With an eye for details and a penchant for gossip, Juliana would help broadcast that information to the entire town before the end of his appointment at the attorney's office. Between Juliana and Martha, the waitress over at Lydia's Café, and the guys outside the barbershop, everyone's comings and goings were grist for the mill.

"You have some legal troubles, Jackson? Maybe I could cook you dinner tonight and you could tell me all about it. You know, I'm a good listener." She smiled at him and licked her pink lips as if she planned to devour him for the main course.

He wanted to laugh. Juliana had proven time and again that she only possessed selective listening skill. No matter how many times he told her no, she failed to hear him. "Sorry, I can't come to dinner. I have a lot to do out at the resort. You know, the vacationers will be showing up in just a few weeks. Your business will pick up, too."

Still smiling at him, she stepped away from his truck, silently accepting his rejection.

"I have to get going. I'll see you around." He pulled away from the curb, giving her a little wave. He watched in his rearview mirror while she waved and bounced; her smile appeared hopeful. He shook his head in complete confusion, making a mental note to drive the back streets out of town today.

Jackson pulled into the circular driveway in front of the law office and parked in the small lot. The sprawling front gardens and the cinnamon brick building were both well maintained. At one time, the building had been a four-bedroom ranch-style home, three blocks north of Main Street. Now it served as Thompson's Law Office, nestled in the middle of a quiet residential neighborhood.

Two cars stood in the driveway, Thompson's shiny silver BMW and Dottie's beat-up, rusted-out, baby blue Taurus. From the hot word on the street, Jackson had expected one additional car.

The gossip mill had been running overtime a few days ago when someone had whispered that a long-lost relative of Ray Lancaster had been found, and she'd be coming into town for the reading of the will. He had this sneaking suspicion that it was Ray and Audrey's granddaughter who'd left in the middle of the night with her mom, Bridget, shortly after Jonathan's death.

He remembered Sophie, the little girl with wild red hair. He remembered her giggles as she chased butterflies, her loud sobs the day she fell off her bike on the gravel driveway, and her soft little voice while she played with her dolls. He also remembered the silent tears that rolled down her freckled cheeks during her dad's funeral service. But all those memories of a sweet eight-year-old girl had been tainted by her utter lack of concern for her grandparents over the past two decades and her apparent gold-digging behavior now at their death.

Jackson stepped through the huge oak door and into the entryway. The law office was decorated in the upscale lodge theme. Shiny, wide plank hardwood floors, rich leather furniture, and wildlife photographs, all originals, hung on the knotty pine walls. He recognized the photographer as Thompson's wife, Sandy. Her north woods nature and wildlife prints sold nationwide, earning her local celebrity status.

"Hi, Jackson. How are you today?" Dressed in business attire far more sophisticated than necessary in small town Krysset, Dottie stepped around the receptionist desk to greet him with a little peck. He swept the petite woman up into a big bear hug and kissed her cheek before he set her feet back on the ground. She giggled, straightening her blouse and skirt.

"You just never give up. Someday you're going to hurt your back lifting me. I'm not getting any lighter, you know." Her manicured fingers fluttered to the elaborate twist on the back of her head, giving it a gentle pat to ensure that his exuberant embrace hadn't destroyed the mysteriously constructed and seemingly permanent up-swoop of hair.

He chuckled. "I plan to give my favorite gal a hug every time I see her until the two of us are old and gray, living in the old folks' home. How's Nate?"

"You are always so kind to ask about my little baby boy. Nathan's fine. He's almost through his second year of college." Dottie's scandalous pregnancy during her senior year of high school had fueled the fires of gossip. Speculation on the paternity of her baby became a town-wide pastime until Daniel Beaumont stepped up and married her. Their hasty and disastrous marriage lasted less than a few months. She'd been alone at the birth of her son and had remained that way all these years.

James Thompson had taken pity on his young niece and her infant son, employing her as receptionist in his small law office. She worked hard, rarely dated, drove a rusted out piece of junk, and focused all her energy and money on raising her son. Jackson respected the woman for the continued sacrifices she'd made to raise a child on her own.

"Oh, I have to show you something." She spun around her desk, reaching for a silver picture frame. She shoved it toward him. "Carl and his wife just had a baby girl, Sarah Jane. Of course, since I'm her auntie, I think she's adorable. Look at all that hair." Dottie's face lit up with a smile, her eyes fixed on the picture of her niece.

Jackson and Carl had graduated high school together, four years after Dottie. "Wow. Carl has a kid." He took the picture frame and gazed at the sweet little baby wrapped in a pink blanket. "You're right; she's adorable." Jackson smiled; without thought his finger caressed the little face behind the glass.

He loved children and had once imagined himself with a houseful. A wife, however, he could live without. He loved women. That wasn't the problem. He loved their soft curvy bodies and their long luscious locks. He loved to kiss them and caress them. He loved their whispered pleas and soft little moans as they came. He loved women, but no way would he commit to one. Not that he feared commitment. The idea of having one special person in his life held a certain appeal to him. But in his experience, when things got tough, women took off, ripping their loved ones' hearts out as they went. And he liked his heart right where it was, thank you very much.

"Mr. Thompson will see you now," Dottie said. Jackson grinned at the professional manner she used to refer to her uncle, and then he followed her down a small hallway to the first doorway on the right.

"Great to see you, Jackson. Come on in." The men shook hands, and Mr. Thompson gestured to one of the chairs in front of his desk, indicating that Jackson should sit. Mr. Thompson returned to his seat behind the enormous mahogany desk in the office that reeked of cigarettes.

James Thompson was a rotund man with a ruddy complexion and numerous chins. In spite of his full head of silver hair, he was Ray's junior by more than a couple decades, but with his pack-a-day habit and his bulging waistline, it was a small miracle the man had managed to outlive Raymond Lancaster.

Mr. Thompson leaned back in his chair. Bushy gray eyebrows sheltered his hazel eyes as he studied Jackson. "Jackson, I am sorry for your loss. I know Ray was not just your boss, but your friend and a second father, too. Ray spoke highly of you. He loved you like a son. I just thought you would want to know that."

Jackson examined his black dress shoes for a moment and cleared his throat a couple times before he said, "Thank you. He was a great guy, and I've missed him a lot over the past few weeks." He cleared his throat again when a soft knock sounded.

Dottie poked her head into the room. "Ms. Lancaster has arrived, sir."

"Great, please send her in," Mr. Thompson said, rising and rounding his desk. Jackson stood as a confident young woman swept into the room.

"Mr. Thompson, hi, I'm Sophia Lancaster. It's nice to meet you." She extended her hand in greeting, and Mr. Thompson grasped her small hand in both of his.

"Ms. Lancaster. It is a pleasure."

"Please call me Sophia."

"I am glad you could join us today. Let me introduce you to Jackson Cooper." He gestured toward Jackson.

His suspicions confirmed. They'd managed to track down Ray's little granddaughter. However, "little" no longer described the full-grown woman who stood before him. Dressed in a conservative emerald green business suit that contradicted her sexy green high heels, "spectacular" was a more accurate description.

Because of the heels, he couldn't be certain of her exact height, maybe five foot three or four. She had curves in all the right places, and that wild, carrot-red hair he remembered from his childhood had softened into a light golden red. And the wild? Well, she'd managed to wrangle most of those unruly curls into a professional style clipped at the nape of her neck, but several locks had slipped free of their restraint as if they had a mind of their own. His visual appraisal stuttered to an abrupt halt at the sight of her full, pink lips that begged to be kissed.

Beautiful and sexy. Never in his wildest dreams had Jackson imagined that the girl from his youth had grown into such a stunning woman. His fingers curled into fists at his side, resisting the urge to free her hair from that oppressive clip and run his fingers through her flowing tresses while he answered the taunting call of her pouty lips.

Visions of touching her silky soft skin, unwrapping the conservative package she presented, and stripping her down to what he hoped would be a black lacy bra and panties slammed through his brain. He imagined her legs wrapped around his waist while he pounded into her warm body. Would she like it hard and fast or sweet and slow? Would she scream his name when she came?

Jackson realized his gaze was fixed on her kissable lips. Great way to make a first impression. He suppressed the self-disgusted groan that rumbled in his throat and lifted his eyes to the vicinity of hers.

"Sophie," he said with a formal nod, noting the slight lift of her brows. Even with his anger and bitterness toward her, she'd always be sweet little Sophie to him.

He needed to get a grip. What was wrong with him? The proper perspective and a quick rundown of her long list of faults should douse his lust-filled thoughts like a cold shower. She'd abandoned her grandparents twenty-one years ago. She'd never called and never returned. She'd left Ray and Audrey to grieve for her until the day they died.

Who did she think she was? She sashayed into the office like she owned the place, dressed in FM shoes and, in his fantasy, lacy black underwear. She was his adversary, not some sweet thing to be picked up at a bar. No matter how luscious her lips appeared, he would not be kissing them, nor admiring her soft curves again. He had no intention of ever forgetting or forgiving the pain she'd caused his dear friend, Ray.

A familiar fury rose within him, anger directed at Sophie for her blatant disregard for his dear friends and her selfish return to collect their money. He recognized the decades-old outrage, but now it was laced with frustration and embarrassment. With himself. He'd allowed his shameless thoughts to wander in an inappropriate way with the enemy.

A onetime mistake that would never happen again.

Jackson waited for the enemy's eyes to lock with his so he could cast an angry glare at her and perhaps bare his teeth in a feral growl. But her gaze darted around the room, and she nibbled on her lower lip. The confident woman who'd waltzed into the office moments before had been replaced by a shy, jittery girl.

When she finally met his eyes, Jackson saw a flicker of fear or perhaps doubt on her face, but in a blink, her expression hardened and the same self-confident, battle-ready woman who'd made her entrance earlier stood before him.

"Jackson." Recognition sparkled in her light green eyes.

Turn the page for a peek at Kate Carley's romantic suspense novel.

Consumed

Thirty-seven minutes after midnight.

Like clockwork, an exquisite stranger sashays into his bar, orders up a shot of Jack Daniel's, and stirs up his curiosity—not to mention his libido. Awaiting the arrival of this mysterious woman, night after night, has Ethan Bearbower growling in frustration.

Or maybe it's her hasty retreat after slamming the whiskey that's driving him crazy. Lord knows her choice of attire isn't improving his condition in the least—one night she's dressed like a shy, sweet nymph, and the next, a seductive dominatrix.

No wonder he's going out of his mind.

But once Ethan uncovers her true identity, his inquisitiveness morphs into a protective streak he can't seem to control. Consumed by this unusual fascination for a woman he's just met and his need to keep her safe, Ethan struggles to reconcile his long-held beliefs with his mounting emotions.

Danielle is searching for the truth, and she's not going home until she's satisfied. But before she can unearth the answers to her biggest questions, she discovers a sexy man who just might derail her quest.

With explosive chemistry and tenderly whispered words of love, their relationship seems destined to last forever…until Danielle's unrelenting search brings danger to her doorstep.

CHAPTER 1

The clinking of glassware and the loud barks of laughter rang through the bar, punctuated by each tick of the clock. The snarling bear face emblazoned on the timepiece mocked him each time he glanced that way. Twelve thirty-one. Only two minutes had passed since he'd last checked. He pulled his cell phone from the back pocket of his jeans for confirmation. What the hell was wrong with him?

Disgusted with his current fixation, he shoved his phone back into his pocket and snatched up a damp towel to wipe down the countertop, maneuvering around Cameron Aasgaard, the bartender on duty tonight. No self-respecting man waited for one skinny brunette to enter a bar already crowded with dozens of willing women. What was wrong with him?

"Hi, Taz Bear. How are you tonight?" Lauren asked. Monsoon-sized swells of anger radiated off her.

"I'm doing well, Lauren. What can I get you? Another rum and Diet Coke?"

"That's what I like," she said.

"I know it's what you like, Lauren, but is that what you want?" Taz asked her.

"No. I want that chick gone," she said, glaring over her shoulder at Ian Davidson and the group gathered around a circular table in the lower level. Although tall booths along the edges hinted at privacy, the entire bar stood wide open for people watching, from one end to the other.

Leaving nowhere for Ian to hide from Lauren's fury.

At the moment, a beautiful blonde was perched on Ian's lap, her tongue stroking the outer shell of his ear—no doubt the source behind Lauren's anger and the vicious if-looks-could-kill glare. Ian and Lauren had arrived at the bar together, looking freshly tumbled, and from the deep scowl that Lauren sported, she'd obviously hoped to leave with Ian at the end of the night.

She turned her attention back to Taz, her delicate brow furrowed and her bold red lips pursed in a pout. "I'll have a Diet Coke, hold the rum." Her words held a forced calm unlike her posture.

"Smart girl," Taz said, filling a tall glass with ice and spraying the dark bubbly liquid from the tap. He topped the drink with a long straw and smiled at the young woman who'd turned twenty-one last month. "It's on the house."

"Thanks, Taz," she said, turning away from the bar.

In curiosity, he watched her strut back to her table, her hips swaying in a seductive manner. He caught her profile when her lips tipped up in a devious grin. Then she plopped her sweet young bottom into Ian's best friend's lap.

Ah, to be twenty-one again. Drinking up a storm and sleeping with any pretty little thing that fluttered her lashes at him. Those were the days. However, at the ripe old age of thirty-two, that type of behavior would kill him in short order.

He snorted at the thought. As owner and manager of the Brawling Bear Bar and Grill, he'd witnessed plenty of drunken behavior and had no time for such nonsense. He drank on occasion—never to excess. As far as casual sex went, he had more than enough opportunities working at the bar.

But nowadays, he found himself searching for something more than a meaningless night of sex.

He scanned the subdued crowd, watching Ian swagger up the steps with his arm draped over the blonde's shoulders. Ian wasn't a big guy, average height with a permanent slouch that was more a statement of his laid-back attitude than poor posture. Always smiling, the sweet talker could woo just about any woman he desired. And he desired every single one of them, regardless of their age or shape, black hair, red hair, blondes, or brunettes. They were all his type, a self-proclaimed equal-opportunity lover.

"Have a nice night, kids." Ian flashed him a huge grin and a thumbs up before they reached the door. Taz shook his head. That same woman had left last night with Ian's best friend, Chaz, who now sat in a corner booth kissing Lauren.

Taz shuddered. Friends should not share that much.

He set another beer in front of Old Sam and glanced at the growling bear that guarded time with a fierce glower and razor-sharp teeth. Two more minutes to go.

For the past three nights at twelve thirty-seven, an exquisite brunette—one he'd never seen before—had entered his establishment, stepped up to the bar, and settled onto a stool at the far right end. Like a shy nymph, she'd gazed up at him from under her lowered lashes, her head tilted in a suggestive fashion, her full pink lips bowed in a demure smile. The look—equal parts innocent and seductive—sent a furnace blast of heat through his blood directly to his groin. A lust-filled jumpstart unlike any he'd had in the recent past. So now, with an eagerness he hadn't experienced since his teen years, he awaited her arrival and the surge of energy she'd induce.

The heavy steel door swung open at precisely twelve thirty-seven, according to the angry bear. And once again, she made her way to her *usual* seat. He snatched up a shot glass, the bottle of Jack Daniels, and a glass of Diet Coke, offering her a smile when she hung her purse on the backrest and settled herself upon the barstool.

"Good evening, beautiful," he said. Her lashes feathered down to conceal her hazel eyes. God, she was sweet. "I brought you your usual, a shot and a diet soda."

"Thank you. I guess I'm a creature of habit." The soft melody of her voice warmed him from the inside out like a double shot of aged whiskey.

"I've noticed you're prompt." A myriad of emotions played across her face. He hoped a smile remained when she realized he'd only been teasing.

Her lips curled in a small grin, and her eyes lifted to his. "I hope you don't mind that I visit every night."

At last, after four nights she flirted back. Perhaps the quiet seductress wasn't an act, but rather a shy woman forcing herself to interact. Had it taken her all evening to work up the nerve to leave her home and venture out to the bar?

"Not at all. I've also noticed you order the exact same drink," he said, splashing Jack into the small glass.

A sad look passed over her face. "It reminds me of home."

He paused a moment and waited for her to explain, but instead she lifted the shot glass to her lips and downed the amber liquid in one gulp. Extending his hand, he said, "I'm Ethan Bearbower. Everyone calls me Taz Bear. Welcome to the Brawling Bear."

"Ethan, it's nice to meet you," she said, placing her cool hand in his. A bright spark of excitement blasted through him at the touch of her delicate fingers cocooned in his larger grasp. "I'm Danielle, but most everyone calls me Dani." She extracted her hand from his with a smile. "So this is your place."

"It is," he said, never taking his eyes off her face. "Danielle. What a beautiful name." For a beautiful creature of habit. He assessed the woman before him. Long, graceful fingers wrapped around the glass of soda, and her soft, plump lips enclosed the tip of the straw. Her cheeks puckered slightly while she sucked down the chaser, and her lashes fluttered against her olive skin. Again, innocent and seductive, and Ethan's body responded with gusto. The woman piqued his interest unlike any other in recent months.

"Thank you." A pink blush crossed her cheeks, either from embarrassment or the warmth of alcohol. She brushed her long bangs back, framing her oval face and exposing her high cheekbones. A golden-red hue cast from the dim interior lights played tricks with the true shade of the shiny tresses that spilled over her shoulders. He'd bet that in the sunlight her hair would shimmer sable or some other rich dark brown tone.

She took a deep breath and looked him in the eyes as if the shot of liquid courage had settled her nerves. In a move that sent all remaining blood from his brain to his groin, the pink tip of her tongue flicked over her bottom lip before her teeth nibbled at the rose-colored flesh there. Then she leaned toward him and said, "Good night, Ethan."

And she was gone.

Ignoring the uncomfortable tightness at the front of his jeans, he glanced at the angry-faced bear that threatened anyone who dared to eye the time. In three minutes flat, Danielle had transformed him from a mature adult male into a randy hormonal teenager again. For the fourth night in a row, his position behind the bar was both a blessing and a curse. Hidden from view, his body's enthusiastic response remained a private matter. His responsibilities to his bar, however, kept him tethered here when the lust-filled caveman inside him growled out that he should follow the beautiful woman.

"Cover for me, Cam?" he shouted at Cameron and raced toward the door, too consumed with his obsession for this woman to think twice.

"No problem, Taz. I'll close up, too."

"Thanks." He escaped the confines of his responsibility in time to watch the taillights of a small sedan exiting onto Main Street, heading west out of town.

His Chevy Tahoe rocketed out of the parking lot, following at a reasonable distance. Not too far away to lose her. Not too close to spook her. He couldn't imagine where she was headed, since so few homes stood between his bar on the westernmost side of downtown Krysset and the edge of Paul Bunyan State Forest.

A short mile out of town, residential Main Street morphed into a dark, winding county road with dense woods on either side. The sliver moon cast deep shadows, heightening the eerie solitude Ethan always experienced whenever he traveled this desolate stretch of pavement. He couldn't help but ponder the fortitude of a woman who traversed this road unaccompanied night after night.

Three miles later, a string of curses fell from Ethan's mouth when her sedan signaled and made a sharp right onto Cougar Creek Lane. No homes existed down this rutted gravel stretch other than a campground, leaving him with a sinking feeling. He switched off his headlights and followed at a safe distance, fearing the worst. Danielle's car crept down the isolated road, past the foreboding "Dead End" sign—a sickening reminder of the young woman murdered at this campground little more than a month ago.

An icy shiver rippled up Ethan's spine that had little to do with the chill of autumn, but rather genuine concern for a woman whose name he'd learned less than an hour ago.

Danielle.

Why any woman would want to stay at a secluded campground perplexed him. But then again, it seemed that everything about Danielle left him mystified. Perhaps it was needless worry, but he still prayed she wasn't staying in a pop-up, canvas tent in the back woods.

He trailed behind her sedan through the Cougar Creek Cabins and Campground, traversing the property by the ambient light of the thin moon and small solar yard lamps sprinkled on either side of the road. An enormous wave of uneasiness swelled from his gut, and his heart threatened to pound right out of his chest. But the foolishly brave woman just drove deeper into the all-but-abandoned campsite nestled in the woods. Finally, after navigating the labyrinth of meandering trails, Danielle parked near a shabby white bungalow.

Sucking in a deep calming breath that didn't do a damn thing to quiet his thudding heart, Ethan pulled his SUV to the side of the dirt path that doubled as the main trail around the campground. He cracked the driver's side door open, thankful he'd procrastinated the dome light repair for the past two months, and quietly unfurled himself from the dark interior of the vehicle.

Closing the distance between them, Ethan watched Danielle make a mad dash from her car and up the few steps to the door of the rental unit. The front porch light illuminated her frantic fumbling. He took one step closer.

In what seemed like a panicked movement, she darted a glance over her shoulder. But Ethan wasn't convinced that she sensed his presence as much as she feared someone—anyone—might sneak up on her with her back turned. He longed to call out to her, to reassure her that he'd followed only to make certain that she'd reached her home safely. But he'd probably frighten her even more. Tomorrow they could discuss her choice of accommodations, but for tonight he simply needed to know that she'd locked herself into the rickety cabin.

After an excruciating battle with the key, the lock surrendered, and Danielle disappeared into the cabin, slamming the door shut behind her just as Ethan stepped into the glowing ring cast by the single bulb lighting the wooden stoop.

He stood close enough to eye what appeared to be the flimsiest door on the planet, no doubt coupled with the cheapest lock in the universe. However, the metallic action of the deadbolt sliding into place was music to his ears. He took a few steps closer, pausing near the wobbly banister leading to the porch.

He resisted the urge to climb the steps and pound on her door, which would only draw attention to the fact that he'd followed her here. He waited and listened, wondering if a killer was lurking in the woods nearby, or worse yet, waiting for her behind the locked cabin door. But he shoved that thought from his mind, dragged a shaky hand over the rough growth on his jaw, and exhaled a weary breath.

Some people couldn't be saved from their own poor judgment. Even beautiful, sexy women like Danielle.

ABOUT THE AUTHOR

Kate spent seven years working as an IT professional before "retiring" to stay at home with her two little boys. Now--two more children and two decades later--Kate is launching her new book series: Changing Krysset.

When Kate isn't writing, she's cooking for her brood. Late at night, you'll find her curled up by the fireplace reading a romance novel.

Kate lives in the Midwest with her husband of twenty-six years and their four children.

Made in the USA
Middletown, DE
08 July 2022

68776504R00186